THE IDEAL GUY

Adam leaned in and asked, "So what do you do? Are you a musician, too?"

"Actually, no. I'm a biochemist. My company's developing a perfume."

"What's it like?"

I scooted over. "I'm wearing it. Can you smell it?"

He met me halfway, eyes dilating black. I knew I shouldn't be flirting. He didn't appear to meet a single one of my criteria and, in fact, actively ticked boxes from the "deal-breaker" list. I didn't want to lead him on only to have to give him the heave-ho in the next thirty minutes.

He lifted my wrist up to smell the fragrance Thanh had given me. "Mmm. That's nice."

Then he brushed his lips across my skin, and an electric current shot up every nerve in my arm. I drew my hand back, shrugging off the shiver that hit me like an aftershock.

"And you? What do you do?"

He laughed and scratched the back of his neck. "Well, I'm a musician."

I blinked back my disappointment.

On my list of suitable professions for my prospective mate, *musician* wasn't at the absolute bottom. There were plenty more embarrassing or unstable career choices. I wouldn't date plumbers or proctologists for obvious reasons. Salesmen either because, well, I didn't like salesmen, but also because their financial situation might be uncertain. Plus they tended to travel. My ideal guy, I'd decided, would be an architect.

I had nothing against musicians. On the contrary, I loved them. I'd supported my brother in his career, but the lifestyle was too precarious for my peace of mind. Even the most talented had a hard time making ends meet. Traveling and selling merchandise became a necessity.

Unfortunately, all the doctors, lawyers, and architects I encountered were usually not interested in jean-clad, concert T-shirt wearing me. This train of thought brought me around to the realization I'd judged Adam for dressing exactly the same way.

Micah saved me from sticking my foot in my mouth when he appeared at our side.

"Adam! I'm glad to see you here. I see you've met my sister." He turned to me. "Eden, do you mind if I steal him for a few?"

Adam threw me a glance. "Will you be here when I get back?"

The jolt of butterflies this simple question gave me came wholly unexpected. "I'll be here. I'm leaving when Micah does."

He flashed a crooked smile at me, and I traced his lips with my eyes. He was going to be trouble.

Some Kind of
MAGIC

Mary Ann Marlowe

KENSINGTON BOOKS
www.kensingtonbooks.com

KENSINGTON BOOKS are published by

Kensington Publishing Corp.
119 West 40th Street
New York, NY 10018

eISBN-13: 978-1-4967-0807-6
eISBN-10: 1-4967-0807-5
First Kensington Electronic Edition: February 2017

ISBN-13: 978-1-4967-0806-9
ISBN-10: 1-4967-0806-7
First Kensington Trade Paperback Printing: February 2017

10 9 8 7 6 5 4 3 2 1

Printed in the United States of America

To Kristin
For singing along with me

Chapter 1

My pen tapped out the drumbeat to the earworm on the radio. I glanced around to make sure I was alone, then grabbed an Erlenmeyer flask and belted out the chorus into my makeshift microphone.

"*I'm beeeegging you . . .*"

With the countertop centrifuge spinning out a white noise, I could imagine a stadium crowd cheering. My eyes closed, and the blinding lab fell away. I stood onstage in the spotlight.

"Eden?" came a voice from the outer hall.

I swiveled my stool toward the door, anticipating the arrival of my first fan. When Stacy came in, I bowed my head. "Thank you. Thank you very much."

She shrugged out of her jacket and hung it on a wooden peg. Unimpressed by my performance, she turned down the radio. "You're early. How long have you been here?"

"Since seven." The centrifuge slowed, and I pulled out tubes filled with rodent sperm. "I want to leave a bit early to head into the city and catch Micah's show."

She dragged a stool over. "Kelly and I are hitting the clubs tonight. You should come with."

"Yeah, right. Why don't you come with me? Kelly's such a—"

"Such a what?" The devil herself stood in the doorway, phone in hand.

Succubus from hell played on my lips. But it was too early to start a fight. "Such a guy magnet. Nobody can compete with you."

Kelly didn't argue and turned her attention back to the phone.

Stacy leaned her elbow on the counter, conspiratorially talking over my head. "Eden's going to abandon us again to go hang out with Micah."

"At that filthy club?" Kelly's lip curled, as if Stacy had just offered her a *non*-soy latte. "But there are never even any guys there. It's always just a bunch of moms."

I gritted my teeth. "Micah's fans are not all moms." When Micah made it big, I was going to enjoy refusing her backstage passes to his eventual sold-out shows.

Kelly snorted. "Oh, right. I suppose their husbands might be there, too."

"That's not fair," Stacy said. "I've seen young guys at his shows."

"Teenage boys don't count." Kelly dropped an invisible microphone and turned toward her desk.

I'd never admit that she was right about the crowd that came out to hear Micah's solo shows. But unlike Kelly, I wasn't interested in picking up random guys at bars. I spun a test tube like a top then clamped my hand down on it before it could careen off the counter. "Whatever. Sometimes Micah lets me sing."

Apparently Kelly smelled blood; her tone turned snide. "Ooh, maybe Eden's dating her brother."

"Don't be ridiculous, Kelly." Stacy rolled her eyes and gave me her best *don't listen to her* look.

"Oh, right." Kelly threw her head back for one last barb. "Eden would never consider dating a struggling musician."

The clock on the wall reminded me I had seven hours of prison left. I hated the feeling that I was wishing my life away one workday at a time.

Thanh peeked his head around the door and saved me. "Eden, I need you to come monitor one of the test subjects."

Inhaling deep to get my residual irritation under control, I followed Thanh down the hall to the holding cells. Behind the window, a cute blond sat with a wire snaking out of his charcoal-gray Dockers. Thanh instructed him to watch a screen flashing more or less pornographic images while I kept one eye on his vital signs.

I bit my pen and put the test subject through my usual Terminator-robot full-body analysis to gauge his romantic eligibility. He wore a crisp dress shirt with a white cotton undershirt peeking out below the unbuttoned collar. I wagered he held a job I'd find acceptable, possibly in programming, accounting, or maybe even architecture. His fading tan, manicured nails, and fit build lent the impression that he had enough money and time to vacation, pamper himself, and work out. No ring on his finger. And blue eyes at that. On paper, he fit my mental checklist to a *T*.

Even if he was strapped up to his balls in wires.

Hmm. Scratch that. If he were financially secure, he wouldn't need the compensation provided to participants in clinical trials for boner research. *Never mind*.

Thanh came back in and sat next to me.

I stifled a yawn and stretched my arms. "Don't get me wrong. This is all very exciting, but could you please slip some arsenic in my coffee?"

He punched buttons on the complex machine monitoring the erectile event in the other room. "Why are you still working here, Eden? Weren't you supposed to start grad school this year?"

"I was." I sketched a small circle in the margin of the paper on the table.

"You need to start applying soon for next year. Are you waiting till you've saved enough money?"

"No, I've saved enough." I drew a flower around the circle and shaded it in. I'd already had this conversation with my parents.

"If you want to do much more than what you're doing now, you need to get your PhD."

I sighed and turned in my chair to face him. "Thanh, you've got your PhD, and you're doing the same thing as me."

When he smiled, the corners of his eyes crinkled. "Yes, but it has always been my lifelong dream to help men maintain a medically induced long-lasting erection."

I looked at my hands, thinking. "Thanh, I'm not sure this is what I want to do with my life. I've lost that loving feeling."

"Well, then, you're in the right place."

I snickered at the erectile dysfunction humor. The guy in the testing room shifted, and I thought for the first time to ask. "What are you even testing today?"

"Top secret."

"You can't tell me?"

"No, I mean you'd already know if you read your e-mails."

"I do read the e-mails." That was partly true. I skimmed and deleted them unless they pertained to my own work. I didn't care about corporate policy changes, congratulations to the sales division, farewells to employees leaving after six wonderful years, tickets to be pawned, baby pictures, or the company chili cook-off.

He reached into a drawer and brought out a small vial containing a clear yellow liquid. When he removed the stopper, a sweet aroma filled the room, like jasmine.

"What's that?"

He handed it to me. "Put some on, right here." He touched my wrist.

I tipped it onto my finger and dabbed both my wrists. Then I waited. "What's it supposed to do?"

He raised an eyebrow. "Do you feel any different?"

I ran an internal assessment. "Uh, nope. Should I?"

"Do me a favor. Walk into that room."

"With the test subject?" It was bad enough that poor guy's schwanz was hooked up to monitors, but he didn't need to know exactly who was observing changes in his penile turgidity. Thanh shooed me on through the door, so I went in.

The erotica continued to run, but the guy's eyes were now on me. I thought, *Is that a sensor monitoring you, or are you just happy to see me?*

"Uh, hi." I glanced back at the one-way mirror, as if I could telepathically understand when Thanh released me from this embarrassing ordeal.

The guy sat patiently, expecting me to do something. So I reached over and adjusted one of the wires, up by the machines. He went back to watching the screen, as if I were just another technician. Nobody interesting.

I backed out of the room. As soon as the door clicked shut, I asked Thanh, "What the hell was that?"

He frowned. "I don't know. I expected something more. Some kind of reaction." He started to place the vial back in the drawer. Then he had a second thought. "Do you like how this smells?"

I nodded. "Yeah, it's good."

"Take it." He tossed it over, and I threw it into my purse.

The rest of the day passed slowly as I listened to Kelly and Stacy argue over the radio station or fight over some impossibly gorgeous actor or front man they'd never meet. Finally at four, I swung into the ladies' room and changed out of my work clothes, which consisted of a rayon suit skirt and a button-up pin-striped shirt. Knowing I'd be hanging with Micah in the club later, I'd brought a pair of comfortable jeans and one of his band's T-shirts. I shook my ponytail out and let my hair fall to my shoulders.

When I went back to the lab to grab my purse and laptop, I wasn't a bit surprised that Kelly disapproved of my entire look.

"I have a low-cut shirt in my car if you want something more attractive." She offered it as though she actually would've lent it to me. Knowing I'd decline, she got in a free dig at my wardrobe choices. We were a study in opposites—she with her overpermed blond hair and salon tan, me with my short-clipped fingernails and functioning brain cells.

"No, thanks. Maybe next time."

"At least let me fix your makeup. Are you even wearing any?"

I pretended she wasn't bothering me. "No time. I have a train to catch."

She sniffed. "Well, you smell nice anyway. New perfume?"

"Uh, yeah. It was a gift." Her normally pouting lips rounded in anticipation of her next question. I zipped my computer bag and said, "Gotta go. See ya tomorrow, Stacy?"

Stacy waved without turning her head away from whatever gossip site she'd logged on to, and I slipped out the door.

As I stood on the train platform waiting for the 5:35 Northeast Corridor train to Penn Station, I heard someone calling "Hello?" from inside my purse. I fetched my phone and found it connected somehow to my mom, whose voice messages I'd been ignoring.

Foiled by technology and the gremlins living in my bag, I placed the phone to my ear. "Mom?"

"Oh, there you are, Eden. I'm making corned beef and gravy tonight. Why don't you come by before you go out?"

I didn't know how to cook, so my mom's invitation was meant as charity. But since she was the reason I couldn't cook, her promise of shit on a shingle wasn't enough to lure me from my original plans.

"No, thanks, Mom. I'm on my way into the city to hear Micah play tonight."

"Oh. Well, we'll see you Sunday I hope. Would you come to church with us? We have a wonderful new minister and—"

"No, Mom. But I'll come by the house later."

"All right. Oh, don't forget you've got a date with Dr. Whedon tomorrow night."

I groaned. She was relentless. "Is it too late to cancel?"

"What's the problem now, Eden?"

I pictured Dr. Rick Whedon, DDS, tonguing my bicuspid as we French kissed. But she wouldn't understand why I'd refuse to date a dentist, so instead, I presented an iron-clad excuse. "Mom, if we got married, I'd be Eden Whedon."

Her sigh came across loud and clear. "Eden, don't be so unreasonable."

"I keep telling you you're wasting your time, Mom."

"And you're letting it slip by, waiting on a nonexistent man. You're going to be twenty-nine soon."

The train approached the station, so I put my finger in my ear and yelled into the phone. "In six months, Mom."

"What was wrong with Jack Talbot?"

I thought for a second and then placed the last guy she'd tried to set me up with. "He had a mustache, Mom. And a tattoo. Also, he lives with his parents."

"That's only temporary," she snapped.

"The mustache or the tattoo?" I thought back to the guy from the lab. "And you never know. Maybe I'll meet Mr. Perfect soon."

"Well, if you do, bring him over on Sunday."

I chortled. The idea of bringing a guy over to my crazy house before I had a ring on my finger was ludicrous. "Sure, Mom. I'll see you Sunday."

"Tell Micah to come, too?"

My turn to sigh. Their pride in him was unflappable, and yet, I'd been the one to do everything they'd ever encouraged me to do, while he'd run off to pursue a pipe dream in music. So maybe they hadn't encouraged me to work in the sex-drug industry, but at least I had a college degree and a stable income.

"Okay, Mom. I'll mention it. The train's here. I have to go."

I climbed on the train and relaxed, so tired of everyone harassing me. At least I could count on Micah not to meddle in my love life.

Chapter 2

At seven thirty, I arrived at the back door of the club, trailing a cloud of profanity. "Fuck. My fucking phone died."

Micah exchanged a glance with the club owner, Tobin. "See? Eden doesn't count."

"What the fuck are you talking about?" After two hours fighting mass transit, I'd lost my patience. My attitude would need to be recalibrated to match Micah's easygoing demeanor.

Micah ground out his cigarette with a twist of his shoe. "Tobin was laying a wager that only women would show up tonight, but I said you'd be here."

I narrowed my eyes.

Micah's small but avid female fan base faithfully came out whenever he put on an acoustic show. His hard-rock band, Theater of the Absurd, catered to a larger male following and performed to ever-increasing audiences. But he loved playing these smaller rooms, bantering with the crowd, hearing people sing along with familiar choruses.

Before Tobin could get in on the act, I blurted, "Can I charge my phone in the green room?"

I made a wide berth around Tobin's plumage of cigarette smoke and followed Micah down the shabby narrow back hall. Dimly lit eight-by-eleven glossy posters plastered the walls, advertising upcoming bands and many other acts that had already passed through. Nobody curated the leftover fliers although hundreds of staples held torn triangles of paper from some distant past. A brand-new poster showing Micah's anticipated club dates hung near the door to the ladies' room. That would disappear during the night as some fan co-opted it for him to autograph, and Tobin would have to replace it. Again.

The green room was actually dark red and held furniture that looked like someone had found it on the curb near the trash. And it smelled like they'd brought the trash, too. God knew what had transpired in here over the years. I tried to touch nothing. Micah flopped down on the sofa and picked up a box of half-eaten Chinese food. His red Converse tennis shoes and dark green pants clashed with the brown-gold hues that stained the formerly whitish sofa.

I plugged in my phone, praying I'd remember to fetch it before I left. I fished out some ibuprofen and grabbed Micah's beer to wash it down. I waved off his interest in the drugs I was popping. "Birth control," I lied.

Without looking up from his noodles, he said, "Oh, good. I was starting to worry you'd joined a convent."

When Micah finished eating, he led me to the front of the club and put me to work setting up his merch table. His band's CDs wouldn't sell, but his self-produced EP of solo work would disappear. Mostly for girls to have something for him to autograph. They'd already own his music digitally. A suitcase filled with rolled-up T-shirts lay under the table. I bent down and selected one of each design to display as samples.

Micah moved around onstage, helping the club employees drag cables and whatnot. Not for the first time, I envied him for inheriting some of Mom's Scandinavian coloring and height, while I got Dad's pale Irish skin and raven hair. Micah repeated "one-two-three check" into the mic a few times and then disappeared around back to grab one last smoke before he had to transform from my sweet older brother into that charismatic guy who held a crowd in the palm of his hand.

Right before the doors opened to the public, one of the guys I'd seen setting up the stage stopped by the table and flipped through the T-shirts and CDs. He picked up Micah's EP and then raised dark brown eyes. "Micah Sinclair. You like his music?"

He wore faded jeans and a threadbare T-shirt from a long-forgotten AC/DC concert under a maroon hoodie. His black hair fell somewhere between tousled and bed head. I saw no traces of product, so I assumed he came by that look through honest negligence rather than studied indifference.

My quick scan revealed: too grungy, probably unwashed, poor. I resisted the urge to pull the merch away from his wandering fingers. But I wouldn't risk the sale, so I leaned in on my elbows, all smiles.

"He's amazing. Will you get a chance to hear him perform?"

"Oh, yeah. Definitely." He set the EP down and held out his hand. "I'm Adam, by the way."

I wrapped my hand around his out of sheer politeness and proper upbringing, but I couldn't help laughing and saying, "Just so you know, my worst nightmare would be dating a guy named Adam."

He quirked his eyebrow. "That's kind of discriminatory."

"My name's Eden." I waited a beat for the significance to register, but I guess any guy named Adam would've already dealt with such issues of nomenclature. His eyes lit up immediately.

"Oh. Seriously?" He chuckled, and his smile transformed his features. I sucked in my breath. Underneath the dark hair, dark eyes, and hobo wardrobe, he was awfully cute. "I'll rethink that marriage proposal. But could I get you anything? You want a beer?"

This was a new twist. Usually, the ladies were offering drinks to my brother. I loved getting the attention for a change. "Sure. Whatever lager or pilsner they have on tap."

He walked off, and I snickered. *Maybe some guys like pale brunettes, Kelly.* As he leaned against the bar, I assessed him from the rear. Tall enough, but too skinny. Questionable employment. Either an employee of the club, a musician, a wannabe musician, or a fan. Shame.

Micah strolled up. "Is everything ready?"

I forced my gaze away from Adam's backside. "Are you?"

He scratched his five-o'clock chin scruff. "That's the thing. I may need some help tonight. Do you think you could maybe sing backup on one song? I was hoping to harmonize on 'Gravity.'"

"Sure." What were sisters for? I had his whole catalog memorized, even the music from his band, although that music ran a little too hard rock for my tastes.

Micah left me alone at the merch table, and Adam returned with a glass. "Did I just miss Micah?"

He'd pulled his hoodie up so his face fell into shadow, giving him a sinister appearance. With the nonexistent lighting in the club, I could barely make out his features. This odd behavior, coupled with his interest in my brother, made me worry maybe he was in fact one of the crazy fans who found ways to get closer than normal, and not, as I'd first thought, an employee of the club. How had he gotten inside before the doors opened?

Before I could ask him, a woman's sharp voice interrupted. "Will Micah be coming out after the show?"

I looked toward the club's entrance, where people had begun to stream in. I took a deep breath and prepared to deal with the intensity of music fandom.

"I assume so. He usually does."

She didn't move. "It's just that I brought something for him." She held up a canister of something I guessed was homemade. I'd advised Micah not to eat whatever they gave him, but he never listened. And so far he'd never landed in the hospital. I knew his fans meant well, but who knew if those cookies had been baked alongside seven long-haired cats?

"I could take it back to him if you like." I made the offer, knowing full well it wouldn't do at all.

"No. Thank you. I'll just wait and give them to him later. If he comes out." She wandered off toward the stage.

I spotted one of Micah's regular fans, Susan something-or-other, making a beeline for the merch table. She looked put out that I was there before her. "Eden, if you like, I'm more than happy to man the merch."

I never understood what she got out of working merch for

Micah. He didn't pay except possibly in a waived cover charge. And she was farther from the stage and possibly distracted from the performances. Perhaps it gave her status. Whatever it was, it made her happy, and I was glad to relinquish the duty to her.

"Thank you, Susan."

She beamed. "Oh, it's no problem." She began to chatter with the other women crowding up to the merch table. I overheard her saying, "Micah told me he'll be performing a new song tonight."

Adam caught my eye, and we exchanged a knowing smile. So okay, he wasn't a fan. He stepped beside me as I walked to the bar to get a seat on a stool. "So you're not the number one fan, then?" he asked.

I smiled. "Of course I am."

Before we could discuss our reasons for being there, the room plunged into near-total darkness, and Tobin stepped onto the stage to introduce the opening act, a tall blonde whose explosion of wild hair had to weigh more than the rest of her.

She pulled up a stool and started into her first song without further ado. Out of respect, I kept quiet and listened, although her performance was a bit shaky, and the between-song banter didn't help. It pleased me that Adam didn't turn to me to say anything snarky about the poor girl or talk at all. I had to glare over at the women hanging around the merch table a few times, though. They'd shut up when Micah came on, but they didn't seem to care that other musicians preferred to play to a rapt audience, too.

In the time between acts, Adam ordered me another beer. At some point he'd dropped his hood back, but with the terrible lighting in the club, I had to squint to see his face. Normally, I wasn't a big fan of facial hair of any kind, but Adam's slight scruff caused my wires to cross. On the one hand, I worried he couldn't afford a razor out there in the cardboard box he lived in. On the other hand, I had a visceral urge to reach up and touch his cheek. And run my finger down the side of his neck.

He caught me staring when he leaned closer to ask me how long Micah had been performing.

I wasn't sure what he was asking, so I gave him the full answer. "He's been singing since he was old enough to talk. He started playing acoustic when he was eleven, but picked up electric when he was fifteen. He formed a metal band in high school, and the first time they performed live anywhere beyond the garage was a battle of the bands."

Adam's expression changed subtly as I recounted Micah's life history, and I could tell he was reassessing my level of crazy fantardness. I laughed and said, "I told you I was his number one fan."

His smile slipped, but he managed to reply politely. "He must be very talented."

Something about the timbre in his voice resonated with me, almost familiar, and I regretted my flippant sarcasm.

Before I could repair my social missteps, the lights faded again, and the girls near the stage screamed in anticipation. A spotlight hit the mic, and Micah unceremoniously took the stage. He strummed a few notes and broke directly into a song everyone knew. The girls up front sang along, swaying and trying to out-do each other in their excitement.

Adam twisted around and watched me, eyebrow raised. Maybe he expected me to sing along, too. I raised an eyebrow back and mouthed the words along with Micah. Wouldn't want to disappoint him. Finally, Adam straightened up to watch the performance, ignoring me for several songs.

Micah performed another well-known song, then a new one, introducing each with some casual-seeming banter. I knew he planned every word he said onstage, but the stories he told were no less sincere for that. He controlled his stage presence like a pro.

Before the fourth song, he announced, "This next song requires some assistance. If you would all encourage my sister, Eden, to come join me, I'm sure she'd hop up here and lend me a hand."

The audience applauded on cue. As my feet hit the floor, Adam's eyes narrowed and then opened wide as he did the math. I curtsied and left him behind to climb up onstage to perform— Micah's support vocals once again. Micah strummed a chord, and I hummed the pitch. Then he began to play the song, a beautiful ballad about a man with an unflagging devotion to a woman. The ladies in the front row ate it up. Micah knew I got a kick out of performing, and I suspected he asked me up so I could live his musician life vicariously.

When the song ended, I headed back to the anonymity of my stool. The hard-core fans all knew who I was, but if they weren't pumping me for information about Micah, they didn't pay much attention to me. There was a fresh beer waiting, and I nodded to Adam, appreciative. He winked and faced forward to listen to Micah. That was the extent of our conversation until Micah performed his last encore and the lights came back up.

Then he turned back. "You were right. He's very talented." He tilted his head. "But you held out on me. Your opinion was a little bit biased."

"I was telling you the truth," I deadpanned. "I am his number one fan."

"You two look nothing alike. I'd never have guessed."

"We have a crazy mix of genetics."

As we chatted, the area behind us, near the merch table, filled up with people waiting for a chance to talk to Micah, get an autograph, or take a picture with him. The lady with the cat-hair cookies had nabbed the first place in the amorphous line. I scanned the rest of the crowd and discovered that Tobin had lost his bet. A pair of teenage boys holding guitars stood on their toes, trying to get a glimpse of Micah over the heads of the other fans, but he hadn't come out yet. They were most likely fans of his edgier rock band, taking advantage of the smaller venue to meet him, pick his brain about music, and have him sign their guitars. They'd still be competing with at least thirty people for Micah's time.

If I wanted to go home with my brother, I'd be hanging out a while. I could still catch a train back to New Jersey, but Micah's place in Brooklyn was closer. I decided to stay. It had nothing to do with the cute guy paying attention to me. I just didn't want to navigate Manhattan alone and drunk.

Adam leaned in and asked, "So what do you do? Are you a musician, too?"

"Actually, no. I'm a biochemist."

"Finding cures for Ebola?"

That caught me off guard, and I snorted. "No, nothing like that." I didn't know what to tell him about what I actually researched, so I half lied. "My company's developing a perfume."

"What's it like?"

I scooted over. "I'm wearing it. Can you smell it?"

He met me halfway, eyes dilating black. I knew I shouldn't be flirting. He didn't appear to meet a single one of my criteria and, in fact, actively ticked boxes from the "deal-breaker" list. I didn't want to lead him on only to have to give him the heave-ho in the next thirty minutes.

He took my hand and kept his dark eyes on mine as he lifted my wrist up to smell the fragrance Thanh had given me. "Mmm. That's nice."

Without dropping his gaze, he brushed his lips across my skin, and an electric current shot up every nerve in my arm. I drew my hand back, shrugging off the shiver that hit me like an aftershock. "And you? What do you do?"

He laughed and scratched the back of his neck. "Well, I'm a musician."

I blinked back my disappointment. From Adam's appearance, I hadn't had high hopes, but he might've been dressed down for a night out. Way down.

On my list of suitable professions for my prospective mate, *musician* wasn't at the absolute bottom. There were plenty more embarrassing or unstable career choices. I wouldn't date plumbers or proctologists for obvious reasons. Salesmen either because, well, I didn't like salesmen, but also because their financial situation might be uncertain. Plus they tended to travel. My ideal guy, I'd decided, would be an architect. But there weren't many of those swimming around my apartment complex in Edison, New Jersey.

I had nothing against musicians. On the contrary, I loved them. I'd supported my brother in his career, but the lifestyle was too precarious for my peace of mind. Even the most talented had a hard time making ends meet. Traveling and selling merchandise became a necessity.

Which is why I never dated musicians.

Unfortunately, all the doctors, lawyers, and architects I encountered were usually not interested in jean-clad, concert T-shirt wearing me. This train of thought brought me around to the realization that I'd judged Adam for dressing exactly the same way.

Micah saved me from sticking my foot in my mouth when he appeared at our side. "Adam! I'm glad to see you here. I see you've met my sister." He turned to me. "Eden, do you mind if I steal him for a few?"

Adam threw me a glance. "Will you be here when I get back?"

The jolt of butterflies this simple question gave me came wholly unexpectedly. "I'll be here. I'm leaving when Micah does."

He flashed a crooked smile at me, and I traced his lips with my eyes. He was going to be trouble.

They headed toward the green room, leaving me as confused as Adam must've been when I went onstage. I didn't know who he was, or why my brother wanted to see him.

I weighed the possible options.

Option one: The most logical explanation was that Micah was hiring Adam to temporarily replace his bassist, Rick, who was taking time off to be with his wife after the birth of their first child. I congratulated myself for solving the mystery on my first try.

Option two: Maybe Adam was a drug dealer. No, other than smoking and drinking, I'd never known Micah to try a recreational drug. And surely, this wouldn't be an ideal location for such a transaction. Besides, Adam already said he was a musician. Option one was looking better and better.

Option three: Or maybe Adam was a homeless man Micah was going to take in out of charity. A homeless man who'd just bought me three beers. I rolled my eyes at myself, but then felt awash with guilt. He probably wasn't homeless, but it did seem like he might be struggling to get by, and I'd accepted three drinks I could've easily afforded. *Good job, Eden. Way to drive a man to starvation.*

Every new option I came up with to explain Adam's presence

here defied logic and stretched the imagination. I gave up and watched the crowd thin. When Micah and Adam came back out, the bar was empty, save me and the staff.

Micah poked me. "We're going over to Adam's. You can come or just go straight back to my place." He bounced on his feet. I looked from him to Adam, standing relaxed up against the bar. From the looks of things, Micah had a boy crush. I might be interrupting a bromance if I tagged along.

Adam stepped toward me. "I have a fully stocked bar, and I don't like to drink alone." His smile was disarming. The whole situation seemed so contrived, and I had to wonder whose idea it was.

Micah stifled a yawn. "Come on, Eden. Just for a drink. Let's go see how the other half lives."

Did he know what that expression meant? "Okay, but let's get going. Some of us have been awake since this morning."

Chapter 3

Adam led us to a walk-up in Brooklyn Heights. As he slid the key into the lock, he downplayed his presence in such an affluent neighborhood with the horrifying excuse: "It's my parents' apartment."

I stifled a groan. *Of course.*

Micah stopped short. "Are we going to be disturbing them?"

Adam threw open the heavy door. "Nope. They retired to Florida and left this to me. It's too much for one person, but whatcha gonna do?"

My head spun with how quickly I mentally unticked the "lives with parents" checkbox.

The apartment did in fact look like a family lived there, not a single man, not a musician. Or more like nobody lived there. It was a mausoleum. The heavy solid mahogany of the dining-room table and the thick red fabric on the upholstery reminded me of a funeral parlor. Gold-framed paintings graced the walls. A Wedgwood vase stood on an end table noticeably absent of clutter or dust.

The whole place was too clean by half.

"When was the last time you were here?" I asked.

His head swung around, "What do you mean?"

"Nothing. I expected to find—"

"Trash on the floor? Dirty clothes on the furniture? Well, you might, normally. But you guessed right. I've been out of town for a little while. If you want evidence I was here this morning, you should see my bedroom."

I blushed. He caught my embarrassment and coughed into his fist. By the way his eyes crinkled, I suspected he was hiding his laughter.

While Micah and I loitered in his sitting room, Adam rummaged through a cupboard that had ornate frosted-glass doors. "I'm going to make you my special island drink."

His mom might take a dim view of him storing his booze in what appeared to be the family china hutch.

Micah dropped heavily into a gold-velvet wing chair, leaving me the outdated and uncomfortable purple divan. If it had been stuffed with phone books, it would've been softer.

"Oh, hey, I've got some cookies." Micah reached into his khaki canvas messenger bag and retrieved the round canister his fan had given him. He popped off the lid and held it out to me, offering me a chocolate cookie. It did look appetizing, but I couldn't overcome my revulsion.

"Nah. I'm good."

He stretched and stifled a yawn, which caused me to yawn as well. I hadn't realized until then that I was wiped out. "Why are you so tired? You can't have been up twelve hours."

"Man, I was up all night arguing with Shane about what songs we're going to use on the next CD. Then Rick called around eleven asking for help building some IKEA crib thing. I got maybe five hours of sleep."

Before I could ask him why he'd agreed to stay out under those circumstances, Adam carried over three highball glasses, precariously balanced, and distributed them. He sat next to me and held his glass out for a toast. "To new friends."

We all took a swig. I was expecting the harsh kick of hard alcohol, but the pale yellow drink was smooth and hardly tasted like booze at all. Micah finished his in three gulps and set the empty glass down beside the Wedgwood vase.

I reached over and moved his glass onto a coaster, tsking. I held my own glass up to the light, as though it might illuminate the recipe. "This is delicious. What's in it?"

"It's a drink I learned to make when I was in Jamaica. It's got some spiced rum, vodka, peach schnapps, banana liqueur . . ."

As Adam rattled off the laundry list of alcohols in the cocktail, I tried to make sense of him. I'd originally misjudged him based solely on his unkempt appearance. I looked around the well-appointed, albeit disturbingly antiquated, sitting room. Adam might be struggling as a musician, but poor and homeless he clearly was not.

The hypocrisy of my preconceived opinions made me snort, and Adam stopped talking midsentence. I bit my lip. "Sorry, I just thought of something."

Micah snorted, too. I glanced over at him to find he'd fallen asleep in the chair. He was slumping toward the floor. "Oh, no. He's such a lightweight." I placed my drink on the glass coffee table. "We should be going."

Adam jumped up. "No, it's okay. There's plenty of room here. Let's help him to a bed."

We heaved Micah up and walked him down the hall to a kind of office with stark white walls and no furniture except two filing cabinets, a cherrywood desk, and a black metal day bed against the wall. I had the uncanny feeling we'd broken into someone else's house. There was nothing to indicate a young musician lived there. Micah sighed when we rolled him onto his side and covered him with a crocheted multicolored afghan.

Adam whispered, "This was my bedroom when I was a kid."

I ran my eyes around the room. Not even a boot scuff marred the walls. "This?"

"My parents converted it. But come here. Let me show you something." He slid open a closet and dragged out a box. "Promise not to laugh."

He lifted the lid to reveal a decade of teenage fandom. I dropped to my knees and rifled through concert ticket stubs and other memorabilia.

I clapped my hand over my mouth, laughing despite the promise. "You kept all this stuff?"

"Technically, my parents did. They didn't know what to keep or what to throw away, so they boxed it all up. Now I find it pretty funny and nostalgic and can't bring myself to toss it out."

A frame peeked out behind the boxes, and I dragged it out to find a replica gold record. It had an inlaid photo of the *At Budokan* album cover below it.

I poked him. "Cheap Trick?"

"Hell, yeah." He said it too loud, and Micah grunted. Adam winced. "Cheap Trick rules," he whispered.

Keeping my voice low, too, I confessed, "I had one of their songs stuck in my head all morning." I held a finger up. "And there it is again."

"Which one?"

It occurred to me how awkward it would be to say that song title to him, so I lied. " 'Surrender.' "

"Good song." He shoved the boxes back in, and the room regained its immaculate appearance.

"It's hard to picture anyone living in here." I stood up. "This is going to sound forward, but can I see proof you still live here? I wouldn't want to be charged with breaking and entering."

He led me down the hall to another bedroom. As he opened the door, he said, "This used to be my parents' room, but I've redecorated and made it my own."

I'd expected more of the nineteenth-century museum furniture, but there was no hint of grandmom anywhere. A king-size bed dominated the space, unmade. A suitcase lay on the floor, spilling out socks and jeans, giving truth to his claim that he'd recently returned from somewhere.

I scanned the rest of the room. I wasn't surprised to see he had a turntable. Micah had been buying vinyl for years. An entertainment unit held a wide-screen TV and a stack of DVDs. I walked over to check out his movie collection. A Netflix envelope sat on top, and I read the address. The name rang a bell.

"Adam Copeland?"

Then I remembered. Stacy and Kelly had crushed on a rock singer with the same name for a few weeks last summer, another impossibly hot guy with red hair. No, wait, that was a different band. I could never keep their celebrity crushes straight.

My eyes went wide. What if this was that same guy? They would die. He was a musician, after all. A wave of nausea crested as I took in my surroundings. The guy certainly had money.

Adam glanced up from a stack of records and caught me staring at him. "What?"

"Your name is Adam Copeland?" My mind raced. The apartment was his parents', so the money was probably his parents', too. If he was a rock star, wouldn't he have some lavish penthouse overlooking Central Park?

He went back to flipping through albums, nonplussed. "Oh, yeah."

I narrowed my eyes. If I asked him straight up, he'd think I was crazy, so I casually sauntered over to the side of his bed and leaned back, facing him. I picked at the hem of my shirt, and then, as though I was teasing, I tested the waters. "So, does everyone ask you if you're any relation to that guy from that band?"

"Huh?" He pulled out a Van Morrison album and then dropped it back down, still on the search for whatever he was looking for.

Then it hit me. "Oh, God. I'm sorry. It must be an incredibly common name."

He froze in place like a deer caught in the headlights, like he had no idea what I was talking about.

This was embarrassing. Awkwardly, I fumbled for an explanation, rambling. "You know that band? They have a song that gets played about a million times an hour." On the spot, I couldn't even remember the band's name. I scraped my brain, tapping my fingers on the bedpost. It came to me out of nowhere. "Walking Disaster!"

Adam rolled his eyes. "*Riiiight.*" He settled on an album and slid the vinyl record from the sleeve.

I hoped I hadn't offended him somehow. Maybe it was an irritating comparison. If someone famous had my name, I'd find it annoying.

What was I thinking? As if some famous musician would just hang out at a club and buy me beers. And flirt. He'd definitely been flirting with me. Guys within my limited reach rarely bought me beers and flirted. How much chance would I have with a freaking rock star? I laughed at myself for losing my head temporarily.

Unfazed, Adam dropped an album onto the turntable. I smiled as a dead sexy Arctic Monkeys song started. "I love this song!"

He sidled up next to me and bumped me with his shoulder. "So you like that band, Walking Disaster?"

Was this a litmus-test question? Like asking someone if they like Nickelback? What if he had a checklist, too? What if he only liked girls who listened to the "right" music and immediately disdained girls who listened to whatever he found uncool? And why did I suddenly care what kind of girls he might like?

I shrugged, reaching for a safe nonchalant answer. "I don't normally listen to them unless they come on the radio. I don't intentionally listen to much current rock music, except for Micah's. But my coworkers gush about that band. They tried to drag me out to see them just recently."

"But you didn't want to go?"

"No, I would've gone. But it was at the Meadowlands, and it was a weeknight. I had to get up early the next day."

"To make perfume, right?" He leaned closer and breathed in. "What's the name of this one?"

"Oh, I don't know."

"Mmm. You should call it 'Irresistible.' It smells nice." He lifted my hand and laid a kiss against my wrist. My brain told me I should leave. I barely knew him.

But I didn't want to leave. Adam's lips felt so good against my skin. His dark eyes sought mine, looking for permission, maybe. The naked desire etched on his face sent a tingle through me. I wanted to feel his lips on mine, but he held back, so I bent toward him. He kissed me soft, and I tasted the hint of Jamaican spiced rum.

He broke away and drew back, so close but too far away. His eyes pierced mine, and his breathing hitched, but he hesitated. I felt tethered there, unable to move back, wanting to move forward. I reached up to touch the stubble on his cheek, then that cord on his neck I'd wanted to touch earlier. Without another thought, I twisted my fingers in his hair and pulled him back to me.

As soon as our mouths touched, he knocked me onto the bed, holding my wrists loosely above my head. He ran his other hand down my shirt until he reached the hem. His fingers roamed uncontested under the elastic of my bra while he kissed me deep, sucking on my lips, brushing his tongue against mine, breaking apart reluctantly. He pressed his body against mine, and I could feel his arousal through his tight jeans.

He released my hands and tugged at my shirt, pausing again, watching me for signs of reluctance. I sat up and let him pull it up over my head. I lightly grazed his abdomen before slipping his shirt up and off. When he unhooked my bra, we sat a moment on our knees, facing each other. Complete strangers.

And for the first time, I saw the inky black tattoos etched across both shoulders and his chest.

The anticipated disgust never registered, but for five solid seconds, I told myself I should stop this. Nothing good could come of it. I couldn't even tear my eyes away from him, let alone get up and leave.

I ran my finger along the star tattooed on his right shoulder. His eyes closed, and his nipples became tiny hard points. I touched one. His movements mirrored mine. My mind kept trying to interject, to make me behave sensibly, but I could no more respond to reason at this point than I could've stopped breathing. My need for him was overwhelming.

Whatever was happening, I let him reach down, unsnap my jeans, and slide them off, along with my panties. He stood to peel off his own jeans, and we stared at one another, brazenly.

He exhaled. "You're so beautiful."

And while he was skinny, he was all tight muscle. *Built* would be the wrong word, but he was sculpted and cut in ways that did funny things to my insides.

"Come here." I held out my hand and led him onto the bed next to me.

He grasped my shoulders, and when we kissed again, he leaned into me so that we fell sideways together.

He traced my cheek before he let his hands explore farther south. "I swear I didn't have this in mind when I invited you here, but I'd be lying if I said I wasn't attracted to you from the moment I saw you."

"From the first moment?" My heart raced as I touched the muscles leading down to his hip. It had been a long time since I'd been with a man like this, and it felt forbidden and dangerous.

"The very first." His hand had reached as far as my inner thigh before turning back. He gently knocked my legs apart so he could slide a finger against me. I let out a soft moan.

He pushed me onto my back, still kissing me, and threw his leg over. My breathing intensified when his erection made contact with my skin.

I whispered, "Adam?" My voice sounded husky. "Do you have a condom?"

He stopped. "I—"

"A condom? In a drawer maybe?"

"No, I—"

"No? How don't you—?"

He rolled slightly away. "I just don't. Can we just—?" He ran his hand down my torso. But third base would've been a huge letdown when we were about to steal home.

I sat up. "Hold on."

My dad always told me ingenuity was the key to success. I doubted he was talking about pickpocketing my brother for protection, but I was sure in theory he'd approve of me slipping down the hall to Micah's canvas bag and stealing not one but two condoms. Micah would never miss them.

I came back to the bedroom, hoping all the heat hadn't vanished. But Adam met me at the door and wrapped his fingers into my hair, drawing me in for an intoxicating kiss. My knees nearly buckled. He caught me and lifted me onto the bed. Our legs twined together, lips inseparable.

He worked the condom without even looking at it, so my fears that he didn't use them were allayed. Once he was set, he nudged me over and sucked on my lower lip as he guided himself into me. I gasped.

My legs wrapped around his back as he thrust and withdrew with urgency. Pleasure exploded throughout my entire body. At the frenetic pace we hit, I knew the whole thing would be over before we'd even begun, but then Adam slowed it down, stopping altogether to touch and kiss. I untangled my legs from him, and he caressed my skin. He reached down between us to run his thumb against me, and I arched my back. When he rocked his hips again, I went over the edge with a hard shudder. His breathing came ragged, broken up by short grunts until he let out one sharp groan and collapsed on me. I could feel his heart thudding in his chest before he fell to one side.

His breathing slowed, and he propped on one elbow, still kissing me gingerly on my arms and shoulders, humming a little tune. Lying beside this total stranger, naked and postcoital, I waited for the awkward slut shame to rush in. In all my life, I'd never had a one-night stand, and I wondered if I was supposed to leave now. But leaving was the last thing I wanted to do. The room hung in suspended animation, cocooned, quiet and still, like the beginning of time.

There was nobody else but him.

He looked into my eyes and then up at my forehead. "Your hair is the midnight sky." He traced my cheek. "Your skin is the light of the moon."

I bit the inside of my cheek, trying not to laugh. "You're calling me pale?"

He placed his finger on my mouth. "Your lips are rose petals on a snow-covered field." He leaned in and kissed me once. He half smiled, playful. "Eden, it's safe to say you are the fairest of them all."

My laugh stopped in my throat. I caught his hand in mine and intertwined our fingers. Words failed me.

But he didn't seem to expect a response. He wrapped his arm around my waist. "Sleep here with me?"

A peace settled over me, and I slipped off, listening to Adam's quiet breathing. It sounded just like music.

Chapter 4

As my eyes adjusted to the morning light, I focused on the clothes hanging in the closet. Where had my wardrobe gone? Disoriented and not quite awake, I inventoried the men's button-up shirts, heavy leather jacket, leather pants . . .

Leather pants?

Movement behind me brought my mind fully awake, and a jolt of alarm shot through me. Oh, God. I'd most certainly had too much to drink the night before, but I didn't think I was drunk at the moment I'd decided to consummate my new friendship with Adam.

Out in the hall, Micah called out for Adam. I threw the covers over my face in case he went around opening doors.

Adam rolled over and kissed the top of my head. Then he slung out of bed, yelling, "Micah? I'm in my bedroom. I'll be right out."

I folded the covers down and watched him pull on his boxers. He looked back at me and flashed that wicked grin. "Stay right there."

My heart thudded in my chest, whether from nerves or residual attraction I couldn't be sure.

As soon as Adam left the room, I followed and put my ear to the door. I needed to know Micah's version of events so I could successfully lie to him as needed.

Micah asked, "Do you know if my sister went to my place or if she headed home? I can't reach her."

My phone! I'd left it in the green room at the club after all. That was going to complicate my day. But at least it hadn't rung in Adam's sitting room when Micah called. That would've taken some explanation.

"I didn't see her leave this morning." Adam bullshitted extremely well.

"Okay. I guess I'll check my place then. I'll call her friend Stacy later if I don't hear from her. Thanks for the bed. And call me later about the gig, either way, okay?"

When the front door slammed shut, I was stark naked on the floor of Adam's bedroom with my ear against the door.

Without any better plan, I climbed under the covers, wishing I'd put on some clothes. It was one of the more awkward moments in my life.

Adam peeked around the door frame. "Are you hungry? I'm going to make some pancakes."

"Starving. But do you mind if I use your shower?"

"One sec." He left and came back carrying my backpack and purse. "How did Micah miss seeing these?" He pushed open the bathroom door. "The towels are clean. Let me know if you need anything."

When he'd left, I dumped the contents of my backpack onto the bathroom floor and surveyed the clothes I had to choose from. I could wear the black rayon knee-length stewardess skirt I'd worn to work the day before or jeans that smelled like an ashtray after a night out with Micah. I opted for the skirt.

I lifted my dirty T-shirt off the floor and sniffed. It also reeked of cigarettes. But my pin-striped button-up shirt reeked of corporate America. Besides, I'd balled it up before shoving it into my bag, and it was wrinkled beyond recognition. I breathed in the fabric of the T-shirt. It was smoky, but I'd been wearing it when Adam first kissed me, so it couldn't be that bad.

I flashed back to that first kiss and sucked in my breath. My eyes rolled back in my head at the memory of his lips on my arms and neck. More to the point, Adam had said he liked the perfume I had on. I dug through my purse and found the vial.

When I finally emerged from the bathroom and took a seat at the kitchen table, Adam frowned. "You got dressed."

I snickered. "Yeah, good eye."

"And now I feel completely out of place."

He still wore only his boxers, but he didn't make a move to go add more clothes. Instead, he flipped pancakes onto each of our plates and sat down kitty-corner to my right. While he scraped butter onto his stack, I passed him through my analysis scanner.

His messy hair was no better or worse than the day before, confirming my suspicion he did absolutely nothing to control it. His dark eyes gave off the impression he was always thinking, but the crinkles around them gave off the impression whatever he was thinking might make me laugh. He wasn't terribly well built, but neither was he flabby or overly thin. It was apparent he used his muscles, though nowhere in the vicinity of a bench press. Maybe he ran long distance.

And he was a musician. A musician living at his parents'. With tattoos.

He pretty much failed to meet any criteria for someone I'd ever want to date.

I shoved a forkful of pancake into my mouth, surprised at how delicious they tasted. I mentally added cooking to the pros list. "Tell me about your tattoos."

He pointed at the star on his left shoulder. "I got this one when I started my first band, Dark Star. We were going to be together forever, as those things go. We actually managed to get a paying gig before we broke up." He pointed at letters spelling *Zoso* on his right shoulder. "This one here . . . yeah, I was kind of obsessed with Led Zeppelin for a while. And drunk."

"What's that one mean?" I pointed my fork at the kanji over his heart.

He looked down, as if he had to remind himself what was permanently etched on his own skin. He laid a finger across the symbol and tapped. "It means 'faith.' "

"Faith in what?" It didn't matter how cute he was. If he turned out to be a religious zealot or a pretentious fake Buddhist, I was out of there.

"More like 'faith in who?'" His playful expression had been replaced by a dark shadow. He looked at me with penetrating eyes, and I wasn't sure if he was going to tell me anything more. He sucked on his upper lip for half a second, as though he were weighing me in a balance. He must have let me pass through some mysterious filter since he finally explained. "This one started out as a reminder to have faith in myself at a time when I'd lost it. But as I tackled that demon, I saw it as a reminder to have faith in others. That's always been a lot harder for me."

"Oh. That's actually really nice." Adam was full of surprises.

"What about you? Any hidden tattoos?"

"Oh, no. I'm terrified of needles." Not to mention my complete snobbery regarding the class of people who got tattoos.

He stretched, and the muscles on his torso grew taut. His hip bones peeked out of the waistband of his boxers. "What do you want to do today?"

I wanted to push down the waistband of his boxers, but instead, I pushed the plate back and looked into the living room to check on the whereabouts of my purse. "I'm going to need to go over to the club pretty soon. I left my phone there."

"Can it wait?"

"I should call Micah before he starts looking for me."

He slid his phone toward me. "You can use mine."

"Then he'd know for sure I spent the night here."

He yawned and scratched his side. "So?"

"Wouldn't that be a bad foot for you to start on with him?"

He cut his yawn short and sat up. "What do you mean?"

Maybe I'd jumped to conclusions. "Aren't you going to be working for him? Is he hiring you to replace his bass player?"

Based on his burst of laughter, I concluded I was way off. I frowned in displeasure at his reaction. "What?"

"I don't even play bass."

"What do you play?"

"Come with me." He took my hand and led me down the hall to a closed door. "Hold on." He left me standing in the hallway as he took a few quick steps and ducked into his bedroom.

I followed him out of curiosity and collided with him as he was pulling a shirt over his head just inside the doorway. When his head popped out the neck hole, he grabbed my wrist and lifted my arm up and back, forcing me against the wall. He caught me in a deep kiss. My body instantly ignited, and I responded to him exactly as I had the night before. My free hand grabbed for his, and our fingers intertwined. He pushed that arm against the wall next to my other, above my head.

He broke the kiss, and his eyes slowly regained focus. "Mmm. There's something about you." He looked at the room and laughed. "You've devirginized my parents' bedroom."

I swallowed. "You don't mean . . . You're not a—?"

"Me?" He stepped back and raked his hands through his hair. "I mean, I've never had a girl in here."

"You've never—?"

"I have, yes. The room hasn't." He blushed. "Not that I—"

"You don't—?"

"I mean, I have but—"

I bit my lip. "You have?"

"I don't usually."

"No, me either."

"I don't want you to think—"

"Or you."

He exhaled. "Follow me."

He led me from his bedroom and opened the door to a room I hadn't been in yet. The walls were sound-proofed. Several guitars—acoustic and electric—leaned against stands. Another framed gold record sat in the corner. Micah used to have one of those hanging on his bedroom wall at my parents'. I guess it gave him something to dream about. Nice to see Adam had ambition, too, no matter how unrealistic.

He picked up a beautiful mahogany guitar and sat down on a stool, one foot propped on the lowest rung. I took a stool across from him and rested my back against the wall as he strummed and tuned the guitar. Then he plucked out a delicate arpeggio and sang. He had a beautiful voice, and I closed my eyes to better focus in on the sounds. I started humming, and when the chorus repeated, I harmonized along with him. I opened my eyes when he finished and found him smiling.

I smiled back. "That was beautiful. One of yours?"

He nodded. "Do you play?"

"I do, but only classical. I'm spoiled for nylon strings."

He jumped up and grabbed another guitar. "Show me?"

I thought about playing something familiar he would know, but decided to play one of my own instead. I rarely had the opportunity to perform my own songs for anyone. As I played, I watched him. He closed his eyes as I'd done and sought the tune. He came in with the harmony, making my song sound far lovelier. Honestly, it was turning me on like nothing else.

When the song ended, there was silence, and we held each other's gaze a moment. Then he jumped up and took the guitar, placing it on its stand. He sat down again. "We should duet."

"You mean like Joy Williams and John Paul White?"

"Who?"

"Um." I searched my mind for something he'd recognize. "Like Robert Plant and Alison Krauss?"

"Exactly." His eyes lit up, and once again his face transformed from cute to beautiful. "I'm serious. We should record some songs together. It would be fun."

"Fun, yes. And expensive." Studio time wasn't something you paid for, for the fun of it.

He scooted his stool close to mine and grabbed my hands. "We should do it."

"Adam and Eden?" I snorted. I was beginning to think maybe he suffered from mania or delusions of grandeur.

"Adam in the Garden of Eden." A wicked smile crept up his face.

I had to admit it sounded exciting. From the tent forming in his boxers, it was clear he felt the same way. My own pulse hadn't slowed since he'd sung with me. My eyes fell on his lips, his luscious lips, and I wanted to taste them again. I loosed a hand from his grip and reached up to run my finger across his mouth.

He grabbed my hand with both of his and kissed my palm. He breathed in deep. Then, as though my arm were a rope, he used his hold to draw me toward him. Our lips met and our hands became free agents again, exploring, exciting.

My pulse throbbed between my thighs, and I groaned, "Unh. I want you so bad."

He stood between my knees and wrapped his hand around the back of my neck. His hardness pressed into me, and I ground against him. His fingers dug into my hair, and he used the anchor to bring my mouth together with his. Out of my control, my hands found his neck, and I tightened my grip to bring us closer still. The attraction I had for him was overpowering.

He reached under my skirt and slid my underwear down and off. I didn't protest.

"Wait here."

He disappeared around the corner and came back with Micah's second stolen condom. "I guess I need to buy some of these."

"Why don't you—?"

He shook his head. "I told you. I don't usually put myself in a position to be so unprepared. I just don't—"

As soon as he was within reach, I grabbed his wrist and reeled him into a kiss. I didn't care to know any more about his history. I ached for him. I dragged on the elastic around his waistband. His skin prickled where my fingers touched. He slid the boxers off.

When he entered me, his eyes rolled back and closed. He moved slowly, arms wrapped around me, kissing my neck. I let him hold me up as I arched my back and took him, faster. The stool wobbled precariously. Still, he didn't slow. With my shoulders against the wall, the stool managed to stay upright. I heard a guttural moan escape my own lips as sheer bliss washed through me. I shuddered, and grabbed his arms. He thrust and let out his breath with a cry and then slowed again. He held me tight a few moments.

My head spun with confused emotions. My feelings for him went deeper than the straightforward physical attraction. I felt as though I'd known him forever, not just one night.

"Adam." I bit my lip, unsure what to say.

"I know. This is going too fast." He tilted his head. "Not that I mind, but seriously, I don't want you to think I'm like this. But there's something, right? It's not just me?"

"No, there's definitely something."

His eyes were soft. "I'm going to call you. Can I see you again?"

"I hope so."

He looked at the clock on the wall. "I'm going to have to get ready to go soon. I have a gig later, and I have to meet up with my band." He sighed, and twined his fingers through mine. "You could come with me."

I bit back the "That's what she said" and the "I already did" comments I might have said under ordinary circumstances. As much as I loved to see his face light up with laughter, I was growing fond of his dark serious eyes, the desire lining his face.

Instead, I considered his invitation. I already knew what it meant to spend a day at band practice. Waiting, ignored, pretending to pay attention when I'm feeling generous, searching for a sofa to nap on when I'm not—not my idea of a perfect Saturday. Also I knew firsthand how bandmates felt about loitering girlfriends.

Besides, I still needed to go find my phone. "Maybe some other time. I should be going."

"Wait. Let me put your number in my contacts. I'm going to call you."

We went out to the kitchen, and I leaned back between the Aunt Jemima and the Land O'Lakes while he punched his phone.

I didn't hang around waiting for him to shower and change

as much as I would've liked to. Another kiss, another brush of skin—like a drug, I wanted more. But I needed to leave, so we kissed good-bye, more than once. I struggled to walk away, but made it out the front door, down the steps to the street, and onto the subway, all the while fighting to keep my legs from shaking.

Chapter 5

My phone had been kicked under a table next to the outlet where I'd left it charging in the club's green room. I knelt on the disgusting floor and tugged carefully on the cable to fish it out, cursing myself the entire time for my forgetfulness.

Tobin stopped me on my way out the back door and asked, "How'd things go with Adam last night?"

I blushed. "Um."

He didn't seem to notice my hesitation and added, "I hope he and Micah hit it off."

"Oh. Right." I exhaled. "They seem to have."

"Hey, you should perform with Micah more often. Or maybe come in and open by yourself?"

"Me?"

"Yeah, why not?"

Why not?

"I suppose I could. I'd never really thought about it. I mean, I work full-time and—"

"Yeah, so do most of these guys. Anyway, think about it."

As I exited the dank, dark club into the clear, bright blue October morning, I dialed Micah's number and woke him up. He kept the hours of a vampire, but in my urgency to cover up last night, I forgot I could've taken my time. It wasn't even noon.

With that task discharged, I immediately regretted turning

Adam down on his offer to tag along with his band. I didn't even know what kind of music they played. I had half a mind to jump on the A-C back to Brooklyn. But reluctantly, I headed downstairs to the uptown tracks toward Penn Station to catch a train home.

Someone had left an empty Snapple bottle on the floor of the subway car. For the whole ride, I watched it careen back and forth slowly, changing direction midroll on the curves or speeding up and ping-ponging against the walls with a *plunka-plunka-plunka-ponk*. I hated being on that subway, alone, with a whole empty weekend stretching out before me. I wished I'd asked for Adam's phone number. I wished I'd stayed with him. As it was, I'd have to wait for him to call or text me.

I sat alone in a three-seater on the forty-minute NJ Transit ride to Metropark. With nothing to do but reread an *Acoustic Guitar* magazine, I stared out the window, watching Elizabeth and Linden pass by. The electrical wires above the train tracks loped up and down, hypnotizing. The events of the night before grew more distant as the sights out the window grew more familiar.

What had that been? A one-night stand? I chided myself for my lack of self-control. I'd never done anything like that before. But the attraction I'd felt for Adam was potent. Irresistible. I wondered what he was doing right then. I wondered if he was thinking about me.

When I got home, I took another shower and then lay down on the sofa, intending to take a quick nap. When the doorbell woke me, I stretched and peered through the security hole, stunned to see Rick Whedon, DDS, standing on my stoop, wearing a white polo with a pair of knit sleeves draped over his shoulders like a sweater scarf.

Oh shit.

I threw open the door and babbled out an excuse. "Sorry, Rick. Come in. I'm almost ready," I lied.

As quick as I could, I threw on some date-night clothes and ran a brush through my hair. Frantic, I looked around to make sure I wasn't forgetting anything.

Teeth!

In the bathroom, I brushed my teeth and sized up my appearance. I couldn't put on makeup at the best of times, but I fashioned my hair into a barrette and rummaged around my purse for some lip gloss. My hand clutched a plastic tube, but when I took it out, I discovered the perfume Thanh had given me. It made me think of Adam, and a deep pang of desire nearly doubled me over.

Right. No perfume.

I dropped the vial in a drawer, grabbed a light sweater, and we were on our way.

Rick walked me out to his Porsche and opened my door. He skipped around to the other side, started the engine, and backed out. He gave it one good loud rev before peeling off through the parking lot at an unnecessary speed. Once on the main road, he punched his radio and tuned to SiriusXM's The Pulse. Pharrell's "Happy" filled the car as Rick tapped his finger along—on the upbeat.

Over the music, he asked, "How long has it been?"

We'd gone to high school together years ago, but even then, our acquaintance was nebulous. Our moms were church friends now, which to them was a good enough reason to fix us up. Almost everything I knew about him I'd learned in the last five minutes.

"I think I saw you at the Beer Room last year." There were only so many places to hang out in central New Jersey without hopping on a train.

He looked over at me. "I was surprised to find out you're still single. You know, I had a bit of a crush on you in high school." The way he said it, with no trace of awkward humility or blushing confession, it sounded like a come-on.

For the first time, I gave him my serious consideration. I tried to picture what he'd looked like in high school. He could've played basketball or captained the debate team for all I remembered.

Rick had classic country-club good looks. His blond hair fell in perfect layers. He probably had it cut weekly and styled it meticulously before heading out. His face had all the hallmarks of generic beauty—blue eyes, straight nose, clear skin, great lips. He obviously had a stable job with a fat paycheck. I bet he owned his own house or condo and vacationed somewhere warm regularly. If I were scoring him on looks and job alone, he'd get high marks.

"So, Rick. How is it you're still single?"

He cut a glance at me. "I just haven't found the right girl, yet. I take commitment very seriously." His teeth were fucking perfect.

Once in a while, Mom set me up with guys who seemed all right on paper. So far a reason always emerged to explain why they needed to be set up in the first place. But since I was being set up too, I tried not to judge.

Nine times out of ten, I managed to find a compelling excuse to head her meddling off at the pass. She was persistent, though. She figured if she threw enough spaghetti at the wall, something might stick. But her notions of unacceptable were worlds apart from my own. While I balked at dating a guy who touched people's teeth for a living, she saw nothing inappropriate in suggesting I give her forty-five-year-old gynecologist a chance.

Finally, we pulled into a parking lot. I looked out the window to discover Rick had taken me to an Applebee's.

After he gave his name to the hostess, we sat, hips pressed together, in the waiting area with a square plastic buzzer. The narrow bench caused me to slide forward, and after a few minutes, I finally asked if he'd mind taking a seat at the bar until our table was ready.

The whole restaurant was crowded with people hollering at the TVs hanging from the walls. I glanced back at Rick to find his eyes glued to the game.

"So my hair caught fire this morning," I said.

"Huh?" He refocused on me.

"I asked if we should order drinks."

"Yeah, sure." He flagged the bartender and ordered a couple of beers without consulting me. It so happened I wanted a beer, so I didn't correct him.

"I don't think I've been to *this* Applebee's." I needed to get my sarcasm in check fast. It wasn't Rick's fault I didn't want to be there.

"Yeah? I come here all the time." The beers arrived, and he laid a single on the bar. "So, what's Micah doing? Is he still playing music?"

Here was a topic I could speak on. "Yeah, he's doing really well actually. I just went to see him play last night."

"God, I haven't seen him in so long. I still remember one time he played at some kid's graduation party or something."

I laughed. "Jeff O'Riordan?"

"Yeah, I think so. And you came up onstage and sang something."

I wracked my brain, trying to recall that night. "Was it 'Piece of My Heart'?"

His eyes lit up. "Maybe. I just remember you were so great. I always thought you'd be the one to do something like that. I mean, Micah was always talented, but you had something. Why didn't you pursue that?"

"Music? That's a hobby, not a career."

He knit his brow. "Does Micah know you look down on his career?"

I choked on my beer and coughed. "Micah knows I support him fully. And he supports me. I actually envy him for taking such a risky path. But I guess I wanted to do something"—I tried to recall how I'd ended up analyzing mouse sperm—"more traditional."

When I first decided to major in biochemistry, it felt like anything but traditional. After years of struggling with my parents' faith-based explanations of the world, I loved that science provided quantifiable answers to the great questions of life, the universe, and everything. But after I graduated, I traded cosmic knowledge for cold hard cash. I knew Anubis Labs specialized in erection enhancement pills, but they seduced me with promises of stability. They operated near my hometown, and I needed to pay off my student loans and start saving money to go back to grad school. But it was a hard sell for my parents.

Penile turgidity in mice is a fun thing to explain to your dad when he asks how your fancy degree in biochemistry has helped you.

Mouse boners have the added bonus of impressing Mom, who's convinced herself that you're still a virgin.

Rick raised his glass. "So what are you doing these days?"

Back to this question. "Mainly just making money to pay my way through grad school. It's always been my plan to go back to school to research genetic diseases." It wasn't exactly a lie. My current ambivalence about that career path didn't negate the goals that got me to where I was.

He swallowed. His upper lip glistened with unconsumed beer. "So you're doing medical research?"

"Sort of." I grimaced. "Turns out all the money's tied up in researching better orgasms."

Rick's face dropped. If this were a movie, he'd have done a spit take. I realized I'd let down my guard, talking like I would to Micah. "What I mean is—"

The buzzer erupted in bright red lights, chasing each other around the square. Rick jumped up, and we headed back to the hostess stand to be led to our table.

When we sat down, I combed through my memories to find something about him I could talk about. He'd been in Micah's class, not mine. But Micah was always popular and bringing his friends over. Most of the kids I knew were his age, and after his class graduated, I felt left behind. I still couldn't remember anything about Rick. Had he played lacrosse? Or soccer?

Rick busied himself looking over the menu, even though he'd probably memorized it. The waitress came, and he told her, "We'll start with the spinach and artichoke dip. Then"—he scanned the Two for Twenty menu and pointed at a picture—"I'll have the sirloin."

The waitress jotted it down. She lifted her eyes off her pad. Before I could speak, Rick added. "And she'll have"—he looked up at me—"the fiesta lime chicken?"

The waitress had already gathered our menus and walked off

before I could recover from the shock. "What made you think I wanted that?"

He shrugged. "You didn't contradict me."

"I'm perfectly capable of ordering for myself." I took a deep breath. "Whatever. It's fine." I stared up at the TV to try to find the time. Rick looked up as well, and his eyes glazed over as though he'd decided to give up and watch the football game.

The chips and dip arrived. I poked at it, struggling for something to say. I brought up my mental checklist and appended new additions to the deal-breaker list. The pros list needed a touch up as well, since I'd apparently left out some vital characteristics, such as "knee-buckling smolder" and "sexy as a motherfucker." God, I was no better than Stacy or Kelly talking about one of their latest celebrity crushes. I liked to think I was more responsible than that. Would I really rate sex over a safe and solid future?

Maybe I was in the right job after all.

I gave Rick another appraisal. Suppose I married this guy. I'd never have to worry about anything. I knew where we'd live, where we'd "summer." We'd have a family, and our kids would have pearly white teeth and names like Emily and Noah. And I'd start drinking at three. And he'd murder me one night in my sleep. And everyone would talk about what a perfect couple we always seemed like.

A waitress passed by, and Rick's eyes dropped down to her ass right as she skirted our table. And that was it. My future husband was already cheating on me.

I nearly asked him to take me home right then, but practicality won out: I was starving. I hadn't eaten since that morning. I hadn't had anything at all since a half-naked Adam had served me pancakes.

I gasped for air.

What was I doing there? With all his perfect hair and perfect teeth, his perfect clothes and perfect job, the man sitting across from me never stood a chance. His eyes connected with mine, and he looked like he might attempt to engage in small talk, but I was done playing the game.

"So, Rick, do you have any interesting tattoos?"

"What?"

"Tattoos? Do you have any?"

His lip curled. "No. Do you?"

"Not yet." I picked up a tortilla chip. "Do you cook?"

He pinched the bridge of his nose. "Of course not. Do you play poker?"

And at that moment, I just quit, as I realized Rick had done from the moment I dropped the O bomb anyway. For a sexist pig, he sure was a prude.

We suffered through our meal with only a few barbed grenades lobbed over the course of the next hour. The fiesta lime chicken turned out to be the best part of the night.

He drove me home to the dulcet sounds of Robin Thicke, walked me to my door, and said, "Thanks for coming out. We'll have to do it again sometime," in monotone. Then without a handshake or a pat on the shoulder, he left.

I never told him he'd had a piece of spinach caught in his perfect teeth for the past hour.

It was early still, so I called Stacy and invited her to come over to watch *Say Anything*. Again. As soon as she dropped her jacket and grabbed a soda, she sat on the sofa and pried into my business.

"How was your date?"

"Soul crushing."

She rolled her eyes. "I'm sure you're exaggerating, Eden. What was today's deal breaker? Did he smell weird or something?"

"I wouldn't know." I tried to remember if I'd even noticed. Instead, my mind drifted, and I could almost recall the way Adam smelled. If I could bottle that up and sell it, I'd make millions. Except I'd probably keep it for myself. But I'd much rather get it from the source. The thought of touching Adam's skin made my knees weak, and I plopped down beside Stacy. "I need to revise my checklist to include 'Swoon worthy.' Rick was definitely not."

"You need to let me see this list. If that wasn't already on there, you've been doing it wrong." She sat up straight. "Hey, so Micah called earlier looking for you. He said you both spent the night at some guy's house, but he didn't know when you left. You weren't here, so . . . where were you?"

"Speaking of swoon worthy . . . You have to promise not to say anything to Micah. Not yet anyway. He'd disapprove."

"You slept with that guy, didn't you?"

The smile that broke across my face refused to be contained.

She sat up straight, eyes wide. "I was only kidding. Holy shit." She knew me well enough to know it was unprecedented, but she segued easily back into prying. "So what's he like?"

"Cute. Very. But he's a bit on the grungy side."

She crossed her arms and cocked her head in friendly condescension. "Like you, then?"

"I'm not grungy. I'm just not as girly as you. Anyway, when we got to his place, Micah fell asleep. Adam showed me his bedroom, and things heated up very fast." Thinking back on how fast, I experienced a secondary wave of exhilaration, like that unexpected hill on the backside of a roller coaster.

"So who is he? What does he do? Does he have a brother? Did you take any pictures?"

I held up a finger to stop her incessant line of questions, cracking up at the image of photographing Adam in the state he was in when I left.

"One question at a time. His name is Adam Copeland." Her face lit up at the name. "No, not *that* Adam Copeland, though he *is* a musician."

"A musician named Adam Copeland, eh?"

"Seriously, Stacy. It's just a coincidence. He was at the club interviewing to play bass for my brother's band." I replayed the earlier conversation and recalled my assumption had been wrong. "No wait, that's not right. I don't know why he was at the club."

Stacy frowned and slumped. "That's too bad. Adam Copeland is seriously smoking hot."

I glared at her. "And you think my Adam isn't?"

"Well, I don't know. How old is he? What's he look like?"

"Not sure about his age, but I'd guess maybe twenty-seven. North of twenty-five, south of thirty, or else he doesn't look his age. He has dark hair, blacker than mine. It looks like he's never met a brush. He's not super tall, but maybe just under six feet."

"Dark hair, huh? How'd he make it inside your perimeter without getting shot down?"

"Well, he didn't. Not at first. But then . . ." I thought back to the night before. When he'd touched me to smell my perfume, something had ignited. But no, before that. When he'd first smiled at me, he'd already breached the fortress.

And those eyes.

"His eyes are brown, I think."

"You think?"

"They're dark, so dark. His lips are . . . God . . . wonderful. Um. Oh, and he has a mess of tattoos."

"Tattoos?" She picked up her phone and started tapping on the screen.

Despite her apparent loss of interest, I answered her question anyway. "Yeah, I know. Deal breaker, right?"

"Can you describe them?" She hadn't taken her eyes off her phone and punched and scrolled all the while feigning curiosity about my life.

"His tattoos?" I made a duck face and rolled my eyes up, as though that would unlock the image in my memory. "Hmm. One was a star. Another was something to do with Led Zeppelin. Then he had some designs across his chest. They were all black."

Hearing myself describe him, I smiled at all the boxes I normally would've mentally ticked to turn away any other guy. Should I mention to Stacy that he was skinny and lived at his parents'? Should I tell her he didn't even keep condoms around? He obviously wasn't a virgin—or even lacking in experience. Maybe he'd had a dry spell. Not that I could judge anyone else for that, given my track record. And quite honestly, I found it endearing.

In fact, despite every mental reservation I should have, I wanted to see him again. Despite his imperfections, he was kind of perfect. And I hoped he'd call me.

Stacy broke my reverie, shoving her phone into my face. "Is this him?"

On her phone, Adam stood outside a restaurant, dressed in a black T-shirt and jeans, with a glamorous woman attached to his elbow. I snapped my eyes back up at her. "How'd you get a picture of him?"

"I didn't. I did a Google image search. That's *the* Adam Copeland."

I snatched the phone from her and scrolled through the rest of the image results. A photo shoot with his band. A fan picture taken from several rows back at a concert. More pictures of him out and about on the street.

My heart jumped into my throat. I scrolled back to the photo-shoot pictures. They made him look a thousand times more beautiful than he was in person. But I'd take the real Adam over this plastic rock star any day of the week.

A picture popped up with him onstage, hands wrapped around the mic, sweat pouring off his face, face twisted in mid-song rapture, one leg bent in front of the other—in those leather pants.

"Oh, my God." A wave of dizziness hit me, and I dropped the phone on the sofa. "Why didn't he tell me?" When I asked him about his name, he'd purposely misled me. He knew I didn't know and didn't correct my misunderstanding. Damn if he didn't know how to tell a lie just so.

I grabbed Stacy's shoulders and shook her. "Why didn't he tell me?!"

Stacy grabbed my shoulders back and leaned her forehead against mine, fixing my eyes with hers. "Eden. Maybe he wanted to make sure you liked him for the right reasons? You know how it is with Micah."

I knew exactly how it was with Micah. Fans often thought they knew him and came on strong, offering themselves up to him with absolutely no provocation. Most of them were pretty cool, but once in a while he'd get a superfan who fell in love with him. Trouble was, they weren't in love with Micah at all. How could they be? They didn't know him. They knew the guy they saw onstage or at the merch table for a few minutes. They knew the guy they'd pieced together from information swapped and shared. But they didn't know my brother.

Micah appreciated his fans and gave them access to interact with him as much as they might like within the confines of his gigs. But he never dated them, not even the cool ones. Outside of his work, he found it tiresome to deal with people who knew more about him than he knew about himself. I'd only experienced it secondhand. Knowing about his sister seemed to be a point on the fandom trivial pursuit.

"You might be right." I sat back and took a breath. "Maybe he'd rather sleep with a girl who thought he was nobody special."

Stacy's eyes opened wide, as though the reality of the situation finally hit home. "I can't believe you had sex with Adam Copeland. Oh, my God. What's he like?"

"Were you even listening? I just got through describing him to you."

"No, I mean, what's he really like? How does he kiss? Oh, my God, what's his *you know* like?"

"Do you hear yourself, Stacy?" I hated to disappoint her, but I wasn't about to recount the graphic details of my night. "He's just a regular guy. You'd never know he was some famous rock star."

"But he totally is. Do you know how lucky you are? Do you know how many people would've loved to swap places with you last night?"

"I guess. I still wish he'd told me."

"Does it make a difference to you? I mean, would you have treated him differently if you knew?"

I replayed the night, imagining I knew he was famous the whole time. He wasn't anybody I'd ever followed, so in that regard, I didn't care. But it certainly would've messed with my self-confidence. Why would someone who could have anyone he wanted pick me?

"I suppose I would have. I might've been nicer about his band. Oh! And . . ."

I reached for my phone and Googled his band. After a few clicks I found what I wanted.

"Holy shit. He's playing Madison Square Garden right now. And he invited me to tag along." I hit my forehead with my palm. "I'm an idiot."

"See? He probably loved that you didn't give a shit about hanging around with his band. But do me a favor and snag me some backstage passes next time. Oh, my God!"

She picked her phone back up, opened Facebook, and began typing frantically. I realized what she was doing a minute before she hit Send.

"Stacy! You can't put this on Facebook!"

Her face dropped. "I wasn't putting anything about the sex."

I grabbed her phone. She'd written, *My best friend got to hang out with Adam Copeland last night. EEE!* And she'd tagged me. I closed the program down before she could send. "No."

She slumped. "Okay, but aren't you dying?!"

Was I dying? Twenty minutes ago, I was dying over an ordinary guy who was totally in my league, if not below it, and who'd made my knees buckle. I couldn't begin to process how I felt about learning someone I wanted was wanted by everyone else. Like finding the most beautiful painting at a garage sale and discovering it was a lost Picasso. I pictured Adam up for auction at Sotheby's. I couldn't even make the opening bid. But for a time, he had been mine.

We sat on the sofa late into the night, running all the scenarios from best to worst.

Option one: Maybe he really liked me and would call again. I hoped this was true but feared I'd never hear from him again.

"Out of my league" was a massive understatement. Oh, God. I'd played my amateurish music for him, a professional musician. I wanted to cry.

Option two: Maybe he liked that I didn't know who he was and wouldn't want to see me once I did. I knew that was paranoid thinking, but it was a possibility. I mean, why didn't he come out and tell me when I asked?

Option three: Maybe he didn't care either way and picked up a girl every night. The state of his condom readiness belied this notion. Although maybe he bought the forty-count pleasure pack in bulk from Sam's Club and had just run out.

I fell asleep and dreamed I was standing outside a concert hall, screaming Adam's name as he waved and stepped into a limousine. I tossed and turned all night. God forbid I should ever wait in line to talk to him like a crazed fan. I'd die of shame.

When I finally woke up on the sofa in the dark of predawn, my mind started racing. Stacy had fallen asleep on the other end of the sofa. I threw a blanket over her and crept to my bedroom to power up the laptop. I had some research to do.

As I suspected, Adam Copeland was a common name, and in fact he wasn't even the only famous one. I narrowed it down to *Adam Copeland Walking Disaster*. God, he had a Wikipedia entry, but all that told me was that he was a Sagittarius from Brooklyn, currently in the band Walking Disaster, and formerly the drummer in some band called the Pickup Artists.

The band's discography shed no light on Adam, but I couldn't resist finding his albums on Amazon and listening to the samples. I downloaded the most recent and set it to play on repeat through my headphones. I was surprised to discover I already knew three other songs on the CD. I'd never realized they were his. I swore I'd heard at least one of those songs in a commercial. No wonder his band was playing the Garden.

I went back to Google and scanned the image results, trying to reconcile this grungy young musician in Brooklyn with the rock star staring back at me. How had I managed to attract *that*? Surely he had women throwing themselves at him on a nightly basis. And even if they weren't, he could certainly shop among the fashion models and other beautiful women of the earth.

I jumped up and appraised myself in the mirror, hoping to convince myself that anything about my appearance could stand up to the kind of competition I'd be facing if I let myself think of Adam Copeland as a potential love interest. Damn lighting. Surely I wasn't that pale? With some makeup I'd be halfway presentable. God, I wasn't even dressed like a girl Friday night.

The articles that came up from my search didn't help my growing inferiority complex. The newspaper gossip page tracked him from lunches with other well-known musicians and actors to shopping trips along Madison Avenue, occasionally mentioning his band or his music.

There was no evidence he was dating anyone, not on the respectable paper's entertainment pages at least. Surely if he was seeing someone, they would've noticed. Still, I Googled *Adam Copeland girlfriend* and came up with several hits. The first few were other Adams. I knew I shouldn't be spying on him, and the uneasy feeling in the pit of my stomach felt like guilt. But he was a public figure, so who wouldn't peek?

On the second page of results, my heart stopped. *Adam Copeland of Walking Disaster Engaged.*

I clicked through to the article. The name of the site wasn't familiar to me, and there was no source given, but they had a picture of Adam with his arm around the singer Adrianna LaRue, both dressed formally, like they were standing at a photo shoot before an awards ceremony. She smiled right into the camera while he glanced off to his right, hand up, waving at off-camera fans. He looked unbelievably hot in a tuxedo. She was even taller than him, with plaited blond hair and perfect facial features.

The article was dated a month prior and claimed that rumors were circulating that the couple had become engaged after the VMAs.

Googling *Adam Copeland engagement* and *Adam Copeland fiancée* brought back tons of hits—blogs, fan sites, fan forums. I read the posts on one forum and found myself nervously caught up in the drama and in-fighting between the faction of jealous teeth gnashers flummoxed over Adam's alleged engagement and the other faction of levelheaded True Fans who proclaimed it was none of their business. As a poster called Di$a$ter put it, *A true fan is in it for the music after all.*

Pumpkin39, presumably a moderator, had stepped in and told everyone the topic was off-limits and locked the thread.

Good lord. What had I walked into?

Googling *Adam Copeland breakup* brought back nothing related.

I closed the laptop and put my head under my pillow. What the fuck had I done?

Had I just wrecked someone else's relationship?

Chapter 6

As if I weren't feeling rotten enough, my mom called at noon to remind me to come over. "It's Indian Summer. Dress for a June lawn party."

It was early October.

Stacy had gone home, and I had nothing better to do, so I put on a summer dress and drove over. Micah's car swung into the driveway right behind mine, and we pushed through the gate into the backyard together.

Both my parents stood to greet us. Mom squealed, "Oh, *Micah* came!"

My brother got his height from her, and as she hugged him, their blond hair intermingled, interchangeable, reminding me how, even physically, Micah would always be closer to Mom.

I cleared my throat. "Yeah, good to see you, too."

Micah shrugged. "They see you every week."

That comment did nothing to make me feel any better.

By the time I got to the patio to hug Dad, he'd already buried his face behind a newspaper, his fingers and dark hair the only visible evidence of him.

"Hi, Dad."

He acknowledged me with a brief nod. I scolded him. "You know you young people should look up from your devices periodically."

Only Micah laughed at my joke.

My mom sat back down on the super-uncomfortable wrought-iron chair next to the umbrella-shaded latticed wrought-iron table. Dotted around the lawn, she'd hammered in croquet wires. On the table, she'd placed pitchers of alcohol-free mint julep. Her Hollywood-style sunglasses dwarfed her face and contrasted oddly with her homely church dress, giving her more the appearance of a recent cataract-surgery patient than a silver-screen bombshell.

"Oh, Eden. I spoke with Connie Whedon this morning. What happened on your date last night?"

"Oh, God."

"Don't swear, Eden."

I fanned my face, regretting my acceptance of her invitation. But who was I kidding? I always came to her parties. What else was I going to do on a Sunday? Watch football? And if I stayed home, I would've made myself sick reading articles and hating myself for willing my phone to ring. I needed the distraction.

I devoutly wished my mom had some alcohol on hand. "Mom, it was fine. We just didn't hit it off."

"Did you at least try?"

"I did, Mom. You might consider that he didn't want to be out with me either."

"Well, no wonder if you're telling him what you do for a living."

I threw up my hands. "What else should I tell him?"

Micah had the stupid grin on his face he got whenever we fought. "You could tell him you're a sex worker. Then you'd get a second date."

"You know, Mom. Maybe I'm not cut out for the exciting life of a dentist's wife."

Micah broke in with the accent of a yenta. "Geez, Eden, you'd think you'd jump at the chance to marry a dentist or doctor. You should be chasing after ambulances."

I kicked his foot, but laughed because his imitation of Mom was subtle perfection. Mom had once quite seriously suggested I hang out in the hospital waiting room more often in the hopes of running into a nice doctor.

She lifted her sunglasses to look at me eye to eye. "You know, it's just as easy to fall in love with a dentist. You should at least give him a chance."

Micah laughed. "Seriously. You're way too picky, Eden. No wonder you never date anyone."

I lowered my voice. "Micah, it was Rick Whedon."

"Ew. You went out with Dick Whedon?"

I turned to go inside and check the fridge for a soda, and threw back. "You know, Micah's single. Why aren't you harassing him?" It was a rhetorical question. Of course he didn't need to find respectable work or look for a wife or settle down. Maybe they had realistic expectations regarding Micah. Maybe it was a compliment to my superior ability to assimilate into society.

Mom coughed. "Eden. You're not Micah."

I stopped dead and faced her. "What's that supposed to mean?"

She tilted her head and pressed her lips together in a downward smile. "Do you remember when we were on the Salvation Bus?"

How could I forget that? A yearlong nationwide mission trip instead of fourth grade? It kind of sticks in the memory. "Yeah, Mom."

"We'd drive hundreds of miles to get from one town to the next, and your brother would sit up front, asking when we'd get there. And once we'd arrive, he'd jump off the bus and run around exploring, making friends with local kids. Half of our contacts were made through him just being himself."

Between stops, he'd spent every minute practicing on a second-hand guitar, when he wasn't complaining. As soon as the bus doors opened, Micah ran around town promoting himself while Mom and Dad contacted the clergy. By six o'clock, he had a small audience. By eight, he had girls trailing him everywhere he went.

"Yeah, so? He was bored on the bus."

"But you weren't. Whenever we'd get to a new town, you'd slink away at every opportunity to get right back onto that bus and work on something you'd started while we were driving. Remember when you found those snails?"

Those snails. "Of course." I'd carried them in a box for a month, feeding them, watching them, fascinated.

"You'd beg us for small furry animals all the time, but we couldn't very well take a kitten on the road. So you found those snails and those were your friends."

They weren't my friends; they were my lab rats. "What does this have to do with Micah?"

"Micah's cut out for the life he leads—the traveling, the new places, the adventure. But you're different. You need a stable home life, Eden. You need to find a nice man and settle down."

I wanted to argue with her, but maybe she was right. I sucked on my lower lip and sulked.

Micah stretched, obviously tired of the lecture. "Whatever happened to Caleb, anyway?"

"Married." I'd dated Caleb in college, and, just when I thought things might turn serious, he announced he needed the freedom to play the field. I announced I needed the freedom to date men who weren't self-serving assholes. "He sent me a wedding invitation."

"Oh." He grabbed a mallet. "You wanna play?"

"Sure."

We walked out to the lawn and tried to figure out the physics of the game. Micah hit one of his balls halfway across the lawn. Trying to compensate for his mistake, my first strike barely moved the ball four inches.

Mom ran out and took Micah's mallet. "Watch me." She laid one ball next to another and, with her foot positioned on the first, gave it a solid whack.

I stood next to Micah and commented under my breath, "Do you realize these sophisticated techniques will likely be completely lost in one generation?"

Micah tapped his ball with a swish of the wrist. "That's because this is the worst game ever invented."

Once Mom had returned to her shaded throne and I had Micah alone, out of earshot of the few other party guests, I casually broached the burning question. "So Micah." I smacked a ball, and it went wide of the target. "Why didn't you tell me who Adam was?"

He'd been lining up his own mallet, but stopped and blinked at me. "What d'ya mean? I thought you knew."

"I had no idea."

"You've never seen him before? Do you live under a rock?"

I rolled my foot over the ball to move it more in line with the target. Micah didn't even notice, so I nudged it a few inches forward. "I don't pay attention to rock musicians. I'm sure I could rattle off names of well-known folk singers you wouldn't be able to pick out of a lineup."

"You liked him though, right? He seems like a genuinely nice guy."

"Yeah, he does. Why were you hanging out with him, anyway? I assumed you were looking for a bass player."

Micah snorted. "You thought I wanted to hire Adam Copeland?"

"Again, I had no idea who he was."

"Fair point. Actually, he's looking for a band to take out on tour with him as an opening act. He said he likes to give talented musicians the exposure."

"On tour where?"

"Europe. A month of concert arenas in Europe." His eyes glazed over, dreamy.

"So what happens next?"

"Nothing right now. Hopefully, he'll call again, and we'll set something up."

I hesitated a moment and then couldn't help myself. "Can't you call him? Don't you have his phone number?"

"Yeah, I have it, but he's hard to reach. He'll call me when he's ready to talk."

My palms slipped on the croquet mallet handle, and I wiped my hands on my pants.

"Micah, could you give me his number?"

He raised an eyebrow, suspicious. "*Whyyy?*"

"Nothing. He mentioned hanging out again sometime, and I gave him my number but didn't get his."

"Oh, so *now* you'll go out with a musician?"

"I didn't say anything about going out with him. Just forget it."

"It wouldn't matter. He never answers his phone. His voice mail is completely full. I've texted him and gotten no response. I thought about trying to message him on Facebook, but he only has a fan page. And Twitter's even worse. The stream of people tweeting at him would be impossible to compete with. I followed him, but he never followed back, so I can't even direct message him. I didn't know he was coming to the club on Friday. I'm at the mercy of waiting for him to call me."

I giggled at his frustration. He sounded like a woman scorned. "You'd think he'd have private numbers for people who matter."

"He probably does. I'm probably not one of them."

I wondered if I was. It hadn't slipped my notice he hadn't called yet.

Mom hollered over. "Dr. Steve is here!"

The nightmare would never end. Reluctantly, I put up my mallet and retreated to the patio to acknowledge the guest. Out of long habit, I ran him through the scanner. His career was a deal breaker for me. It might be shallow and wrong, but I'd never have been able to get past the fact that he was a gynecologist. The image of him crouched with a speculum between a pair of paper-gown-shrouded knees had already formed and could not be unformed. Aside from that, he wore button-up shirts he didn't button up all the way. Nor did he wear an undershirt. The result was a clear view of his 1970s chest curl. He was just missing a gold medallion and a pair of white slacks to complete the deal.

While I poured a drink to have something to hold, Steve flirted with my mother, and I added another demerit to his checklist.

Mom's sugar smile was plastered to her face as she informed me Steve had recently bought a time-share in Ocala. "That's in Florida."

I closed my eyes so as to keep them from rolling out of my head. Searching for anything to respond to this news, I blurted out, "Isn't that completely landlocked?"

Mom swatted at me and then returned her smile to Steve, covering a slight underlying grimace aimed at me.

Steve didn't seem to notice the undercurrent as he directed his comments toward my dad.

"The price differential on a condo in Ocala as compared to Orlando is worth checking into."

Mom added philosophical complexity to the conversation. "It must be quite warm in Florida at this time of year."

While Mom had Steve's attention, Micah grabbed my elbow and waved for me to follow him. He went around to the front of the house and dropped onto the porch swing. Once I was settled, he kicked back with his feet. We both pulled our legs up and closed our eyes. It took me back years. We'd spent a lot of time sitting on that swing when we were kids. It was where I tried my first—and last—cigarette.

After a few minutes, Micah took a deep breath, and I braced for the big-brother lecture.

"Eden, what are you still doing here?"

I knew what he meant, but couldn't help purposely misunderstanding. "It's still early. I figured I'd stay through dinner."

He looked up at the sky, exasperated. "Seriously, you don't belong here. You're twenty-eight and Mom's fixing you up with Dick Weed? God, I hated that guy when we were teenagers. I can't imagine what a douche lord he turned into."

"I tried to refuse her. You know how she gets."

"That's just it, though. You shouldn't need to refuse her. You shouldn't be here. Why haven't you applied to grad school, Eden? You were supposed to go back this year."

I sucked my teeth. "Oh, so Mom's not supposed to interfere with my life, but you can?"

He sighed. "Eden. You've got so much potential. Unlike Mom, I don't want you to settle. I want you to get your ass out of that groove and take some chances. You're too young to let your life become Saturday night out with some mustache and Sunday afternoon at Mom's."

"Mom was right, though. You're the adventurous one. What happens if I try something new and fail?"

He shrugged. "So what if you fail? You'd learn something and maybe have a good time in the process." He wrapped my hand in his. "And I'll tell you a secret. We're all afraid of failing. We're all scared of adventure."

"You?" A laugh burst out of me.

"Yeah. What if I don't go out with Adam on his tour? What if I go with him and we suck? What if that's the only shot we ever get? What if I spend the rest of my life chasing a dream?"

"So how do you do it?"

"It's not always easy, but I love what I do. You need to figure out what you love, Eden. Everything will fall into place when you do. But please tell me you haven't found it here."

I reached over and gave him a hug. His arms came around me and pulled me in tight. "Thanks, Micah. I'll think about it. I'm glad you came out here today."

There wasn't enough coffee in the world to make Monday morning bearable. I had to go through the pep talk to remind myself why I got up at seven thirty to go to a job that didn't fulfill me in any way other than to replenish my coffers so I could one day get a better job doing more of the same. My pep talks sucked.

Thanh grabbed me the second I got into the lab. "I figured something out over the weekend. Come with me."

"Good morning, Thanh."

He took me back down to the holding cells, where the cute blond twiddled his thumbs to the backdrop of *bow-chicka-wow-wow* music.

"Do you have that vial I gave you?"

I reached into my bag, but then remembered that I'd tossed it into a drawer in my bathroom. "I'll try to bring it in tomorrow."

"Please, do." He seemed agitated. He produced another vial. "Can you put this back on?"

"Thanh, what does it do? You never told me last week."

His shoulders slumped, and he sighed dramatically. "I told you to read the e-mails." He handed the vial out to me.

I gave him the stink eye, but I put the perfume on. "Still nothing. What's it do?"

"I'll tell you in a minute, but I want you to go into the test room and chat with the guy in there for a little while, okay?"

"All right."

Thanh turned off the soft porn and opened the door. I slid a chair over so I faced the guy. Our knees nearly touched.

"Hi. I'm Eden."

He seemed as unimpressed with me as he had the week before. Whatever Thanh was up to, this was a bust. "I'm Glenn."

"Nice to meet you. What do you do for a living, Glenn?" I wagered ten bucks against myself that he was a software developer.

"I work at Sam Ash."

Even though I lost my bet, my smile was genuine. "The one in Edison? I go in there all the time."

His eyes grew wide, and he looked at me for the first time like I was a person, not just a lab tech. "Yeah? I've never seen you in there."

"I normally just buy my guitar strings there." I never would've pegged him for a music store employee. "If you don't mind me saying, you're dressed really nice for Sam Ash."

He looked down at himself and ran his hand along the buttons on his shirt. "I recently moved up to manager. I'm trying to get the respect of my coworkers. They still treat me like a cashier sometimes. Do I look managerial?"

I nodded, but now I was curious about the rest of my assumptions. "I noticed you've got a bit of a tan. Have you spent any time at the beach recently?"

"Oh, yeah. I went to Hilton Head a couple of weeks ago. My parents have a time-share down there."

"Did you vacation with your parents?" I tried to keep the judgment out of my voice. I couldn't begin to imagine traveling with my parents. Not since I was a kid.

He scratched his head. "Well, they paid for it."

Wow.

There was a tap on the window, and I said good-bye to Glenn and returned to the observation room.

Thanh was beaming. "I knew it."

"What did you know?"

"It came to me over the weekend. The chemicals might work fine for mice, but people are social. You need a connection before the rest of the synapses fire. Check it out."

I looked over the metrics Thanh had gathered. Our boy Glenn had a hard-on for me. Literally.

"What is this stuff, Thanh?"

"It's a pheromone-reception enhancer."

A laugh escaped. "What? Like whale sperm or ox musk or the urine of a cat in heat?"

"Nothing like that. Tell me, how do you feel? Honestly? Did you feel any attraction, too?"

"None."

Thanh's face dropped, and I covered quickly to soften his disappointment. "But Glenn's not my type."

Neither was Adam, but my synapses fired like crazy for him. Was it due to this sex ba-bomb? That was ridiculous—those pheromone perfumes were nothing but snake oil.

But why would an international rock star be attracted to me?

"Thanh, could you show me your research?"

When we got to Thanh's lab, we ran into our manager, Keith, and his John Stossel mustache. It was as if he wanted to say, *This is the most mustache a lip can support.* He reached out his hand. "Congratulations on the FDA approval, Thanh. Are you all ready to start the trials?"

While they discussed the schedule for human testing of, I assumed, the perfume I was now wearing, I walked around the lab. When I'd gotten hired, I started in this same lab. I'd been brought in as a lab assistant, based on my undergraduate minor and future desire to work in genetic testing. The field had so much promise to crack wide open mysteries of the human condition, from curing diseases to understanding how the mind works. I'd been excited to do some real-world experiments, but there was one major problem. It turned out I was terrified of mice. I claimed that I had a moral aversion to testing on animals, and they shunted me down to run analysis on the blood work collected in other parts of the company. And there I'd languished for the past several years.

As I took my trip down regret lane, I ran across a thick binder on the counter. I flipped open the jacket to glance at the research. Thanh's name was typed across the front page along with the title: *Genetic Biosynthesis of G Protein–Coupled Pheromone Receptors in Mice.*

I shot up. "Excuse me." Thanh and Keith continued to confer. I raised my voice. "Excuse me."

Thanh stopped talking. Keith turned around and asked, "Can we help you?"

I held up the research paper, hands shaking. "Is this—?" I stopped to control my breathing. "Are you altering my genetic makeup?"

Thanh crossed the room in two steps and snatched the paper away. "Eden, you shouldn't be reading this."

"Answer my question. I never signed up for genetic testing."

He pulled up a stool and sat beside me, unfazed by my anger. "Eden. Stop and think. We can't alter your DNA. The chemical we're developing targets specific proteins that control the on/off switch for certain signals in your cells. When those cells eventually die, your body will produce new cells that will continue to behave as before."

I laughed in relief. Then it hit me. "So this shit's real?"

Thanh stood and snapped. "Of course it is. Ten years of my life went into this research."

I had one last question. "Thanh, how long does the effect last?"

He shrugged. "How long does it take a cell to regenerate?"

The answer to that question was: It depends. Granulocytes take hours to days. Bone cells could take thirty years. "What's your best guess?"

"A day or two?"

"Show me."

He scooted over so I could see a set of cages. "Meet Rob Roy and Cosmo." Thanh had apparently named all of the mice after cocktails. "All the mice in the lab were sent through a cycle of tests without our serum before they were brought together in the presence of the chemical. When any of the tests show positive for an attraction, the pair is isolated for further evaluation. I like to call this the 'sexperiment.' " His goofy grin seemed disproportionate to the quality of his joke.

I didn't hear the rest of what he said as I was lost in a fog of confusion, thinking back to Friday night when Adam had breathed in the perfume on my wrist. Was it possible the drug Thanh was peddling could magnify an attraction so much that the moon could attract the sun?

When I wasn't wearing the perfume, I couldn't even attract a dentist from Middlesex County.

I spent the rest of the day going over the past weekend. My mind ricocheted between hope, doubt, regret, and gratitude. Hope that the perfume had nothing to do with the connection Adam had clearly felt for me. Doubt that I could have attracted someone like Adam on my own without even trying. Regret that I'd experienced something that amazing only to lose it immediately. Gratitude that I'd experienced something that amazing.

After considering every angle, I came to the conclusion Adam had been momentarily tempted by the power of lab-engineered sexual chemistry, but once the air had cleared, he had come to his senses or forgotten about me. Either way, he had never called. I figured I should just chalk the whole experience up to a lesson learned: Never trust Thanh.

So when my phone rang at three p.m. with an unknown number from the Brooklyn area code, I was already halfway down the hall before I hit the answer button on the third ring.

"Hello?" I shouldered through the glass doors, looking around for the most likely place to have a quiet, private conversation.

"Eden?"

"Yup." The bench in the smoking area was empty. I cut across the grass. My heart raced either from exertion or excitement.

"Hey. It's Adam. Sorry I didn't call sooner."

"It's no problem. How are you?" I slowed to get my breathing under control.

"I'm good. Listen."

My heart flipped. *Here we go.*

It was too good to be true. Now he'd tell me about the engagement and the mistake he made and how sorry he was, what a great girl I was. I sucked in a lungful of air and prepared for the worst.

He cleared his throat. "I'm coming out to New Jersey tonight."

"You are?" *Whatever for?*

"I am. I wanted to know if you're free. I know you don't do weeknights or date guys named Adam but hoped you might make an exception. On both counts."

I also didn't date guys who were involved with other women. I silently apologized to my sisters the world over, rationalizing it would be easier to ask him about it in person. "What time?"

He laughed. "Good. Let's make it a real date. I'll pick you up at whatever time people who date go out."

"And . . . What time would that be?"

"You're funny. I'll come by around seven thirty? But I need to know where you live."

I gave him the address, and then he said, "I'll see you tonight."

As soon as I hung up, I wished I'd thought to ask him what to wear. I flipped the phone open and stared at the call log. I stored his name and number in my contacts, and for a moment I was tempted to call his number to see if he'd even answer. Maybe I could compare with Micah later. Or not. I wouldn't want to give out a private number to just anyone.

Floating on air, I went back to work and stared at the meaningless numbers while I fantasized about going on a date with a rock star.

I imagined he'd pick me up in a limo with champagne chilling in the back. He'd whisk me into Midtown Manhattan to one of those restaurants I saw him at on Page 6. Paparazzi would shoot pictures of us as he tucked my arm around his elbow. We'd wave and laugh at a private joke. Then later, he'd take me home, and we'd have monkey sex. I wanted to have monkey sex with a rock star, but, like, aware of it this time. Was that wrong of me? Maybe we'd have monkey sex in the limo.

Then my fantasy turned bleak. Neurotically, I thought of everything that could go wrong, starting with him never showing up.

Or he'd show up, but he'd change his mind and decide he didn't even want to go out with me at all when he saw me again.

Or we'd go out, but he'd figure out how ordinary I was. I wouldn't live up to his memory of me, such as it was. And we'd have nothing in common. Nothing to talk about. What did I have to say to someone living his lifestyle?

And he was going to get angry at me for asking about his engagement because there was no way I wasn't going to ask.

But even if the date went well, what if . . . oh, God, what if he didn't want to have monkey sex with me again? Friday night could've been a total fluke. And what if the entire thing was based on a hyper-enhanced sex appeal? I sniffed my wrist. The residual odor from Thanh Phanh's pharmaceutical pheromones lingered.

How bad of a breach of ethics would it be to knowingly seduce a man with a biochemical agent? Was it any different from Stacy in her miniskirts or Kelly with her stiletto heels and push-up bras? And why did women wear perfume in the first place if not to appear more attractive to men?

The angel on my shoulder whispered, "Eden, you know the difference. He has no chance against chemical warfare."

The devil showed up on the other shoulder in a cloud of dust and boomed, "But you have no chance without it."

The devil was right. I had no chance with Adam without the added kick of the perfume. That should've been a good reason to scrub my arms in bleach. Have a nice date out with a nice guy and then let him go on with his life.

Stacy caught me staring off into space. "He called?"

I bit my lip and nodded. "We're going out to dinner tonight."

Telling her turned out to be a dumb idea. She "dropped by" at seven fifteen to make sure I looked presentable for my date.

"You can't be going out like that."

I looked down at my going-out clothes. "Why? What's wrong with this?" I didn't normally wear skirts outside of work, but the one I had on looked as good as any other. Granted, it covered my thighs.

"Have you seen your hair?"

"Oh, shit!"

I'd taken a shower, using an industrial abrasive to scrub the perfume off my wrists. Then I'd stood in the bathroom for a good twenty minutes, debating the merits of wearing the perfume—on purpose.

Did scrubbing it off make any difference at this point? What if the effects from Friday night hadn't worn off yet?

What if they had?

In the end, I decided to compromise and dabbed the smallest amount on the back of my neck, right where he'd have to be kissing me to even smell it. Then I tossed the vial back into the drawer. In a daydream, I'd eventually wandered out to find clothes. My hair had air-dried in whatever messy form it'd taken after I toweled it.

"Let me fix that." Stacy grabbed a brush and combed so quickly and so hard, black strands fell to the floor.

"Ow. Stop it! Let me do that." I wrestled the brush from her and worked it from the ends up. Once my hair was detangled, Stacy ran her fingers through it and caught it up in a barrette in the back. The hair that hung loose had a pronounced wave and curled under where it touched my shoulders.

"Thank you. Can you imagine?"

"Oh, we're not done yet. You haven't put on any makeup. Do you even know how to win a guy?"

I burst out laughing, and she smiled. Then she worked magic with whatever makeup she could find in my bathroom. My mascara had turned to dried cake since whenever I'd last tried to use it, so she gave up at my lashes, but the eyeliner, blush, and lipstick were perfection.

She pointed at the clock on the DVR. "He's late."

"Five minutes. He could've hit traffic. And who shows up

right on the minute anyway? Wouldn't that be weird? Also, why are you still here?"

"Moral support." She dropped onto the sofa and picked up the magazine I'd been reading, pretending to be engrossed in it.

There was a tap on the door, and she sat bolt upright, giddy with excitement.

He actually showed up. My number one fear allayed, I prayed Stacy wouldn't embarrass me too badly. I shot her a look and mouthed, "Be cool!"

I swallowed down my nerves and calmed my breathing. *Showtime.*

Chapter 7

I opened the door, and my heart melted. He wasn't a rock star. He was just Adam, wearing a pair of nice black jeans and a button-up shirt with the sleeves pushed up. He'd shaved and combed his hair in some approximation of control. And he was wearing cologne. He ducked his head and brought his eyes up to mine. "Hi."

At his apparent shyness, my anxiety dissipated. "Come in. Someone wants to meet you."

I turned around and ran smack into Stacy, who was hovering at my shoulder. Did she think he would disappear if she didn't trap him?

He looked from Stacy's hyperbeaming expression back to mine. I feigned nonchalance, one eyebrow raised, mouth turned up at one corner, smirking at Stacy and her crazy behavior.

"Um. Adam, this is my friend Stacy."

Adam leaned forward and whispered, "You found out."

I snickered. "I have no idea what you're talking about."

Stacy finally burst. "I know this is incredibly bad form." She bounced on her toes. "But Eden, would you get a picture of me with Adam? Please?"

The expression I'd been feigning became genuine. My raised eyebrow now pointed at her in disapproval. Adam must've had a Pavlovian response to fans because before I could react, he already stood beside her, sidling for a tight one-armed hug. Stacy handed me her phone, and I counted to three and snapped the picture. Jesus, he was perfectly photogenic. Stacy looked a mess.

"Let me do that again." They posed again, and I clicked another. Adam looked completely one hundred percent identical to the previous picture. Stacy's picture would have to do. She came around to grab it. I glanced at him. "Do you practice posing for pictures or what?"

He chuckled. "Busted. But the first few times fan photos turned up online, I wanted to hunt them down and have them burned. So I hired a photographer to help me out. You know, with some practice everyone can learn a pose that works more or less all the time."

"I never thought of that. If you take Micah along with you, I hope you'll teach him stuff like that."

"Whoever comes with me will get a crash course."

We left Stacy standing starstruck in the doorway of my apartment. Adam walked me out to his car. His car. Not his limo. Just a plain old Acura. It was a nice car, but not my fantasy date ride. I recovered from disappointment when I made eye contact with Adam and he sucked in his breath, squashing my fear that he might've changed his mind about me.

He opened the door for me. When I bent to climb in, he laid his hand across my back, and a chill of nervous adrenaline shot down my spine. He grasped my upper arm, spun me, and pressed me against the inside of the passenger door.

"I'm sorry, but I can't wait an entire date for a kiss."

His fingers twined in my hair, grazing the nape of my neck. My skin prickled from his touch. He drew me to him and kissed me deep, somehow both confident and needy. I felt such a surge of desire, he could've fucked me against the side of the car at that moment.

He backed away instead and laughed. "That might've been a miscalculation." My eyes landed on the bulge in his pants. "I hate to be so forward, but will your roommate be there when we get back?"

My stomach flipped. "She's not my roommate. And no. She better not be there."

"Thank God. Let's go eat."

Adam followed the GPS and chatted about how he rarely drove anymore and hoped he wouldn't get us lost.

"Where are we going?"

"Do you like Italian?" He reached over and took my hand. We veered onto 287 West.

"Of course. Who doesn't?" I was having a hard time keeping myself from staring at him.

"A friend of mine has a place close to here, over in Bound Brook."

Not Midtown. Plain old Bound Brook. We couldn't get more suburban than that. And I was pretty sure I knew which restaurant we were going to.

There certainly wouldn't be any paparazzi in Bound Brook.

At that thought, it hit me again who I was with. Jesus, this guy had played Madison Square Garden two nights ago. My lungs sought oxygen. My hands trembled.

He glanced over. "Is everything all right?"

"Why didn't you tell me?"

"Oh." He frowned. "Does it make a difference?"

"Well, yeah. A little bit. It makes a little bit of a difference." My voice sounded shrill, panicked.

"And that's why." He retracted his hand and gripped the steering wheel with both fists.

"I'm sorry. I know it shouldn't matter. It's kind of hard to process. It was hard enough to process before."

He drove silently for another few minutes, and I didn't speak either. I hadn't realized how upset the whole thing had made me until I'd confronted him. I stared out the window, trying to find the words to ask him about Adrianna LaRue as well, but then decided I'd rather fight one battle at a time.

He turned off the road into the restaurant's parking lot and switched off the ignition. In the dark, quiet car, he shifted to face me. "Look, Eden. I can't help the way things are. I would've given anything to put whatever this is between us in a bubble until we could sort it out like regular people. When I realized you thought I was someone else—"

"Is that what you like? The novelty of slumming it with someone ignorant of your celebrity status?"

"Honestly, I do love that—having someone see me for myself. But until you started talking about it, I had no reason to think you didn't know who I was, and I know for a fact I was drawn to you before you were ready to give me the time of day."

"So you're into indifference."

He laid his hand on my knee and dragged his finger in a slow line along the exposed skin. The hem of my skirt rose.

"I'm definitely not into indifference." My shallow breath redoubled as the electricity climbed up my leg. "But I'm also not into idol worship."

He drew his hand back, and my disappointment was total. He opened his door. "Do you think we could go inside? We have a reservation."

The maître d' greeted us. If he recognized Adam, he gave no sign. He escorted us to a corner table and pulled a chair out for me so I'd be facing the restaurant. Adam would be shrouded in mystery with his back facing any prying eyes. Not that it mattered. The place was practically deserted. I couldn't help but wonder if Adam had brought other dates here before me. Was this a regular spot where he could go to escape the paparazzi? Or to cheat on his fiancée? I shook my head. I was going to drive myself crazy.

We ordered, and then Adam took my hand in his on the table. "So . . ."

I pressed my lips together, trying to think of anything interesting to say. He was about to discover how boring I was. "So . . ."

Then I thought of something and asked, "How do you know the guy who—?"

At the same moment, he asked, "How long have you known your—?"

I laughed, awkward. "Sorry, you go first."

"No, go ahead."

"Just . . . How do you know this place?"

He shifted in his seat. Was he nervous too? "The owner's son, Bobby, used to work as a roadie for us."

Right on cue, the kitchen door swung open, and a large man hurried over to our table. Adam stood and shook hands with him. The man reeled Adam in for a bear hug.

"Adam! It's so good to see you. It's been too long. What brings you out this way?"

Adam gestured at me, and I stood, not knowing what else to do. "Anthony, this is Eden. I wanted to take her out for the best Italian food in Jersey."

"In *Jersey*, you say? In the world." He laughed, but his hands flew about as he talked, and he seemed harried. "You know Bobby always talks about the days when he worked with you. Whenever he hears your songs on the radio, he tells everyone he knows you."

"How is Bobby?"

"Eh. He got married." He burst out laughing again. "But otherwise he's just fine."

Adam smiled politely. "It's so good to see you again, Anthony."

"Don't be a stranger." As he turned to go, he told the waiter standing at attention to bring us a bottle of something nice.

Adam and I sat down, and the tension broke. We smiled privately at the bombastic encounter, waiting for the waiter to uncork a red and pour it out. Adam looked into my eyes, and my stomach did things that made me question my ability to keep my food down.

Finally alone, I mustered my courage. "Adam, there's something I have to ask you."

"Oh, no." He took a bite from one of the rolls the waiter had left.

"You're not engaged, are you?"

He coughed violently. I was about to jump up to help him, when he hacked extra hard and started to breathe. He wiped his eyes with the napkin. "You've been doing some serious research."

"And?"

"No. Definitely not engaged." He narrowed his eyes. "Can I tell you a secret?"

"Probably not, but I want to hear it anyway."

"Okay, but I'll know who leaked it because only three other people know this."

I leaned in, curious.

He glanced around dramatically and bent closer. "I made it up."

"You what?"

"Or we made it up—Adrianna and I."

"You made up the engagement?"

He forced a tight smile. "Yeah. See, we were at this awards ceremony. She gets a lot more tabloid attention than I do, and she was complaining about all the backlash because of that music video. You know the one, right?"

I shook my head. I hadn't watched a music video, on purpose, since I was in high school. And until very recently, yesterday in fact, I'd never paid attention to entertainment news.

"It doesn't matter. We just thought it would be funny to give the gossip rags something to talk about and leaked out news of our engagement. We made a point of doing this in the shadiest way possible so it could never be more than mere speculation. But I regretted it almost immediately."

My eyes were probably saucers. "Because you couldn't date anyone after that?"

"What? No. Not at all. It's just that I hadn't thought about the ramifications of hitching myself to Adrianna's star. It raised my profile, which was something I'd rather avoid. I mean, I want my band to succeed, but personal fame isn't something I'd wish on my worst enemy."

"That makes sense," I said, as if I'd ever struggled with fame. I blushed, embarrassed by my own gawking. "I'm sorry I looked. It's kind of impossible not to."

"Yeah, I understand. But promise me you'll ask me before you take anything you read at face value."

I was relieved he hadn't gotten angry with me, both for snooping and for confronting him. "I promise."

"So now, you know everything about me, and I want to know everything about you."

"Oh, no. I only know that you're thirty and a Sagittarius."

"Okay, so what are you?"

"Twenty-eight and an Aries . . ."

The waiter placed our salads on the table and ground pepper over them. I pushed some around with my fork, thinking of something to talk about. "What were you like as a kid, Adam?"

He shrugged. "Not very interesting. I wore braces and played the drums in the marching band."

"Not guitar?"

"Guitar, too. Like Micah, I started playing early, but I was better on the drums. I was the drummer in the band until we found Hervé."

"Was that the Pickup Artists?"

He smiled. "So you did find out more. It's actually the same band. We renamed it when we changed the lineup."

"How'd you end up the lead?"

"That's a good question. The guys should've kicked me out. We already had a charismatic lead singer who played rhythm guitar. I served no earthly purpose once Hervé replaced me. I'd started to place ads on craigslist for bands in need of a drummer."

"So what happened?"

"Well, I played guitar better than Chris. And he was a bit of a diva, ya know? Turns out the guys in the band just liked me better. And since I'd been one of them for a long time, mistreated and ignored, they knew I respected them and would never forget my place. And besides, I'd started writing songs by then. So they were patient with me while I learned how to perform. Very patient. It was a step back for us as a band, and I sucked at first."

I'd gotten so comfortable talking to him he could've been telling me how he got into law school. "It's the age-old story. Average boy turns rock star."

As soon as the words left my lips, I felt a wave of panic begin to surge again, but he smiled. "I'm still an average guy."

That put me at ease, and the panic subsided, replaced by the other churning in my insides. What would happen if I grabbed his collar and tore his shirt open? I imagined tracing my fingers across his tattoos right here in the restaurant. I fanned myself with my napkin. Was it getting hot?

The chicken parm came, and he asked, "What about you? What were you like?"

I took a deep breath. "Well, my childhood was far from average."

"I was wondering how you ended up with a name like Eden. And Micah is unusual, too. Were your parents very religious?"

I laughed out loud. "Yeah, you could say that. When I was nine, we crisscrossed the country on a mission to prepare everyone for the imminent apocalypse."

"Are you serious?"

"Unfortunately. That lasted about a year, and then we went back to normal suburban life. I wore braces. I played the violin in the orchestra."

"How does that work, exactly? They just tore you out of school and threw you on a church bus?"

"Pretty much, yeah. The Salvation Bus."

"What about school?"

"My parents taught us the important things: arithmetic and Jesus."

"And then they just quit their mission? Wow."

I poked at my spaghetti, trying to find a way to explain. "End Times cults end with a bang or a fizzle. You know, when you spend a year spreading the word the end is nigh and the end never comes, you only have a few options."

"Kool-Aid?"

I closed my eyes and shook my head, chuckling at the inappropriateness of the joke. "That would be one way. And at least that way you never have to admit you were wrong. It's kind of mortifying to be so monumentally mistaken, you know."

"So the world kept turning, and your parents moved to Edison, New Jersey?"

"Woodbridge. But yeah, my dad went to work as a claims adjuster, and my mom made sack lunches and went to PTA meetings and church socials. Normal life."

"That must've been hard to have a mission to save the world, and then just go back to regular day-to-day life."

"Oh, she still has a mission." I tore off a small piece of bread and popped it in my mouth.

"Yeah? But not the end of the world still?"

"Well, to her it is. She won't rest until she's married me off to a doctor. Or possibly a lawyer. Currently, she's working the doctor angle. Gynecologist to be exact."

Adam laughed into his napkin. "Really?"

I nodded.

His whole gorgeous face was alight with his laughter. "Oh, she's going to love me."

"She will. She loves Micah after all."

"She'll love a nice Jewish boy?"

"Yeah, she mellowed out a whole lot after the world failed to end. You put a ring on this, and she'll start a cult around you." I heard the words as they left my mouth and wanted to reel them back in. "I mean—"

"You're completely fascinating. You know that?" Before I could think of a response to that, he changed the subject back. "So what was it like for you and Micah after all that?"

"Micah started a band, smoked cigarettes, snuck out at night, and basically turned into your stereotypical bad boy. Nobody was surprised when he decided to become a full-time musician and moved out. He always loved the adventure."

"But not you?"

"Nope. I hated our nomadic life. It convinced me early on I needed some stability." Tired of hearing my own voice, I asked him, "What about you? Did you have a religious upbringing?"

"Sort of. I mean, we went to synagogue and observed the convenient holy days. I had a Bar Mitzvah. But we were more culturally Jewish, you know? My mom was a big socialite."

Our plates were cleared, and the waiter brought out two coffees. I sipped on mine and continued to ask him questions about his family and found out he had two older brothers.

"Daniel followed in Dad's footsteps and became a pediatrician." He chuckled. "I better not let your mom meet him."

"Daniel's your oldest brother?"

"Yeah. Joshua moved to LA to try to break into acting. You may have seen him in that movie about that talking bear? And then there's me."

"The rock star."

"Tell that to my parents. They worried I'd end up destitute and tried to get me to learn something more practical, but I always came back to music. That's why I'm the one who got the apartment. That and because they'll always think of me as the baby."

"But you're doing very well."

"Yeah, I am. But who knows if our band will last? We could be a flash in the pan. You see it happen all the time. I'm socking everything I can away in case. Honestly, I took my parents' apartment because I'm afraid to jinx my success by moving out to my own place." He saw the smile cross my face. "What's so funny?"

"Nothing. I find it ironic I've avoided dating musicians my whole life because there's no financial security in it. The first one I go out with is stinking rich."

He grew serious. "It may not always be that way. But I'm thinking ahead. I don't want to ever need money."

"I didn't mean to imply that wealth is all that important. It's the freedom that comes with having enough money. It's one less thing to worry about, right?"

He nodded. "Yeah, that's what I meant, too."

I laid my hand on the table, palm up, and he reached over and clasped my fingers. I squeezed back. "But you have to know that even when I assumed you were a poor struggling artist, I was attracted to you."

The boyish smile lit up his features. "Is that so?" He turned around and flagged the waiter with the universal hand gesture for *check, please*.

On the drive back, an awkward silence grew up between us,

couched by the music on the radio. It happened as he took the exit for Edison—his song came on. I sang the first verse, " 'In the beginning, there was only you.' "

He laughed and sang along, too. " 'A part of me. The world was new.' " His voice doubled in stereo. It was completely surreal.

I was surprised I knew all the words to this song, but it seriously played all the time and was catchy as hell. When it ended, he reached over and took my hand. "I thought you didn't like that song."

"I *never* said that. It just plays so much. Don't take this the wrong way, but I prefer your voice without the production."

"Why would I take that the wrong way? I have to perform that song live practically every day, so I hope I sound good enough without the studio help." He released my hand and dragged his finger up my thigh a little. I was dying. If he weren't driving, I would've climbed over the center console and dropped his seat back. He kept up a steady stream of conversation, but the splotches on his cheeks gave him away. "Just between you and me, I've been sick of that song for a year or more."

"But it just came out a couple of months ago."

"You only heard it a couple of months ago. I wrote it several years ago, and we'd already performed it a thousand times before we recorded it. And nobody ever wants to hear new songs. So we'll be playing that one until we die."

He parked next to my apartment and walked me to my front door. Before I invited him in, I thought maybe I ought to fess up about the perfume. I slid the key in the lock and started, "Adam, I need—"

At the same moment, he said, "I know—"

We laughed, and I said, "You know what?"

He asked, "No, what were you going to say?"

"You first."

"I was just going to say I know you have to be up early tomorrow."

"You're dropping me off?" A knot formed in my stomach. Of

course he'd lost his attraction to me. Why hadn't I doused my-self in that perfume? I tried not to sound petulant. "I'd hoped you'd come in."

Without waiting for a formal invitation, he leaned forward and kissed me. I wrapped my arms around him, no longer inter-ested in confessions or any other conversation, either. My weight pushed the door open, and we fell into my apartment. I tore at his jacket, and we were half naked by the time we reached the living room. The rest of our clothes hit the floor of the bedroom, and we lay down on my bed, a tangle of arms and legs and lips and skin.

I had a moment's worry. "Um. Adam? Do you have a condom?"

"I do!" Then he sighed. "Wait here a second."

I stifled a laugh. "We're making steady improvements."

Chapter 8

Only one of my wishes for my fantasy date had come true—the best one. But late night monkey sex with a rock star comes at a steep price when you have to be up at seven thirty. My alarm screeched what felt like minutes after I'd closed my eyes. I smacked the snooze and then tentatively rolled over, searching for a cool spot on the pillow.

A hand reached across my stomach and pulled me tight. My back pressed flat against Adam's front. He gently kissed between my shoulder blades, with a soft "Mmm."

I peeled an eye open. It was seven fifteen. "I have to get ready for work."

"Can't you call in sick?"

It was tempting. "I would, but I have to measure corticosterone levels today. Very exciting."

"It's so sexy when you talk chemistry." His kisses roamed across my back while his hand explored everywhere else.

"Biology. They put me in charge of analyzing blood samples because I hate testing on the animals."

He yawned. "Why do they need to test perfume on animals? Is it toxic?"

I'd forgotten I'd told him we made perfume, so I just laughed it off. "Yeah. Gotta fend off the FDA at the border."

His hand had roamed farther south, and he traced a finger across the lowest part of my stomach, venturing into the bikini island. "You're gonna have to fend me off at the border."

I relaxed into him. "You are making this very difficult."

"You can be late, right? Can't you have car trouble?"

"In fact, my car has been acting very strange." I was rewarded with his erection against the top of my thigh. I surprised him by turning and pushing him onto his back and then throwing a leg over him.

He reached his arms toward the headboard. "I'm all yours."

"Um, Adam?" I bit my lip.

"Right." He dug his hand under the pillow and produced the condom he'd preplanned, like a mint from the turndown service.

"Better."

I straddled him and gazed down, memorizing the image of him in my bed in an agony of ecstasy. I knew this couldn't possibly last, but at least I'd have this memory to keep me warm on cold nights. I laid my hands on his torso and rocked forward, turned on further by the groan that escaped him. Mine matched his when I rocked back, and he thrust to meet me. I tried to keep my eyes on him, but they involuntarily closed, and my head fell back as pleasure consumed my body.

And then my alarm went off again. Adam swung an arm out and knocked it hard against the wall, where it shattered, squawked once more, and went silent.

He winced. "Sorry."

"I don't care about the fucking clock," I panted. I leaned down and ran my tongue along his lower lip, and he forgot about the clock, too.

We moved together in a rhythm, caught up in an irrepressible desire.

At last, I reached climax with a seismic wave, but I kept moving, watching him. I don't know how I hadn't seen how beautiful he was the minute I'd laid eyes on him. I'd thought he was cute, but his features were a masterpiece. I might have to buy a *Tiger Beat* magazine later and hang his posters on my wall.

He cried out and wrapped his hands around me to draw me down into a tight embrace. The gesture made me feel wanted and safe. For a moment in time, I didn't worry about his celebrity or about my potential future heartbreak. He was just Adam, and I could lie in his arms forever.

After an eternity and no time at all, I broke contact with him and fell across the bed. "I have to get dressed. Can I get you some breakfast?" I grimaced. "I only have cereal or oatmeal. But I can make coffee."

He rolled over. "It's so early. You get up at this time every day?"

I gathered some clothes together and left to get a shower. When I came out, he'd set himself up in the kitchen. Eggs sizzled on a griddle, and coffee brewed.

"How do you not have bacon?" He moved the eggs onto a plate and placed it on the table.

I slid into the chair while he poured a cup of coffee. "I don't usually eat breakfast."

"What? But it's the most important meal of the day. I eat breakfast for lunch and dinner, too, sometimes." He settled in across from me, stifling a yawn. "But usually not for breakfast. Who gets up this early?"

Even though I hated scrambled eggs, it pleased me inordinately to share breakfast with him in my own apartment, and I ate every bite. "So what's your schedule like? I can tell you mine in one sentence—I'll be working every day."

He walked over to his jacket and returned with his phone. He scrolled through to the calendar. "Dunno. Let me see if I'm supposed to be somewhere right now."

I stood up and leaned over the table to get a look. "Jesus. How do you keep up with all that?"

"Jane. Our agent. She keeps our calendar online. So okay, today, I'm free until this evening. I have to go out to see another band we're considering for an opening act."

"Don't bother. They suck." My mom would've chastised me for talking with my mouth full. "Micah's band is way better."

"You wanna come with me? Oh, never mind. School night."

I poked at his phone. "What about the rest of the week?"

"It looks like I have some interviews, and we start rehearsing for the European leg of the tour. And . . . Oh, shit."

"What?" The words "European tour" echoed around inside my head and made me miss him before the fact.

"We have to fly to Atlanta Thursday for a show. Then we'll drive back up Friday and Saturday for shows in Charlotte and DC." He winced apologetically. "Sorry. I'm erratic."

"Must be crazy." I'd almost completely forgotten he was a big deal, sitting here having an innocuous breakfast with him. I finished eating and checked the time on the microwave. "You're free to stay here, but I have to go. Uh, thanks for dinner and . . . uh . . . everything else."

I strolled into work with a swagger nobody saw and powered up my computer. Exhaustion hit me hard. Four hours of sleep couldn't possibly get me through this morning. I caught up on my e-mails and finally read about Thanh's research, but my brain couldn't process it, so I logged onto Facebook.

Adam and Stacy's picture came up right at the top of my feed. Stacy had tagged herself and some fake Adam Copeland profile. She posted the caption, *Look who I met!* My blood pulsed with rage. I was going to kill her.

The comments piled up with the obvious congratulations and *How did you meet him?!* and *Who is that? He's gorgeous!* and *OH MY GOD I LOVE HIM!!11!*

My stomach hurt. I couldn't even "like" Stacy's picture. I didn't recognize the emotion I was feeling. It was like I was jealous of her, but that made no sense at all. Of course she'd post it. Why wouldn't she? She'd just met a celebrity, one she'd had a massive crush on, and who wouldn't want to share that?

Instead of stewing, I considered my immediate options.

Option one: I could pretend I had no idea about the origin of the picture, "like" it, and comment, *Awesome!* Stacy would get the irony. But that would leave a bad taste in my mouth.

Option two: I could ignore it completely. At the moment, that seemed like the best plan.

Option three: I could comment, *She's at my apartment be-*

cause I was up all night fucking him. That would be immediately satisfying, but in addition to the fact that my mom would see it, I knew I couldn't do that for so very many reasons.

Option four: I could comment, *Actually, she met him through me.* That seemed attention seeking at best. At worst, it would lead to a hundred questions I wasn't ready to answer.

Option five: Or I could text Adam and ask him to meet me for lunch.

I picked option five. *If you're still around and awake, would you meet me for lunch?* I sent it and waited. And waited.

While I had Facebook open, I searched for Adam's page. Micah had said he only had a fan page, so I'd never bothered trying to find it before. When I pulled it up, the wall of promotional info, tour dates, and videos revealed nothing personal at all, as if his agent maintained his account.

I logged on to Twitter and found his profile. It was all verified and everything. I clicked on Follow. Though the tweets were few and far between, they weren't promotional. In the past week, before I'd met him, he'd asked his followers, *It's 3 am. Should I go for a donut or finally get some sleep?*

I giggled at how cute Adam-before-he-knew-me was. And most of his tweets were similar—glimpses into the male psyche.

The replies to his pivotal donut dilemma were infinite. Donuts held the lead, but the competition was fierce and included such lofty professions as *I love you!* and *I love donuts!* I ran a search on his Twitter handle to read his general replies. Micah was right—it was way too much for anyone to read. Adam was almost completely inaccessible online.

I was just about to close the program and start doing some real work, when I noticed a tweet from Adrianna LaRue from sometime Sunday. It said, *In the best of times :)* I clicked View Conversation, and thunder filled my ears.

Adrianna had tweeted: *I can't overstate the importance of friends who really know you. I hope you're all blessed with at least one. #amgrateful*

Adam's reply read: *Especially in times of war.*

Adrianna's *In the best of times :)* was the final tweet. The sideways smiley face looked like a smug asshole. Sunday, I'd been suffering at my parents' house and wondering why Adam hadn't called. Where had he been?

I took a deep, calming breath and then, without much premeditation, I clicked the Follow link on Adrianna's profile.

The door to the lab opened and interrupted my stalking. Stacy and Kelly entered together, arguing.

Kelly complained. "I don't see why you can't just tell me."

Stacy grabbed her elbow and hauled her over. "You tell her, Eden. I didn't think I should steal your thunder."

"*Whaaat?*" I asked slowly, looking from one to the other.

Kelly huffed. "Um. Stacy won't tell me how she met Adam Copeland and said I'd have to let you explain it."

"Yeah." I wasn't sure how to begin. "Sooo. We're kind of seeing each other?" It was still a question in my own mind.

"Kind of? How in the hell did you manage to land someone like that?"

Again, not sure how best to explain it. "Uhh. Chemistry?"

"Chemistry, huh? That hardly explains how you even know him." She shifted her weight from one foot to the other.

"I met him at Micah's show last Friday. It's no big deal."

"At that club?" The disdain Kelly had shown a week before was replaced by disbelief.

Stacy beamed. "She didn't know who he was. Can you even imagine?"

Kelly pursed her lips. "Right. You didn't know who Adam Copeland was." Her laugh was hollow.

"Why's that so hard to believe?"

She slung her purse over her shoulder and stepped toward the door. "Well, good luck. I'm going to get some coffee."

After she left, Stacy's mouth hung open.

"Why's she acting like such a bitch?" I asked.

Stacy laughed. "She's *so* jealous. We're both so jealous. Come to the cafeteria with me and tell me everything. Please?" She handed me my purse. "You can start with that kiss I saw him give you at the car before you'd even left for your date. He had you *pinned* against the car. Damn."

We grabbed some coffee and found a table near the far wall, away from prying ears. She immediately started in with the questions, but instead of giving her an account of my date, I asked, "Stacy, would you think it weird if I took a picture with you going on a date and posted it on Facebook?"

Her face dropped. "Oh, you're mad I didn't ask if I could post that picture of Adam?"

"I'm not mad, but you should have asked first."

She shrugged. "But, Eden, it's not the same thing. Adam's a celebrity. Surely, he's used to having his picture posted everywhere."

I sucked on my teeth for a second, trying to find a way to get through to her. "Stacy, was Adam performing last night? Was he at a concert or at some kind of arranged meet and greet?"

"Huh?"

"Look. I know it's hard to separate your knowledge of Adam from before with the guy in my apartment last night, but when he's out on a date, he's just a regular guy. Okay?"

"Ha. As if." She shook her head and snorted.

"When he's with me, he's just Adam. And when you post pictures of him in *my* apartment, it's an invasion of *my* privacy."

"You're overreacting, Eden. It was just a picture. He agreed to pose with me."

"And did you consider how it might impact me? Did you notice I didn't respond? How was I supposed to respond?"

"You could've commented."

I tilted my head at her. "Why couldn't you have kept it off Facebook? What did you get out of posting it?"

She scoffed. "What would be the point of taking the picture if it wasn't going to be shared? Who would've known I'd met someone famous?"

"Bingo. And that's what we call name-dropping, Stacy."

Her expression changed from surprise to shock to anger in a flash. "You're accusing me of name-dropping? I was just sharing a cool thing that happened to me. You know, it must be pretty easy to feel smug from your vantage point."

"That cool thing that happened to you wasn't about you."

She rolled her eyes. "Jesus, don't worry, Eden. He only had eyes for you. It was like I wasn't even there."

I blew my lips out in frustration. "Well, Stacy. He was *my* date." I changed tactics. "Would you like to ever meet him again?"

Her eyes grew wide. "God, yes!"

I waited a beat.

She slumped. "Oh. Yeah, okay. I get it. Am I cut off? Will you ever let me near him again?"

"Stacy, I have no idea where things are going with him. Would you just agree to tone it down for now? If things go well, and I hope they will, maybe once we're a public couple you can post pictures of yourself with him. Or if you run into him in your own apartment. Please?"

She twisted her mouth. "Okay, but damn it, that was the best thing to happen to me all year."

I sipped my coffee. "Me, too."

At ten, Thanh grabbed me and took me down to the testing area. Before he had a chance to trick me into playing human guinea pig, I said, "Thanh, you should've told me what your perfume did before asking me to wear it. You know I sometimes leave the lab. Did you stop to think what might happen if I went into the world wearing a man magnet?"

His eyes lit up. "Did you?"

I dropped into a chair, considering how much to tell him. "Look. I may have met someone."

He pulled up a chair. He'd never looked so interested in anything I'd had to say before. "Wearing the perfume? And?"

I shrugged. "I don't know. It might have triggered something. I can't be sure. I'm worried that—"

He laid his hand on my forearm. "Could you bring him in? Please?"

"What?"

"Bring him in. I want to interview him. Find out his reaction. Maybe get some blood samples. You could be my Tristan and Iseult."

"Tristan and who?"

"We're starting clinical trials. We've got a whole array of male test subjects to observe, but it would be very useful to have a couple this stuff actually may have worked on." He was off in his own world, making plans, ignoring me. I could've set my hair on fire, and he might not notice for a few minutes.

"Thanh, listen. I don't want to be a part of your experiment, okay? Have you considered the ethical ramifications of this perfume? It's like an airborne attack on the unsuspecting. And you didn't even tell me what it was. You have no idea what you've done."

He clapped his hands to his mouth. I was making his entire day. "So it must have really worked, huh? Tell me this, was it mutual? How long did the feelings last?"

I banged my head against the table. "Thanh, I am not a guinea pig. This is real life."

"You really like him, huh? Very exciting."

Irritated, I stood and left the room. I jumped on the laptop to Google this Tristan and Iseult. They were legendary lovers, but their story had about ten billion versions. I managed to glean that Tristan had unwittingly drunk a love potion that made him fall passionately in love with Iseult against his will. I couldn't shake the guilt I felt for continuing to see Adam without telling him about the perfume. I vowed I would tell him at lunch. Let the chips fall.

For the rest of the morning, I buried myself in my work. I only checked my phone every thirty or forty seconds. Before noon, he texted me. *Something urgent came up. I had to head back into the city. Keep Sunday free?*

Disappointed in my failed lunch plans, I threw myself into work to shut out the voice insisting I'd managed to sign up for the exact kind of boyfriend I'd always avoided—distant and inaccessible. A traveling salesman.

A quieter voice fought back, defending Adam, saying, *It's not his fault.* And when he was with me, he was truly with me. And he was worlds better than Mom's gynecologist.

Once I got home, I looked around for the scant traces of Adam's existence—the dishes drying by the sink, the unmade bed. I grabbed a pillow and breathed in the smell of him for a few minutes. Aside from Stacy seeing him in the flesh, nobody would likely believe me if I told them he'd been there. The air did not in fact spark with latent electricity.

I flopped down on the sofa with my laptop. My Twitter app was still up, and I checked the notifications. My gloom lifted when I saw Adam had followed me back. Out of curiosity, I went to see who else he was following and hugged myself when I discovered he only followed about one hundred other people.

The gloom completely dissipated when I scrolled his feed and found a tweet from earlier in the day that read, *Spent the night discovering some beautiful parts of New Jersey.*

Oh, my God. I loved him.

Wait, stop the presses. What?

That wasn't possible. I'd known him less than a week. I'd only seen him two times.

I shook it off. I couldn't love him. It was just an expression. I loved that he tweeted about me. That was all.

But what did I feel for him exactly? Lust for sure. There was no denying our physical chemistry. That went way beyond mere attraction.

Aside from the sex, I really liked him. We got along easily. Maybe we'd discover some irreconcilable difference in time. For now, at least when he was with me, I felt more relaxed than I'd ever been with any other guy.

The responses to his cryptic tweet had me cracking up. Hundreds of people sent him pictures of New Jersey, insisting he come visit their neck of the woods. Others wanted to know what he was doing in Jersey. So many people asked him to follow back, or begged him to tweet at them, or told him weird and random things, saying the same thing over and over in different words: *Notice me.* I'd be shocked if he ever read any of it.

It was impossible for me to judge them, though. I wanted him to notice me, too. In fact, I ached for him, and that worried me.

Insecurity and jealousy came calling as soon as I found myself alone, and I couldn't tell whether I was jealous by nature or if the circumstances were playing with my head. We each had our own cross to bear.

I'd never know for sure how much that damn perfume had factored into his feelings for me. And he'd never know for sure how little his fame factored into my feelings for him.

Chapter 9

My lesson about Adam being a regular guy clearly didn't sink in because the next morning, before work, Stacy called me, gushing. "Your boyfriend's about to be on the *TODAY* show!"

I grabbed the remote and started scrolling through the DVR guide. "Oh, that's right. He said he had an interview today."

Stacy coughed. "An interview? The *TODAY* fucking show! His band is going to perform. Are you going to record it?"

"Duh."

"Okay. I won't bother then. Can I come over after work?"

When I got home, I set up the recording and waited until Stacy showed up with two fast food salads. She glowed. "This is so exciting! I've never known someone on TV!"

We snuggled up with our salads as the show started. After the first fifteen minutes, my salad was gone, and they'd only talked about some lady whose cat had saved her life. My brain hurt. "Is he on at the end of the three hours, or whatever?"

She poked at the last bits of lettuce, pushing the cherry tomatoes uneaten from side to side. "Can you fast forward? What if we miss teasers?"

I pressed the double arrows until I saw Adam sitting in a chair and then, over Stacy's freak out, backed it up to the commercial.

Carson Daly started talking. I was baffled. "Since when is Carson Daly on the *TODAY* show?"

"Shut up!" Stacy leaned forward, listening close to every syllable.

"Jesus. It's not like Carson is going to—"

"SHUT UP!"

"—*band The Walking Disaster hit #1*—"

I snickered, "*The* Walking Disaster."

"SHHH!"

"—*charts this week with their song 'Expulsion.' This is their third Top Forty song. They've been selling out concert arenas worldwide. And they were nominated for a VMA earlier this year. Stick around for their performance a little later in the hour, but right now we're pleased to welcome Adam Copeland, songwriter and lead singer for the band to our program.*"

The camera panned out to show Adam had been sitting in a chair to Carson's right the entire time. He swiveled slightly in the chair and smiled his practiced endearing smile. It was uncanny to see him being treated like any other celebrity. He was dressed in black jeans and a Supertramp T-shirt with the *Breakfast in America* album cover on it. I recognized the album because Micah played it to death for months when we were in high school. I recognized those jeans because they'd been on my floor the day before.

Stacy sighed. "God, he looks great. I can't believe he was *right here* two days ago."

"Yesterday," I whispered.

Carson asked, "*Adam, your latest single is sitting at number one. How do you feel about that?*"

I groaned. "What a stupid question."

Stacy grabbed the remote and hit Pause. "If you don't shut up, I'm going to ask you to leave."

She started it again as I mumbled, "But it's my apartment."

"*Carson, it's an incredible feeling when your song connects with people.*" He looked at the camera. "*When I perform that* song and see someone singing along with me, it gives me such a charge."

"Is he smoldering?" I was cracking up, thinking about that ride in his car.

"HUSH!"

A woman broke in. I had to ask, "Who's she?"

Stacy snapped, "Natalie. Be quiet."

"*I've always wondered how you came up with the name of your band.*"

Adam licked his lips and hit her with those eyes, and Natalie absently adjusted the hem of her skirt. "*It was my mom's nickname for me growing up. She always said I was a 'walking disaster.'*"

"*Well, I'm sure she's proud of you now.*"

"*Yeah, she is. Hi, Mom!*"

Natalie and Carson exchanged a glance. Natalie said, "*How sweet,*" then changed her line of questioning. "*Now Adam, I understand you're no longer eligible. There's a rumor circulating you were recently engaged to pop sensation Adrianna LaRue. Is there any truth to that?*"

I nearly burst out laughing.

Stacy hit Pause. "Did you know about that?"

"He told me about the engagement, but it's just a farce. A trick played on the tabloid media." I clapped my hands to my mouth. "You can't tell anyone that. I promised to keep it a secret."

Stacy giggled. "Looks like the joke has taken root." She hit Play.

Adam smiled, coy. "*I'm not prepared to make a statement on that right now.*"

Natalie continued. "*And you were seen last night leaving a restaurant with Adrianna—*"

I stopped laughing.

Adam cut her off. "*Yes, well.*"

Natalie changed the subject. I was only half listening to his trivial commentary about his fashion sense and plans for touring. He was supposed to be going to see a band play last night, but he was out with Adrianna?

I willed myself not to cry.

When the interview ended, Stacy asked, "What's the deal with Adrianna LaRue anyway? Why's he going out with her if it's just a joke? After that video she put out, I always thought she favored women."

"He told me they're friends." I took a huge breath. "He told me not to trust what I see in the news. I should ask him."

"So ask him. It's probably nothing." She tilted her head. "Eden?"

I waved away her concern but sat dazed while Stacy forwarded to his band's performance.

I kept myself calm, but as soon as Stacy left, I opened my laptop and found the story. He had in fact been out with Adrianna. There were photos of them on the sidewalk in front of the restaurant. Just like when he took me out, he was wearing those black jeans and a button-up shirt. I shook my head. He wore jeans out with her while she was dressed to the nines.

Before I knew it, I was watching her videos and falling more and more into misery. Even in the controversial video, where she'd dressed like a man in a full tuxedo, at least where her body parts were covered, she was air-brushed perfection with exotic features and hair as blond as mine was black. Her body could pose on a pedestal at the Louvre. She was talented, glamorous, rich, and famous. And fascinating. What was I?

I went to bed that night playing out every scenario, but the one that hurt the most was the one that liked to come around with the most frequency. He was fucking around with me, but courting someone else. How could I compete with a superstar?

I tossed and turned, debating my options, assuming I ever saw him again.

Option one: I could do nothing and pretend I hadn't seen anything, just let it go. This seemed like the best, most mature plan at present. It would eat me up inside, and maybe one day in the distant future, we'd be walking across a parking lot after a lovely date, and, without warning, I'd scream, "*Why'd you lie to me!*" Still, bottling it up seemed like the most adult way to behave.

Option two: I could passive-aggressively text him to tell him I saw him on the *TODAY* show and leave it at that. That way I could look like an adult, and the ball would be in his court to give me some kind of explanation. It was an appealing option. But if I let it go so easily, he might read that as implicit permission to keep two-timing me. Not that we had an agreement, but still. He should've known it wasn't cool, and if he didn't know that, then we had bigger problems.

Option three: I could hit it head-on and ask him. On paper, this was a responsible, brave, and grown-up way to approach the issue. And he'd invited me to ask him about anything I saw in the press. Surely there was some explanation. But if I nagged him about every interview, I'd come across as a harpy. If I wanted to drive him away, that would be a great way to do it.

I picked up my phone and scrolled to Adam's number on my contact list. I stared at it, wanting to call even if it was just an excuse to hear his voice. Instead, I tossed it on the table and buried my head under my pillow.

The phone rang an hour later—Micah paying me back for disturbing his sleep the weekend before.

"Hey, lil' Sis! Guess where I'm going?"

"Micah, what time is it?"

"Oh, shit. Sorry. But guess where I'm going?"

I sighed and sat up. "Disney World?"

"Better! Adam called me last night and asked me over to his rehearsal. He's formally invited my band to come on tour with him to Europe!"

"Wow! Congratulations!" I meant it, even if I yawned while I said it.

"You should've been there. Oh! And he invited me to ride with them in the tour bus for the next few days!"

I could picture that. A bunch of rowdy guys partying in a rolling vehicle. "You'll have a great time."

"You should take off work and go with us!"

"No, you're their guest. But I expect you to tell me all about it. Will you be at Mom's on Sunday?"

"Maybe." I could tell he wasn't even thinking about his answer. He was too excited about his good fortune. "What if he lets me get onstage and perform with them?"

As I listened to him dream about the next adventure in his career, I wanted to feel nothing but pure happiness and pride for him. He'd worked long years and developed a talent and a fan base of his own. He deserved to be recognized and find a smidgen of the success Adam enjoyed. In any other circumstance, my feelings would've been unadulterated, and I hated myself a little for the twinge of jealousy that played along the edge of my joy.

And what was I jealous of? It wasn't like Adam would've invited me on the tour bus if he hadn't invited Micah. And if Micah hadn't introduced me to Adam, I wouldn't even be in the situation to feel jealous. I owed him for that. And he didn't even know it. I wasn't sure how I was going to tell him. But not tonight.

Maybe I was slightly jealous Micah's gamble was paying off. His career would become ever more exciting as mine remained always the same. Safe, but boring.

After Micah had told me his itinerary, he wound down. I took advantage of a lull in his gushing. "Promise me you'll take pictures. And *please,* try to make it to Mom's on Sunday. I seriously will want a full recap."

He let me go, and I sat in bed, dissatisfied with the prospect of the next three days, trying to imagine what those boys were up to. I picked up my phone and pulled up Google, hoping that, if there was a God in heaven and He loved me, I might discover Adam Copeland had posed for an underwear commercial.

One advantage to dating a rock star is that you're never quite alone in your stalking. Thursday after work, I created an account on that site where Pumpkin39 held sway. My username was Alice2. *Alice* because I felt like I had fallen through a rabbit hole. And 2 because some other Alice had beaten me to the registration.

I found an "Introduce Yourself" thread and posted, *Hello. I'm Alice. I'm a new fan of the band. I've only recently discovered this forum. I'm hoping to find some concert video.*

The other members greeted me with friendly excitement. They seemed to enjoy bringing a new fan, or "walker," up to date. They competed with each other, linking me to songs, music videos, and concert bootleg they all loved.

I'd seen rock shows before, so I watched the live performances with a preconceived notion of what they'd entail. I expected to see a band of four or five guys on a stage with some smoke and lights for atmosphere. And that's exactly what I encountered. However, I wasn't prepared for how sexy Adam would be when he performed. He held his microphone so intimately, it bordered on obscene, and I grew a bit jealous of an inanimate object. Those leather pants might've made me swoon had I not seen them hanging in his parents' bedroom closet.

If he'd ever sucked at performing, as he claimed, that must've been a very long time ago. He had rock god pretty much nailed.

Some simpering fan girls pointed me to their treasure trove of collected photos and, oh, my, they did not disappoint. I admit I saved a few to my computer. No underwear ads, but the fans had captured images from a music video in which he appeared briefly without a shirt. When I hit *Save As* . . . I noticed the file was called "My Imaginary Boyfriend.jpg." I laughed but slowly backed out of that thread and went looking for the music discussions.

In the topics about Adam's discography, not every fan welcomed me with enthusiasm. Some fans had been following the band for several years and seemed perplexed by the rise in their success. They were happy to have their own fandom vindicated, but the influx of new fans both thrilled them and pissed them off. They argued over whether or not the latest hit song was too commercial. Had the band sold out?

A user called Janeway invited me to a chat room. I wanted to see just how far this rabbit hole went, so I took the red pill and followed her link.

Once I entered the chat, another user, Copelandia, asked if I

knew about the "cellcerts." He—or she—explained that someone at a show would hold a phone up to capture the performances while others conferenced in to the call and listened to a
free show from the comfort of their own living room. A few
people involved promised it would sound more like aliens having sex with broken violins than recognizable music. I had nothing better to do, so I poured myself a beer and dialed in.

As I listened to the Atlanta show, or more accurately, as I listened to the distortion of the Atlanta show with a dozen other
fans, I would've loved to know what Micah was up to. I hoped
he was living the dream and wished I could be there to watch
for him onstage. I asked the chat room what the odds were
some video would turn up online from this show.

Stick around, Alice2, posted Pumpkin39, who'd graced the
chat room with her illustrious presence. *We WD fans supply the
crack.*

When the concert ended, I temporarily forgot I was mad at
Adam because of his interview and texted him. *Guess what? I
listened to your show over someone's cell phone! Is that too
weird?*

He texted back. *It's better if you're in the same room with the
band.*

This was followed directly with, *Or alone with the lead
singer.*

The entire experience left me with a sense of vertigo. One
minute gushing with fans over this unreachable celebrity. The
next flirting with him via text. I fell asleep with a Cheshire grin,
but I felt about as sane as the Mad Hatter.

Friday morning, as I got ready for work, I thought back on
my foray into the fan forum. It was fun, but I wouldn't make
that a habit. It confused me way too much, like trying to make
sense of a fun-house mirror.

There were two distinct Adams in my life: the one the world
saw and the one I knew. It was taking some time to reconcile
them, but if I concentrated, I could make my mind go back to
our first night together, before I knew who he was. That Adam
would've been enough for me.

I chided myself that after all this time I would've been happier with a poor, struggling musician than with this insanity. It would mean he was mine, here, now—instead of theirs, out there, away from me.

My daily work routine had become exceedingly boring over the past week. I kept trying to steal time to check my phone for texts or to go online and watch videos. I wished I could hang out with Adam all day instead of staring at a timer, waiting for the centrifuge to finish.

Thanh begged me to come back down to chat with Glenn, but this time without any perfume on. "I want to see if there's any lasting connection. Humans are weird."

"And what are you then? A robot?"

But it was fun to talk to Glenn. When I mentioned Micah, his eyes lit up with recognition. "Oh, Micah. How is he?"

"Good. He's actually traveling right now with that band Walking Disaster. Do you know them?"

"Oh, yeah. I've been listening to them for a long time. Before they were well-known." He looked pleased with himself. I half expected him to say they sucked now that they were popular, but he added, "I'm always happy when nice, talented musicians get a break."

"Are you talking about Micah or Adam Copeland?"

He flashed his perfectly white teeth. "Both."

I narrowed my eyes, assessing him. "Wait. Do you know Adam?"

He chuckled and crossed his hands over his knees. "No. But I'm also a musician, and I often hear things. I could've played with Adam once, a few years ago. I always heard he was very professional to work with. I hope his success doesn't change that."

"From what I can tell, he's pretty levelheaded."

I'd totally forgotten I was sitting across from a guy with a sensor attached to his dick. Glenn's demeanor was so relaxed and personable, it took me by surprise when he said, "Hey, if you're free later tonight, I'd love to take you out to see a local band playing at the Stone Pony."

"Uh." I put my weight on my feet, preparing to get up.

He shook his head. "It's okay." He glanced up at the one-way mirror and leaned in, whispering. "It's odd. Maybe it's the constant monitoring, but ever since I've come here, I've been very aware of an attraction to women I normally wouldn't notice. No offense."

I shrugged. "No big deal." But this was deeply concerning.

The wires sprouting off his johnson bounced for a second. "But hey, I saw you with a pretty blonde the other day. Maybe you could introduce us?"

Kelly would love to hear that she was inspiring boners at forty paces. Was it Kelly and her Barbie doll good looks, or had Thanh concocted something that made men cocksure? I tried to do the math on how many women were currently within grabby hand distance of Adam. Maybe it was just what Glenn suggested, and all the testing made him hyperaware of his own sexuality. But what if exposure to this perfume turned guys into prowling horndogs?

If I'd told Micah we were seeing each other, he would know to keep Adam honest. But I wasn't ready to do that yet.

It occurred to me the fan-forum people might know whether Adam had a habit of hooking up at concerts. But even I couldn't snoop that low. I was curious as hell, but I knew you couldn't trust what people said on the Internet. I'd have to wait until he got home and try to assess the damage. Plus, I still had the situation with Adrianna to sort out.

How was I going to survive this?

I survived Friday night, barely, by going out with Kelly and Stacy to their favorite bar. The guys there were all beefcakes from the local community. Once more, Stacy had lied when she'd told me jeans and a T-shirt would be acceptable attire. Stacy's skirt was the size of a washcloth. Kelly's was longer, but then again so were her legs.

Kelly was busy making herself available for anyone who wanted to buy her a drink or engage in light flirtation, but she could multitask and grilled me at the same time. "So where's your boyfriend?"

"He's not my boyfriend. I just met him, and to be honest, I don't know what's going on between us. I haven't even talked to him today."

She scooted close. "You should text him right now."

I gave her my best *eat shit* look. "He's literally right this moment performing onstage in front of two thousand people in"—I searched my brain—"Charlotte. I think."

Stacy snorted. "Eden, Adam's band plays for twenty thousand people, easy."

Ice water crept down my spine. "I'd just assumed . . ."

Kelly had a one-track mind. "Could you text him?"

"Yeah."

"That's so hot."

I shrugged. "I suppose. He might not text back."

"Still. What's he like in bed?"

"Really, Kelly?"

I looked around the bar for someone else to talk to. I made eye contact with some guy and regretted it immediately. How could any guy stand a chance next to the memory of Adam?

My phone buzzed, and I fished it out of my purse. Micah wrote, *I just got offstage!!*

Kelly leaned over. "Is it him?"

I shook my head. "Micah." I texted him, *Did you play?*

Stacy flirted with a skinny guy in a plaid shirt, and I prayed she'd remember she was my ride and wouldn't leave me stranded. The night wasn't a total bust. A guy named Fox who claimed to be an aerospace engineer tried to buy me a drink, but I cock-blocked him. A week ago, I would've taken the drink at least as a down payment on my self-esteem. But I wouldn't have gone home with him even then. I mean, his name was *Fox*. And until last week, my record for one-night stands was zero.

But Adam was at least a two-night stand. My patience wore thin, and I nagged Stacy to take me home. She slumped in disappointment but understood.

Once I was alone at my place, I wondered if anyone might've posted any videos of the concert. I would've loved to see Micah onstage. But the search brought back nothing. I thought about that fan forum and logged in to ask if anyone knew of any concert footage.

At the top of the page, a thread title caught my attention: "I fucked Adam Copeland."

Before I could stop myself, I clicked it. The sharp taste of acid coated my tongue.

The first post showed a bleached-blond twenty-something-year-old wearing a tight sweater standing next to Adam in the standard side-hug photo op. Adam had the same smile on his face he put on for everyone. Under this, a girl calling herself Mirabelle posted her claim.

That's me. See the backstage pass?

I studied the picture. She wore some kind of lanyard with a pass hanging off the end. It was plausibly a backstage pass. I wasn't unfamiliar with meet and greets.

She continued, *Adam told me to wait near the exit til everyone else was gone. A lady came out and took me back to his tour bus.* She then went into graphic detail about their sexual encounter, with creative spelling.

Below this post, another poster, Total Disaster, wrote: *Cough*BULLSHIT*Cough.*

Mirabelle defended her claim. *Think what u want. I just had the best fuck of my life.*

That last statement gutted me. I didn't want to believe her, but if she'd been with Adam, then she wouldn't be lying about that last bit.

I hit Refresh to see what other posters would say but I got an error—the thread had been removed. Curious, I sent a private message to Total Disaster and asked, *Hey, do you know why that thread about Adam was deleted?*

She—or he—wrote back right away. *I flagged it and Pumpkin took it down. She doesn't tolerate that kind of bullshit here.*

But you didn't think she was telling the truth? I replied.

She could of been. She's an attention whore so I called her out. If Adam wanted to shag a fan, he could of done better then that hosebeast.

I thought about it for a little while and then hit Reply. *Do a lot of women claim to have slept with him?*

Total Disaster wrote, *Ask Pumpkin. She's the one cleaning up the forum. I seen a few, but they're crazy stupid. Dude's business is his own. He could be fucking feral cats at the animal shelter for all I care.*

That made me laugh despite the crushing depression. Should I call Micah and get the scoop? Should I ask Adam? Should I stop reading things people said online?

Hopefully Micah would show up at Mom's party on Sunday, and I'd grill him there. Subtly.

Chapter 10

My weekend was a shit sandwich. Friday night, I drowned my jealous sorrows in a gallon of ice cream, which caused me to wake up so sick I prayed I would die.

And in a way I did because on Saturday, Stacy dragged me to the Jersey Gardens mall, which was my definition of hell. On the far side of the purgatorial parking lot, I caught a glimpse of the shimmering halls of IKEA, paradise just out of reach. She spent the afternoon boring me with discount shoes, and I repaid the favor by whining incessantly about my perceived woes.

Her advice to me was, "Don't get upset about nothing. Talk to Adam."

My advice to her was, "When are you ever going to wear those?"

And then on Sunday morning, my mom asked me to join her for church. There was literally nothing I wanted to do less. I'd almost rather do my taxes than spend an hour sitting in a wooden pew listening to contemporary Christian music performed by a volunteer band. But my dad wasn't feeling well, or so she said. And if I didn't go with her, she'd never let me hear the end of it.

I yawned for a full hour. There came this moment where I knew I was going to fall asleep, and every single thing I did to counteract it only made sleep more imminent. I slapped my face, and my eyes rolled back in my head. The minister droned on and on and on about salvation. It made me want to kill myself.

My mind drifted.

When I was a lot younger, I took everything on faith. My religious fervor back then was based more in a fear of eternal damnation than any real understanding of church dogma. But I didn't question what my parents taught me. It seemed important at the time to travel the country sharing the good news that Christ's return was nigh upon us. I earnestly feared for the lost souls in Dubuque, Iowa. I never knew what caused my parents to realize they were on a fool's errand. Maybe it had simply come down to an argument between adults. Whatever happened, they pulled us from the bus, rented a car, and drove straight to Mor-Mor's. The only explanation my mom gave me was that everything I'd been taught was still true; she'd just gotten the timing wrong.

After that, I questioned everything. I excelled in my science classes because I had a genuine curiosity about the world, about my body, about all of creation. As a result, my religious conviction had diminished to absolute zero. But as I figured out that my new objective beliefs could turn out to be fundamentally wrong, I'd lost my passion for science, too. Lately, I'd felt nothing more than an itch to create.

When the service ended, I stood up and tried to shake the cobwebs from my head. I hadn't heard a single word of the previous hour, but my mom seemed excited about whatever wisdom Reverend Chen had imparted.

"Come with me." She dragged me down the aisle toward the double doors.

The flock exited in a single-file line, shaking the minister's hand, and saying, "Lovely sermon."

When my mom and I approached him, Mom said, "Reverend Chen, this is my daughter Eden. She's twenty-eight and single."

Oh. My. God. My mom was trying to set me up with a church official. She was completely unaware I should've burst into flames by setting foot through the door. I wanted to say, *No, thanks, Mom. I'm fucking someone already,* but it wasn't the reverend's fault my mom had no couth.

Reverend Chen was a good-looking man, pretty even. With his pale skin, dark hair, and delicate features, he could almost pass as a girl—or a vampire. He looked like somebody's girlfriend. Somebody's vampire girlfriend.

I snorted as it occurred to me that I was fairly translucent myself. We could have a paranormal romance.

Not that it mattered. He took the hand I offered in both of his, and his dainty fingers lightly closed together. His eyes were muted, like he purposely refused to see me. Maybe we all blended together after a while and made no impression on him. Or maybe he sensed I'd tempt him into sin if he met my eyes. Maybe Reverend Chen was savvier than my mom.

He thanked us and blessed us and sent us onward. Christian soldiers. Mom marched quickly toward the car. She would find me a nice man, come hell or high water.

She started up the Buick, and looked over her shoulder, before backing out at a snail's pace. "I think Joey Franco might come by the house today."

Joey had an advertisement on TV for his law services. I covered my yawn with the back of my fist. "Can we just go?"

When we got to her house, she enlisted my help in making unappetizing foods, like ham loaves and soup casseroles. Wieners simmered in barbecue Crock-Pots. She'd Jell-O'd the mayonnaise the night before. In the backyard, she'd erected our old badminton set. I should've told her nobody needed a theme to have a party.

The first guest to arrive was Dr. Steve, the gynecologist. Maybe I'd given him some hope the week before. I couldn't imagine how. Our entire conversation had revolved around the sun and how unusually warm it was.

He settled in across from me on the patio and immediately engaged me in a very serious conversation about the latest in biochemical discoveries. I got the creepy impression he'd been researching me. Talking about biology with a gynecologist gave me uncomfortable memories of sex ed classes in junior high.

I smiled politely in response to his voice but watched people enter the backyard through the gate on the side of the house. Other neighbors trickled in, and after a while, I heard my mom squeal in that particular way that let me know the crowned prince had arrived. I couldn't wait to get Micah alone and find out about his trip.

The gate swung open, and Micah walked through, looking five hundred percent more relaxed and grungy than I'd ever seen him. I wondered if he'd bathed once. I wondered if he'd taken drugs.

He held the gate, and a figure in black strolled into the yard behind him. Micah had brought Adam. Adam was at my mom's badminton party. And I was wearing a dressbarn dress and flats.

I counted the exits.

Dr. Steve had shut up about folic acid for a moment, and I excused myself. I stood and took two steps toward the sliding glass doors to get my ass into my parents' living room when I heard my name.

"Eden!"

I stopped and turned back. Micah shoved his sunglasses on top of his head. Mom fussed over him, but he pushed past her, his eyes on me. Adam kept his head down as he followed Micah. He'd nearly reached the patio when Mom finally spoke out and forced her order on the situation.

"Micah! Would you please introduce us to your friend."

We all froze where we were like we were teenagers caught breaking back into the house. Adam stood in our yard two feet behind Micah. With his dark sunglasses, his thin frame, his unkempt hair, and the all-black shirt and jeans combo, he could've been Derek or Todd or any one of Micah's friends from back in the day.

It took me back years.

When we were in high school, Micah was forever bringing

home guys to play music in the garage. My mom had drawn the line at letting them smoke in her house, and so eventually he'd gone to his friends' houses to practice. And then one day, he'd moved away completely.

I'd looked up to Micah like a hero-worshiping little sister does. I used to come out and sit on the driveway, cross-legged, watching them perform. They weren't good, but I thought they were legends. After a while, he'd handed me a guitar, but the steel had hurt my fingers, so he'd restrung an old one in nylon and shown me how to make chords. Once in a while, when he wasn't showing off to his friends by calling me names, he'd let me hold a microphone and sing with them.

Later, after I'd practiced an awful lot, he'd dragged me up on-stage and made me play the classical guitar parts of some of the metal songs. Our audiences were usually limited to the local kids, but one time they'd gotten a gig at a hole in the wall, and he'd called me, crying from nerves. He'd made me show up to perform with them, thinking for some reason I'd be less nervous. In a way, I was because to me it was fun. For them it was their dream.

It might've been mine too, if I'd ever seen it for anything other than a long, slow path to failure.

Adam stepped up beside Micah. I took him in from head to toe. Adam.

He was a total mess. Totally not my type. Barely tall enough, dark hair, dark eyes, and covered in tattoos. And though I knew that under that black T-shirt, his lean, wiry frame was taut with muscle, to the naked eye, he had the build of a skinny, struggling musician.

Okay, so he wasn't starving, but his career had already proven inconducive to a regular dating life. How could anyone settle down with his schedule? And would we forever be hiding in dark corners?

He was a walking deal breaker. A literal walking disaster.

But the sight of him brought a smile to my face.

He slipped his sunglasses off and met my eyes. The heat in his gaze melted some of the hurt and anger I'd stoked the past few days.

Micah slapped Adam's shoulder and said, "Mom, this is my friend Adam. We've been touring the East Coast together since Thursday."

He might as well have told her he'd gotten first place in a trumpet assembly race. She looked blank but said, "Isn't that nice." She turned to my dad. "Howard, this is Adam."

"I'm sitting right here, Peg." My dad hid behind a double-wide newspaper, the only person alive who still had them thrown on his porch every Sunday. I suspected he did so for the camouflage.

Broken from my trance, I remembered I'd intended to escape into the house before my mom's shrill voice had trapped me in its power. Now, I wasn't sure where I wanted to go. I slumped into a chair.

Dr. Steve picked back up. "So as I was saying, it's the folic acid that—"

Adam pulled a chair up right next to me and dropped into it. "Hey."

Without turning my head, I looked at him from the corner of my eye. "Hello."

"D'ja miss me?"

"Well, I suppose that all depends."

He laid his foot along the side of mine, under the table, completely visible through the slats in the wrought iron. He dragged it slowly up my ankle. "Depends on what?"

I suppressed a chill. I couldn't let him see me crumpling under the gravitational force of his magnetism—the power he held over me and probably every single woman who passed through his orbit. I slid my leg away. "I saw the interview you did on Wednesday."

My mom heard part of that and turned her crystal-blue gaze on him. "Interview? Are you looking for work, Adam?"

"No, ma'am." He sat up straighter. "I work with your son."

He did have a way of lying just so.

My dad folded the corner of the paper down, his pale Irish skin meeting the sun for the first time this century. "Micah does very well. You could learn a thing or two from him. Make sure he looks after you."

I snorted. "Seriously, Dad. Adam does well enough. Leave him alone."

Dad took shelter behind the paper, but Mom continued where he left off. "Micah's band released a CD last year. You can't do much better than that." She pursed her lips, and I knew she'd soon be asking him who his parents were, where he went to church, and whether he'd gone to college. Never mind that Micah never had.

I decided to save Adam from this farce and stood. "Would you come with me? I'd like to show you something inside."

He followed me through the sliding doors. I wound through the kitchen and dining room and up the carpeted stairs to the second floor. Down the hall, my own childhood bedroom had never been converted into an office. A four-poster canopy bed still filled most of the space. A bookshelf lined one of the walls, and an extra-long set of dresser drawers flanked the other. The dresser was littered with two decades' worth of collections from the practical swivel mirror and earring holder to the childish figurines made in art class.

I grabbed a heart-shaped pillow off the bed and dropped it onto the toy chest under the window. I sat down to face Adam. His eyes bounced around the room as he scrutinized the vestiges of my youth.

After all my Internet stalking, interview recording, fan-forum diving, cellcert listening, Google image searching, YouTube watching, and self-inflicted mind fucking, it was uncanny to see larger-than-life rock star Adam Copeland standing beside my purple satin princess cone hat, picking up my blown glass elephant. But that's not who I wanted to talk to. I needed to find my way back to the guy I thought he was before all that.

"We need to talk. Would you mind?"

A shadow passed over his face, but he slid a glossy pink and white chair away from my desk and settled in. "Okay. You want to talk about the interview?"

Squeezing my fists for courage, I pressed on. "That's a good place to start."

"Eden." He bent forward, resting his elbows on his knees, hands clasped. When he brought his eyes up to meet mine, I steeled myself for the worst. "I can't tell you not to follow my public movements. They're public. I can control what I say and do, but I can't control how people will report it, or what they'll say about it."

He wasn't answering the question, so I took a direct approach. "Were you out with Adrianna LaRue on Tuesday?"

He didn't hesitate. "Yes."

I sat for a moment, staring at my feet, weighing my options. I didn't have any right to grill him about any of this. But I didn't have to stay involved with him. It was his right to see both of us, but I didn't think I wanted to share him or anyone. I nodded and made up my mind.

"Thank you for being honest." I stood up and started to walk out of the room, but when I went to pass him, he reached out and took my hand. A jolt of electricity shot up my arm, and my ankles wobbled.

"Eden. Stop."

I stopped. He pulled me closer, and when our knees touched, the physical contact nearly broke my resistance. I fought the temptation to sit down on his lap and forgive everything. I reminded myself I was worth more than that. I deserved better. With considerable effort, I wrenched my hand free and stepped back, arms crossed. It was a convincing display of hostility. I nearly fooled myself into believing it, but my eyes fell on his lips, and I was a heartbeat away from caving.

He exhaled. "I wish we could go back to that time when you thought the Adam Copeland in the news media was someone else. When I was me, and that was him."

"But you are him."

"I am, but I'm also not. My image is there for people to manipulate and use to sell things—newspapers as well as music. When you have me, right here, you have me. Please believe me."

"Adam. I do believe you. You have a way of saying things that are very precisely true. But having you right here, right now, doesn't mean I have you when you're out there. When you're with others. Sleeping with your fans or whatever you do when you're on tour. That's the Adam I can't control. And I don't want to control you. But I also don't want to be a part of that world."

He raked his hand through his hair. "Sleeping with fans? Is that what you think I do?"

"Well, I—"

"Eden, I tried to tell you when I met you that I don't normally jump in bed like that with anyone. I can see why you wouldn't believe me after how fast things went with us. But you had such a hold over me. I thought you felt it, too."

My conscience pricked me as I thought about the perfume I'd worn that night. I hadn't meant to seduce him, but what if I'd inadvertently made him do something so against his own nature? How could I be angry with him? I parsed his words for any hidden meaning. "You don't normally. But you have?"

"Yes, I have. A very long stupid time ago."

"But not last Friday night with a fan at a meet and greet?"

He laughed out loud. "That's pretty specific." Then his eyes widened. "Were you reading fan forums?" I took a step back, and he laughed again. "You *were!*"

"I was looking for concert footage of Micah onstage." My cheeks heated up with the embarrassment of getting caught. "I'm sorry. I shouldn't have clicked the link, but—" I threw up my hands. "What would you do if you saw someone making claims like that?"

"And you believed it?"

The tension broke, and my shoulders slumped. "No. Not really. But Adam, I've barely known you a week, so how could I be sure?"

"Eden, I've been surrounded by extremely ardent fans for years now. I can handle myself."

"But it's constant."

"So were you having sex with your coworkers the whole time I was gone?"

I rolled my eyes. "That's hardly a fair comparison."

"It's fair to me. Dating fans would be like dating my employees. Only weirder. It would be like dating a magic mirror that only shows me what it thinks I want to see."

I thought of Micah's aversion to dating fans. I affected a teasing tone to cover my insecurities. "So you don't collect notches on the bedpost?"

He frowned. "Hardly. But it was hard at first. Nobody prepared me for the sophistication of girls who get turned on by fame. Those girls used to find ways to get backstage to my dressing room or onto the bus. And the propositions they made would curl your hair."

"They don't now?"

"No, now we have bodyguards everywhere. I promise, I don't mix with fans."

"But you said you did?"

I could see I'd made him uncomfortable, and he shifted in his seat, but answered. "Once. It was one moment of weakness before I'd come to terms with how much my life had changed. One girl managed to tempt me by playing into every need or insecurity I had back then."

"And you slept with her?"

"Well, I didn't *sleep* with her."

I'd signed up for this with my prying, but I didn't like to think of him with anyone else. Even before me. Even once. When had I become so jealous? "Tell me the sex was terrible, and you took a vow of chastity."

"The sex was sex. Not terrible, not great. Impersonal. And when it was over, she left and shared her experience with the world."

"Oh, God." I remembered worrying Stacy might post something innocuous about Adam and me on Facebook. I would've died if someone spilled graphic details about my sex life, like that girl on the fan forum. "But why didn't she just lie about it if all she wanted was to impress people?"

He shrugged. "I don't know. I guess she wanted some kind of boost to her self-esteem from contact with me. Maybe it made her feel like she was someone special for a moment. Not because I'm this great catch, but because I'm a difficult catch."

"And that made you feel like prey?"

"No, it made me feel like a predator. It took no effort on my part to get with her. And I looked around me every night and saw more of the same. Girls wanting me to validate them in some way that I couldn't. And I didn't want to hurt any of them or me. All they saw in me was the bullshit rock-star image and the fame and fortune. Not me." He smiled. "So *then* I took a vow of chastity. Sort of."

So many things made so much more sense. "That would explain your lack of condom preparedness."

"Yeah, it's a lonely business, this fame thing. And that brings us back to Adrianna."

My heart skipped a beat. I'd already forgotten I was mad about her, too. "Go on."

"Do you remember when I texted you that something urgent had come up?"

I nodded.

"Adrianna was that urgent something." He fished out his phone and Googled. He held out the photo from in front of the restaurant. "Did you see this?"

I nodded again.

"What did you think after you saw it?"

I hesitated. "I thought you were leaving a restaurant after eating dinner with Adrianna Tuesday night."

He handed me the phone. "Look. Are we sitting in a restaurant?"

"No, you're out on the street."

"What am I wearing?"

I shrugged. "You're wearing jeans, like you always do."

"Do you recognize that shirt?"

I looked more closely. It couldn't be. "You don't mean?"

"Yeah. It's the same shirt. Eden, I hadn't been home yet."

"But you had to leave before lunch, so where were you all that time?"

"One last question. What do I have on my face?"

"Sunglasses." I stared at the picture. Behind them, a man walked a dog. He had on sunglasses, too. Another lady carried bags, like she'd come from shopping. Shadows darkened the sidewalk. Comprehension dawned on me, and my eyes darted up to Adam's face. "What time was this?"

He smiled. "Now we're getting somewhere."

"They can do that? Isn't that libel or slander or something?"

"Read the headline again."

"Adam Copeland and Adrianna LaRue. Dinner for two?"

He tilted his head toward me. "Where's the lie in that? It's presented as speculation, not fact."

I jerked my finger at the image, incensed. "But the picture! They fudged the picture so it would look like night!"

"Look, Eden. I could maybe sue for libel. Maybe. I'd lose. And what would be the point? The newspaper wouldn't stop printing misleading stories."

"That must drive you crazy!"

He relaxed and sat back. "It used to. I've found the easiest course of action is to smile and say nothing. It blows over."

"Shit. I'm so sorry. I shouldn't have jumped to conclusions." I handed him his phone. "You're exhausted and come home to the third degree."

"I expected it, actually."

"Really?" I climbed up onto my bed and crossed my legs.

He got up and sat next to me. "I figured you'd either see it, or someone would say something. I expected one of three things to happen."

I laughed. He sounded like me. "What were they?"

He took my hand. "You might've pretended like nothing had happened. I'm glad you didn't."

"I almost did. I didn't think it was my business."

"But it is, right?"

Hearing him say that warmed my heart. "So what's the second thing?"

"I thought you wouldn't talk to me at all. When we first got here, I thought you were getting ready to walk in the house and shut me out."

I grimaced. "It had crossed my mind."

"Ouch. Still better than pretending you're not mad."

"And what's the third thing?"

He squeezed my hand. "This. Just talking. You should've just called and asked."

I flashed back to Wednesday night, staring at his number in my contact list and wanting nothing more than to call. "I thought about it. It was the third option in my list. I held the phone in my hand and—"

"So why didn't you call?"

"Because you're—" Because he was an international celebrity, and I wasn't.

He closed his eyes and let his head fall back. "Shit."

"Well, if you knew I'd be mad, why didn't you call me? Why didn't you call and explain?"

He winked. "I thought about it. It was the third option. I held the phone in my hand and—"

I laughed at his echo. I reciprocated. "So why didn't you call?"

"First, because there was a chance you wouldn't have seen the interview, and I didn't want to open a can of worms for nothing."

"That makes sense."

"Second, because I might've made myself look guilty by claiming innocence before I was even accused."

"Thou doth protest too much?"

"Yup. And third, because I don't want to have to call to explain every time a news story puts me in an unfavorable light. I'd be calling you every five minutes. And honestly I'm unaware of most of the accounts."

I beamed, proud of myself for having come to that conclusion already. "I did think of that."

"But mostly, because I was afraid you'd hang up on me."

"Oh. I didn't think of that."

"I did. But Eden, can we talk about why you didn't call me?" His hand left mine and traveled up my arm. He gently circled my shoulder when he asked, "Can you forget about all that, please? I'm just a regular guy."

Goose bumps visibly popped up everywhere his finger went. "But, Adam, everyone wants you."

"No, they don't. They want that guy. And I'm banking on the hope that you're not into that guy."

I shook my head. "No, I'm mystified by that guy."

"Truth? I am, too." His thumb tickled the side of my neck, and my head fell in that direction. "I'm the guy who spent hours learning to play guitar and then sang poorly with my friends in a basement in Brooklyn, over and over until we got decent. I love music and want to make a career of it. All this other stuff is confusing and isolating." His fingers ran across my lips, and I kissed them.

He leaned forward and kissed me, and my lips curled in a wicked smile. "My bedroom's a virgin."

He looked around. "Yeah? Can we do something about that?"

Against my strongest impulse, I dragged myself away from him and went to check out the window. My parents were sitting on the porch together. Dr. Steve was nowhere to be seen. Micah lay passed out on a lawn chair. I didn't care about any of the other neighbors. I walked over and locked the door. Then I returned and pushed Adam backward.

As I worked his shirt up, I breathed him in. "You smell good."

"You seem surprised. I did have time to shower before coming here."

"It's just that I've missed you. Is that too weird?"

"I hope not because I've missed you, too. And—" He reached into his pocket, waggled his eyebrows, and revealed a square black envelope, like it was the Hope diamond.

Chapter 11

On the way to my apartment, Adam and I stopped and picked up a giant bucket of fried chicken and mashed potatoes. We were both starving from avoiding the food at my mom's. Adam moved around my kitchen like it was his, gathering plates and silverware. We plopped down at the table and silently put back the calories we'd burned off in my childhood bedroom.

Halfway through the bucket, there was a knock at the door. Stacy stood on the landing and came in without being invited.

"I saw your car and—" She cleared the entrance and encountered Adam sitting at my kitchen table. She stopped dead, as though she were on an African safari and had come across a polar bear. She stared at me, slack jawed.

"Want some chicken?" I asked her, pushing back a chair.

She came over and sat at the table, staring at the wing in Adam's hand like it had magical properties.

"You should turn her into a newt," I suggested.

Adam waved the wing at her. "Hi, Stacy."

"You know my name!" She bounced a little in her chair.

He looked at me, as if to say, *See?* But to her he said, "Of course. We took a picture together."

She squealed and hit me. "He remembers me!!"

Frankly, I was embarrassed by her behavior, but Adam kept

eating, so I spooned more mashed potatoes on my plate. "You wanna watch TV?"

He shrugged. "Not much on."

I grabbed the remote.

Stacy gawked. I snapped my fingers. "Stacy, do you want some fried chicken? I don't think we can finish it all."

I picked up the bucket and moved it over to the coffee table. Adam stretched and propped his feet up. I sat down and snuggled against him. He wrapped one arm around my shoulder and the other across my front, locking his hands together, hugging me. Stacy zombie-staggered over and dropped onto the love seat. Slowly, she seemed to thaw.

"So . . ." She was watching us instead of the TV.

I threw my eyes her way. "Spit it out, Stacy."

She blinked. Twice. "What's going on with you guys?"

I tilted my head. Seriously? "Well, we're sitting on the sofa, watching whatever this investigative report is. We're both sleepy. What's going on with you?"

Adam's arms tightened around me. I let my head fall on his shoulder. I was tempted to nuzzle his neck, but we had company to perform for.

I desperately wanted Stacy to snap out of it and behave like her normal self, but she seemed perpetually dazed by Adam. She couldn't seem to shake the celebrity crush she'd had on him before. Surely, she could see he wasn't made of gold. There was nothing I could say to reach her, but maybe in time, her false image of him would be replaced with the reality of him.

I was starting to understand how frustrating it must be to actually be him.

When the chicken was gone, and we'd lost interest in the TV show, and Stacy hadn't left, Adam went into my bedroom and found my guitar. He sat cross-legged on the sofa and strummed. I shut off the TV and joined Stacy on the love seat. She squeezed my hand hard and whispered, "Oh, my God! Private concert!" Okay, so she *thought* she was whispering.

Adam tuned the guitar by ear and asked Stacy, "You wanna hear something?"

Stacy flailed against me. "Holy fucking shit. Can you play 'Dam Burst'?" She dug her phone out of her purse, but I laid a hand on her arm and shook my head.

"No videos, Stacy. Remember our conversation?" She'd made some improvements, though. She hadn't tried to take a picture of Adam eating fried chicken. She hadn't pocketed his half-eaten fried chicken.

Adam found the chord and strummed a rhythm. Then he sang. I didn't even know the song, but Stacy clearly did. She mouthed the words along with him, swaying and grabbing my hand. I worried she might have an orgasm right there on my sofa. I had no clue she was that much of an ardent fan. It would've been funny if she turned out to be Pumpkin39.

Adam, for his part, lost himself in the song. His eyes closed, and his voice held so much emotion, I wondered where he'd gone to. I'd always held this cynical suspicion that pop/rock music was written in a factory and that the people singing it were puppets—this despite watching Micah struggle to write his songs and get his music out there.

When he finished singing, I asked, "When did you write that?"

"Ages ago. All our songs got changed when we went into the studio. I like playing them acoustic sometimes. It reminds me why I wrote them."

Stacy said, "We should call Kelly over." Then, without taking a breath. "Can you play 'Expulsion'?"

Adam shook his head. "Maybe later. I wanna hear Eden play."

Stacy blew a raspberry. She'd heard all my songs. I could sky-rocket to the top of the charts, play Madison Square Garden, get interviewed on the *TODAY* show, and Stacy would never see me as any big deal. I guess she'd be the one who kept me grounded through fame and fortune. While treating my boyfriend like a mythological creature.

I took the guitar. I'd never tried to play "Expulsion" before, but I'd listened to it about forty-seven times since the night I sang it in Adam's car with him. I strummed the first chord and sang, "In the beginning . . ."

Adam chuckled, and Stacy started singing along. As soon as Adam joined in, I found the harmony and slowed it way down.

When I set the guitar down, Stacy grinned like a giddy school-girl. "That was so much fun! And oh, my God, Adam, your voice is gorgeous." Her eyes widened, and her hands flailed like she'd had one too many lattes. "You, too, Eden! You guys sound amazing together."

Adam raised an eyebrow at me. "See? We should duet. Right, Stacy?"

She bounced. "Yes! And I'll stand behind you guys and play the tambourine."

I handed the guitar to Adam. "Maybe we should listen to you for a while."

Eventually, Stacy left. Adam put the guitar back, and I gathered up the fried chicken trash. Stacy hadn't asked Adam to autograph any of it.

Adam hummed and followed me into the kitchen, wrapping his hands around my waist from behind. He laid his head against mine. "I've got a great idea. Let's record a song together tomorrow."

I twisted around to face him. "What? Where? I have work tomorrow."

"I know. I mean later. When you get off work, let's drive to Brooklyn. My drummer Hervé will let us use his studio. It'll be great!"

I gulped. "Are you serious?"

"Dead. Think about it."

He helped me get the kitchen straight and then sat down on my bed while I jumped in the shower. When I came out of the bathroom, I discovered Adam fast asleep on top of the covers. I went around and took his shoes off, laying them on the floor. Then I helped him get under the blanket. I turned off the light and climbed in next to him with my head snuggled against his chest. His arm came over and circled me. I drifted off to his rhythmic breathing.

That was our third date.

Adam didn't wake up early and make me breakfast. He didn't wake up and snuggle with me, making me late for work. He didn't wake up at all. I slid from the covers and threw on some clothes. He snorted and rolled on his side. I grabbed a granola bar and snuck out the front door. I tried to blow my mind with the knowledge that a rock star was sleeping in my bed, but it had lost its impact. I'd watched him scarf down a bucket of fried chicken.

An entire eight-hour workday lasted approximately ninety-two hours. Adam texted me starting around eleven, asking me to meet him for lunch, then coffee, then begging me to come home and spend the afternoon taking a "nap" with him. He tormented me with offers of hot-oil back rubs and promises to serenade me. Every single text made me ecstatic for exactly ten seconds.

In the first second, the phone beeped, and my heart jumped.

I spent the next two seconds in optimistic hope that it wouldn't turn out to be Micah.

Second number four brought the confirmation that Adam had hit Send on a text just five seconds earlier.

The next three seconds were the best because everything Adam wrote was perfection.

Knowing he was thinking about me sustained me all the way through a bonus eighth second.

Seconds nine and ten were spent fighting the urge to grab my keys and drive home. But I couldn't. There was work to do.

So the eleventh second brought a crushing loss and an immediate addictive need for another text. I reread the old texts until they lost the power to distract me from the never-ending day.

Every time my phone dinged, Kelly moved closer. After a while, she said, "I can't stand it. It's him, isn't it? What's he saying?"

That time the text didn't say anything too personal, so I read it to her. *I just found your perfume in the bathroom. Reminds me of the first night we met.*

She nodded. "Yeah, you did smell pretty good when you went out that night. Where'd you get that perfume? I could use something new."

This conversation spoiled my mood. Thanh had made me spend some time with Glenn earlier in the day, but Glenn no longer showed any interest in me. In fact, Glenn was downright surly. I chalked it up to him feeling embarrassed from the scorning of the week before.

Thanh suggested an alternative. "When was the last time I got you to wear the chemical in here?"

"The perfume? It's been a week, Thanh."

He picked up an iPad. "Hmm. A week." He glanced at a spreadsheet and typed something in.

I grabbed his wrist. "What happens when it wears off?"

He pulled his arm free, oblivious to my internal distress. "We'll see. I'm currently running longevity tests on the mice." He widened his eyes. "Oh, but guess what? They're starting trials on actual people for the first time this week!"

"You mean, other than me?"

All of Adam's texts throughout the day gave me cause to shrug off some anecdotal evidence that the chemical might have kicked off a one-week fling. I knew I shouldn't worry that Adam would lose interest in me as fast as Glenn had. After all, Glenn had no reason to carry a torch. It's not like I'd ever licked the back of Glenn's neck.

And when I came home from work, Adam was sitting on the front step with my guitar on his knee, strumming and humming. People drove through the parking lot or walked along the sidewalk, oblivious to the guy who, in another context, would have thousands of people screaming for him.

As soon as he saw me, he jumped up. "Can we go now?"

We drove across Staten Island, alternately singing along with the radio and asking each other dinner party questions.

"Okay, so you're stuck on a desert island." I looked over my shoulder and changed lanes. "One book, one album, and one food."

"One food! That's impossible."

"Answer, please."

He sucked on his lip, thinking. I was glad to see he took it so serious. "My book would be, uh, *The Lord of the Rings* trilogy. No, wait. *Game of Thrones*. All of them."

"Cheater. What's your album?"

"You know, Eden, they have these devices now called MP3 players. I could bring an entire library of music. What am I supposed to play an album on?"

It took us a little over an hour to get to Brooklyn.

Adam didn't bother to knock on the front door of the brownstone. We followed a beckoning sound down the hall to an open door that led to a basement.

A short, muscled bald man with a circus mustache stood up from behind a drum assembly. "Adam!"

We walked across the room, and he put his hand out. "Hi. I'm Hervé. You must be Eden. I've heard so much about you."

He winked at Adam, and I blushed furiously. What on earth could he have told someone about me after such a brief period of time, except—

"It's nice to meet you, Hervé. Thank you for letting us use your studio."

He laughed. "Anything for Adam. I have to admit I'm excited by what he wants to do."

I raised my eyebrow at Adam. "What does he want to do?"

"He said you're going to do an acoustic duet version of 'Expulsion.' That's going to be killer."

Adam picked up a guitar. "I've been thinking about it all night. What you did with that song yesterday. It turned the song around."

"But I just came up with that on the spot. I hardly planned it."

"Can you do it again?"

I shrugged. "Probably. It was fairly simple. I'm not sure why—"

He took my hand and led me into a glassed-in booth. "We're going to sit in here. See the soundboard there?" He pointed at another glassed-in room.

I nodded.

"Hervé's going to be there recording. We may need to do this a few times, but if we can get it in one take, we can post a video to YouTube tonight."

My stomach hurt. "YouTube?"

Before I could protest, he placed a black guitar into my hands. "Can you play this?"

It was a classical guitar. I sat down on a stool in the booth, put the strap around my shoulders, and set the guitar on my knee. It felt okay. "Yeah, I guess."

"Great."

It was moving way too fast. I couldn't think. How could I record a song without practicing? I wasn't sure I'd remember the words. He didn't tell me what to do. He closed the booth door and stood outside the window. A tinny voice came through a speaker. "Okay, Eden. Can you start playing so we can set the levels?"

Relief. This wasn't the take. I had a moment to practice. I strummed the chords to the song and hummed a couple of bars of the verse. Then I started to sing it. The lyrics came easy once I got going. I closed my eyes and kept playing, strumming or picking arpeggios as it felt right. The structure of the song was beautiful. Some of that was lost under layers of production on the radio version. When I finished the song, I looked up. Nobody had told me to stop.

Adam beamed on the other side of the glass. I spoke into the mic. "Are we ready to do this now?"

Hervé's voice came through the speaker. "I think we got it."

"What? But that was just practice."

Hervé came out of his booth, so I got up and met the two of them in the main room. Adam was picking up a guitar as Hervé gave him directions. "I think it will work best if you can add in the rhythm guitar and sing the bass lines. Can you work with the vocal?"

I stood back as Adam disappeared into the booth. He put on headphones, and at Hervé's go, he started to play. It was odd to listen to him because his vocals alone didn't sound like a song. But when he was done and Hervé played it back, the result was stunning.

"That's us?" I couldn't believe it.

"I told you we should duet."

Hervé shook his head. "Your voices complement each other so well. This is gorgeous. What are we going to do with it?"

"Can we mix it and then overlay the video?"

"What video?" I hadn't seen a camera anywhere.

"Up there." Hervé pointed into the booth. The camera was blatantly mounted on the wall. I hadn't bothered to look.

I glanced at my phone. The entire process had taken less than forty-five minutes.

Hervé promised he'd continue to work on it and would have it up on YouTube later that night. We didn't need to hang around unless we wanted to.

Adam laid his hand on my shoulder. "Hungry?"

"Starved." We hadn't stopped to eat any dinner.

"Do you want to go to my place? I may have some food there." He raised his eyebrows, grinning expectantly.

If I went to his place, I wasn't sure if I'd ever be able to leave again, and I needed to be at work in the morning. "Can we grab something nearby? I need to be getting home soon. Some of us have a day job."

He sighed. "Yeah, I know a place."

We walked six blocks to a dark bar, and he ushered me to a corner table. I scanned the menu, and the waiter took our order.

When we were alone, I had to ask. "Are we always going to date in clandestine out-of-the-way restaurants?"

He shrugged.

I continued. "Because I know you don't always hide when

you go out." I leaned forward. "You don't have a problem being seen with notable people." *Or Adrianna.*

His eyes grew big. "You think I don't want to be seen with you?"

My turn to shrug. "Seems that way."

"Oh, God. Eden, no. It's just that—" He looked up at the ceiling. "You don't know what you'd invite in if you went out with me in public."

"You're about to post a video of us on YouTube."

"It's hardly the same thing."

I didn't understand at all. "How so?"

"Well, first of all, gossip rags don't give a shit about what I do professionally, and they won't pay much attention to that video. Fans will. They may not like it, and they may say horribly nasty things about the song, but they won't find out where you live and go through your garbage to figure out your worst secret."

"And if I go out with you publicly, you think that will happen?"

"Yeah. Maybe. I don't want to find out. You can't put that genie back in the bottle. Are you ready to climb into this bubble with me?"

I relaxed. It sounded reasonable. "But you know, I don't want to hide forever." I heard the presumption in that statement and was glad the dark hid my blush. "I mean, if—"

He caught the meaning. "Oh, right, well, if—"

Thankfully, our food arrived and saved us from an avalanche of filler words.

After we ate, he walked me back to where I'd parked my car. It wasn't too late, but driving home would take time, and I'd gotten up early. He held my hand as we walked. "What are you doing tomorrow?"

"Working. You?"

"Not much. I'll hook up with Micah and make sure they're getting ready to come with us. My guys will meet up to rehearse later this week, but we've been touring the U.S. for the past eight months, so most of our prep will be in the logistics of getting our stuff to Dublin."

We reached my car. "How long will you be gone?"

"A month. We'll start in Dublin, and then we go elsewhere. I'll have to pay attention so I don't say 'Hello, Frankfurt' when I'm in Paris."

I laughed. "A month doesn't sound too bad. But do you realize I've known you less than two weeks?"

He pushed me against the car. "I know. I don't know what it is about you, Eden Sinclair." He dropped my hand and traced up my arm to my neck. He leaned in for a kiss, and my knees buckled. I knew I needed to get in the car and drive home, but my hands were under his shirt, running up his back. He pulled me in tighter and dragged his fingers through my hair.

I turned my head to kiss his wrist and smelled something familiar, something . . .

"Adam, are you wearing my perfume?"

He hesitated.

I pulled his arm closer and breathed in. "You are, aren't you?"

"No. I mean, just a little." He shrugged. "I was missing you, and I found it, so I touched a little here. It's not that weird."

It smelled different on him somehow. It smelled delicious. I kissed his wrist again, then pulled him closer, kissing his lips, wanting him.

He drew back. "You sure you can't come to my place? It's not far."

My breathing came ragged and fast. "I can't stay the night. I need to be at work this week." I fumbled in my purse for the key and pressed the Unlock. All the doors clicked open.

He took a step back, and I reached for the driver's side door. His lips grazed the nape of my neck, and I shrugged my shoulders up.

"You smell so nice." He spun me around and took my shoulders, kissing me so hard, my back pressed against the car.

He stopped and looked at me. "Is this normal?"

No.

"Have you ever—?"

"No, never—"

He ground himself into me "Do you want—?"

"Yes . . ."

My legs trembled. There was no way I'd be able to drive away, safely anyway. I turned, despite his groan of disappointment. But I opened the back door and pushed him to get in.

When the door closed behind us, I wiggled out of my pants and unbuttoned his. He let me undress him. I glanced out the window onto the deserted street and sidewalk and yanked his pants to the floor. The physics of the backseat worked against me, but Adam didn't seem daunted. He sat there with his erection pointing sky high. His eyes were dilated, and his face was splotched.

"Shit. Condom." He panted the words.

I cuffed my purse and knocked it upside down, shaking the contents everywhere. There in the pile of pens and movie stubs, I spied the corner of a wrapper. I snatched it up.

"I come prepared."

He laughed, ripping the envelope open. "Yes, you will."

He took my hand, and I straddled him, kissing him, sliding down on him. We gasped at the same time.

"Eden. Oh, my God."

"Adam. Ah."

We rocked together, releasing an immediate need. He came quickly, and we separated reluctantly. I wanted to follow him home and stay up all night touching him, kissing him. Instead I dropped him off at his place, and we kissed good-night for a lot longer than we should have. Then I headed home.

Alone in my bedroom, I opened my laptop and searched for videos on Walking Disaster's YouTube channel. Our video had uploaded, and it had three-hundred-some-odd views already.

The video blew my mind. Hervé had managed to splice in cuts of both Adam and me singing. The audio was mixed and overlaid our videos. It sounded amazing. I read every single comment below the video. They weren't all complimentary, but most of the negative comments were directed at the speculation that Adam Copeland was gay and that his music was gay. I laughed at those. Plenty of people asked who I was, but by the time I went to bed, the overwhelming commentary was that the song sounded cool like that, and that I had a lovely voice.

I fell asleep with a smile on my face.

Chapter 12

Nobody at work had any clue I was an Internet sensation. Probably because I really wasn't one, although I did wake up to two thousand views of our video. I couldn't possibly read all the comments and get ready for work in time. People had devolved into political arguments somehow, anyway.

Still, I couldn't refrain from checking the fan site one time to see if anyone there had noticed the video. Someone had created a thread to discuss it, and it already had seven pages of comments. It was surreal.

And those fans knew how to stalk. The video was titled *"Adam Copeland w/ Eden Sinclair—Expulsion (acoustic)."* With my name to work with, they'd linked me to my brother, who they already knew would be opening for Walking Disaster in Europe. I clicked to the next page and was rewarded with some video footage of Micah onstage in Charlotte. They'd also found video of Micah and his band performing. And one savvy fan had located a recording of me singing backup for Micah.

The speculators had arrived at the apparently obvious conclusion that I was a musician, too, and that maybe Adam was planning on working more with me. The discussion stayed on this track for a couple more pages. The burning question was whether Adam was putting together an acoustic CD. Lots of tiny dancing emoticons lined these posts: a little yellow smiley holding up an electric fan to cool off, a little yellow smiley melting into a puddle, a little yellow smiley falling flat on his face in a dead faint.

A couple of people complained they didn't like this direction for Adam's music at all. It had already veered too pop for their tastes, and they'd have to find someone else to follow if he was going to turn into a folk act.

Then someone posted a link to my Facebook page. *Is this her? It doesn't appear she's a musician at all. She lives in New Jersey and works at some place called Anubis Labs.*

I was relieved I hadn't posted anything about Adam on there. But they also found my Twitter, and someone pulled up Adam's tweet from the week before about discovering the beautiful parts of New Jersey, and speculation took off like a thoroughbred in heat.

Their relentless hunger to find out everything they could about me weirded me out. I wanted to post, *Knock it off! I'm just an average girl. I'm just like all of you. Nothing to see here.*

But Pumpkin dropped a reminder not to dig into Adam's personal life, and that was the end of that. I had half a mind to send her a private message to thank her. She had an uncanny ability to let the posters run free without allowing them to venture into truly invasive territory. And her posters for their part seemed rather well trained. I wondered if Adam had any idea who she was. If so, he should be sending her backstage passes and fruit baskets.

The last comment in the thread, from AnimeFan, asked, *Didn't Adam say in an interview last year he was trying to find a female vocalist to work with? Looks like he found one.*

The apparently innocuous comment rattled me more than it should have. Maybe because Adam's attention to me had gotten so much friendlier after I'd joined Micah onstage that first night. Maybe because he'd handed me a guitar the very next day and hinted at duetting without any more to go on than that. Maybe because he had me in the studio after three dates.

Dates. They weren't even dates. We'd gone to dark, out-of-the-way restaurants, or to his place, or to mine. His explanations for hiding from prying eyes rang true, but he had a knack for saying the truth without being honest.

Maybe he'd seduced me with his sexy sexiness to trick me into performing with him. That thought was so ludicrous it made me laugh out loud. He could've always just asked me to perform with him first without all the hocus-pocus.

Still, it troubled me that he'd put me onstage professionally while keeping me hidden privately. But I swallowed back the doubts.

I brought up my Facebook page and discovered that Stacy had posted the video on her wall. *Listen to my friend Eden Sinclair singing with Adam Copeland. How cool is this?*

The buzz from the positive responses charged me all the way into the office, a place of unending normalcy. I was bursting with this secret that wasn't a secret at all, except for the fact that you don't just blurt out, "People are watching me perform on YouTube!" without sounding a bit full of yourself.

But when Kelly entered the lab, even she was nice about it. "Stacy sent me your video with Adam. *Wow.*"

At lunch, when I took a break, I had a dozen text messages on my phone, my Twitter following had increased by sixty people, I had several strange friend requests on Facebook, the view count on YouTube had increased to six thousand, and my mom had left me a voice-mail message.

Holy shit.

I found Adam's number and called him. He picked up on the second ring, "Hey, superstar," he yawned. It didn't register until later that he must've been asleep.

"Have you seen it?"

He laughed quietly. "I told you."

"I can't believe it. Everyone is trying to reach me today. My phone keeps buzzing."

"It'll die down. Enjoy it while it lasts. But Eden, don't go hunting down comments and read everything."

"Too late."

"I doubt you've read everything. Seriously though, it's tempting, and when you read nothing but good things, you'll get high on the ego-feeding reactions. It can be addicting."

I recalled how buzzed I was driving into work and could see what he meant. "But what's wrong with that?"

"It never lasts. Tomorrow or next week or next month, that video will be old news. The best possible outcome would be that you go from reading thousands of nice things about yourself and then suddenly nothing. And you'll want another hit. Next thing you know, you'll be wanting to make more videos, and that will lead to the slippery slope of trying to make a career out of music. And you wouldn't want that."

I laughed. "So what's the worst possible outcome?"

"This would never happen, I'm sure. But people can turn nasty on a dime. If you read too much about yourself, you're going to eventually find some pretty terrible opinions. And that can be miserable."

"You mean like how gay your music is?"

He didn't laugh. "Like how someone wants to beat my skull in with a blunt instrument so they don't have to hear my shitty music anymore."

"Ouch."

"It gets ugly. So just . . . try not to read too much, okay?"

"Okay."

"But what are you doing tonight? Can I take you out on the town to celebrate?"

Surely, he only meant another trip to Bound Brook. But a butterfly flew loose in my belly. "You just said yesterday—"

"I know what I said. If I'd taken you out in public last night, you'd have been my date with all the gossip that goes with it. When I take you out tonight, you'll be Eden Sinclair, up-and-coming musical sensation, and my colleague. It's a different class."

"I thought the paparazzi wouldn't see that YouTube."

"They haven't. They will as soon as they see you on my arm. It's what they do, Eden."

I was useless the rest of the day. My nerves came and went. I'd forget about how nervous I was, and then my body would remind me. And when my body forgot, my mind picked up the slack. It was a tag-team effort to keep me completely distracted.

In the afternoon, I had to get up and move before I made myself crazy. I took a walk over to Thanh's lab and found him occupied with a pair of mice. He acknowledged me with a wink. I came up behind him and gathered that these were in fact the same mice he'd shown me the week before.

I watched as Thanh pinched Rob Roy's neck and inserted a syringe to draw blood. Then he placed Rob Roy on a treadmill near Cosmo and started a stopwatch. After several minutes, he drew blood again. He handed the vials to me without a word. While I ran the blood samples through the centrifuge to test for the presence of elevated corticosterone, Thanh got Rob Roy ready for the ejaculation testing. I stepped out of the room to get another cup of coffee. They were just mice, but when he explained what came next, so to speak, I felt like we were dealing in pornography.

When I returned, he was studying the blood work. "Fascinating."

"What?"

"I haven't injected the serum into Rob Roy for a week. His interest levels are dropping off." He scribbled some notes on his clipboard.

"What does it mean?"

He set down the clipboard. "Your question before about cell regeneration was spot-on. Seems like the receptor gene is finally closed for business. If only we could get such promising results with the airborne topical agent . . ."

"Wait, but you said a day or two. Oh, God." It had been over a week since I'd put on the perfume. But Adam was wearing it just the day before. "Thanh, how does it work that I'm not attracting every guy I pass when I wear the perfume? Why am I not attracted to every guy after I've worn it?"

"Don't you remember before with Glenn, how he didn't react to you until you talked to him? My theory at the time was that you need to have some connection, maybe a latent attraction, though I'm not sure to what extent. Honestly, we've gotten mixed results in our human trials. I'm trying to control for things like natural chemistry, but you know, humans are more art than science."

I left his lab more confused than when I'd arrived.

Adam was waiting outside my apartment when I got off work. He actually wore non-jeans, a light suit jacket thing and, wonder of wonders, a tie. "Where are we going?"

"Somewhere nice. Dress nice."

I called Stacy immediately. "Help!"

She raced over and glanced at Adam with an "Oh, hi" so casual as to seem rehearsed. I tried not to laugh. We pulled out everything that might pass as "nice" and settled on a soft black sweater with three-quarter sleeves, a tweed miniskirt, and chunky black heels. I let her do my makeup, without trying to hide from Adam that I had no idea what I was doing.

"This is what you signed up for, okay? Do not laugh."

He laughed. "It's cool. I don't know how to put on makeup either."

"Oh, I know how. But she can make me look good."

"You always look good."

Stacy stopped for a minute. "Aw. Points for that."

Traffic going into the city wasn't a nightmare, and we made it to the restaurant with time to spare. He parked and walked me out to the street. As we strolled together, I wrapped my hand around his bicep and bumped him with my shoulder. "We clean up pretty good."

He put his hand on mine and stopped me. "Are you ready for this?"

"For what?"

"Fasten your seat belt. And take a deep breath."

He dropped my hand as we turned the corner. Right out front, a small crowd waited to go in. A man leaned against the wall nearby, noticeable in that he clearly wasn't dressed to dine at the restaurant, he was alone, and he held a very expensive-looking camera. Adam and I cleared the corner, and the man straightened up and started shooting pictures. He crossed the sidewalk and walked along beside us. "Who's your date, Adam?"

We kept walking. Adam ignored the man. Undeterred, Mr. Paparazzo spun around and walked backward down the sidewalk right in front of us, his camera *click-click-clicking* the whole time. I couldn't help notice Adam didn't put his arm around me or in any way demonstrate we were together. It hurt a little, but I figured he knew what he was doing. When we got inside the door of the restaurant, he lightly touched my back, just between my shoulder blades, and spoke to the maître d' who ushered us in. For a change, we didn't go to a corner table in a dark room. We were right out in the open.

I scoped out the restaurant and saw some people who looked familiar. I sucked in my breath. "Isn't that—?"

Adam's eyes never left mine, but he smiled. "Probably."

Picking up my cloth napkin, I flapped it against his hand. "You don't know who I was going to say."

He shrugged. "Doesn't matter. It probably is whoever you think it is."

From the corner of my eye, I noticed a couple staring in our direction. When I glanced over, they looked away quickly. But the girl's eyes crept over again, and she whispered feverishly to the guy with her. Her date might be saying, "*Probably. It probably is Adam Copeland.*"

That thought put me in my place, and I stopped gawking at other customers and focused on the menu. There were no prices. Oh.

I cast my eyes up at him to find him watching me with a devilish grin. "What?"

"Nothing. Just enjoying watching you. You're completely fascinating."

Okay. Other than him, nobody had ever said anything like that my entire life. "Me? How about you?"

"Why? Because people know who I am?" He put his forearms on the table and leaned in. "I've made music my entire life. Like your brother, I started playing at battle of the bands and wherever we could get someone to give us the time of day. I played small clubs. My band toured in a broken-down van and played in front of five people. That song on the radio now? I wrote that years ago, but nobody gave a shit."

I scooted forward so we could talk closer, more quietly, more privately. "Yeah. Music's a fickle business. I've watched my brother scratch and claw to make a living from it. He's so talented, but so are a million other people competing for the same dollar. And he doesn't even care about the money, but he has to."

He listened, nodding. "Exactly. People say we sold out. I don't know. We studied the business and adjusted our performances to build a grassroots fan base. And we hired producers who could make our music more radio-friendly. We worked on our stage presence. It was work. None of it came easy, but when it paid off, it left me a little disillusioned. A little bitter."

"Because you had to bend to the industry to succeed?"

"Yeah. I'm grateful to be able to make a living this way. But when we set our sights on success, we were thinking about playing more gigs at slightly better venues. None of us expected this."

"Careful what you wish for?"

He laughed. "Exactly. You know, most people would pull out the world's smallest violin about now. I have nothing to complain about, right? It's what everyone wants."

"But not you?"

The waiter interrupted us to take our order. I'd barely scanned the menu. "Um." I looked up at Adam for help. "What should I get?"

"Do you like steak?"

"Of course."

He asked the waiter to have the chef prepare his best cut of meat and whatever he thought best to pair with that. Then he asked the waiter to choose the wine. The waiter smiled appreciatively and walked off with a mission.

Adam watched him go. "I didn't know what to order either. I'm not sure why, but it always seems to make waiters happy when I let them pick the wine. Maybe they just grab the most expensive. I can't really tell the difference."

I put my hand out on the table toward him. He hesitated, but took mine and asked, "Living on the edge so soon?"

He ran his finger across the side of my hand, lightly, barely noticeable to the naked eye, but it set fireworks off inside my body. My eyes rolled back in my head, and I had to drag my hand back across the table and set it in my lap for fear of making far too obvious what we were still trying to keep hidden.

I coughed and squared my shoulders. "Back to what you were saying. What do you want out of all this, Adam?"

"I want to take you out to dinner without some creepy little troll trying to find out if I'm cheating on the fake fiancée invented to foil a different creepy troll. And I want to make a career out of making music. Why are those two things incompatible?"

"They aren't, though. Not as much as you think."

His eyes narrowed. "What d'ya mean?"

"How many people could pick Hervé out of a crowd? Doesn't he play the same gigs as you?"

"Oh, so you're saying I cultivated this because I'm the front man?" He sat back in his chair and considered that. "Yeah. That's true. Part of our marketing put the target on me. And then that stunt with Adrianna didn't help." He sighed. "I'm sorry. I didn't mean to come here and be all sour grapes. This was supposed to be about your YouTube success today."

I found a roll in the basket and tore it in half. "How did you know that would come out so well?"

"You really don't know how talented you are, do you? Hervé heard it right away. Micah must know, he asks you to come up at the last minute and throws a mic in your hand. You have an amazing voice and an instinct for songwriting."

I ducked my head behind the roll in my hands, unsure how to take the compliment. "I've always loved music."

"You could've made a career of it. You still could."

The waiter came and poured us our wine. He let me taste it, and I pretended I had a clue what I was doing. "It's fine."

When we were alone again, I revealed to him things I rarely even confessed to myself. "Adam, I'd love to have a career in music, if it could provide a steady paycheck, if half the job didn't involve hustling. I can keep a day job and make music as a hobby, and that's more than a lot of people get."

"But how did it feel when we were playing together? How did it feel when other people saw that and loved it?"

Without thinking, I touched his hand again, clasping his fingers in mine. "When we played music together? I've never been more turned on in my life. And then when other people *liked* that?" I looked up at the ceiling. "God. I still can't believe that. What's wrong with all those people?"

He nodded, eyes wide-open. "Right? I ask myself that question all the time. But wait. Back up. It turned you on to sing with me?"

"The first time? That was the hottest five minutes of my life."

His face fell. "What? Seriously?"

I caught the insult and made an attempt to recover. "Apart from being with you the . . . what? Four times?" My face burned as I replayed what I'd just said. If my mother knew.

The rest of our dinner, we talked easily about ourselves, and by the time dessert came, Adam had charted out an entire music career with us writing music and touring together. He made me laugh, anyway.

When we left the restaurant, our new friend followed us for about a block. By now, the clever little troll had found out who I was, like Adam had predicted. He walked lockstep beside me and rattled off questions.

"Eden, what's your relationship with Adam? Are you collaborating on an album?"

I swallowed and kept my eyes forward, determined to pretend he wasn't there.

But he was practically breathing down my neck. "Are you dating? Does Adrianna know about you?"

My head jerked toward him when he asked the last, mainly because I was so horrified someone would have so little decency than to ask one woman about another.

The momentary hesitation fueled his energy, and he asked, "Are you aware Adam's allegedly engaged? Care to make a comment, Adam?"

My every instinct told me to stop and tell him off for the evil little fuck face he was. But I followed Adam's lead, and we ducked into the garage and fetched his car.

As we pulled out of the garage, Adam started laughing. I was on the verge of tears, so his reaction angered me for a full minute. But he said, "You handled that so perfectly. God, those people are fucking scary."

I relaxed and faked a laugh. "Doesn't that freak you out?"

"Yes. It totally does. But you can't let them see it, or they smell it on you and rush in for the kill."

When Adam dropped me off at my apartment, he jumped out of the car and walked me to my front door. Before I could turn the key in the lock, he rubbed the back of his neck and said, "I had a nice time."

"You're not staying?"

He cast his gaze down and shuffled his feet. "Eden."

It would've been adorable if my heart hadn't leapt into my throat. Was this it then? He'd gotten his duet out of me and paid me with a nice dinner out. Would we part ways? I'd see him from time to time on the TV and remember that brief romance I had with someone I could never approach again. Except by using Micah to reach him.

Not that any of that would matter. If he didn't want to see me anymore, it wouldn't matter if he was the guy next door. That would be that.

He brought his eyes up without lifting his head. My nerves broke. "Adam? Are we—?"

His eyes opened wide. "What? No. I just thought—"

I didn't know *what* he just thought and knit my eyebrows into a question. "You don't want—?"

"No, I do. God, I totally do." He exhaled. "This is going to sound so dumb."

I crossed my arms. "Try me."

He took my hand. "I want to back up."

"Back up?"

"I don't even know if it's possible, but when you mentioned at dinner we've been together four times, I realized tonight was our second real date. And I thought I should walk you to the door and kiss you good-night."

"A true gentleman."

"Usually, yes. But everything's happened so fast. Can we start over? Move a little slower?"

"Get to know each other?"

He squeezed my hand. "Yes. Do you realize we've run this relationship in reverse?"

I thought about it for a minute. "Oh, my God. You've already met my parents!"

"I bet you don't remember that the first time we met, I failed to propose to you."

The memory stirred. "That's right. Wow. So what happens when you go on tour next week?"

"It's a complication, but not a permanent one. We can stay in touch, and when I get back, I'll have more time. And I'd like to start making music with you."

"That better be a euphemism."

He chuckled. "Maybe."

"Can I have a kiss good-night?"

He pulled me close and kissed me once, chaste, with his lips pressed together. Even still, it set me on fire, and it took every ounce of willpower to take a step away from him. "When will I see you again?"

"Can you come to Hervé's on Friday after work? We'll be in rehearsals all week and packing up."

"Friday? That's years away."

He arched an eyebrow and smiled his wicked smile. "Then you'll miss me?"

"Nope. I'll just watch concert videos, and it will be like you never left." I hoped my flippant tone would hide the crushing anxiety his sweet gesture had crippled me with.

Chapter 13

An incessant droning woke me early Wednesday morning. I got up to investigate and discovered the culprit was my phone. I pulled down the notifications to see who was trying so hard to reach me.

That couldn't be right.

I had twenty-five voice-mail messages, four hundred and two new Twitter followers, over eight hundred Twitter mentions. . . . I couldn't process this. Facebook friend requests, direct messages, e-mails, text messages. I threw my phone in my purse. I'd deal with it later. I needed to get to work.

I almost expected to find someone hiding in the bushes outside, but the parking lot was clear. I made it to my car unmolested.

When I got to work, my manager Keith called me down to his office. "Eden, is this you?"

He turned his laptop toward me and showed me a large photo of me standing next to Adam. There was no question it was me, so I nodded. "Yeah."

"Look. I can't tell you what to do in your free time, but please make sure your extracurricular activity doesn't compromise our work here."

My eyebrows shot straight up. "Are you serious? Keith. Why

would you think my *extracurricular activity* as you call it would compromise anything? Does yours?"

He puffed up his chest. "Eden. I'm not hanging out with someone who wears leather pants to work."

"It shouldn't matter if Adam wore no pants to work. My private life is none of your business."

"Your private life has become public. As you know, we're right in the middle of our clinical trials. This is a critical time for our research, and we want to shield ourselves from public scrutiny. We don't want to give our competitors an edge. Make sure you aren't adversely impacting the confidentiality of your work here."

Resisting the urge to slam his door, I left his office and flew to my computer to find out what he'd been reading. I found the gossip column with a byline from Andy Dickson. That had to be the creepy troll who'd accosted us. At least the picture wasn't too unflattering. I wasn't yanking my underwear out of my ass or anything. Nor was I mugging for the camera. It was clearly an unsolicited picture of two people walking down the street together, but not necessarily together. Adam knew what he was doing after all. Nobody could say we were dating from that picture.

And yet they did. The tag under the picture was provocative but by no means definitive. "*Adam Copeland with Eden Sinclair, his latest protégée. Or romantic interest?*" The rest of the story lacked anything resembling evidence about the second claim but did question the reliability of rumors about Adam's alleged engagement. I wished Adam would put those rumors to rest, but I supposed he had his reasons. I'd considered asking him, but until right at that moment, it seemed like Adrianna and I had inhabited completely separate planes of existence.

I could deal with being labeled Adam's protégée. My brother could claim the exact same title. And now at least I understood why my phone had exploded. Last I checked, it was still vibrating. How much worse would it be if we were a confirmed couple? Adam had been right all along about that. As it was, I was going to have to uninstall some programs or figure out how to disable notifications. Or maybe delete every account. I groaned at the thought of going dark on the Internet. It would be more than just a slight hassle.

My voice mails were from my family and friends. I called my mom and told her to calm down. Yes, it was the boy Micah had brought home. No, I didn't think he had a college degree. Yes, he was treating me very well. I called Micah before I remembered he'd be asleep. I hung up. I ignored the calls from everyone else.

Then I turned to Facebook. I didn't know a single person trying to friend me, so I deleted those. I scrolled through the private messages, but there was nothing there from anyone I knew so I deleted those. Twitter was going bananas. I disabled that app completely. Nobody I knew would try to reach me there.

Out of curiosity, I opened the laptop and typed in the url of the fan site. I could hear Adam warning me not to, but I needed to know how things stood. The first thread was titled "Eden Sinclair." I hesitated and then clicked the link to read the pages.

Those people weren't stupid and knew up front without further ado the girl from the gossip page was the same girl from the YouTube video. That was child's play. But what they seemed to need to suss out was who I was to Adam. They started with the protégée moniker and considered romantic interest. The question of Adrianna came up again and again.

Total Disaster posted, *I never bought into the whole engagement thing. Adam has never made a public statement about it.*

Balls to the Walls wrote, *When was the last time Adam was seen on a date? I'm convinced he's gearing up to start a side project.*

Shy Guy said, *But she's not a professional musician. And she's a fucking knockout. I vote for romantic interest or at least short term hookup.*

Adams Apple quoted the second sentence in Shy Guy's post and added, *QFT.* I had to Google that to learn it means "quoted for truth." I giggled. Nobody had ever referred to me as a knockout before. Not that I knew.

The curiosity over me had reached a fever pitch before the thread was locked. And they hadn't uncovered any more than they knew before.

Small victories.

When Stacy got to work, she rushed over. "I've been trying to reach you all morning. Didn't you get my messages?"

Kelly came in while I was fishing out my phone. I held it up so they could witness the insanity. "It's been like this all night. I've given up trying to weed through everything. I'm going to have to uninstall Facebook and Twitter until this dies down."

Kelly snorted. "Must be rough."

"You know what, Kelly? It is."

"Yeah, cry me a river."

Stacy broke in. "How are you holding up? I didn't even see the article until people started asking *me* what *I* knew about it. I didn't even know what to say. What do I tell people? *Are* you publicly dating?"

I dropped on a stool. "I don't know."

Stacy pulled up beside me, shaking her head. "What was he thinking, taking you out like that if he's not ready to make it public?"

"He's trying to establish me as a musician, I think. After we posted that video, he thought it would be okay to be seen in public. Plausibly, we're just colleagues." I sighed. "This whole thing is tiresome."

"Oh, boo hoo," said Kelly. "Do you like the guy?"

"Yes. Very much."

"And he likes you?"

"He seems to." I neglected to mention his initial interest in me might've been biochemically engineered. I neglected to mention his continued interest in me might be professional.

"Then what's the problem? Everyone deals with noise. Ignore it."

I stared at my hands. "Yeah, that's good advice."

Stacy frowned. "Is he worth the headache, Eden? Even I'm getting a little freaked out by how many people have come out of the woodwork to try to get information from me."

My stomach twisted. "God. I'm so sorry, Stacy. It never occurred to me how this would affect everyone else."

She laughed. "It's okay. It's crazy how one little thing could make people go bananas. But are you willing to put up with it for him?"

I didn't have to think about that. "Definitely."

"Then give it some time. Everyone you know is going to have to wrap their heads around it. And seriously, ignore the strangers." She added, "I still can't believe you're dating him."

She didn't see the parallel in the over-the-top reaction about me and her own continued idol worship of Adam, so I spelled it out for her. "Oh, Stacy. He's no different from you and me."

Adam was right that the chatter concerning me slowly died down by the following day as our outing together became old news.

My mom had come to the conclusion that Micah's friend was a tad bit more successful than her son and optimistically convinced herself I was helping Micah's career somehow by going to dinner with "that skinny rocker." When she invited me to her pre-Halloween party, she added, "Did you know Duncan Lewis is recently divorced? I'm trying to get him over, but honestly, that newspaper article about you isn't helping any."

"Mom, Duncan Lewis is a known alcoholic."

"He's a surgeon." She nearly harrumphed with her trump card.

"Okay. Bye, Mom. I'll see you Sunday."

I posted vague statements on social media in response to all the questions I'd run across there.

On Facebook, I wrote: *I'm sorry I've been out of touch online this week. It's been crazy around here. Thanks to everyone who left me a message.*

On Twitter, I said, *Loved performing "Expulsion" with Adam Copeland earlier this week. Thanks for the kind comments.* Adam retweeted it and then asked how many of his followers would like to see us do some more duets together. The response was overwhelmingly positive. It didn't quite make up for the circus that my life had become, but it helped to know so many people out there were encouraging even if their first instinct was to channel that into an unhealthy interest in Adam's private life.

I peeked at the fan forum, but with speculation shot down by the moderator, the comments had moved on to talk of the upcoming European tour. My gut twisted. I'd been trying to forget Adam would be away for several weeks.

His own Web site had a listing of tour dates. The band would be hitting more than a dozen cities: Dublin, Glasgow, London, Paris, Antwerp, Amsterdam, Hamburg, Copenhagen, Stockholm, Oslo, Berlin, Munich, Vienna, Rome, Nice, Barcelona. They'd be gone until mid-November. A whole month. They had some downtime scheduled in there, but still they'd be playing and traveling almost nonstop. He'd never have time to call or text. Hopefully, he wouldn't have time to canoodle with anyone else either.

Stacy's response to my concerns was to beg me to take her to the party at Hervé's as moral support. And since I was super nervous about it, I hesitantly agreed. Other than Adam, neither of us had any experience with celebrities, and Adam had hinted some big names might show up.

When we climbed the front steps to the brownstone, Hervé's door was wide-open. We followed another group of people into the crowded townhouse. A large man in the vestibule stopped us and asked for our names.

"I'm Eden. I'm with Adam." I pointed my thumb at Stacy. "And she's with me."

He broke out in a toothy grin. "Oh, Eden. Hey. I'm Jackson."

"Nice to meet you, Jackson. Where is everyone?"

He laughed because everyone was literally everywhere. "If you're looking for Adam, try the basement."

We dodged and weaved through the hallway to the stairs. I recalled the first time I'd come here, when the place was completely empty aside from Hervé in his studio. I grabbed Stacy's hand and made sure she stuck with me. Compared to the upstairs, the basement was relatively deserted and quiet. Instruments lined the walls, all packed in their sturdy black cases, tagged and ready to travel. Adam sat on a stool with one of the guitars, picking out a tune. His eyes were closed, and I stopped where I was to observe him, so beautiful. His voice sent a shiver up my spine.

A small but solid guy sat on a box and leaned forward to beat out a rhythm between his legs.

Stacy elbowed me and whispered in my ear, "That's Mark Townsend." I shrugged, and she clarified. "He's the bass player."

"I haven't met him."

"Didn't you look up his band?"

It'd never occurred to me to. "Was I supposed to?"

"Seriously? There's four guys in the band. Adam on rhythm guitar and lead vocals, Mark on bass, Hervé Diaz on drums, and Charles McCord on lead guitar. But as you can see, they switch it up sometimes."

I shook my head at her. "Tell me you can behave yourself tonight."

When he finished playing, Adam saw us and smiled. He waved us over and introduced us to Mark. For a wonder, Stacy acted like a normal human being when I introduced her. She was pinching my arm pretty hard though, and I could tell she was losing her shit.

With all the people moving around, Adam and I ended up in conversations in groups. We may have been talking to other famous musicians, but I was clueless and recognized nobody. Stacy relaxed after a couple of beers. We found Micah in the kitchen, chatting amiably with Hervé. I saw some of Micah's band scattered here and there.

The talk often turned to the tour plans. They'd all be flying to Dublin in the morning. They'd hit Glasgow and London before leaving Great Britain toward the end of the week.

Micah was excited to play Wembley Stadium. He'd been to Canada, but never across the pond. "Tomorrow night, we'll be busy getting ready for our first show. It's happening so fast. But Sunday's free, so I can get out and do some touristy stuff in Scotland. I can bring you back something!"

As the night wore on, I lost track of Stacy but thought I saw her laughing with Mark in the kitchen at one point. I worried I'd never get a moment alone with Adam. There was always someone else who wanted to talk to him. And occasionally to me. Some people had seen our video and commented on it. Adam must've trusted everyone there, because the entire night, he had his arm draped over my shoulder or around my waist when he wasn't twining his fingers through mine. But he hadn't cornered me in any dark rooms or even grazed my cheek with a kiss.

Late into the party, I heard a high-pitched titter and turned around to find a tall, platinum blonde entering the kitchen. She had colored streaks through that platinum and so much makeup on she looked more transvestite than girl. She walked straight over to Adam and leaned in for a hug, almost peering down on him from her height.

"Oh, honey," she said. "I'm sorry I'm so late. We had to go to Carmen's party."

I knew this was Adrianna LaRue, but up close she looked different than on her videos. She was glamorous and beautiful in her way, but it was entirely plastic. Around the edges of that pancake makeup, her skin was the soft color of driftwood.

She was a tour de force and totally out of place in an ordinary Brooklyn townhouse. She made me feel totally out of place.

Adam touched her arm and said, "Eden, this is Adrianna. Adrianna, Eden."

Adrianna's eyes lit up, and she cooed. "Oh, this is the one?"

Adam blushed. "I've told Adrianna about us."

She laid a hand on my shoulder. "I'm so sorry about any trouble I've caused you with our little fun. I'm incorrigible at best."

"So did you bring the paparazzi with you?" asked Adam. "Or did you give them the slip?"

She laughed, and her mouth was a flash of unnaturally white teeth. "They're out front. Careful if you go outside to take a whiz."

"That wouldn't be the worst picture ever. God, remember when they caught me with my hand on my ass?" He rolled his eyes. "They made it look like I'd had the world's biggest crack itch."

No, I didn't remember that. But Adrianna's mouth was wide with laughter. "Or when they caught you with your hand on *my* ass." She fluttered her incredibly false eyelashes and then covered her mouth. "Oh, dear." She bent toward me. "I'm only joking. That never happened."

I fought the jealousy rising as they interacted. It made me feel better to know he'd told her about me, but he'd never talked to me very much about her. She was nothing like what I'd expected.

Adam touched my elbow. "Seriously. If it had, that picture would've been everywhere." He waved his hands in the direction of *everywhere*.

Was he defensive? Surely he wouldn't have told her about me if they had anything going on, but who knew how she might feel about a casual relationship?

I forced a laugh. Not that they noticed.

"So what do you have planned while we're on tour, Ade? You gonna head back to California?"

Adam stood closer to me than to her. Absently, he'd touch my arm or lay his hand on my back. If I leaned toward him, he'd lean back. But his eyes were focused on her.

"Actually, I thought I'd go play in Europe for a little bit. See where the tide brings me."

I sucked in a lungful of air and held it.

He nodded. "That's great. Maybe we'll cross paths."

She tilted her head. "Actually, I was hoping I could beg a ride over to Ireland with you. I can find my own way from there. That is, if you have room on the plane."

At last Adam broke eye contact with Adrianna, checking in with me instead.

Given what he'd said about sharing a bubble with her, maybe they had an arrangement. Maybe they were fuck buddies. I counted to ten, then exhaled. There was nothing I could contribute to this conversation. If I asked him to refuse her, I'd be the jealous girlfriend.

I checked the time on my phone, shocked to find it was nearly two a.m. "What time do you guys have to be up tomorrow?"

Adam sighed. "In six hours. These guys are going to have to be poured onto the plane."

I pretended to stifle a yawn. "Thanks for inviting me, but I think I need to go home. It's been a long day."

He didn't ask me if I wanted to come to his place to sleep, but he did walk Stacy and me to my car. With a glance up the street to check for lurking cameramen, he took my hand in his and brushed my lips with a kiss, but whether because Stacy was standing right there, or because we were starting over, or because he'd lost his passion for me or had some side thing with Adrianna, he stepped back and let me climb in the car.

He stopped me from closing the door to tell me he'd miss me and would call me when he got to Dublin.

I started the car, fighting back tears. I didn't even know if I was sad because he was leaving or because he didn't seem to care.

Stacy and Kelly took me out on Saturday night to cheer me up, but I was terrible company, staring at my phone every time it buzzed, hoping to get some word of Adam. I knew he'd arrived in Dublin because Micah had texted me pictures from the private jet. I'd begun the automatic addition of five hours to the time that would become a knee-jerk reaction for the next several days. When my phone showed ten p.m., I simultaneously held in mind that it was three a.m. in Ireland. They'd likely all be asleep by now. And still no word from Adam.

Maybe my total lack of interest in anyone at the bar made me more desirable than usual. For some reason, more than one man asked me for my name, where I worked, what I was drinking, and other questions designed to hide their ultimate question: *Can I take you home tonight?*

I tuned them all out.

Kelly snickered, and I pulled my eyes away from my phone. "What is it?"

"Hold on. Just listen."

I waited. Then the song came on overhead. She'd managed to get someone to put "Expulsion" into the music mix. It sounded weird coming out over the loud speakers that usually played country or pop. The radio version of "Expulsion" had a hard edge to it. Underneath the crunchy guitars and heavy drumming, it was a trite love song about lost innocence and falling into temptation before being cast out of paradise together. But the lyrics were allegorical and clever, a fact that was lost when the drunks in the bar sang along with the chorus.

Kelly hid her mischievous smile and nudged me. "You're not laughing. What's wrong?"

I forced a fake smile. "Stacy and I were out late last night. I haven't caught up on my sleep yet."

She had to know I missed Adam. It seemed kind of shitty to remind me by having his music play. It had been a mistake to come out here with them. I excused myself and went home.

The silence had started to eat at me. When I left the bar, it was four a.m. in the UK, and I knew he'd be sleeping, and I knew he'd been busy. Last night he'd been onstage, meeting fans, sleeping. Or sleeping with fans.

I knew he wouldn't, but I stared at my phone and willed him to text. It wouldn't be the same as a conversation. Or his presence. Or his kiss. But it would ease my mind.

Writing or calling him myself became a more and more distant option as time passed. I could hear him in my head telling me to talk to him, but that was the Adam who snuggled next to me on the sofa on a lazy Sunday with nowhere else to go. The more people reminded me of the disparity in our leagues, the more I needed him to make the first move. The more I needed him to be the one to call or write to me.

Not much of a role model for women's lib.

But it wasn't because I thought I couldn't call him. I knew I could, but that wasn't the point. I didn't worry I'd annoy him. I could control this one thing, waiting. And that meant waiting to follow his lead. That might be perceived as giving him all the power, but he already held all the power in this relationship. My power play was to make him work for it. If he couldn't call and let me know he was alive, I wasn't about to make it easy on him.

Chapter 14

When I woke up Sunday morning, I checked my phone immediately to find that Adam had written me an hour after I'd gone to sleep.

Subject: Hi

I bit my lip and clicked through, always a little leery of the breakup speech. Now that we were separated, the complete absence of the physical chemistry that had sustained our relationship felt like the sword of Damocles. I couldn't see any way he'd remain interested in me apart from me. Sooner or later, he'd wake up.

> Eden,
> I'm sorry I didn't call last night. When we got to Dublin, we had some major issues with the arena. As soon as I arrived, I was on the phone with Jane until we got everything resolved. We had to scramble to get our set built and at last put on a show. Don't go looking for reviews. I'm sure it was pretty shaky. But we pulled it off. We're heading to Glasgow right now. Thankfully, Jane

scheduled a day between our first two shows for
just this kind of hitch. It's not uncommon.

But I still should have called you. It's the middle of the night there now, so I don't want to
wake you.

I'm sitting alone on the front of a bus that's flying through the darkness. All I can see out the
window are the divided lines in the highway
shooting us like lasers. All I can think of is you.
And I can't sleep.

I hope you're thinking of me.

Adam

That was all the invitation I needed to call. It was one p.m.
Glasgow time.

He answered on the second ring.

"Eden?" His voice gave me goose bumps.

"Good morning . . . or, I mean, good afternoon. I just got
your e-mail."

"Yeah?"

"Yeah."

"I'm glad you called. It's great to hear your voice."

"How'd Micah do in Dublin?"

"Awesome. He's opening now, but I predict he'll have his
own tours within the next two years. The crowds love him."

I relaxed and settled in to talk to him. We talked casually for
an hour. He told me about the tour antics that had already
started. They had to find ways to kill the long hours between
shows, and the tour usually began with fun camaraderie, pranks,
and group mayhem—all of which would slowly die down as the
exhaustion and boredom of four weeks on the road ground on
them.

"When I opened a drawer to pull out a pair of boxers to sleep
in last night, there was nothing but diapers."

I giggled. "What did you do?"

"I went commando."

"So right now—?" The image of him sitting half naked on the tour bus might push me from vaguely missing him all the way into physical pain.

"Sweat pants. Very attractive."

"That's good. I was about to book a flight."

His voice changed. "You should."

Not that it wasn't tempting, but . . . "Can't. Work. Besides, I'd be in the way."

"No, you wouldn't. For now, everyone is still filled with excitement, but after two days on the road, I feel more alone than I remember it being. It's hard to explain. I'm surrounded by people constantly, and half the time, I want to get away to myself. I enjoy the guys, but . . ." His voice dropped, quiet. "I guess I'm just missing you."

"You better. At least you have something fun to do. Same old same old here."

"Come here. Meet us in London. Or Paris. Come see the show and travel with us. Doooo it, Eden."

I laughed. How many women would jump at the chance? The idea seemed so crazy, but I said, "I would if I could."

He wasn't laughing. "If you change your mind, contact my agent, Jane. I'll send her instructions to take care of you. Think about it."

Later in the morning, my mom called and told me she needed my help getting together the Halloween decorations. Dad was carving a pumpkin when I arrived. It always surprised me that my mom got into Halloween at all given her feelings about the underworld. But any theme she could mine for a party seemed to fall into the realm of the acceptable. She avoided anything that touched on witchcraft or devilry and stuck to the more savory spooks—bats, skeletons, cobwebs, spiders, tomb stones. Death and creepy crawlies were just a part of life.

I recalled one year when Micah had wanted to dress up like a warlock, but my parents said there was no such thing as magic and made him choose something else. He ended up going out dressed as a Jedi Knight. I still didn't understand their logic.

As I was stapling the cobweb netting to the front-porch overhang, Dad came out and asked if he could be of any assistance. He stood beside the ladder, one hand bracing the side. Ever so casually, he dropped his payload. "Mom's a bit concerned with some of the rumors going around."

I finished putting up the decoration and climbed down and thanked him. "Dad, there's nothing for her to worry about."

"I'm sure." He looked down at me, saying more with his dark eyes than he ever would with words. He patted my shoulder, an overwhelming sign of solidarity and affection. "Maybe you should go talk to her?"

"Thanks, Dad."

I found my mom upstairs, putting her hair up. She didn't take her eyes from the mirror. "Oh, Eden. Could you hand me that comb?" She put a bobby pin in her mouth, and I grabbed the comb from the edge of her vanity.

I sat on her bed, one leg under the other, and ran my eyes across the room. She'd changed minor things over the years: the comforter, the curtains, the carpets. But the furniture and wall hangings had been the same since we moved into this house. The bright red wooden horses from Sweden had stood silent watch for a decade. The only significant change had been in Mom. I leaned over and placed a finger where she'd been pinning her hair. It used to be blond with hints of white. Now the roots were silver with a few golden holdouts. If I took after her in any way, I'd have a pretty shade of gray to look forward to. But I didn't. I was Dad's kid all the way. I'd have black hair until I was wearing dentures.

She finished and held the hand mirror to inspect her handiwork. Then she turned around with a deep exhale. "Eden, I know you're dating that musician."

I snorted. That was going to be impossible to deny. "Well, yeah."

Her eyes narrowed. "It's not serious, is it?"

"A little. He invited me to fly to Europe and tour with his band." No big deal. I dropped that on her and stood up. I didn't like where this was heading.

"You're not considering it, are you?"

162 Mary Ann Marlowe

Micah was right. I needed to get out of there. "It's none of your business, Mom. I'm twenty-eight. I can make my own decisions."

"Eden, sit down." I leaned against her bed, neither sitting, nor standing. She scowled, but let it go. "You can be so obstinate. All I ever wanted was for you to be happy."

I took in the fine lines under her eyes, the deep groove between her brows. Did she have matching etches in her cheeks when she smiled?

"Are you happy, Mom?" I hadn't meant it to come out like a challenge, but my hackles were up.

Her frown deepened. "Of course, I am. Why would you think otherwise?"

Because you focus so much attention on my life? And always have. At least since—

"Mom, whatever happened on that mission trip?"

"What?"

"Why did you take us off that bus and come here?"

She shifted. "That was a very long time ago, Eden."

"But you've never explained it to me."

"Eden, we weren't supposed to be on that bus for more than a month or two."

I chuckled. "Because the world was supposed to end?"

She looked at her hands. Was she embarrassed about that chapter in her life?

"I'm sorry, Mom. Go on."

"I began to realize that we were neglecting our responsibilities to you children. We had a tutor on hand to keep up with your school work, of course. But Micah was becoming so wild."

"So you came back?"

She exhaled. "Not at first."

"So why?"

Her shoulders dropped, and she made eye contact with me. "We ran out of money."

Something clicked into place in my brain. "We were broke?"

She nodded.

"So that's why we lived with Mor-Mor until Dad found work? Did you move us here so we could be resocialized?"

"That's a harsh way to describe it. But yes, I wanted to move on and make sure you kids had a healthy environment to grow up in."

"After you realized we were actually going to grow up?"

"Something like that."

"You do know that I've grown up now. You don't need to keep protecting me."

She smiled weakly. "I just don't want to see you get hurt."

I bit my cheek. "You know you can't control that."

The groove in her brow deepened. Maybe I'd put it there. "I'm not sure why you waited so long to turn wild. But you of all people should know those musicians don't lead the kind of life you need. They don't know how to keep a relationship going."

"Ugh, Mom. I haven't gone wild, and anyway, half the guys you set me up with are divorced."

"But they've got homes and stable careers." Her hands were tiny fists in her lap. "Go on then. I guess you'll have to learn from experience. The door is always open here."

There was so much I wanted to say, but my mom's prejudices about me were as fixed as the Dala horses guarding her night-stand. Her notion of my Mr. Right couldn't encompass someone like Adam. And I'd let her worldview influence my own.

As much as I'd fought against her attempts to settle me with a man of her choosing, I'd inherited her myopic assessment of people, even if I'd twisted it to create my own arbitrary standards. Was I any better than my mom for ruling out entire groups of people because of their career? Or for writing off so many people as unsuitable for me based on something as superficial as their hair color or their tattoos?

And had it all come down to something missing in her life? I knew she loved my dad, and he'd provided for us, but as a claims adjuster, he didn't give my mom whatever she thought I'd find with a wealthier man. Maybe all she really needed was a kitchen remodel and a new bedroom suite, and she'd leave me alone.

Micah was right all along. I'd been a jackass.

Going to work the next morning should have given me something to do to keep my mind occupied. All the publicity from the week before had died down, and so I couldn't even pass the time by reading the forum to find out which of the competing theories about my continued existence was in the lead.

I walked into the lab, expecting to attempt to bury myself in mundane analysis, but both Thanh and Keith were waiting for me.

Keith's mustache said, "A reporter came around this morning asking questions about you."

The blood drained from my face. I felt light-headed. "A reporter? Here?"

He scowled. "That's not good, Eden. Not for you and not for us. Fortunately, he approached Thanh first thing, and Thanh called security."

I rested my weight against the stool. "What would he hope to find out about me? This is where I work."

He laid a hand on my arm. "This is what I meant before. With you gallivanting about with celebrities, it's bound to come back to us here. We're just hoping you don't bring further scrutiny to our research. Prying eyes could lend an advantage to our competitors, Eden." He pinched the bridge of his nose, and when he looked back at me, the lines on his face and the red in his eyes told me he hadn't been getting his beauty sleep. I'd had no idea there was so much pressure over this project. "You haven't left anything in your trash at home, have you?"

"What? You think they're going through my trash?" Oh, my God. Adam had warned me. I couldn't get a full breath. "But. No. Nothing." I watched Keith rub his thumb and forefinger together, a nervous tic. What was he so afraid of? An idea struck me, so beautiful in its simple genius, I had to refrain from blowing the execution with enthusiasm. "Would it be helpful if I took some time off? I've been thinking of traveling."

His breath released from his lungs in an explosion of relief. "That's not a bad idea."

Thanh frowned. "I'm sorry, Eden. But thanks for all the help on my project." Then he turned his head. "Kelly, can you come with me?" And just like that he had a new lab assistant. Glenn was going to love this change in circumstances.

Once they'd left the lab, I placed a call to Jane, who didn't seem surprised to hear from me. "You held out longer than I expected."

A knot formed in my stomach. "Why? Has Adam done this before?"

"Oh, no. Call it intuition. When can you leave?"

"Immediately."

She said she could get me to the London show on Thursday, but suggested I aim for the Friday night in Paris. "Travel can be disrupted. It would be easier to catch you up to the tour from there if things go wrong. I'll try to get you out on Wednesday, okay?"

I trusted her with the logistics, but the extra day worked out in my favor. Tobin texted me on Tuesday morning, asking if I could fill in for a late cancellation that night. I didn't need to be asked twice. Normally a Tuesday night was completely out of the question, but I would be flying out of JFK the next morning, and I could stay at Micah's.

Sure. Opening act? I could get out of there by ten.

Main. 10-12. Will feed you. Please?

My stomach flipped. I'd never be able to do two hours of my own material, but . . . *Can I do covers? Can I sing Micah's songs?*

You can sing "Wheels on the Bus," for all I care. Just need a body.

Flattering. But it sounded like fun and would help burn away the hours that seemed to have come to a crawl since Adam had left.

Sure. See you there.

I couldn't believe I had my very own show to prepare for. The butterflies were waiting in the wings to tear my stomach apart, but I immediately set about creating a possible set list. I knew I could handle it. Ignoring the fan sites, the gossip columns, and the Internet in general helped me sustain my optimism throughout the day. I left work a little early so I could practice playing every song I thought might get me through two hours.

Then I packed my suitcase for every contingency—T-shirts, jeans, sweaters, skirts, makeup, hairspray. When I opened the drawer in my bathroom and saw the vial of perfume, I stopped short. Should I leave it there? I couldn't throw it away, not after Keith's panic attack. But then again, what if someone broke in while I was away? Unlikely, but I didn't need to be stressing about the possibility from three thousand miles away.

I threw the tube into my purse and drove over to the lab. I knocked on Thanh's office door, then tried the knob. He must've gone to lunch and locked up, so I went down to find Stacy. From the hallway, I could hear her and Kelly arguing and listened for a minute before opening the door.

Kelly said, "I doubt someone like Adam Copeland would consider Eden over Adrianna. Don't you even read the papers?"

My hands clenched. But then Stacy rose to my defense. "You haven't seen them together. He's completely smitten. It's totes adorable."

"You know he's slumming."

I shouldered the door open hard enough for it to bounce against the wall. "Stacy, you got a minute?" I shot a glance at Kelly to shame her, but she made duck lips and turned back to her microscope.

Stacy hopped off her stool. "I thought you'd be gone by now."

"I was packing, but I came across something that belongs to Thanh." I reached into my purse and found the vial. I grabbed her wrist, thrust the perfume into her hand, and closed her fist over it tight. "Could you please return this to him?"

She unfurled her fingers and looked at her palm. "What is this?"

"Something he lent me. I forgot I had it. He'll know what it is."

Kelly didn't bother to look over. "I bet I can guess what it is."

Stacy eyed me. "You want to tell me what's going on?"

I grabbed her elbow and pulled her out into the hall. "Look. Thanh gave me this perfume without telling me what it does."

"What does it do?"

"I'm not sure it does anything. But it's supposed to amp up pheromone reception. Like a love potion."

Her eyes went wide. "You've been wearing this around Adam?"

"Only a little. I didn't know what it did. What it's supposed to do."

She whispered, "Maybe you should keep it. I mean, until—"

"Until what?"

"Does Adam know?"

My stomach twisted in a knot. "No."

"Oh. Wow." She wouldn't meet my eyes.

"What?"

"I hope you know what you're doing."

Her reaction troubled me, but she'd only gotten the brochure version of my all-expense-paid excursion into moral ambiguity. How could she understand? "If you give me a ride out to Micah's, I'll tell you all about it."

She followed me home so I could drop off my car and transfer my bags to her trunk. On our way to Brooklyn, I filled her in on how I'd accidentally worn the perfume twice, and how I'd worried about it. "What if it hasn't worn off yet? What if it has?"

She promised me it would sort itself out. "There's no way a drug is coercing him to want to be with you, Eden. But I still think you should tell him. I'm sure he'd understand."

"Maybe." I wasn't so sure. "I'll see how things go when I get there."

We said our good-byes on the sidewalk, and then I dropped my things off at Micah's and took a subway to Lower Manhattan.

When I arrived, the familiarity of the club made the prospect of performing less daunting. That didn't stop my nerves from turning my heart into a battering ram, but I knew I could conquer that fear. I'd been on that stage many times. I could pretend Micah was there with me. The crowd promised to be small in any case.

I'd seen the guy who was opening for me around before. Ricky Levine or something. He slipped in late, so I didn't have a chance to run into him preshow. He'd missed the sound check. He had no merch. No wonder he hadn't been promoted to the main act. The original main act had to cancel due to a motorcycle accident. The audience was fairly sparse as it was. I'd be lucky if I made enough money to pay my subway fare.

After about ten songs, Ricky packed it in. He had virtually no stage presence, hadn't interacted with the audience at all, and all of his songs had been about beer or sports. I came to understand the Tuesday night lineup wasn't a gig anyone should aspire to.

Tobin climbed up on the stage and requested some applause for Ricky but was met with halfhearted clapping. I scanned the crowd. Why were these people here anyway? Were they just that bored?

The microphone popped as Tobin said my name. He located me near the side of the stage and stretched his hand out my way. The people sitting nearest me craned their necks as they watched me climb up the stairs. The awkwardness of performing for people who had paid the cover to hear another musician intensified. But I was committed now.

I grabbed my guitar and pulled the strap over my shoulder. Then I stood before the mic and said, "Hello. I'm Eden Sinclair. I'm filling in for Raven Crowe." The high pitch of feedback squealed momentarily.

I coughed nervously and then launched into one of the songs I'd written. The song I'd played for Adam a couple of weeks before.

My eyes closed as I drifted into the music. My fingers instinctively picked out the chords, strummed, plucked, carried the song from the guitar, which had become a part of my body. When the song ended and I came back to myself, I remembered the crowd and watched for their reaction, always a secondary motivation for my music. But the performance was why I'd been hired, and I needed to check in with my audience.

Sometime during the song, the front row had filled with women ranging in age from young twenties to possibly forty-something. They beamed and clapped. A phone camera flashed as I leaned into the microphone, and I was effectively blind for the next few minutes.

"Thank you very much. This next song is one my brother Micah wrote. If you've come to see him perform, you may know it. Feel free to sing along."

The upbeat song encouraged the women to stand and clap along. Some did sing, so I knew at least a few of them were his fans. Maybe they'd heard I was playing and came here to get closer to Micah or to support his sister. It didn't disappoint me. How would I have any fans of my own?

I hooted the nonverbal parts of the song—the crowd-pleasing oohs and aahs everyone could join along with. Micah had a genius for building those hooks into his music, and they paid off. By the time the song ended, the people who'd been hanging back in the bar had moved closer to the stage. They swayed and bobbed their heads in time.

"Thank you. I'm glad to see some of Micah's fans out here tonight. If there's anything you'd like to hear, I'd be happy to give it a try." I knew his whole catalog. It was unlikely they'd stump me.

I finished the night mostly singing requests along with a few other songs I happened to know. Some standards. Some old folk songs. It was an erratic set, but I got through it. Eventually, I set my guitar down, said good-night to the crowd, and exited stage right. Finally in the green room, I dropped onto that nasty sofa and heaved a huge sigh of relief.

Tobin knocked on the door and stuck his head in. "Do you think you could come back up front? There's a crowd of people waiting to talk to you at the merch area."

"Me?"

Five people stood by the nonexistent merchandise. Hardly a crowd, barely a line. The first person to talk to me was a younger girl, college age by my guess. She wore a gray sweatshirt and jeans, with her hair secured in a tight ponytail. A girl after my own fashion.

"Hi, I'm Amanda." She glowed as she babbled a mile a minute.

"I saw your video online and loved it. Will you be performing here again? Do you have a CD for sale?"

I swallowed a guffaw. I'd learned once if you want to make someone talk quieter, you talk quieter. I wondered if that might work with fast talkers. Calmly and deliberately, I told her, "No. I haven't recorded anything just yet. Other than that YouTube video you saw."

It didn't work. "Oh, my God. What was it like to perform with Adam Copeland? Do you, like, know him?"

I was thinking, *Biblically*. But I said, "We're colleagues. I'd love to work with him again." *In the backseat of a car. In the green room. In his parents' bedroom.* How could I miss him so badly already?

The man behind Amanda coughed, and she had a moment of self-awareness. "Would you mind if we got a picture together?"

Amanda handed her camera to the man. I hadn't practiced that perfect smile, so right when the camera flashed, I had visions of grabbing her phone and smashing it into a million pieces before she could upload the picture to Instagram. No wonder Adam had practiced the perfect pose. But this was part of the job. As an entertainer, I had to build a connection, a rapport with the audience. That connection ended for me when I stepped off the stage, but not for them. I understood it completely. It just felt surreal to be on the receiving end.

I pasted on a smile to greet the next total stranger. He put his hand out, strong, confident, and we shook, businesslike.

"Hi, my name is Brian Hawkins." He held out a card to me. I scanned it without seeing it. "I represent several musical acts and would be interested in talking to you about representation. Have you considered working with an agent?"

My throat had dried up. I caught Tobin's eye and made the universal gesture for *get me a drink*. I gave Brian my attention and frowned. "Mr. Hawkins—"

"Brian."

"You must be under the impression I'm a professional musician. I'm just filling in here for the night."

"Did you get paid?"

I'd get paid, but it would be peanuts. If I got a percentage of the door, it might come out to fifty dollars at most. Plus dinner. And drinks. Nothing compared to working the same amount of time at a lab.

"Look. I'm flattered. Let me take your card, and if I change my mind, I'll know where to find you."

He nodded. "Understood. But call me before you call anyone else. Do some research, and you'll find I'm very reputable. I have a number of clients you may have heard of."

My brother had an agent. If I needed one, I could work with her. But why would I need one?

Brian left me, and I faced two eager women and a fidgety blond guy. The women just wanted to tell me they were fans of Micah and that I'd done a great job, and the guy wanted permission to upload video he'd shot of the show to YouTube. I didn't know people asked permission for that sort of thing.

I shrugged. "Sure. Go ahead." It could disappear into the millions of other live performances uploaded every minute.

"Could I ask you the name of that first song?"

" 'Midnight in the Garden.' "

"Oh, that's great. Nice song."

"Thanks."

I'd written that song in college. A friend of mine had been through a terrible experience with a bully of a guy. The song wasn't exactly about that, but it was about taking control, being strong. It was filled with platitudes. Still, for some reason, I liked to sing it, mainly because the chords came so comfortably to me, and that allowed me to make variations and intricate little flourishes as I performed it. It was a good song for me to start with to warm up.

He jotted the name down on a slip of paper in his hand. I leaned in to read what else he'd written. "Is that a set list?"

"Yeah." He didn't lift his head until he'd finished writing. When he did, he locked eyes with me. He had cornflower-blue eyes. "I'd planned to shoot Raven's set, but when he didn't show, I figured I'd stick around and record yours anyway. I'm glad I did. You were phenomenal."

He glanced over at the bar. "Could I buy you a drink? I'd love to talk to you about this more."

It was late, and as a performer, my drinks were free anyway. And this guy looked like he was pushing twenty-one. His offer flattered me, but no. "Thanks, but I'm going to head out now."

His head dipped, but his eyes stayed on me. If he dug his toe into the ground and wrung his hands together, he'd be the picture-perfect image of a Precious Moments figurine. "Maybe next time then?"

"Okay," I laughed. "Next time."

As if there would be a next time. Although, I wouldn't turn Tobin down if he needed another substitute. I'd had a surprisingly great time.

"By the way, my name's Jacob." He wrote something down, ripped off the corner of his paper, and handed it to me. I expected a phone number, but it was a nonsense word.

I held it up and looked at him quizzically.

"My YouTube username. It might take me a couple of hours to upload these, but watch for them tomorrow."

"Thanks. I'll do that."

Before heading out, I took a mental image of my night. For once, I'd gotten to taste what it was like to be Micah, in the spotlight, center stage. As much as I'd loved it, that momentary glimpse into the world of a full-time musician would have to hold me. Unless I was prepared to throw away everything I'd worked toward, my path didn't include that fork in the road, except as a temporary diversion.

Chapter 15

Jane got me a first-class ticket to Paris, arriving Wednesday night. A limo met me at the airport and delivered me to an opulent hotel next to the stadium. The long thin building looked like a silver ship sailing through the city. The mirrors on the modern structure reflected the older architecture in the surrounding area.

When I got to my room, I discovered a bouquet of flowers with a handwritten note that read, *I can't wait to see you after the show. Adam.*

My ticket and backstage pass sat in an envelope next to maps of Paris Adam had apparently faxed. He'd used some clunky paint software to draw lines and mark places I should visit. He'd typed at the bottom, *Thursday morning. Follow the route and text me from each of the places. It will be like taking a tour of the city together.*

Since the boys were in London Thursday night, I had the day to myself. I woke up and was about to go for breakfast with the map tucked in my purse, but when I checked the first stop, I noticed he expected me to have breakfast at a specific restaurant. So I grabbed a taxi and had them deposit me near the base of the Eiffel Tower.

When I went in to order, the cashier asked if I was Eden. He told me to select anything. It was all paid for. I took a picture of my Nutella crepe and sent it to Adam. I couldn't believe he was awake that early, but he texted, *That looks amazing!*

I sat outside, staring up at the massive steel structure on the edge of the Seine. I would've liked to go to the top, but my tour didn't leave room for a side excursion. I promised myself I'd come back the following morning and go up.

The rest of the morning was filled with a similar mix of delight and frustration. I loved that he'd planned for me to see so many sights, and if he'd been with me, I'm sure we would've deviated from the plan. Besides, if I was honest, I would've holed up in the hotel, or, at most, I'd have spent the entire day hanging around the Eiffel Tower if he hadn't encouraged me to sally forth.

And on Friday, I made my way back to the places I'd wanted to explore further. All in all, I was proud of myself for familiarizing myself with a foreign city. And I bought a new skirt to show off that night.

Back near my hotel, I found a street vendor selling long baguette sandwiches and Coca Light, which looked a lot like Diet Coke. The Bercy sports arena sat across from my hotel, directly on the Seine. It was a crazy modern building with grass growing along the angled outer walls. I ate while walking around the outside of the stadium, trying to see if the tour buses had pulled up.

My phone buzzed, so I had to find a bench to set my drink on. Swallowing as much of my bite of sandwich as I could, I slid my knuckle across the screen. "Hi, Stacy. What's up?"

"It's lunchtime here. I wanted to hear about your trip."

I filled her in on the romantic scavenger hunt and sent her a picture of my new skirt.

"I approve. Very chic. So you see him tonight, right?"

"After the concert. Yes."

She made a sound that reminded me of a frightened pig. "That's so exciting. I'm so jealous. And please take pictures!"

"Go online, Stacy. There will be plenty of pictures and video."

"Not of the concert, Eden. You got backstage passes right?"

"Uh-huh."

A semi with the Walking Disaster logo on its side turned the corner and passed right in front of me. I peered into the cab windows, but the truck passed by too fast. Sun glinted off the glass, and I put my hand across my forehead to shade my eyes, squinting.

"I think their gear just arrived." I got up and walked down the sidewalk, but a metal barricade had been erected between the street and the area where the buses would park. I wondered if Adam's bus would soon arrive.

Stacy had kept talking, but I missed what she was saying. I put the phone back to my ear. "What?"

"Are you going to tell him?"

The trailer doors swung open, and a large man wearing a black T-shirt, with sleeves rolled up to better display oversized muscles, stepped out. I didn't recognize him. Someone handed down a long black case. Probably a guitar.

Stacy broke into my mesmerized rubbernecking. "Eden?"

"Oh, yeah. I'm gonna tell him." I hadn't decided, but I was distracted by the imminent arrival of my boyfriend and his entourage.

"Tonight. Okay? Don't wait or you won't do it."

More equipment descended through the open truck door. "Good advice," I muttered. The buses would have to come this way. I watched the entrance to the street, disappointed at every car that turned toward me, forgetting to speak to Stacy.

She got the hint. "I'll talk to you later. There's something going on here anyway. They've been really weird whenever they see me on the phone."

Remembering how they freaked out on me for drawing a reporter's attention, I figured I'd brought on a police state. "I'll call you after the show. Or whenever I can."

When I hung up, a man wearing a badge around his neck approached me and said something in French. I shook my head. "English."

"You cannot stay here," he said with a heavy accent.

He looked anxious, like I might cause a scene and have to be forcibly evicted. God, how embarrassing. "No problemo."

I walked back to the hotel to change into my new skirt and pick up my ticket and backstage pass. Nervously excited, I headed toward the arena a little early. I thought about trying to skirt the barricade by the buses, but after my run-in with one guard, I didn't think I should risk it. Besides, crowds already streamed in from the street, and so I fell in line.

My outfit had two immediate drawbacks. First, I hadn't realized how chilly an October night in Paris would be, and I had to wait in a long, slow line to get through the security checkpoint. Second, while the middle-aged woman ahead of me passed through the entry with a quick peek inside her purse, I was the recipient of a full-body pat down accompanied by a wink.

Once inside the arena, I scanned around the sides of the stage and saw an entryway backstage, but it had taken me so long to get through the checkpoint that the lights had begun to dim, and I hurried to find my seat. I couldn't wait to see Micah's band perform in this huge arena. My excitement matched the growing enthusiasm of the fans cheering in anticipation. The seats around me remained mostly empty as Micah's band came out, one member at a time, starting with his drummer, Shane.

Shane started a beat, solo, and the audience clapped in rhythm. Then the bassist came out and laid down a riff. He was a replacement bassist I'd never met, but he sounded great. The guitarist, Noah, came in with a crazy lick. Finally Micah walked out.

Even though I was fairly certain nobody there had ever heard of Theater of the Absurd, the crowd cheered as Micah started playing rhythm guitar behind the center mic. I sang along with all their songs, so excited to see him in this huge venue. He knew how to work the crowd and had everyone on their feet by the time he introduced his last song.

"Thank you, Paris! We're so glad to be here in support of Walking Disaster! How excited are you for them?" The decibels in the place doubled. "We're Theater of the Absurd. This is our last song tonight. Thanks for being such a great crowd!" Cheers again.

People had slowly trickled in during their performance. Two men squeezed past me and took the seats to my right. They stood back up again since everyone else was on their feet. One of them pressed far closer to me than he needed to, and I threw him a warning glance.

As Micah left the stage, people sat. The man to my right leaned over and said, "*Eh, bonsoir, madame.*" His eyebrows raised a little. "*Ou mademoiselle?*" He flashed what might've been a toothy grin, if he hadn't been missing molars on either side, giving him the appearance of a horse in need of a bit.

How obvious was it that I'd come alone? The couple to my left huddled together over one of the colorful concert programs I'd seen for sale when I came in.

The horse-faced man continued his efforts to engage me in conversation, though I couldn't understand a word. I interpreted his aggressive lechery easily enough. I gave Mr. Ed one dismissive shrug and kept my eyes focused forward on the empty stage. In a minute, Adam would be there. I craned my neck around to take in the entirety of the arena. People in the upper deck had hung poster-board signs professing their love for the band or their desire to marry Adam.

Without warning, the lights shut off completely, and the screaming hurt my ears. Phones lit up all around, and shadowed silhouettes appeared on the stage. If anyone in the band had uttered a "one-two-three-four" intro, it was lost in the white noise of the crowd. The drum and bass started playing in time. Everyone in the stadium, already amped up on adrenaline, immediately clapped and stomped along with the beat.

A spotlight illuminated Adam at the exact moment he came in with the guitar. I'd been watching concert footage all week, so this did not surprise me, but the audience ate it up. He stepped up to the mic and went right into a crowd favorite. I'd become familiar with all of their songs from following them, and I sang along with the band and thousands of other strangers.

Adam was a god. All the video in the world couldn't have prepared me for his stage presence. And he'd let his facial hair grow into a rapscallion scruff that made me want to throw my panties at his feet.

Up on the jumbotron, he seemed to gaze down on me personally. I knew it was an illusion, but one shared by many. The stage jutted out into the audience, and Adam used that walkway to surround himself in the outstretched arms reaching out to touch him. He approached the edges, but the moat created by the venue prevented anyone from reaching up onto the stage.

The man to my right ground into me, and I took a step to my left. The jostling increased with each song, and the people in the audience were beginning to move out of their seats and push toward the stage. People jumped up and down along with the rhythm. I worried about my safety. The man to my right put his hands on me.

I lurched away from him out into the aisle and pushed through the crowds, out into the hall. I found some stairs going up and walked all the way up to the highest nosebleed back row seat in the arena. The stage looked tiny from there, but there was nobody around me. I sat down and propped my feet on the seat in front of me.

The crowd below pulsated and swelled. The number of men at the show dwarfed the number of women. I knew women came because they posted about Adam on the fan forum. But the guys dominated, and no wonder. This music wouldn't have appealed to me at all if it weren't for the fact that I wanted to get into the leather pants of the lead singer. Along with all the other women here.

So it was a surprise when the band left the stage and Adam sat down alone at the mic with a classical guitar and plucked an arpeggio. The song he played wasn't just soft for Walking Disaster, it was soft for AM radio. He hadn't done this at the previous shows.

As he struck the opening chords, he spoke to the crowd, saying, "I wrote this song earlier this week. And Paris, I knew you were the only crowd I could play this for. This song is called 'Compulsion.'" If the crowd was about to turn ugly from the sharp left turn into light rock, this statement brought them back to him, and the phones came out, lights waving over heads.

He played four more bars and then came in with the vocal.

> Wandering alone in the desert
> For forty days and forty nights
> A mirage in a short skirt
> Led me back
> Back to the garden's delights.

The chorus came in, and then he repeated it.

> Two weeks in paradise
> Under October skies
> Drawn to the tree of life
> For one more bite

I didn't need to hold my phone up because my blush had to be lighting up the entire top row. I let my head fall back against the concrete wall behind me and hugged myself.

There would be no doubt who that song was intended for. Adam had essentially outed me to anyone with more than half a brain cell. The fan forum would be active tonight. It occurred to me that some of those fans might be in the audience below. I was so glad I'd moved up above the crowd, where nobody would recognize me, where I could drink in the thrill of hearing a song written for me without worrying. I couldn't wait to get Adam alone and show him how much that forbidden fruit liked him right back.

On the second verse, a female voice wove in with Adam's. The figure of Adrianna LaRue appeared on the edge of the stage as she sang her way to the front and placed her mic into the stand. The crowd screamed, while I slumped into my seat. The duet sounded great, but I couldn't understand what she was doing there. Why was he singing that song with her?

In a heartbeat, my elation turned into irrational jealousy. I told myself it didn't mean anything. She was just singing with him, but they had some kind of history. The green monster whispered in my ear, *He wrote that song for her, you fool.* But reason prevailed. He knew I was going to be here. He wouldn't shove another woman in my face. There was an explanation. I'd ask him. I relaxed, thinking about how fun it would be to find him backstage in a short while.

Eventually, the concert came to an end, and after calling the band back for an encore, the crowd began to stream out. I fought my way down the stairs to find out how to get backstage. A number of other people stood at the barricade, begging the security guards to let them have access. I fished out my pass and showed it to one of the guards, and he let me through. The fans around me grabbed at my clothes, as if they could hitch a ride.

My heart raced as I stepped across the boundary between the fans and the musicians.

The corridor running behind the stage wasn't narrow, but it was constricted with all the people moving around. Several large men in black carried equipment around, but there were others with less obvious associations to the band. I passed through this crowd, looking for some sign of Micah or Adam.

I caught a glimpse of Adrianna coming out of a doorway and started in that direction. When I saw Adam's unmistakable mess of hair, I called out after him. At that exact moment, many other female voices shouted his name. I turned back to see a group of fans corralled at the end of the hall, peering down the corridor toward where I stood.

A hand landed on my shoulder, and I thought I was about to be groped for the second time that day.

The tall bald man stepped in front of me. "Where are you going?"

I showed him my pass. "I'm looking for Micah Sinclair or Adam Copeland?"

He shook his head. "Sure you are. Along with all of the others. Let me show you to the meet-and-greet room."

I stopped him. "What's your name?"

"Paul."

"Paul. I'm Micah's sister, Eden. He's expecting me. I'm trying to find Adam."

"So are half the other girls here." He blocked my way and herded me back the way I'd come. "Look. I'm sure you are who you say you are, so it shouldn't be a big deal to wait until one of them comes out. If they recognize you, then you're good to go. I hope you can see my point of view here. I can't let every girl who has a pass wander back to the dressing rooms."

I gave up. It made sense, and I was glad to know that the fan girls wouldn't be rushing in on Adam while he was changing after a show. I let Paul take me down to the waiting area to crowd in with the fans exuding simultaneous excitement and impatience. They all held programs or CDs or T-shirts. Every one of them clutched a Sharpie. I sent texts to Micah and Adam and tapped my foot anxiously, but with all the commotion, they probably weren't fixated on their phones.

After about thirty minutes, a stadium employee led us into a small room, and we lined up behind a red velvet rope. A door opened, and necks craned. Adrianna walked through first, followed by Adam. Everyone, including me, stood taller and pushed forward a little. The rest of Adam's band came through the doors, and they all sat down at a table to start signing autographs. With every group, they'd have to stop long enough to take a picture with the fan. Then the line inched forward.

I couldn't wrap my mind around the ridiculous fact that I stood in a meet-and-greet line, waiting for a chance to get closer to Adam. Fans shoved me from behind, and I shuffled along, hoping Adam would eventually see me. It might've been a mark of bad character, but it would've done my pride a world of good to get plucked from this line before I found myself in the presence of Adrianna.

But while I hid among the fans, I got to spy on Adam interacting with strangers who thought they knew him. He took his time, asking people their names before signing whatever they'd brought. With one eye on his signature, he kept up a steady stream of questions or responses depending on the situation. He was completely adorable.

A pair of girls managed to talk him into coming around the table to give each of them a hug. They giggled and squealed, then hugged each other as they left the meet-and-greet room with a story to tell their friends.

Eventually, when there were only a few fans left ahead of me, his eyes landed on me. He broke out in a huge smile and stood up from the table.

"How'd you get in here?" He stepped past the waiting fans and grabbed my hand. "Come back here."

I walked behind the table and leaned against the wall. The remaining fans looked up at me, perplexed for a moment, but then focused back on getting their own time with Adam. He signed and smiled and posed and chatted for a little while longer. His T-shirt clung to his body. I inched closer, hoping to smell his sweaty concert musk. My fingers itched to touch the exposed skin on his neck.

Stacy would have lost her shit, standing behind the band at a meet and greet. I grabbed my phone out and snapped a picture of the back of Adam's head and texted it to her. *Look where I am.*

A few minutes later, she wrote, *Swoons!* followed by, *Did you tell him yet?*

I wrote back, *Just got here. Haven't had time to. I will.*

But Adam smiled back at me so sweet, with eyes lined with unhidden desire. I caught my breath. Would he look at me like that if he knew?

Finally, the line dwindled. The band stood and stretched and made their way through the door.

Adam grabbed me and wrapped his arms around my back. "Why were you in here?"

I breathed him in. He must've been sweating pheromones stronger than anything Thanh could concoct. "Ask Paul. He brought me here."

He jerked his head back and twisted his face. "Who's Paul?"

I had no answer. "Isn't he some kind of bouncer?"

"Maybe. But come on with me." He took my hand and practically dragged me down the corridor, past the crowds, and into a narrow room that held a sofa, some clothes, and a mirror with lights. His dressing room, I presumed.

As soon as the door clicked shut, he spun me and pushed me back against the wall. "God, I've missed you."

Without another word, he kissed me. His hands were on my

face, then down my arms, then pushing up my shirt. I responded immediately. My hands reached for his neck, fingers locking into his hair.

I heard Stacy's voice, warning me I had to tell him about the perfume now or never. I broke away with difficulty. "Adam."

His breathing was deep, heavy. "Oh, God. Eden." He reached down to the hem of my skirt, lifting it up and reaching for the edge of my panties. They slid down an inch. His fingers found their way into me, and I groaned. He had to feel how badly I wanted him, but he'd never come on this strong before. We hadn't even had a chance to say hello.

I put my hands on his shoulders and pushed him back. "Adam!"

His eyes were nearly black. His shirt stuck to his skin where I held him. I twisted my fingers into the cloth and pulled myself closer, breathing in his sweat and musk and sex.

He moaned and seized my wrist. He held it above my head against the wall and kissed the side of my neck. I was insane for him, but there was something fan stalkerish about the whole encounter.

I elbowed him aside and took a seat on the sofa. "Can we—?"

My question ended with a groan when Adam knelt at my feet and kissed my inner thigh, the scruff on his cheeks rough against my skin. He nudged my knees apart, and his hands roamed back up under my skirt. The crotch of my underwear slid to one side, and his thumb connected. His kisses were nearing the same destination.

I wanted nothing more than to feel his tongue against me, but I gathered my strength and scooted back.

"Adam."

He lifted his eyes, and his gaze bore into me. "What is it, Eden?"

He'd transformed into the rock god who'd looked down from on high as twenty thousand fans worshiped at his feet.

"I wanted to talk to you," I rasped. My skin burned where his lips had just been, and I writhed, betraying my own declaration.

"Can we talk later?" His fingers wandered back under my skirt, and my resolve weakened.

"Yes."

He wrapped his hands around my thighs and slid me forward until I was flat on my back, with my everything hanging off the edge of the sofa. And his tongue ran right up the pleasure zone. His fingers entered, and my strength broke.

"Oh, my God." I closed my eyes, gurgling with the intensity of it. And I totally succumbed to him. I bucked once as I came.

Before my body shook a second time, his hands grasped my hips, and he pressed hard against me. His unzipped leather pants scratched against my thigh.

"Adam. Do you have a condom?"

On his knees, he rocked forward, and I moaned. He hadn't bothered to remove my panties and was on the verge of entry.

"Adam! Condom?"

"Fuck. I don't—" He looked like he was coming out of a drugged stupor. He cast about the room, apparently searching for likely stashes of prior rock stars. "Just a second."

He started to get up, but I locked my hand on his wrist, and laid a finger against his lips. "Hand me my purse."

I dug in the pocket and produced a black square envelope.

"Smart girl."

"I learn from experience."

He took my hands and gently tugged me forward until I slid off the sofa and onto his lap. Any thoughts of fighting him had long abandoned me. I gave in to him completely. My legs wrapped around him, and I stared into his eyes as he entered. I lifted my hips slowly and watched his face agonize. My fingers traced the skin along his neck, and he grabbed my hair at the back of my head and pulled me forward to suck and bite my lips in what passed for a kiss.

The need was mutual. An earthquake wouldn't have been able to tear me away from him at this moment.

An earthquake was exactly what it felt like when my body jolted and jerked a second time. My nails dragged into his skin, and he came with a cry. I slowed my rhythm and lay my head on his shoulder, hugging him against me.

Once I'd caught my breath, I asked, "Adam, what happened to taking a step back and waiting?"

He held my shoulders and leaned me back to face him. "Eden, I can't get you out of my mind. Did you hear the song I wrote for you?"

I nodded. "Nobody's ever done that for me. It was beautiful."

"I looked for you in the audience but didn't see you out there. I thought you were going to be in the first few rows."

"Yeah. I moved. The crowds were getting a little rough out there."

"When I didn't see you, I had a moment of panic that maybe you hadn't come after all. Maybe you wouldn't be here tonight. Maybe it was relief, but when I saw you at the meet and greet, all I could think of was how much I needed you. I was signing autographs, thinking the whole time about taking you back here and ravishing you."

"Adam."

There was a knock at the door and someone called, "Adam! We need to load up the bus. We're leaving in thirty minutes."

He moved under me, and I rolled off him. I was going to need thirty or forty showers to wash all the nasty off me.

"Can we talk for a minute, please?"

He pulled his pants back up and rummaged around the room, throwing his things together. "We're on a tight schedule. Driving to Antwerp tonight." He turned back. "You're going with us, right?"

"I want to talk to you. Can you give me a few minutes?"

"Let's get on the bus. We can talk there."

I sighed. "My stuff is back at the hotel. I didn't bring anything with me."

Adam opened the door and stuck his head out. "Shane! Hey, man. Can you find that driver?"

He got my hotel key and exchanged a few words with another guy named Seamus, who had instructions to pack everything away and to check the bathroom, the drawers, and under the bed. I wanted to go back to the hotel with him, but Adam said he'd rather take the time to show me our berth on the bus.

Things were moving faster than my mind could keep up with, but for now, I gave up. I didn't want to start an argument with Adam while we were pressed for time. And honestly, what I wanted at that moment was to go with the flow and experience his rock-star lifestyle—if only for a little while.

Chapter 16

The crowds in the corridor hadn't diminished, and when Adam and I stepped out of his dressing room, a dozen heads turned. All eyes went from him to me and then back to him. If his song hadn't clued everyone in to our relationship yet, seeing us with our sex hair leaving his dressing room together was a pretty strong indication we were together. Provided he didn't have a habit of leaving his dressing room trailing a hot bimbo. And if his hair didn't already always look like he'd slept with a bear in heat.

As we passed from the corridor of theoretically vetted people toward the exit doors, the quality of noise changed from the in-dustrial behind-the-scenes buzz to a crazed-fan-girl anticipation. We were about to leave the bubble of normalcy and enter that world where Adam became someone else again.

"Take a deep breath," he said.

"That's what you always say."

We walked outside into the cool Paris night air. The buses sat several yards away, engines running. To one side, dozens of fans flanked a barricade, waiting patiently in the hopes they might get a moment of Adam's time. They didn't have meet-and-greet passes or any sure way to know he'd even take the time to walk over to meet them. But they'd come and stood outside in the cold. And it occurred to me I was the reason they'd waited so long. I blushed.

"ADAM!" they called, sometimes in small bursts of unison, mostly in total cacophony.

I leaned over. "Which is our bus? Can I just disappear now?"

He put his hand on my back and pointed. "First one on the left. Go on. We've got a little time. I'm going to try to meet as many of these people as I can. Micah should already be on board."

With one last glance at the girls crushing against the barricade, I stepped away from Adam. He dove right into the fray, and I admired his ability to juggle this part of his life. I couldn't imagine what would cause anyone to stand outside in the cold waiting for a chance to meet a performer. But they were the entire reason he was able to make a career doing what he loved, and he treated them accordingly.

Two enormous bodyguards stood positioned on either side of the bus doors and scrutinized me as I set my foot onto the steps. One blocked my way, but then Micah shouted from inside the bus.

"Eden!" He came down and grabbed my wrist. The bodyguard retracted his hand and faced the mob again. I was relieved that they were there to make sure Adam would be safe. The level of adrenaline outside the bus eclipsed anything I'd ever experienced at Micah's shows.

Micah glowed from his after-show excitement. "Did you get to see us?"

I followed him past the front seats to a small kitchenette in the middle section of the bus. A fold-out table blocked my way, and I squeezed around it. I sat across from Micah and gushed.

"You were amazing. You know you're never going to be able to perform those small clubs again if you keep this up. You're going to leave this tour as big a rock star as Adam."

He laughed. "I seriously doubt that, but this trip has been incredible already." His eyes grew big. "Wait. Are you coming with us to Antwerp? Don't you need to get back home?"

I shrugged. "Apparently not. My manager said I could take up to two weeks, so I could theoretically travel with you guys as far as Munich."

"Seriously? Excellent!" He raised his hand for a high five, and I didn't leave him hanging. "Hey, would you be willing to sing with us?"

I gave him my "No, my brother" face. The one I'd worn when he'd asked me to steal money out of Mom's purse. "Um. No way. You're gonna have to get your own backup singer."

"Why not? Come on. Did Adam already stake a claim?"

"What? Of course not. No way am I getting up onstage in an arena. This is way too big-time for me. But thanks for asking."

Adam lunged up the steps and down the aisle to join us. His hair stuck out in every direction, and he had lipstick on every inch of skin across his cheeks and on his neck. I started to speak, but he lifted a hand. "Don't even. It's really not my fault."

He grabbed a couple of napkins and rubbed it all off. I couldn't blame the fans for wanting to lay their lips on him. I already regretted the lack of privacy we'd have on this bus for the next four hours. And I supposed even longer because it wasn't like we'd get off the bus and find a hotel once we arrived in Antwerp. We'd likely just sleep here.

As if he'd read my mind, Adam took my hand and said, "Come with me." He pointed out the benches along the walls. "These open out a little, but it's far from comfortable."

Farther back, we came to the rock-star suite. A platform had been installed to support a somewhat thicker mattress, and a flimsy cloth hung down in the opening to give the small alcove some privacy. "At night, we generally all squeeze in here because it's better than the bunks. During the day, it makes a great place to get away and nap."

I snickered, trying to reconcile my image of the rock-star tour bus with this reality. "You and Micah have been sleeping in here together for the past week?"

"Some. We have the three buses, plus a trailer for our gear. Micah's bandmates are on one, and my other bandmates are on the other. We sometimes mix up the arrangement to give everyone a break from the sardine cans."

The sound of someone climbing onto the bus interrupted my

tour. Seamus shoved my suitcase in the middle of the aisle, saying, "One sec. I'll be back."

He returned a few moments later with bags slung over his shoulder and dropped them each on the front seats.

"Thank you, Seamus," I said.

When he'd gone, Adam explained I could get some things out of my suitcase and put them into the few drawers near the back so the suitcase could be stored below the bus. While I picked out the few clean clothes I had left, Micah announced he'd go bunk with his bandmates for the night. So apparently he approved of my romance with Adam. That was good to know. I still hadn't talked to him about it.

The bus doors closed, and we were alone with the driver, who paid us no attention.

"Are you hungry?" He began pulling things down from the cabinets. "One of our guys keeps these fully stocked, but it's not a five-star restaurant. We've got peanut butter and fruit. Cheese and crackers? Or do you want something to drink?"

That's when I realized this was his house—disguised as a bus. He was trying to make me feel like I was at home too, so I obliged him. "Can we have some of that cheese? And do you have a beer?"

As the bus rolled out of the parking lot and onward toward Antwerp, he went around gathering food. I would've loved to spy on the normal routine on this bus. Guys all jostling one another for space and food. Nobody serving someone else, as though they were a proper guest, unless they also brought girls on board. But if I'd thought a rock-star life was conducive to getting laid, I was disabused.

Sure, the dressing room had worked out for us, and tonight we had the bus to ourselves. But the other guys? They were going to be very horny by the end of this tour. Or maybe they weren't clearing out for Adam because he was their diva. Maybe they all did that for one another. I'd love to stick around long enough to know.

He never stopped bustling around the cabin while I sat and ate. He picked up his food and then went back to find blankets.

He tossed those into the bed alcove, grabbed his beer, and then opened a drawer to get clean clothes.

"Oh, and look!" He slid out a basket and displayed an assortment of colored square envelopes.

"Oh." The muscles in my face dropped into a frown. I didn't want to read too much into the fact that he kept condoms on his tour bus.

He shook his head. "I thought you'd be glad I thought ahead. Not far enough obviously. I thought we'd at least make it onto the bus."

When the food was gone, and he'd cleaned it up, he said, "I'm beat. You can stay up if you want, but I'm going to lie down. Or you could join me." His smile was equal parts cute, shy boy, and hot, smoldering rock star.

"You are irresistible," I said.

I could see Adam wasn't kidding about being exhausted, so I gathered a change of clothes for sleeping. As I glanced up, Adam tugged his shirt over his head, bearing his tattoo-covered torso, his taut abs, and the trail of hair running into his shorts. I followed him into his alcove and lay down beside him. He drew me in against his chest and caressed my skin until he slipped off to sleep. I lay there, listening to his deep breathing and worried the day would come when it would forever be out of my reach.

I woke up to the sound of Adam speaking in the front of the bus. I crept to the curtain at the entrance to the alcove and listened.

"Come on, Adrianna, it was so much better with you."
Pause.

"Maybe. She doesn't have as much experience, though. I'm pretty sure she'll refuse."

I took a deep breath and pushed open the curtain. Jealousy smoldered below the surface, but I wasn't going to jump to conclusions without an explanation. He knew I was on the bus.

"Good morning," I said in a cheery tone.

Adam leaned over as far as he could and stretched his hand out to me. "Hey, come out here."

Then to the phone, he said, "Okay. Maybe we'll see you farther south."

When he hung up, he reeled me onto his lap and kissed my cheek. "Adrianna wondered whether you might want to duet with me tonight in Antwerp."

"Me?"

Adam chuckled and rubbed my hand. "I told her you'd refuse."

"Then why are you bringing it up?"

"Adrianna ditched us in Dublin, but we caught up with her in London. Then she wanted to hitch a ride to Paris. I told her she could if she would duet on 'Compulsion.' She worked on it on the bus with me all day yesterday. We only practiced it once onstage for the sound check. Not bad, right?"

I nodded, unable to form a coherent response.

"But she doesn't want to ride all over Europe with us just to perform one song."

The idea was insane. "You want me to sing with you? Onstage?"

His lips found my neck, and he laid small kisses on me, sending chills down my spine. "Why not? You've sung onstage."

His warm breath tickled my skin. But he couldn't convince me so easily. "Not in front of a crowd that large."

"So we start you off slow. You could sing in the shadows. Did you see how we hid Adrianna last night at first? If you're game, it could totally work out. Adrianna could head south, and I could keep performing that song with your help."

We only had a few hours to practice "Compulsion," and he put me on a crash course. I had no intention of going onstage to perform it, but I went along with his plan because who wouldn't want to learn a song written about her with the guy who wrote it?

While we were camped out in the Antwerp Sportpaleis parking lot, people constantly came and went. I had no time alone with Adam while I learned the lyrics. And then Adam wanted to work out the harmonies and go over it so many times that even if I got cold feet, practice would kick in. Compared to the insanity of the after concert the night before, I found the day hanging out with the guys relaxing and fun. They all got along with each other well. One of the drivers went out and brought back a ton of food, so when we weren't practicing, we were eating.

Fans already camped out near the barricades by the buses, and whenever the guys moved about, the shrill shriek of thrilled girls followed us across the parking lot. Micah had started imitating Adam and took a page from his notebook by going over to the barricades and greeting all the fans. He came back glowing from all the adulation. I no longer recognized my brother; he was growing into the rock star he was always meant to be.

Adam went into the arena to lend a hand with the crew, so I called Stacy to fill her in on my latest news and catch up on the antics back home.

"The bus is cramped," I told her. "And smelly. And fascinating."

"Gah. I can only imagine riding around with a freaking rock star in a rock-star tour bus."

"And Adam wants me to sing with him tonight."

"Like onstage?"

"Yeah. You sound about as confident about it as I do."

She chuckled. "You'll be great. Just picture everyone in their underwear or whatever."

"Funny." I sat down on a giant black trunk. I had no clue what it held, but it felt warm and made a comfortable perch to watch the crew move around while I chatted. "Are you going out with Kelly tonight?"

"Actually, no. Your mom invited me over to dinner tonight. I get the feeling she'd assumed you'd be back already and set this up. She told me Rick Whedon was coming over."

"Oh, God." My mom's house seemed so far away from this world. "You don't have to go."

She hesitated. "Well, it's okay. I think it will be nice."

"Okay, but you do not have to entertain Rick Whedon, DDS."

"Why do you do that?"

"Do what?"

"Just because you don't like him doesn't mean I won't."

My stomach lurched. "Oh, Stacy. You can do so much better."

"Eden, you accidentally landed the hottest man on earth. But it's not practical for me to expect more than what's around here. Rick has a good job. He's kind of cute."

I didn't want to tell her what to do. "Swoons, Stacy. Don't talk yourself into a guy who doesn't make you swoon. Remember?"

"Speaking of your swoon-worthy boyfriend—"

"Haven't told him yet." I understood her point of view, but I'd weighed out the options and had more or less decided not to tell him. The harm it could cause far outweighed the good. It'd been over a week since either of us had worn the perfume, and there were far too many other things in this life waiting to derail our fledgling relationship. Why add one more?

Shane crossed the parking lot, and a dozen girls called over from the barricades. He waved, and I noticed his eyes lingering, like he was shopping for a groupie. So many girls wanted to cross that barricade. When they looked at me, their smiles disappeared, clearly unsure what I'd done to get to hang out with the band. At best they might look at me like a rat in a cage—someone to study to figure out how to reproduce the results. At worst, they looked like they wanted to take me out and take my place.

Stacy had continued to ramble on about something while I'd been paying more attention to the crew. "—and I have to confess that Kelly and I went out last night and tested your perfume."

I sat bolt upright. "You did what?"

"Don't freak out. We were just curious. But oh, my God, did we get a lot of attention at the bar."

My teeth ground together. "Of course you did. You always do. You're two attractive girls in a sea of testosterone. On a Monday night." My heart rate sped up. "And you were supposed to give the perfume to Thanh."

"I did. I swear. But Kelly was there, and she asked if she could have it. He happily let her take it."

"Of course he did. Guinea pigs in the wild." I couldn't find any words to say that didn't seem hypocritical. "Just promise me you won't wear it anymore."

"You afraid I might land my own world-famous rock star?"

"Don't." I didn't appreciate the implication that I'd attracted Adam that way. Mainly because I couldn't be sure I hadn't. And her teasing amped up my insecurities.

"Fine, but then don't scold me if I try it out for myself."

I had no argument against that, so I navigated us toward our good-byes. "Tell my parents I said hello and that I'm still alive."

"And you tell Adam I said hello and that you met him while wearing a sex bomb."

As soon as I hung up, Seamus jogged over and asked if I wanted to use the stadium facilities. Throughout the day, the guys had taken advantage of the showers provided for the band. They prepared for the sound check while I finally got a chance to clean up. Nobody warned me that traveling with a rock band could be so gross.

Adam walked me out onto the stage, and we did a final sound check together to an empty arena. Micah recorded it on his phone, and when he played it back, I had to admit it sounded great. But I warned Adam repeatedly he shouldn't count on me. He just kept moving things one step closer to inevitable.

The energy increased as the arena filled, and that special hum of thousands of individuals creating a single voice grew louder. The guys felt it too, and they all moved around like they were amped on amphetamines. They were all superheroes in their own minds for a little while.

During the show, I sat ringside, mesmerized. The lights and the sounds intoxicated me. Micah's band brought the crowd to their feet, and then Adam's band went out and brought them to their knees.

For that night, they'd rigged up a mic offstage so I could sing facing Micah and a small makeshift audience rather than the entire stadium. When it came time, I nearly conquered my fears and climbed onto the stage, but then my nerves went into overdrive. I paced until the adrenaline wore off. Shaking my hands and wiping my sweaty palms on my jeans, I stood in front of the hidden mic and waited for the song to start.

Adam sat onstage in the hushed auditorium, just him, his guitar, and the spotlight. He strummed and began to sing. I shut my eyes and listened to him, and then, like we'd practiced, I wove in the harmonies. It was just his voice and mine, intertwining, making love with each other in front of the whole world, invisible to everybody but us.

The song came to an end, and Adam surprised me by calling me out onstage. "She's a little shy, so show her some love."

The roar of the crowd grew louder, and my nerves returned with a vengeance. I hesitated at the side of the stage until Micah put his hand on my back and said, "Go on. They don't bite."

I stepped out next to Adam, blinking to adjust my eyes to the light. If I'd thought there was a charge to be had seeing fourteen smiling faces beaming up as I sang in a small club, I was unprepared for the raw energy of fourteen thousand people cheering.

For me.

I couldn't make out any individuals except maybe right in the very front. They were an undulating sea of forms. Lights from cameras sparkled all over, like stars twinkling in the night sky, and signs waved high in the nosebleed section, impossible to read from my vantage point. I raised my hand up to the people up there.

And then I was coming off the stage, stepping down into the weird normal world of entertainers.

When Adam came offstage after another five songs, he found me and wrapped his arms around me. "You were hot."

The crowd chanted and stomped for an encore. Adam gave me a kiss and said, "Hold that thought." He bit his lip and raised his eyebrows. "Think I'll get an encore with you tonight?"

His hand was the last thing to leave me as he was sucked back up onstage with his band.

"Please hurry back," I groaned.

I was still high off that one moment in the spotlight. I could imagine it would be like a drug to those guys, night after night, performing their own music to the adulation of thousands.

Adam had worked up to this level of success over a long time, but still, it amazed me he hadn't succumbed to his own press. He should've been an insufferable prick, living with this kind of undiluted worship.

The tour moved on to Amsterdam's Ziggo Dome, a far smaller venue than the Antwerp Sportpaleis, and Adam begged me to come sing onstage. "It's no different than last night. Close your eyes and pretend you're backstage."

My hands shook as I stood at the microphone under the spotlight, so I took his advice and shut my eyes, listened to Adam, and went with it. After a while, I opened my eyes and found a face in the audience to focus on. One person. It reminded me the crowd was made up of individual people. I could sing to them each, rather than picture them as a mass of humanity. It tricked my brain enough to allow me to relax and enjoy performing the song. But during the third verse, the trick wore off, and I couldn't tell myself I wasn't singing in front of thousands of people. I lost the lyrics for a heartbeat. If anyone noticed, nobody said.

After that show, the entire band was exhausted. Fortunately the next day was free.

We woke up in Hamburg. Adam got up and made me a breakfast of English muffins and peanut butter. Then he told me to get dressed so we could explore. We wandered around Hamburg, and nobody seemed to know who he was. Or maybe they just didn't care.

We ate fish cake sandwiches and strolled along the river, hand in hand. He stopped as we crossed a bridge. I leaned against the rail to watch the boats pass underneath, and he came up behind me and wrapped his arms around me. His breath against my neck made my hairs stand on end.

"We should move here."

I laughed. "Just pick up and move to Hamburg?"

"Why not? It's beautiful here. And nobody takes pictures of us for walking down the street together." He turned me to face him. "I can totally do this right here." He put his hand on my back and kissed me.

My knees weakened. "Is this your idea of going slow? Moving to Hamburg together?"

"Why do you think I want to go slow?"

I leaned back to give him my *are you shitting me* look. "Are you shitting me? Don't you remember wanting to slow down, stop having sex every time we met. Date?"

"I don't think that worked. And besides, I didn't like it."

"Nor did I."

I bit my thumbnail, pondering Stacy's admonitions. If I'd wanted to tell him about the perfume, this would've been about as good a time to confess as I'd likely get. The whole idea of it might even seem preposterous, standing on this bridge so far from New Jersey. He'd laugh, and it would be behind us. I cast my eyes down the length of the bridge, desperately searching for the right words, but Adam touched my chin to draw me into a kiss. Then he grinned at me, and I knew Adam and I were fine. Our life was complicated right now, but our relationship was real and getting stronger all the time. It would be stupid to risk all this on something that wouldn't matter in the long run.

A couple passed by us, and I caught the girl craning her neck. Either checking out my hot boyfriend or gawking. Maybe Adam wasn't totally unknown here.

Adam bounced in his Vans. "Let's do it. Let's move to Hamburg. Or Paris."

His insane proposition completely derailed thoughts of confession. "And what about your band?"

"I could quit the band." He ran his finger along my cheek. I was starting to think it was a bad idea to be so far away from the bus.

"Are you high? You wouldn't quit your band."

"I could start a new one." His hand found mine, and he squeezed it.

The one complication that rankled me was our continued secrecy. I wrested my hand free.

"Adam, do you really have to move to Hamburg and quit your band to kiss me in public?"

He jerked his head back in surprise. "Of course not. I've kissed you in public. Haven't I?"

"No. You haven't. Not in broad daylight."

He slid his arm around my waist, tilting his head at me, all charm. "Can I make up for lost time?"

I fought through my building desire. I needed to say what weighed on my mind. "Adam, are you ever going to stop the rumors about Adrianna?"

He walked to the edge of the bridge and stood beside me, peering over. "Actually, she and I talked about that. I told her it was unfair to you to keep letting people speculate. Especially after she was in Paris. It's gotten out of hand."

"And?"

"And she's going to make a statement."

"When?"

"I don't know. I'd hoped she would do it yesterday, but she's not the most reliable person in the world. Soon." He made eye contact. "I promise, if she doesn't say anything by the time you go home, I will. Okay?"

I believed him. I leaned against him and let him pull me close. "Okay."

"But, Eden, all that stuff I warned you about before? If we go public, you'll be in my world, in this bubble. You're going to have to learn to live with the bullshit that comes from living in the limelight."

"I thought we were moving to Hamburg." I winked. "You could stop being so famous."

"So you want my band to fall into obscurity?" He snuck his hand under the hem of my shirt and dragged it along my waist-line.

"Yes." It came out half whisper because he was driving me insane. I reached up and traced along his collarbone.

His eyes rolled back just before his lids closed. "You want me to get a job in a small town as an accountant?" He leaned in and laid gentle kisses all down the side of my neck.

I groaned out, "Architect," and slipped my fingers into his

belt loops so I could pull him closer to me. Evidence of his own mounting excitement pressed against me.

"I have to start by studying a modern masterpiece." His hands wrapped around my waist as he ground into me. "Would you mind if we cut this walk a little short?"

"I was hoping you'd suggest that." If he was half as turned on as I was, I didn't know how he managed to walk.

And despite the fact the perfume must've finally worn off, he spent the next several hours proving that his attraction was powerful and, to my great relief, enduring.

That evening, the drivers parked the buses in a square, making a small central area where we could hang out without anyone watching us. Without a concert to put on or an audience to perform for, we set lamps around and unloaded folding chairs out from under the buses. The guys grabbed their guitars and cajón drums, and we all began to sing cover songs. It was a magical time.

Chapter 17

The next day it was back to the usual preshow activities. Despite the hiccup from the Amsterdam show, I felt ready to get back onstage. The fix of anonymous love from Adam's fans temporarily overshadowed my fear of performing if I didn't think about it too much.

The Hamburg show started out like any other. Micah's band energized the crowd. Adam's band brought the intensity up a thousandfold. But my phone buzzed right before my cue to go onstage and broke my concentration. Stacy had picked the worst possible time to try to reach me. I ignored her call and tossed the phone into my bag, trying to shake off my nerves and get back into the zone. A moment later, Adam called me out onstage to sing "Compulsion" with him.

I missed my opening, but recovered immediately. The faces in the front row were solemn, and I couldn't find a single friendly fan to focus on. I worried I'd wrecked the song, which only made me screw up again. My hands trembled as nervous adrenaline impacted my vocals. Cameras flashed everywhere, and what once looked like the twinkling of stars suddenly felt like what it was—thousands and thousands of people watching me fuck up epically. When the song came to an end, Adam held his hand out to me, as though the performance had been flawless.

He told the crowd, "Eden Sinclair, everyone." The reception felt muted.

I walked down the steps, my knees wobbled, and I collapsed onto the concrete.

When I came to, Micah was at my side, calling some of the roadies over to help me up. He laid a hand on my forehead. "Eden, are you okay?"

My voice faltered when I said, "Just got dizzy."

"Come on, let's get back to the bus." He led me toward the exit, probing me with questions the whole way. "Did you get enough food today? Were the lights too hot?"

I stopped him. "I got overwhelmed."

"By what?"

"All of this. I'd rather stay back here and watch you guys."

"The last two nights, you seemed to love performing."

"I do, Micah. But it all suddenly terrified me. It's miles outside of my comfort zone. I need to work up to this."

"I'm sure Adam would understand if you talk to him."

He walked with an arm around my waist as we exited the arena. The fans near the barricades screamed in anticipation, but there was an undercurrent I'd never heard. Some of the fans were booing. I glanced over to see what had caused their reaction and discovered they were all watching me.

And booing.

So much for moving to Hamburg. Fans had never greeted me with warmth, but I was baffled by their hostility. Micah accompanied me onto the bus, and I asked, "What the hell is going on?"

He frowned. "I was hoping we could get out of town without you noticing, but there's a story about you in the local paper today."

"What?"

I grabbed my laptop and searched for "*Hamburg Eden Sinclair*." An article in a gossip rag popped up in German. It showed a clear picture of Adam and me on the bridge in Hamburg in a very hot embrace. Under it, the text read something I didn't understand, so I threw it into a translator.

The gist of it was simple. Adrianna, Adam's supposed fiancée, had allegedly left the tour in tears when this interloper, that would be me, had dropped in on the tour in Paris. Fans reported seeing me show up in the meet-and-greet line to insinuate myself onto the tour bus. Since then, Adrianna had reportedly headed south to lick her wounds.

I Googled out of a sick curiosity and discovered the story had been picked up stateside. I was an international villain.

Holy fucking shit.

Micah sat next to me and put his arm around me. "It'll be okay, Eden. Trust me."

It was easy for him to say. This kind of personal invasion scared the shit out of me.

"Micah, I don't know if I can do this anymore."

He closed the lid of the laptop. "It's just a bullshit article, Eden. You know it isn't true. That's all that matters, right?"

"Doesn't all that horrify you? You might think it's no big deal to have your life on display, but even though I know it's all lies, real people will read it and believe it." My hands clapped across my mouth as I realized my parents would see this. "Oh, God, Mom's going to have a field day, Micah."

"Don't worry about Mom." He took both my hands in his. "Just ignore it, Eden. It will blow over. It isn't real life."

I tilted my head and looked at Micah. He'd grown more confident every day on this tour. Every day he'd performed to screaming audiences. Every day he'd soaked up declarations of love from new fans. Every day more and more girls vied for his attention.

"Micah, your real life is here, and you live a charmed fantasy. My real life is back home where this kind of story matters." I squeezed his hands. "I can't live in this fish bowl."

"What do you want to do? Do you want to go home?"

"I don't know." What did I want? "I want to be with Adam, but I also want to be able to go out in public with him without always worrying about all that." I pointed at the laptop. "Is it too much to ask for?"

My phone buzzed again. I looked at the screen.

"It's Stacy. She must have seen the article." My notifications showed that I had seven voice messages and over twenty missed calls. I hit Answer.

"Eden! Oh, my God. There you are finally."

"Hey, Stacy. I guess you saw the German papers?"

"German papers? What?"

Micah crooked a brow at me, inquisitive. I shook my head. "Never mind. What's up?"

"It's about the perfume. That reporter came here today."

My hands went numb, but all I could think to say was, "Okay." This must be what it felt like to listen to a doctor revealing the prognosis of a biopsy. At that precise moment, things could have turned out to be no big deal. Or my worst nightmare might have been coming to life.

"And did they send him away again?"

"Oh, Eden." She sniffled. Was she crying? "They paid Kelly to spill." Her voice spiked an octave. "I don't know what she told them. She said she's got a gag order and can't talk until after the story comes out. But you have to assume the worst, Eden."

"The worst." I couldn't even conceive of the worst. "You think they're going to reveal what the perfume does?"

"I think you can count on it."

The fans outside the buses cheered as the band began exiting the stadium, and I knew when Adam was on his way out by the deafening shrieks. Our life was about to get a whole lot more complicated.

"I have to go, Stacy. Thanks for the heads-up."

"Good luck, Eden."

I implored Micah with wide-eyed little sister eyes. "Can you give us some space? I need to talk to Adam."

He gave me a hug and said, "Everything will be all right."

Moments after Micah left, Adam bounded up onto the bus with the evidence of brazen fan affection stamped all over his cheeks and lips. I didn't even feel up to teasing him about it. The ground beneath my feet had opened up, and I was fighting not to fall through.

He scrubbed at the lipstick on his skin as he moved toward me. "You scared everyone." He lifted my hand and kissed my fingers. "Are you okay?" His look of concern warred with a sexy half smile.

I pulled him onto the bench beside me. "I'm okay. But we need to talk. I have to tell you something, and it's serious." I swallowed hard. "And you might be mad."

His smile slipped. "Are you leaving?"

"What? No. I mean—"

"Is this about Adrianna? Shane told me there was an article in the tabloids. I'll take care of it tomorrow. Okay? Promise."

I laid a finger across his lips. He kissed it. I said, "Shhh. Please listen."

He sat still and listened.

"The company I work for—" I looked into his eyes; they were so dark, like the deepest night. "I told you we make perfume. And we do, but I didn't tell you everything."

He leaned against the bench and propped his elbow across the back. "So tell me."

Nervously, I continued. "I work at a lab that specializes in drugs to enhance, you know. Romance."

"You make boner pills?"

"That, among other things." I breathed in and out. This was the moment. "They're also developing a perfume to carry a pheromone-reception enhancer."

He scratched his cheek, where a day's worth of scruffy beard gave him an advantage far more unfair than any drug. I resisted the urge to lay my hand on his face.

"English, please?"

"It's a chemical that would flip on a gene to make someone more responsive, you know, sexually."

"So—what? You're creating a boner perfume?"

I smiled a little. "Not exactly. But the perfume is meant to increase attraction, chemically. Adam, I had it on the night we met. Do you remember when I let you smell it on my wrist?"

He laughed. "You think I was attracted to you because you were wearing some kind of love potion?"

"I don't know. It's a drug, Adam." I blinked, surprised to feel a tear fall from a lash. All the crazy emotions of the day were catching up to me. "I swear I didn't know what they were developing until I'd already worn it out."

He lifted my arm and kissed my wrist. "Is that why I can't resist you?" His lips moved up my forearm to the inside of my elbow.

"Adam, listen."

He chuckled. "I can't. I'm under a spell, Eden." He nuzzled my neck and bit my earlobe. Then he whispered, "I can't control myself. It's all your fault."

"Adam, would you stop? This isn't funny." I pushed him.

His lips curled into that wicked smile. "It's kind of funny."

"You don't understand." I scooted away before he could kiss me again, but he reached over and laid his hand on my thigh. I ignored him and pressed on. "Adam, a reporter found out about the perfume and interviewed one of my coworkers. This is all going to come out in the tabloids tomorrow. I'm pretty sure the story will include something about us."

He jerked his head up and frowned. "What kind of story?"

"For sure about the perfume and my company." I choked back my fear. If I'd told him about the perfume a week ago, this part of the conversation wouldn't be making me so sick. "It's probably going to mention me. And you."

In one fluid motion, his hand moved from my thigh back to his. "You mean I was going to find out everything you just told me tomorrow anyway?"

"If not tomorrow, soon." My fists clenched tight. I thought he'd be mad about the perfume, but I knew he'd be livid about a self-serving confession.

He narrowed his eyes. His face had lost all the softness. "Is that the only reason you're telling me this now? You're trying to get in front of a story?"

"Listen." I held up my hand. "Adam. I always meant to tell you about this, but—" I edged closer to him, gently, as though he were a skittish woodland creature that might bolt at any sudden movement.

"But you didn't."

"No. I told you you'd be mad."

He looked at his feet and rubbed the back of his neck. "I don't know if I'm mad. I wish you'd told me sooner." He met my eyes. "It makes me wonder why you didn't. It didn't seem like that big a deal. Now—"

"I'm sorry. I should have." I picked up his hand. "Can you forgive me?"

He drew his hand back and stood. "I need some time to think about it." He walked back toward the alcove and started sorting through his drawer, taking out a fresh T-shirt and boxers.

"Adam?"

He tossed a pillow on the bench. "You can sleep in the back."

A lump formed in my throat. I got up and touched his shoulder. Goose bumps prickled his skin. "Please don't stay mad. Come sleep with me."

He looked into my eyes, and for the first time, I didn't see unfettered desire hiding there.

"Yeah, okay," he said, without much enthusiasm.

We got ready for bed in silence. When he climbed in next to me, I lay my head on his chest, but he didn't wrap his arms around me, and after a few minutes, he rolled onto his side away from me. I pressed up against his back and fell asleep listening to his heart beat, hoping Micah was right and everything would work itself out.

Sunlight streamed through the windows. I stretched out and wrapped the blanket tight over me, coming to awareness slowly. The bus wasn't moving, so I figured we must be in Copenhagen. I sat up and folded the curtain back a little to peer outside. The blinding light hurt, but I adjusted slowly. It was a parking lot outside another arena. If there were any fans about, they were well camouflaged and probably freezing.

Adam must've woken up earlier. It was taking me forever to adjust to the time difference. I rubbed my eyes and followed the sounds from the front of the bus, hoping he'd made some coffee. I found him on one of the benches, hunched over his phone. He scratched the back of his head.

"Adam?" I yawned.

His eyes lifted to meet mine. Cold. "Now I see why you never told me this before."

"What? What are you doing?"

He ran his thumb across his screen, scrolling. " 'She acted as if she didn't even know who he was . . .' "

My heart rose into my throat. "Is that it?"

He tossed me his phone. I read the headline on the top of the gossip site. It was titled "Sex Drugs and Rock 'n' Roll."

My hand flew to my mouth. There was a very real possibility I might throw up. I searched out the byline and was not surprised to discover Andy Dickson—that weasel from the night we went out to dinner. I scanned the article. It was all there. Kelly had fed the gossip magazine a story that made me look bad from every angle. I dropped on the bench, reading.

> Coworker Kelly Wilcox confirms the company has invented a drug that switches on a genetic signal to amp up pheromone reception. "Eden had been testing the perfume before she left, and I took over her role. I know what that drug can do. And she knew it, too. And she used the chemical to her advantage. How else could she land someone like [Adam Copeland]? [. . .] And then she acted as if she didn't even know who he was. Can you imagine?"

This was bad. This was very bad. My boss . . . Oh, God, this was going to get me fired.

And Adam. Oh, God. Adam.

I looked up at him, trying to assess the damage. Last night, he'd been a little upset, but he'd found some humor in it. Maybe today, he'd shrug it off. But his expression was so dark. Hurt and anger resonated from his stiff body language, heavy breathing, and red eyes. Had he been crying?

"So did you really not know who I was?" He ran his hand over his face, exhaling a shuddering breath. "Tell me you didn't know I was meeting Micah at the club that night."

"Huh?" It took me a full second to catch up to how Adam would have read the exact same article. "Is that what you think?"

He leaned forward, elbows on knees. "Tell me what else I can think, Eden." His head dropped forward, his face in his palms. "I knew this was too good to be true."

"Can I explain?"

He fixed me with his eyes, pleading. "I wish you would."

"I didn't have any idea you were meeting my brother." I moved to the berth across from him and reached over to take his hand. He didn't pull away from me. That seemed a good sign.

"I wasn't even interested in you until—"

"Until what?" He stood up and paced the length of the aisle. He wasn't listening. "You even told me you don't date musicians. And all this time, I'd let myself think you saw past everything. What kills me is that I thought you liked me despite all this." He shook his head. "Oh, the irony."

This was way worse than I'd anticipated. My stomach twisted into knots. "Adam, I was attracted to you way before I even knew who you were."

"Your coworker seems to think you already knew. It doesn't add up, Eden. I was meeting your brother, and I've seen how close you two are. He must have told you." He closed his eyes tight, and for a second, I thought he might faint. He set his hand on the table for balance. "Why would you lie to me about that?"

"I never lied. Adam. I didn't know you. Ask Micah if you don't believe me. I thought Micah was hiring you." My voice was rising with panic. "And the scientist I work with asked me to wear that perfume without telling me what it did. I was just as clueless as you were."

He laughed bitterly. "Was I part of their experiment? Or was I just a bonus?"

"Adam."

"God, I feel like an idiot. The night I met you, I thought it was fate." His breath came shallow and fast. Red spots blotched his cheeks. "How corny is that?"

I raised my voice. "Adam. It's the tabloid media. Please believe me. They're twisting things to sell papers. You of all people should understand that. It isn't true."

His shoulders relaxed. He sat down across from me and took a breath. "So the whole thing was a fluke? You only wore the perfume that one time? And you didn't know me?" His voice had calmed. "Swear it to me."

I held out my hand, and he took it. I exhaled, relieved that our argument might blow over, and we could move on in complete honesty. Complete honesty. I sighed. "I wore it once more." A tear formed on the edge of my eyelid and hung there. I blinked, and it fell.

"When?"

"On our first date. The restaurant. But it was only a little. I just panicked."

His eyes went wide. "You panicked?"

God, I was making things worse. I hadn't prepared for this at all. "Yes. I'd just discovered who you are, and I panicked. I'm not proud of that."

"Because you discovered *who I am?*" His jaw tightened, and he squeezed his fist. I had no idea how deep this emotional iceberg went, but I seemed to be driving straight into it.

"It's more than that. If you knew . . . How could I compete with thousands of women?"

"Who do you think I am, Eden? If you really thought I randomly picked you out of thousands of women, why would you even want to be with me? Why would you want to trick someone like *that* into staying with you?"

My voice cracked. "But how could I be sure you really liked me for who I am?"

He whispered. "Trust, Eden. You start with trust."

"I trust you, Adam."

He leaned toward me across the open space. "But I'm not sure I can trust you anymore."

I reached out and touched his cheek. Like an involuntary reflex, he turned his head toward my hand, brushed my wrist with his nose, and breathed in. Electricity arced up my arm, and I nearly pulled him into me. There was no need to, though, because he followed the magnetic force until his face nearly touched mine. His lips were a butterfly kiss away, but he just stared into my eyes.

"Damn it." He dropped my arm and stepped back. "Is it that chemical making me want to kiss you even when I'm so confused and angry?" He raked a hand through his hair.

"I'm sorry." I stood and moved toward him.

He backed up until he reached the doors. "I need to get all this out of my system."

"Adam, please, don't go. I never meant—"

He shot eye daggers at me. "You never meant what? To make me fall in love with you? Well, you did anyway." He snorted. "And you know, I really believed you were different." He laid his hand across his chest, over his heart, where I knew he'd tattooed the kanji for "faith." Had he lost his faith in me?

I took a hesitant step toward him. "Adam, you were right. I am." I closed the gap and placed my hand on his wrist, but he jerked his arm free.

"Eden. I can't do this." He pushed open the door. "I'm sorry."

I dropped to my knees. "Adam, please, don't go."

The last thing he said before walking off the bus was "Don't follow me."

And he was gone. I stared after him, wanting to chase him. I'd had my chance with words, and they weren't enough. I'd lost him anyway.

Overwhelmed by sorrow and anger, I asked the bus driver to grab my suitcase out from under the bus. While he did that, I emptied my clothes out of the drawers, dripping snot and tears all over the clean shirts. I wiped my face with a Vampire Weekend T-shirt. I had the irrational thought that I'd forgotten to buy any T-shirts from this tour and made a crazy mental note to ask

Micah to get me one. I shoved everything into the suitcase once it was delivered.

It wasn't as if I hadn't known this was the way things would go. This was always more than I could handle. More than I deserved.

The suitcase bumped down the steps to the cement. I panicked because I didn't know how to call a taxi in Denmark. I didn't know how to call a taxi to come pick me up in the middle of a fucking parking lot. I drag-rolled the suitcase behind me over to Micah's band's tour bus to talk to the one person who had to love me unconditionally. He sat inside, eating a bowl of Cheerios. My stomach rumbled. He pushed over an empty bowl, and we ate in silence for a few minutes while Shane and that new bass player argued in the back of the bus. The Cheerios might as well have been Styrofoam.

"I'm leaving," I said.

Through the half-opened blinds, the sun slanted across his face, leaving black and yellow stripes. He blinked rapidly and then put his hand up a makeshift visor. The light shone through his palm, turning it bright red.

"What happened, Eden? Did you fight?"

My mouth twisted into an ugly frown. The tears fell hot and fat. I faced the window and bit my lip to get control over myself. Roadies unloaded equipment from one trailer and dragged it across the expanse of parking lot. The show must go on. "We broke up."

Micah handed me a napkin. "Do I need to kick his ass?"

I laughed through fat blubbering lips and hid my face in my hands. "It's not his fault."

"Are you sure you should be leaving?"

I nodded without looking up.

"Do you want to talk about it?"

I shook my head. Forming words and keeping myself from sobbing seemed to be mutually exclusive activities. When I felt in control of my shaky voice, I said, "Can you help me figure out how to call a taxi? I need a ride to the airport."

"Taxi? Haven't you noticed these people only need to snap their fingers to get anywhere?" He leaned back. "Hey, Shane!"

The raised voices in the back abruptly silenced, and the curtain parted. Shane's head appeared. "Yeah?"

"Find Seamus."

"On it!"

Twenty minutes later, Seamus called into the bus, asking who needed a ride. I hugged Micah and promised to text him when I got stateside. "And promise me you'll look after Adam. I'm afraid I've made a mess of things. Hopefully, he'll get over it." I wiped another tear from my cheek. "I don't want him to get over me. Make sure he's okay."

I hugged him one more time and climbed off the bus. A limo sat outside a barricade of wooden sawhorses that encircled the buses. Seamus heaved my suitcase into the open trunk. I laid my hand on the passenger door.

"Eden!" Adam emerged from around the tour bus, running toward me. My heart lurched. I couldn't dare to hope he'd forgiven me so quickly. He jogged up and took in the whole scene.

"You're leaving?"

"I—"

"You couldn't come find me first?" He held his palm toward me. "Go on then. Have a safe flight." He turned toward the buses, head down.

"Adam. Wait."

He stopped and spun toward me, and I imagined hope in his eyes. "Yes?"

I waited for him to tell me why he'd raced over to catch me. "What did you want?"

He halved the distance between us, stopping short of the idling limo. "Eden. I thought—"

My heart hammered in my chest. "You thought—?"

His eyes fell on the waiting limo, and he shook his head. "But it doesn't matter now." He twisted his hands together and said nothing more.

After it became apparent he was waiting for me to leave, I

backed slowly toward the open car door, hoping he would stop me. His expression was inscrutable. When I could go no farther, I gave him one last chance to ask me to stay and finally said, "I'll see you around, Adam."

He sucked on his lower lip and then said, "Have a good life, Eden."

He might as well have punched me in the gut. I climbed in the limo, and Seamus closed the door behind me. The sanctuary of the backseat allowed me to hide the anguish that twisted my face at those words. I mastered my expression and looked out the rearview window. Adam lifted his hand. I held mine up as the car drove away.

Chapter 18

Seamus whisked me to the Copenhagen airport in twenty minutes, but the flight took almost nine hours, direct to Newark. The plane touched down, and I lugged my carry-on out through the mass of bodies jamming up to go through international security. Practically sleepwalking from emotional exhaustion, I handed my passport to an official and answered his questions with a yawn. Once cleared, I shuffled along with the crowd, hoping to find Stacy and get home and sleep for the next month. The wheels on my carry-on wobbled, and the bag nearly overturned several times. I didn't expend any energy to fix it.

As soon as I cleared the security checkpoint, I heard a distinct, "There she is."

All at once, cameras encircled me, and voices clamored for my attention.

"Eden, how did you seduce Adam Copeland?"

"Did Adam kick you out?"

"Do you have the perfume with you?"

"Have you seen Adrianna's statement?"

I stopped for a second and took stock of the situation. There were only three reporters, but somehow they'd managed to create the impression of twice as many. Their shadows might as well have taken on a life of their own. One cameraman ran several feet ahead, then turned and knelt right in my path, shooting pictures of me while coaxing me to "look over here, Eden."

I ducked my head and kept walking until I'd made it to baggage claim. I looked up and saw Stacy right away. When she realized I was the center of the commotion, she rushed in like a professional manager and began demanding the paparazzi step back and give me space. They began interrogating her as well.

"Holy shit," she said to me. "I can handle this. Let me wait for your suitcase for you." She scanned the area and pointed out a restroom. "Go hide."

"It's the red suitcase." The panic in my voice surprised me.

Grateful, I rushed for the restroom, trailing reporters behind me. They didn't pursue me past the door, and I relished the sudden privacy. I stood at the sink, wetting my face to wake up, and considered putting on some makeup so I wouldn't look like a mugshot in the gossip rags. The door swung open, and a young lady moved to the sink next to me. She laid her phone on the counter and began to wash her hands.

"Crazy out there," she said.

"Mmm hmm."

"Were all those reporters following you?"

She pulled out some paper towels and dried her hands. I didn't answer.

"Why are they so interested? Are you famous?"

I looked at her in the mirror. "You didn't even use the bathroom."

"Excuse me?"

I took a step toward the door.

She grabbed her phone. "Eden, come on. Just give me a statement."

I grabbed the door handle, weighing the relative evils of my current situation.

"We'll pay you. Tell me your story."

I opened the door and bolted for the exit. Stacy caught up to me before I fled into the safety of the parking garage. "Let's go to my car. I'll come back for your suitcase."

She left me alone in the front seat of her RAV4, where I spent the next fifteen minutes hunkered down out of sight. When she finally got back, she just said, "You hungry? Did they feed you on your flight?"

She went straight to a drive-thru. Food had been the last thing on my mind. "Could you get me . . ." I stared at the wall of food choices, blinking back tears. My stomach growled, but the thought of eating made me want to vomit. "Just get me a salad."

Stacy turned the radio down and yelled the order out at the speaker. A disembodied arm held cash out of the black SUV before us, and then several huge bags of food left the open window in the brick wall. Red taillights flashed as the SUV braked then drove away. Stacy rolled up, and a teenager with two-tone hair and a too-big smile asked how we were this evening. Stacy ignored the question and held her debit card out in the air.

She handed me my salad and jammed hers between her knees. She navigated the parking lot with one hand and mixed her salad with the other. She merged onto Route 1/9. "That was insane. Has it been like that the whole time?"

In her car, safe from the intense scrutiny, I'd calmed down considerably. Thank God for the normalcy of Stacy. "It's been quiet. But when that story broke—"

She bounced in her seat. "Oh, I have news. Kelly got shit-canned." She grabbed a napkin to blot the dressing off the steering wheel she'd spit there when she'd said "shit."

That only made me feel slightly better. I chewed my food slowly. "What the hell was she thinking? How much did they pay her?"

"I don't think it was a lot. I told you she was jealous of you."

The knot in my stomach made it difficult to keep eating, but I knew I needed the food. I grabbed her soda and took a sip, hoping to settle the queasiness. I leaned my head against the glass and stared up at the nothingness of the dark black sky.

Stacy reached over and laid a hand on my knee for a second. "Are you okay?"

"I don't know. Everything's too recent."

"Tell me about the tour."

"The tour was going well. I got to perform onstage with the band. Micah's having a great time, and Adam's amazing on-stage."

"Yeah. I saw him that one time when they played here. I re-member how hot Adam was. And you know, you totally mocked me for having a crush on him."

"Did not." I'm sure I did. The debilitating depression lifted slightly at my false memory of that earlier time. Perspective changed everything.

"But I wasn't asking about the concerts. How was it touring with Adam? Spending so much time with him?"

"It was better than I would have imagined. We roamed around Hamburg yesterday morning just like a regular couple, and I thought things were just about perfect. And then the gos-sip started, and here I am."

She rolled her eyes as wide as a cow's. "Well, yeah. But it's ob-viously bullshit. All that talk about you drugging Adam? Don't those awful gossip columnists have anything better to do?"

My head grew light, and I reminded myself to breathe. "Stacy, what are they saying over here? Am I a monster?"

"What? Oh! You haven't seen! Get out your phone and Google yourself."

I fished it out of my purse and searched news reports. While I was in flight, Adrianna had released a press statement to clarify that she was not now, nor ever had been, engaged to Adam Copeland, nor was she distraught over his relationships with any other women. The article I had up went on to say Adam could not be reached for comment.

"Oh, my God. That's—" That would have been perfect twelve hours ago. Now? That asshole troll of a weasel fuck face might've run the story about my involvement with the perfume anyway. But without the original story connecting me to Adrianna, no-body would've had any incentive to dig up dirt about me in the first place. Without the initial story in the German tabloid, no-body would've cared.

Stacy kept her eyes on the road. "Surely you guys aren't fight-ing over these obvious lies. Did you guys fight?"

"Yeah." I thought back on the conversation we'd had. "No. Not exactly. It wasn't a fight exactly." More like an inevitable collapse.

"So he asked you to leave just because you had a nonfight?"

"He didn't ask me to leave. Not exactly." But he hadn't told me to stay. He'd said, "Have a good life."

"You're not making this very clear. I'm starting to think maybe you created some drama for yourself."

"Really, I wish that's all it was. I'm afraid we're done."

When she stopped at a traffic light, she turned toward me. "Look. I don't know what the problem is. Maybe you discovered he never wants to have kids. Or maybe he grew a mustache. But unless it's something so obviously bad, I can't believe you guys would call it quits over one fight."

"What if he thinks I intentionally went after him because he's famous? What if he thinks I meant to trick him into being with me?"

The light turned green, but I could see her expression from the side. Her lips flattened in disgust with me. She looked at me from the corner of her eye. "Eden, I'm going to guess that if you'd stayed with the tour, you two could've talked this out. You have a tendency to judge things too quickly. Do you really think he believes all of that?"

"I do. I think it's exactly what he thinks. And he didn't want me there anymore, Stacy. The last thing he wants is to feel like he's being used." I could picture his face as all his fears about me crystallized. "You were right. I should've told him right away. But now, he's never going to trust me again."

"Give him some time, Eden. He'll come to realize you aren't just another groupie."

I laughed, but she'd only identified one half of the problem. Adam had sucked me into his orbit, immediately and like nobody I'd ever known. But his orbit was as suffocating as outer space.

"There's more. It's kind of ironic that I was starting to lose my shit about the exact thing Adam must think I was after. I couldn't hack living in his world. It was moving too fast."

"Well, he was pushing you pretty hard."

"But I don't think he realized it, you know?"

"Oh, Eden. He totally knew exactly what he was doing."

"Okay, but he didn't mean any harm."

"And neither did you. He'll see that."

Stacy parked the car in front of my apartment and helped me drag my suitcase in. The apartment smelled like nobody had been there in a month. It felt empty and lifeless. I turned on the TV to fill the void. On her way out the door, Stacy asked, "You wanna go out tonight? We could hit the watering hole. Get your mind off everything."

I stifled a yawn. "I'm beat. I never had a chance to get used to European time, but it's like—" I did the math. "It's two a.m. in Denmark now. I'm going to go to bed early."

When she was gone, I moved around my apartment, trying to find something to do to keep my mind off my immediate worries. When I heard myself humming "Compulsion," I gave in and fired up the laptop. I searched on YouTube for any video from the show, but coming up empty, I ventured into the land of the fans.

The activity on the forum centered around the tour. There were threads up for all different tour dates, but the one that caught my eye right away had the title: "New song—Compulsion."

I knew Pumpkin39 wouldn't let people speculate about Adam's private life, so I could at least avoid all the idle gossip about Adam if I focused on the music.

I clicked through to find what I'd been hunting for—shaky phone video from the Paris show. The intro was cut off. The poster explained, *I hadn't intended to record anything tonight, but as soon as Adam said it was a new song, I pulled out my phone. Apologies for the sound quality. I'm in the nose bleeds and this is zoomed in as close as I could get.*

The video jumped all over the place, and the sound was tinny and distorted, but I could make out the song. I couldn't believe the fans were so dedicated as to upload videos and post on the fan forum during a concert.

I noticed another video had been posted with better quality soon after. The poster added, *I've got all the videos in hi def, but knew you'd all want to see this one right away. It was incredible live. God, Adam's a sexy beast.*

The post following the video with good audio quality asked, *Can anyone make out the lyrics? I've got this for the first stanza.*

Each successive post added more until the entire song had been transcribed. Then the analysis began in earnest.

Adams Apple wrote, *I've always wondered about the biblical allusions in "Expulsion." Obviously, the first line "In the beginning" and the word "expulsion" refer to the Garden of Eden. Now this new song has very explicit language about returning to paradise, and tree of life, and implies forbidden fruit not to mention the word garden in the first verse. The Garden of Eden. Things that make you go Hmm.*

God, these people were too quick by half. I glanced at the date on the post. At the time this was posted, Adam and I would've been getting it on in a Paris green room.

Marco Polo replied, *What the fuck is this anyway? A shitty love song? Jesus, if he's in love and writing this garbage, I hope he gets his heart stepped on real quick. Give me his angry breakup music every time.*

Crazy4Copeland weighed in. *I think it's sweet. I love it when he breaks out the acoustic. I hope this is proof he'll be doing more songs like this. His voice gives me shivers. I do wonder though if 'Expulsion' was written about the same person as this new song. I know we aren't supposed to speculate on his personal life, but it is curious.*

Adams Apple wrote, *Exactly.*

I looked up the lyrics to "Expulsion" to try to understand what they were talking about. I'd sung them a hundred times but never stopped and paid attention to what it was I was singing. Adam's lyrics tended toward the allegorical, and while not shrouded in mystery, it was easy to assume the words were just telling a fictional story. Why hadn't it occurred to me Adam's lyrics were telling his story? "Compulsion" was obviously based on real life. When did he say he'd written "Expulsion"? Years ago. Why had he written it? Was it based on a real girl?

> In the beginning
> There was only you
> A part of me
> The world was new
> Free of shame and taboo
> And jealousy we never knew
> Expulsion
> And ejection
> Apart from you
> There's no connection

The crunchy guitars and the heavy drum beat covered over a very obvious fact—this pop ballad wasn't a trite love song. It was a breakup song. Someone had hurt Adam very badly at some point. How had I never heard this song for what it was?

My misunderstanding hinged on the double meaning of the phrase "apart from you," which I'd always interpreted as "other than you." Read that way, it was a song about finding the only person in the world you connect with. After all, Adam and Eve were expelled together into the world.

But now it occurred to me that "apart from you" actually meant "away from you," which was slap-my-forehead obvious, given the title of the track. But the meaning turned on its head. This was so clearly a song written in great pain, hidden in a pop alt rock song.

He once told me they'd changed it to make it more commercial. How had it sounded when Adam had first written it? Whenever I'd played it acoustic, I'd played it with major chords. That explained why he found that so intriguing. The song was probably written in the saddest of all keys.

I grabbed my guitar and tried the same song again, but this time in E minor. The plaintive and haunting twist hit me hard. It echoed the pain I felt after leaving Copenhagen. Who had done this to him?

The posters on the forum were smart to make a connection to me, given the biblical link between the songs, but I knew better. I wondered if anyone knew the true story.

Total Disaster showed a green online icon by her username. I hesitated and then hit Private Message.

Hi,

Remember me? I had another nosy question if you wouldn't mind answering. I noticed some talk on the forum of "Expulsion" as a breakup song. I'd never thought of that before. I know nobody will talk about it openly, but is there a known story?

Maybe I shouldn't be prying. Maybe I should find a way to ask Adam himself. But if the story was out there, it was out there. And I couldn't contain my curiosity.

I hit Refresh again and again until the link changed from *"0 messages"* to *"1 messages"* and opened it up.

Hey,

Yeah, I'm not really sure anybody knows. Adam's fiercely private, but it may be about this one girl he dated in college. The timing adds up, but nobody really knows. It's ancient history.

The new song has a lot of fans asking, off the forum, if she's back in his life. Or if the song's about that singer he's been dragging out. My money's on the new girl.

I wrote Total Disaster back to thank her, or him, for the information, no closer to understanding what had happened. The *who* of the situation didn't interest me so much as the *why*. It didn't surprise me one bit that the fans had figured out the new song was about me.

Little did they know that "Expulsion" right at this moment

could be sung about me as well. Ironically, Eden was cast out from the Garden of Adam.

It hit me a second later. Did Total Disaster say Adam had gone to college? I'd always assumed he hadn't, because Micah never did. We didn't know anything about each other. Was our entire relationship based on a physical attraction that wasn't even real?

There were half a hundred things I wanted to ask him about. If I'd stayed with the tour, we would've had hours to do nothing but talk. Adam had once asked me to come to him first with any questions, and instead, I'd fled the scene. His open offer was likely forever closed now.

He'd be asleep, but I started to text him anyway. I typed out, "*Thinking of you.*" It wasn't at all what I wanted to say to him, but how could I say everything I wanted to say to him?

I deleted the message and laid my head down. Nothing could fix this mess. Adam believed I was the worst kind of opportunist, winning him over through nothing more than a chemical reaction. Words weren't going to win him back. It had always been only a matter of time before this came to a crashing end. And I deserved it. I deserved to lose him. It was going to hurt for a very long time.

Chapter 19

On Tuesday morning, I'd been standing on a bridge in Hamburg with Adam, talking about our future. On Tuesday night, I'd been singing with him in front of twelve thousand people. On Wednesday, I was on a flight home from Copenhagen in disgrace. And on Thursday, I sat in the parking lot at Anubis Labs, a regular nine-to-five employee, seeking motivation to drag my ass into work.

Nobody was expecting me to come straight back since I'd asked for vacation. But I didn't see any reason to burn my days off twiddling my thumbs at home. Ten minutes after I sat at my desk, Keith stuck his head into the lab.

"Good morning, Eden. Welcome back."

I nodded, waiting for him to clarify why he'd stopped in.

"Could you come with me?"

With a growing sense of trepidation, I followed him into the corridor. As we walked, he made pleasant small talk with me about some place in Italy he'd visited once. But as soon as we were in his office, he closed the door and gestured toward an orange plastic chair.

He sat at his desk with his fingers steepled. "So we have a problem."

I waited for him to continue.

"Yeah. We need to talk about the media."

Ice water flooded my veins. They couldn't think I talked to reporters. "That wasn't me. I've never even discussed this research with my family."

"Oh, I know that."

"Then, what?"

"Remember our talk about the importance of keeping a low profile. We're very sensitive to the press. Not just on this project, but others. And whether you intended it or not, you've brought international attention to our company. Negative attention."

I looked at my hands. "I'm sorry, Keith. I—"

"Eden. I'm sorry to have to tell you this, but we're not going to be able to retain you." He crossed his hands together on the desk and leaned forward. "Listen. You've been with us for six years, and we know you've provided value. We're prepared to offer you a generous severance package for up to three months of your salary."

"You're firing me?" Why didn't this upset me more? I squared my shoulders. "I understand. And that's very generous of you. I hope I can count on you for a positive reference when I find a new position."

"Of course, Eden. We're going to miss you."

No, they wouldn't.

On my way to collect my things, I took a detour through the boner wing and caught Thanh at his laptop. He shoved plastic safety glasses way up on his head. The indentation gave him the look of a professional skier. "Eden. What's up?"

"I wanted to tell you I was sorry for causing any trouble with your product."

He smiled. "Oh, you didn't. I mean, you did, but it was indirect."

"Thanks for everything. I always enjoyed working with you." I took a step to leave.

"Hey, wait a second." He reached into a drawer and pulled out a metal case. He handed it to me. "You said you liked how this perfume smelled, right?"

I opened the case to find a dozen or so vials of the gold liquid. I slammed the lid shut and held it out to him. "This stuff's already caused me too much trouble, Thanh."

"Oh, well. It's completely useless to me." He shook his head, eyes rolled up to the ceiling. "Completely worthless. Can you believe it?"

"How is that possible?"

He sat down. "It's strange. The injectable form of this same chemical showed positive results both in the lab tests and in some of our further research. But who would want to inject a chemical intended to make you more receptive to another person's pheromones? We considered an ingestible form, but you can't just go around slipping a pill into someone's drink. We'd hoped that we could translate the effects to a topical product. But apart from some anecdotal results, we can't draw any conclusive proof that it's anything more than a lovely perfume."

"It's just perfume?"

"Just perfume."

The ramifications of this revelation sank in. "Then how . . ." I stopped.

"Oh, right. You went and got involved with some guy." He nudged my shoulder. "What do they say? Even a blind squirrel finds a nut. But yeah, I don't think this stuff gave you much of an edge there. You know, you're not completely unattractive."

My face grew warm, thinking of the uncontrollable sex I'd had with Adam that first night. "It was real?"

"Real?" He scratched his chin. "I don't know what that word means. But if you're asking whether you landed a guy through some kind of magic, relax. This stuff apparently works about as well as toothpaste."

I hugged Thanh good-bye and walked out of the lab without a job. I waited for the expected sadness to hit me, but the knowledge that the chemistry with Adam had been based on our natural attraction elated me. I had to refrain from punching the sky, freeze-frame style. I could almost hear the Simple Minds sound track playing as I crossed the parking lot.

Driving home, I let my mind race with the information I'd learned. I didn't worry about myself. I could find another job, and honestly, the thought of analyzing blood samples in that building for another year did not fill me with excitement.

I'd managed to save up a small fortune working there. And with three months' salary, I could find a better job. My rent was my biggest expense, but my car was paid off. I still paid student loans every month, but a large amount of my paycheck went into savings intended to fund grad school. Savings I never touched. I mentally calculated how much money I'd squirreled away.

It should be enough to sustain me while I hunted for another job. But that was the last thing on my mind. My only concern in the world was how I could let Adam know his feelings for me had been free of chemical seduction. How could I tell him that I hadn't trapped him? He might not care. He might still accuse me of having sinister intentions. But at least one thing was clear: Adam's attraction to me had been one hundred percent genuine. If only I could convince him of the reverse.

I pulled into a parking space at my apartment and sent him a text. *Just spoke to the researchers at the lab. The perfume doesn't work. It never did anything.*

After five minutes, he hadn't responded, so I went into my apartment and paced around, waiting. I located his number, hit Dial, and listened to the phone ring. No answer.

Desperate to get word to Adam, I sent Micah a text. *You there?*

I figured it was afternoon wherever he was. Berlin maybe? No, that would be later. Oslo? Either way, they should be awake by now.

A few minutes later, my phone buzzed with Micah's response. *Yes.*

Hey, how's the tour going?

Do you mean to ask me how is Adam? He knew me too well. *Maybe.*

He's putting on shows. Seems to be doing okay. Hasn't said anything to me about you. That stung.

I sat down on the sofa to think of what to ask. *Is he around? Could you tell him something for me?*

Sure.

Tell him the perfume never worked.

Will he know what that means?

I think so. Can you go tell him?

Okay. I have to go find him.

I went outside and sat on a bench in the apartment complex community lawn. I stared at my phone, hoping against reason that the next text I'd get would be from Adam. But it wasn't.

He said it doesn't matter. It never mattered.

What does that mean?

I don't know. I thought you would.

Okay. Thanks.

The words made no sense to me. It didn't matter. Why not? Because it was too late? Because I broke his trust in me when I lied to him in the first place? It never mattered? What never mattered? Everything? Us?

I threw my head back and stared at the blue sky for an answer. The clouds floated past innocent and cheerful. They were the same clouds I'd watched float past when I'd lie on the driveway, listening to my brother in the garage practicing the chords to another metal song. Until he'd say, "*Come stand over here, Eden. I need an audience to chant my name.*" And I'd shake myself out of my reverie and become my brother's biggest fan.

I was so proud of him now, out on tour with a huge rock band, performing before huge audiences who would know his name soon enough. Good for him.

The stab of jealousy hit me unexpectedly. I inhaled and let the breath out slowly. I wasn't jealous of his career path. I was jealous that he could walk over to Adam and pass along a message. He could hear Adam's voice when he responded. I was jealous of his proximity to everything I wanted.

The blue sky was pissing me off. I needed to go inside and start searching for a job. I needed to figure out what I wanted to do with my life.

Monster.com listed five openings in the Central Jersey area for lab technicians. I threw Brooklyn into the search location, lying to myself that I only wanted to broaden my opportunities, not to find work closer to Adam.

Would I ever be able to get close to him again or would there forevermore be bodyguards directing me to stand in line with the other gawking fan girls? I didn't even know how often he stayed in Brooklyn. For all I knew, he had a house in LA for the months he wasn't on tour. I couldn't plan my life around the location of an apartment where a guy I'd barely dated might or might not live.

I e-mailed my resume to the New Jersey companies even though it was really time to take the next step and start sending out grad-school applications. But I no longer felt remotely enthusiastic about that prospect anymore. My entire future lay out before me, and it looked like someone else's.

My mom cajoled me into coming over for her "Ring in November" faux New Year's Eve party. I decided to kill two birds with one stone and used the party as a chance to spend some time with Stacy. In retrospect, I should've spared the birds and thrown the stone at myself.

Mom eagerly led us toward the kitchen, where Duncan Lewis, the alcoholic surgeon, leaned against the kitchen island. He wore completely acceptable beige Dockers and a safe, plain navy sweater. He had to be at least forty.

I stayed on the other side of the divide, feigning interest in the variety of chips my mom had laid out. I poured myself a strawberry soda out of a champagne bottle into a clear plastic flute, and we made awkward small talk, but I must've glanced at the clock on the soffit about two hundred times. It wouldn't be midnight for another eight hours. It wouldn't be New Year's Eve for as many weeks.

Duncan used to be good-looking. He had that kind of left-over leathery skin from too much golf sun. He'd had a great life, before—a nice house in Metuchen, a lovely wife. Or so we'd pieced together from conversations my mom had had with him. After the divorce, he'd lost a fortune. But he didn't stop drinking until the accident.

My mom asked him if she could get him anything. She fluttered around the kitchen, straightening things that didn't need straightening and throwing out topics that might spark a deeper conversation between us. "There's a possibility of rain in the forecast."

Finally, she moved out of the kitchen to check on my dad, and Duncan quipped, "I hear your company made a product to help horny ladies get laid. Did you really drug that guy?"

I pinched Stacy's hand. Hard.

Stacy sipped her soda and casually asked, "How's that malpractice suit going, Duncan?"

Mom must've had some kind of sixth sense, because she was in the kitchen in a heartbeat, saying, "Eden, Dr. Lewis just came back from Europe. Where all did you go, Duncan?" Her voice oozed sycophantic wonder. It was like she was starstruck. By Duncan.

He rounded his lips, preparing to regale us with whichever destination he'd recently visited, but I cut him off. "Mom, *I* just got back from Europe."

She flapped her hand dismissively. "She spent a week in a bus."

"I got to perform at a couple of huge arenas, Mom. It was really exciting."

Duncan piped in. "I used to play music."

Mom batted her eyes. "Did you?"

Oh, good lord. Was she trying to catch these guys for me or for herself?

She threw a pointed glance my way and then told Duncan, "Eden's broken up with that rock star you may have read about in the news." She sighed and smiled at him in a shared *bullet-dodged* sort of way.

"Mom, we didn't break up." *Not exactly.* "In fact, we're going to get married and have little rock musician babies. We're going to live in a grungy cockroach-infested apartment in Brooklyn and spend all our time touring small venues across America together."

Her eyebrows shot up. "Eden, you're not funny."

"Seriously, Mom. Stop interfering."

"Eden." She flashed a look at Duncan. "She's only joking. She's always had a strange sense of humor. Did you know Eden works in a medical research lab. Isn't that interesting?"

I nearly choked on my corn chip. She chose an impeccable time to exhibit pride in my place of employment for the first time ever.

Dad entered the kitchen. "What's going on?" He meant well but picked the wrong time to ask.

"Merm." I swallowed the food down and took a swig of the mercilessly nonalcoholic champagne. "I've been terminated."

"What? Eden! Why didn't you tell us? When?"

"Thursday."

Dad sat on a stool beside me. "What happened, Pumpkin?"

My mom pointed a finger at me. "I knew something like this would happen. We've seen the gossip pages, Eden. Do you think Elsie Lockwood could refrain from asking about it?"

I drained my sparkling soda and crushed the plastic flute. "Could you give me a break, Mom? You shouldn't be reading the tabloids."

Mom snapped, "How else can I find out what's going on with you?" She turned to face Duncan, saying, "She's usually not like this," but he'd cleared out at about the same time I'd started losing my shit. She narrowed her eyes. "Do you know how hard it was for me to get him here? Well, consider that bridge burned."

I crossed my arms. Somewhere between 4:06 and 4:09, I'd turned into a twelve-year-old.

"Oh, my God, Mom. Stop trying to force these poor guys on me. They are *not* interested. I am *not* interested." I was done with it all. I bit back all the words jumbling in my head and settled on the one thing that felt like truth. "You've got to stop trying to plan my life out. You've got to stop trying to fix everything. Mom, you can't live vicariously through me."

Stacy's jaw dropped, and my dad scowled.

My mom looked very disappointed in me. "Oh, Eden. That isn't funny."

"Mom, I wish I was even kidding. You think you know what I want out of life, but you don't. You and I don't want the same things." I pulled over a stool and sat, pleading. "You can't protect me forever. I could do everything right. I could get the right job, meet that mythical perfect doctor, buy a house in the suburbs, and find complete stability. And still be unhappy."

Dad shifted to face me. "Do you have any leads on your next job?"

I knew he meant well, but he couldn't hear me. Irritated, I gave him a smart-ass answer.

"Nope. And as a matter of fact, I'm not looking for another job. I'll play music on the streets for twenty bucks a day and live with Micah until I can produce a CD that will languish on a merch table in the back of a club while I play music to small crowds. And I'll finally be happy." That would get their goats. What was good enough for Micah would never be good enough for me.

My mom blanched. "Oh, Eden. You're not twenty any longer. You can't spend the next five years hanging around bars. You'll never get married."

Even though I'd fully expected that, her response fueled my annoyance. "Mom, chances are that wasn't going to happen anyway. I think I'll be happier doing something I love."

"Until you run out of money."

Dad leaned over and reached for his back pocket. "Do you need money?"

"No, Dad. I'm fine. I've saved. I'll be all right."

Mom threw her hands up. "Honestly, ever since you met that boy. Well, your room is here for you when you need somewhere to go."

"Thanks for the vote of confidence, Mom." I gathered my

things, grabbed Stacy's elbow, and leaned over to give my dad a kiss. "Stacy and I are just gonna—"

"Okay, sweetheart. Keep in touch, and let your mom know you're okay. It wouldn't hurt to let us know what's going on with you once in a while."

That statement made me chortle, because it did hurt. Every single time.

Chapter 20

When I'd told my parents I was going to move in with Micah and become a musician, I was yanking their chain. But now, the temptation to use my savings as a source of income while trying out my hand as a real musician began to grow and take root. I couldn't stop toying with the idea of spending my days writing songs and my nights performing them before my very own fans.

Adam was right. The lure of the feedback was as addictive as anything I'd ever encountered. Except for the lure of Adam himself.

I pulled out my guitar and started playing Micah's songs. The nylon strings made them sound different than when he played them. Especially his band's harder rock songs. I struck an odd chord and liked the sound of it, so I strummed it a few times and then added another. As I strummed new chords one after the other and back again, I hummed. This was something I did occasionally to relax or warm up, and once in a while, a new song came to life.

And that meant I needed a recorder because, shamefully, I couldn't write music at the same time I composed it. Chords I could notate, but the melody of the song lived in my head. I could read sheet music, and later I would figure out which notes to write down, but it was a messy business that would get in the way of immediate creation. I opened my laptop, ran a cord from the guitar to the adapter, and then opened the microphone.

After I'd laid out the first verse, I recognized what I'd been humming as a variation on the theme of Adam's new song that had crept into my subconscious. It wasn't the same song, but there was an echo. It sounded like an answer to his song. And I knew what I needed to write.

I'd only known Adam for a few weeks. In that time, we'd spent very little time together and much of our relationship could be characterized by lust. Still I felt a deep emotional connection with him. And beyond his sexy self, I liked him. A lot. He was kind. He was honest in his own weird way. He made me laugh. I'd never felt so comfortable with another man. In a short time, he'd become a good friend, and it sucked because I just missed him. Not the sex. Well, yeah, the sex, too. But not just the sex. Much more than the sex.

And if the perfume didn't work, and, therefore, the perfume hadn't coerced him into wanting to be with me, then that meant he liked me too, and he'd liked me from the very beginning.

I hummed, "In the beginning, there was only you." Only him. Only me. None of this other bullshit. The electricity that had seemed too powerful to be real had been real all along. And like a fuse, I blew it.

My vision blurred from the tears brimming but not falling from my eyes. How had I fucked this up so much?

Lyrics weren't my strong suit, but with the imagery in mind from Adam's own songs, I began to set down an apology of sorts. If he wouldn't listen to me, I could address the universe at large. Things needed saying.

> Tempting and enchanting
> One apple
> Fell from the tree
> Promising seduction
> But it felt like love

The words flowed easily. I'd been ignorant of the seductive power the perfume was supposed to hold, but when I found out, rather than confess it, I'd held it out to him. Even though the "apple" in question turned out to be innocent. As soon as I *believed* it had power, I should have told him. Instead, I used it again and led him into temptation. My knowledge damned me.

But that was the end of my sins. And Adam of all people had to know that the gossip media fed off half truths, creating a plausible story out of smoke. And my anger at the media fed the second verse.

> Lying but convincing
> One snake
> Hissed in the tree
> Creating suspicion
> And I lost your love

The chorus came as an apology.

> It could have been paradise
> In the beginning
> There was only you to entice
> Love before reason
> Ignorant and innocent
> We took the first bite

I packed up my guitar to let the song sit. As I slept, more ideas would hit. Obsessing over the song helped me stop obsessing over Adam, but I knew I wouldn't sleep well until I'd finished it.

I woke up Monday morning with new ideas for darkening the chords. I flew out of bed so I wouldn't lose them. Once I'd saved the newest version on my computer, I practiced some older songs of mine I didn't usually play anymore.

Then I texted Tobin. *Can I take you up on your offer to open one night? I'd love a chance to perform.*

Tobin got back to me soon after, *Absolutely. People have been requesting you. Can you open Friday night?*

I'll be there at seven.

I sat down to figure out my set list in earnest. I didn't need to practice Micah's songs all the way, just enough to remind myself how they went.

Since I didn't need to be at work, I grabbed my guitar and hopped the train into the city. I roamed around Chinatown, eating most everything that looked good. Then I strolled over to Battery Park and watched people. A couple of live statues amused the tourists, who'd clearly never seen anything like it before. When a group of singers packed up to leave, I sat down in their abandoned spot with my guitar case opened and played songs until the sun fell low in the sky.

Tourists took my photo. Children broke free of their parents and stared glassy-eyed at me, or wiggled to the music, or climbed into my guitar case until their parents caught up. Parents with a sense of shame about it tossed me some loose change. Those without warned their children to stay away from the filthy homeless musician. More than once, someone recognized me from the paper and waited until I was between songs to ask for my autograph. Only one person admitted she had mistaken me for someone else.

With seventeen extra bucks in my back pocket, I wound my way up toward TriBeCa to the club, figuring I could get dinner and watch whoever performed, calling it research.

That was Monday.

On Tuesday, human resources representatives called about my job applications. I had to do some soul searching as I made the decision to turn down every interview. If I wanted to make a go at the music career, I had to commit. It terrified me. Financial security beckoned to me like a beam from a lighthouse. Sailing into the dark, I might be headed right into the rocks. But there was no way I could balance both a full-time job and a real attempt to break out on my own.

And without a job to keep me tied to one spot, I placed an ad to sublet my apartment. Stacy said I was acting rash. She was right of course, but the funny thing about irrational behavior is that hasty decision making feels like a positive side effect. It's easier to shoot the moon with guns fully loaded.

On Wednesday, I called Micah's agent, Sandy, and set up an appointment to talk to her about booking gigs and recording demos. Then I took the subway to Brooklyn and visited apartments I'd found on craigslist. Most were near Micah, but one was in a high-rise on the edge of Brooklyn Heights. The apartment was out of my price range, too small, and on the eighth floor. It smelled like cheese and overlooked the Brooklyn-Queens Expressway.

I weighed the options. On the one hand, it was a block south of an A-C subway stop and seven blocks north of Adam's apartment. On the other hand, it was the worst place I'd looked at all day.

Without a job and a steady paycheck, the owners rejected my application anyway.

On Thursday, I moved my belongings into storage, gave my keys over to a new tenant, and then texted Micah. *Can I use your apartment until you get back?*

By Friday, I was unemployed and practically homeless.

Friday night, Tobin had a plate of chicken wings sent to the green room along with a tall Stella. I still didn't trust the nasty sofa, so I ate standing up and then helped with sound check. Tobin had scrawled my name onto the posters for tonight's show, hoping it might attract whoever had called asking specifically for me. It felt good knowing I had some fans already, though I had no idea where they might be coming from. Either they'd seen me perform here last time, saw me on Adam's YouTube, or knew me through Micah.

For a Friday night, the crowd seemed kind of thin. Most people would likely show up later for the headliner. Tobin announced me, and I took the stage to a totally different reception than the Tuesday night when I'd played the main set. The seats remained relatively empty while a group of women talked loudly at the merch table. Fans of the next performer, I presumed. Still, a handful of nice people sat and paid attention as I collected myself before launching into the six songs in my set. I wasn't even the opener. I was the opener to the opener. Friday nights. Three acts.

I sat on a stool behind the mic and said, "Hi. I'm Eden Sinclair. This is a song called 'Midnight in the Garden.' " No screeching feedback this time at least.

While I played, people chatted among themselves. Ice clinked in glasses. The chairs in front of me filled, or people laid down their jackets and then moved back to the bar or merch area. The talking in the back competed with my own vocals.

I finished playing that first song and said thank you to a pathetic few hand claps. I started to introduce my next song when someone cried out, " 'Expulsion!' "

Faces were shrouded in shadow. I peered through the spotlight into the dark place in the crowd where only their bodies stood out against the void. "I'm sorry?"

"Yeah! 'Expulsion!' " a different voice called.

The first person chanted. " 'Expulsion!' 'Expulsion!' "

The people milling in the back picked up the chant and stomped their feet in time.

It was overwhelming. I repositioned my hands on the strings and said, "This is a song written by Adam Copeland." I swallowed back an unexpected lump in my throat.

Oblivious to my emotional turmoil, the crowd applauded and hushed almost immediately, but not before a sharp cry of "Yay!"

With the guitar propped on my knee, I picked the arpeggio. Apart from my guitar, the room was still.

The people requesting must've all seen the YouTube video, and they'd be expecting that version of the song, but after last week, I couldn't play it as a pop song, as a throwaway love song.

The minor key transformed the song. I fell into it, the emotion coursing through my lungs. I heard the cracks in my voice but turned them to my advantage, pushing the plaintive yearning of the song to its apex. When I strummed the chorus, I ran my eyes over the rapt faces looking up at me. I had them all. They were mine, and I carried them to the end, quietly bringing the last chorus to a heart-wrenching close. When I plucked the last note, a pin drop would've sounded like thunder. Then the applause broke the silence.

"Thank you very much."

I adjusted the guitar, appreciating the fact that the seats had filled and most of the people gave me their full attention now. They waited for what I'd do next, and I wasn't sure where to take them. On my set list, I had most of Micah's more popular songs, since I figured I'd chicken out at the last minute and play his songs anyway. But my fingers moved across the strings as I thought, and then they were playing the song I'd written Sunday.

"I hope you'll indulge me a little. I'm working on a new song. Would you like to hear it?"

Genuine approval met me. "Sing it, Eden!" It was a man's voice. I scanned the crowd to find a handful of guys in the audience. They could've been Micah's fans, but it was unusual to see more than the husbands or boyfriends of the fan girls who came out for Micah. They may have been coming out to see the performer I was opening for. That would make the most sense.

"This will be an interesting experiment."

Coming on the heels of "Expulsion," it made me feel guilty and ashamed. But the song expressed my sorrow, my hope for atonement. It said, *I know what I did was wrong. Can you ever forgive me?* It said, *You and I are victims of the same deceptive vultures in the media.* But all of that was buried in allegory. To the naked ear, it was a song about temptation, innocuous and common as tropes go. To the naked ear, it was a derivative rip-off of Walking Disaster's latest hit song, which was what I was banking on.

I finished the set with three more songs—one of Micah's by request and two more of my own. It wasn't like standing in a stadium of thousands, but captivating any audience fueled that addiction to perform. More and more, I thought getting fired might've been a blessing in disguise.

The line of fans near the back waiting to meet me after the show thrilled me. They pressed in around me, wanting pictures, autographs, conversation. A few asked me straight up about the gossip in the news, about sex drugs, about Adrianna. It crossed my mind that their interest in me was pure fascination. But it also struck me that all news was publicity. I understood now why Adam and Micah brushed it all off so easily. If it got people into the seats, who cared what they were saying in the gossip column? My true friends knew the truth about me. What else really mattered?

I recognized some of Micah's fans in the line as well as some of the regulars who hung out at the club all week. I wasn't surprised when the blue-eyed blond from my last show stood before me with his scrap of paper and his felt-tip marker.

"Hey, Eden. Great set."

"Hi, Jacob. Thanks."

He smiled. "You remembered my name. Could I ask you for the title of the song you sang? The new one?"

That song had no name. I bit my lip and considered. He stood waiting. Finally, I spit out, " 'Atonement.' "

"That's great." He scribbled it. He brought his eyes up to me and half smiled. "Now, about that drink."

Until that moment, I'd forgotten I'd promised him he could buy me a drink if we ever met again. "Don't you have to set up your camera for the next act?"

He shook his head slowly. "I came here to see you."

I sighed, laughing at the same time. "Give me a minute. There are people still waiting to say hi."

We sat down at the bar on the same exact stools where Adam and I had once sat. Jacob was a good-looking guy. He had mussed-up blond hair with the slight hint of hair product crinkle. He had the kind of cute face that would start to look odd at age forty. Boyishly charming forever.

He pushed the beer he'd ordered in front of my stool. "I'm so glad you were able to come out tonight. That new song of yours is incredible. You should record it."

"You don't know how much I appreciate that."

"After your last show, I made sure the club knew to get you back here. The videos I uploaded have gotten a ton of traffic."

I sipped my beer, a little embarrassed by the compliments.

"So Jacob, what do you do when you're not bootlegging concert video?"

He chuckled. "Student actually. NYU."

"Not bad. What are you studying? Music? Film?"

"Actually, no. I do love those things, but I'm majoring in architecture."

I closed my eyes and pinched the bridge of my nose. "Architecture?" Why couldn't I have met this guy a month ago?

"Yeah. When I was a kid, my parents took me with them to Habitat for Humanity projects. I developed a passion for it."

"For humanity?"

He snickered. "For construction. But I didn't want to spend my life with a tool belt on and my butt crack hanging out, so I applied for scholarships and got lucky."

"You got lucky? You don't get lucky to get scholarships. You must've had a great application."

"I wrote good essays." A dimple appeared in his cheek as he flashed a one-sided smile. I imagined he charmed his way into that scholarship.

"I'm sure you did."

Tobin announced the second opening act. A tall musician named Liam took the stage with his banjo. I'd known Liam for a long time. He was kind of an asshole, but he gave a good show. He could play a banjo, but he didn't play original songs. His shtick was transforming popular songs into bluegrass.

Out of fellow-musician camaraderie, I focused my attention on the stage.

Jacob whispered, "I've seen this guy before. He does a hilarious cover of 'Let It Go' from *Frozen*."

"I don't think it's supposed to be funny," I said back. We were breaking a cardinal rule, talking during the show. I vowed to keep my mouth shut for the rest of the set. Liam started playing a cover of Katy Perry's "Roar."

Jacob leaned forward. His breath tickled my cheek. "Do you think he'd do 'All About That Bass'?"

I snorted. "Stop."

He stopped talking but didn't move back into his space. He

remained inches from me, and I could sense the electricity coming off him even though he didn't touch me. I knew he was there. When Liam played his third song, Jacob leaned in closer still, and his lips brushed against the nape of my neck. I held my breath, waiting for the butterflies to hit me.

Nothing.

Jacob's hand slid around my waist gently. He whispered, "Do you have to stay through the rest of the show?"

I weighed my options.

Option one: If I left now with Jacob, I was reasonably sure he'd expect us to end up either at his college dorm in a twin bed or back at my place, which tonight would be Micah's. Either way, Jacob probably expected to work up to a night together.

Option two: If I lied and said I had to stay, he'd just wait here, moving his hands tighter around me, mistaking silence for consent.

I turned around and said, "Jacob."

He drew his hand back. "I'm sorry." He dragged his teeth across his lower lip. "I didn't mean to push you. I'd really like to get to know you better."

I threw a glance at the stage, at Liam yodeling "Royals." Fuck it. I was going to break my own rule.

"Jacob, look. You seem like a nice guy. Maybe at another time—"

"That's what you said last time. Is that your default letdown phrase?" He wasn't pouting. In fact, his expression was disarmingly charming. That half smile might've won me over. But I wasn't feeling it. This kid was playing with dynamite, but Adam played with nuclear warheads. There was no way this kid could reach me where I lived.

"You misunderstand me. I'm not saying maybe another time in the future. I'm saying maybe at another time in the past, I might've been interested. But right now, I'm not in the market."

"You're seeing someone?" He narrowed one eye, still charming. "Are you really dating Adam Copeland?"

The question jarred me on several levels, not the least of

which was the casual nature with which Jacob had admitted to gawking at my private life. Granted, my private life had been made public thanks to that gossip columnist, but nobody had forced Jacob to click the link.

And just like that, I felt the hypocrisy of my judgment. Had I been any better when I'd started dating Adam?

"No, we're not dating." *Not exactly.* "It's just that my head's not in the game."

"Fair enough. I'll ask you again next time then." He flashed that grin again. Bonus points for backing off without a fight. Or at least not much of one.

"Thanks for understanding." If he'd caught me a month ago, a gorgeous guy with a future in architecture and a history of charitable work? On my back in minutes.

But my perfect guy had been rescripted, and what I needed was a brown-eyed, black-haired, tattoo-covered, thin, grungy rock musician named Adam. Too specific?

If I'd been impossible to please before, I was destined to be a spinster. I couldn't see how any guy would ever live up to my new standards.

I left Jacob and went looking for Tobin. I needed to have a word with him. He was out back, smoking with Liam.

"Nice set, Liam," I said robotically. Liam was one of those people who could sift through a pile of criticism to find the one positive comment, so I didn't think he'd hear the lack of enthusiasm in my voice.

"Thanks, Eden. Those girls were really eating it up." He took one last drag, dropped the cigarette, and then stubbed it out with his shoe.

When he'd gone in, I rounded on Tobin. "So, about those people wanting me to come out to play . . ."

"What about them?"

"How many calls did you get, Tobin? One?"

"There were at least three."

"Did they all sound the same? Were they all college-aged boys named Jacob?"

He averted his eyes. "I don't know. I didn't take the calls."

"So maybe the same person called multiple times? Is that possible?"

"Look, Eden. You're early on in your career. Don't worry about it. You'll build up to something."

"I'm not worried about that. I'm trying to ascertain, *Tobin*, whether or not I have a stalker."

Tobin snorted. "After one show?"

It did seem ridiculous, and I laughed, too. "Okay, maybe *stalker* is too strong a word. But listen, do you think you could get me on as the main act again sometime?"

He shrugged. "If someone cancels last minute, I'll give you a call. You're welcome to play the first opening act next Friday if you like."

It would have to do. "Thanks, Tobin. I'll let you know."

I left the bar alone and took the subway to Micah's, thinking over the night. I knew I had a long way to go before I could make a living as a musician. I knew I'd have to have my own CD and my own fans before Tobin would consider letting me headline unless, like before, he was desperate for anyone to fill the time slot.

And yet, with as low a profile as I had, there was Jacob, calling the venue to bring me back. If he hadn't revealed that slightly creepy bit of overinvestment, and if I hadn't removed myself completely from circulation, how flattering would his attention have been?

If Adam never forgave me and I had to go out on the market again, I'd forever question the motives of the guys offering me drinks. And it would likely only get worse if I made a name for myself. That was what I was signing up for.

I chuckled thinking back on how I'd naïvely chided Adam, telling him he could combine a career in music with a normal low-profile life if he wanted to. Because Hervé could. As if he could somehow play the role of his drummer, simultaneously in the limelight and nearly anonymous. And I understood why Adam would've been charmed by my complete ignorance of his celebrity. It was the same reason I was relieved to discover Thanh's tonic was inert, for the knowledge that he wanted me for who I was.

But I understood it all too late. And now I was going to have to find a way to win him back with all the baggage that came with being a simpering fan girl—distance, lack of access, and an idol-like worship of his sexiness.

Chapter 21

Micah's apartment sat along a lovely street with a trendy coffee shop on the corner. With nowhere else to be, I threw on jeans and my warmest sweater and camped out at a table in the back with my laptop, a latte, and an apple-cinnamon scone.

My headphones drowned out the clink of dishware as I listened to the videos Jacob had faithfully posted the night before. He did good work, and the videos were high quality with excellent audio. I clicked through them quickly to check the view count and get a sense of the comments. I couldn't bear to watch them if everyone was panning them. But they had a surprisingly high number of views, especially "Expulsion," but that could easily have been from people searching for Adam's version.

A woman asked if she could borrow a chair, and I slid my headphones off to hear her question and waved my permission. Then I disappeared back into the night before. I was pleased with how clearly the lyrics to "Atonement" came out.

The comments below were fair, mostly complimentary of the song and my voice.

Great song. Where can I buy this?

I saw this show last night. Check out the other videos. She killed it.

Catchy tune. Great voice.

Is this the same girl that sang with Adam Copeland a few weeks ago?

There were some insulting comments mixed in as well, but they seemed to mostly focus on me as a person rather than the song. *She should open her eyes when she sings.* Or *Is that the bitch shagging Adam Copeland?* And of course, as expected, a few people called me a homewrecker and linked to articles about how I'd trapped Adam with an evil spell. Still others linked to Adrianna's press release in defense.

My favorite comment came from someone who thought I should get hit by a bus before I ruined Adam Copeland's music career and attempted to butcher any more of his songs. At least he hadn't suggested my skull should be bashed in to stop me from performing my own shitty music. I took a deep breath and remembered Adam admonishing me not to read the comments for too long.

I copied the video links into an e-mail to Micah, along with a note telling him I'd performed the night before and hoped he'd listen. Secretly, I hoped Micah would pass the links to Adam. Then Adam would see the new song and know how sorry I was. And then maybe everything would be okay. I hadn't heard from Adam the entire week, so deep in my heart, I feared the breach was irreparable. All I could do was apologize.

It would be afternoon wherever they were. I checked the tour schedule. They didn't have a show tonight, so they were either in Frankfurt or Vienna, or somewhere in between. I double-checked the calendar. They only had one more week out on tour. Their last show was the following Friday, and then they'd come home. And then what? Would Adam come find me? Would we work things out then?

I ordered another latte and watched videos from the Walking Disaster tour from after I left. Adam had stopped singing his new song altogether. On the forum, in the threads from the Copenhagen show, the fans zeroed in on the lack of Adam's new song and speculated vaguely about its absence. Why had he performed it in only four cities with two different women?

In some ways, their sleuthing pained me, but other times it amused me. Their conjectures could veer into crazy town, but usually at least one person hit on an explanation very close to the truth. The minute they brought up my name or Adrianna's, they risked Pumpkin locking the thread, so they spoke in code. Or possibly off the forum.

In another subforum devoted to musicians Adam had performed with, they had posted the videos from my own set the night before. They didn't make a fuss over my version of "Expulsion" except to say it made sense I'd play that since I'd already performed it before with Adam, and since the video started with the audience clamoring for it. Nobody analyzed the lyrics of my new song for any added meaning. They just dropped the videos and pointed out I'd returned from the tour and was back in NYC—*in case anyone was interested*. Off-site, in the chat rooms and private messages, they'd probably already discussed the coincidence of my leaving the tour at the same time Adam stopped singing the new song.

My phone buzzed. Micah texted, *Congratulations! How'd you end up playing again?*

I texted back, *I asked Tobin for a chance to perform and he let me!*

Now we'll never get you off the stage. I wish you were still here with us. But only one more week and we'll be home!

That made me smile. I started to put my phone away, when it buzzed again. *Hey, can I share those videos with Adam?*

Bingo. That was what I was waiting for. *It's a free country. They're public, aren't they?*

True dat.

Perfect. I daydreamed a little about Adam listening to the song, recognizing it for an apology, and forgiving me for leading him astray. He'd have to know I never intended to. He'd have to know that when I did intend to, it was only because I was so afraid of losing him so soon.

But if my daydream extended to Adam picking up his phone to call me, or text me, or send me a long explanatory e-mail, I was destined for disappointment. The morning dragged on, and he remained silent.

I texted Tobin to find out if he had any openings at the club, but after a couple of hours of radio silence, I got the message. I called Stacy to invite her over, but she had plans with Rick Whedon, DDS, despite my misgivings. I thought about calling my mom, but we hadn't spoken since the week before. I didn't even know where to begin. I spent the night alone in Micah's apartment, eating my weight in pizza. I missed Micah a lot. I missed Adam more.

Sunday morning, I woke up in Micah's bed disoriented, feeling untethered. I'd made a mess of everything, and I was pretty sure I knew where I needed to start to repair things. I drove across Staten Island and pulled into my parents' driveway just after noon.

When my mom opened the door, she arched an eyebrow, but then her face softened.

"Eden."

"Mom." The word came out like a croak, and I couldn't hold back the tears.

"Oh, Eden." She pulled me into a hug. "I told you this would happen."

I fought the urge to argue with her and wiped my eyes with my sleeve. "It's not what you think, Mom."

She led me inside. I dropped onto the lopsided sofa and pulled myself together. "I came over to apologize for last week. I shouldn't have lashed out at you. I was just—"

"You were just embarrassed that you'd made a mistake. It's okay. I'm sorry that you had to learn the hard way. I did try to warn you."

I choked back my usual venom. "I wish it was just a mistake, Mom. It would make things a whole lot easier."

She sat beside me. "But I thought you were done with that whole rock music thing. The news—"

"Mom, don't even read the news. They lie. Like a lot."

She exhaled. "Okay. So tell me."

The fact that she was at least trying broke down some of the barriers between us, and I started from the beginning. I told her everything—almost everything—from when I'd first met Adam until that moment. About the perfume and how I'd worried he only liked me because of some man magnet. About how he thought I only liked him because he was famous. About losing my job. About losing Adam.

"And I thought he'd see my video and forgive me." My voice cracked. "But he hasn't."

She interrupted me. "Do you love him, Eden?"

"What?" I wiped a tear off my cheek with the back of my hand.

"Are you in love with him?" She pressed her lips together, and I knew she was making an effort to listen rather than advise.

I shook my head. "I don't know. How can I know that? I've never been in love before." I ran my hands through my hair and looked into my mom's clear blue eyes, so much like Micah's. "It's only been a month. How could I fall in love with someone in such a short time? It's ludicrous."

Mom waved her hands. "Time doesn't matter. For some people it takes years to figure out. For others, it's as obvious as night and day. Do you think you love him?"

I thought back over the past month and remembered things Adam had said or done. I missed him so much it hurt.

"Yeah, Mom. I think I might. I'm not ready for it to be over. But I blew it. He thinks I tricked him, and he won't even talk to me."

Mom's worried expression never changed, but she took my hand. When had her skin turned so paper thin?

"Eden, I know you've dismissed my advice in the past, but hear me out. I don't know if this boy is right for you. He seems like trouble to me, and here you are nursing a broken heart." She frowned, revealing deep wrinkles in the corners of her mouth. "But, Eden, if you're in love with him, you're going to have to get out of your comfort zone and show him."

I sighed. "That's the thing, Mom. I don't know how."

"If it's meant to be, God will send you a sign." She squeezed my hand. "I'll be praying for you."

That was as much of a blessing as I could hope for. "Thanks, Mom."

As I drove back across Staten Island and then Lower Manhattan, my phone dinged with incoming messages. Every time it dinged, I held out the always unsatisfied hope for something that so far hadn't come—a text, or a voice mail, or an e-mail from Adam.

When I parked the car, I pulled the phone out and scrolled through the notifications, stunned to discover the e-mail right at the top of the list.

Subject: Atonement.

My heart rate sped up. He'd sent it twenty minutes earlier, while I was driving. Wherever they were, he would've sent it just before his show.

Did I want to read this now? Did I want to read it at all? I'd waited more than a week to hear what he had to say, but I dreaded what he had to say. What if he told me to leave him alone? Still, I dared hope he'd say he forgave me and wanted to work things out.

I opened the e-mail.

> Eden,
> Micah showed me the songs you performed
> last night. You look stunning btw. And your new
> song is gorgeous. The message in it wasn't lost on
> me. I've had a long time on this bus to do nothing
> but think about the conversation we had before
> you left. I'm glad you're thinking about it, too.
> When you left, I was angry and confused.
> Listening to your new song, I realized you're

under the impression I was angry at you for luring me against my will into temptation. Do you really think some love potion could have created feelings I wouldn't otherwise have had?

Eden, people take heavy drugs to feel as good as I felt when I was with you. If somehow you had enticed me through chemistry alone, I'd be hard-pressed to ask you to stop. And yeah, it's even better to find out that what you thought was a drugged reaction was completely natural. It's good to be sure the attraction was genuine, but seriously, I don't care. It doesn't matter. It never mattered. How I felt with you always felt real to me.

Even if I had been angry about any of that, I would have forgiven you. The second I stepped off that bus in Copenhagen, I knew I'd overreacted. A lot hit me at once—from the revelation that you'd lied to me about what your company did, that you'd never told me about that perfume, that you might have lied about knowing who I was. It confirmed my worst fears.

Micah told me you didn't know I was coming to the club that night and that you really hadn't ever heard of me. I'm sorry for accusing you of lying about that.

But there's still a fundamental issue, Eden. You didn't trust me with the truth. How can I trust you if you don't trust me?

I don't know where your head is. I'm not sure where mine is anymore.

It's funny. I saw your video for 'Expulsion.' Damn, it hurt hearing you sing that song the way I'd originally written it. Congratulations for unlocking that, btw. Ironically, you hit closer to the mark with that song than with your apology song.

Good luck with everything,
Adam

I read through his letter twice, trying to make sense of it.

I closed my eyes and held a mental dialogue with him, painfully wishing he were with me instead of halfway around the world. There were so many things I thought of writing back, but his e-mail didn't invite conversation.

And honestly, he'd made it clear when I left that he was done with me. He hadn't exactly begged me to stay. I recalled his words. *Have a good life.* They stung still.

I snorted, thinking about how good my life was since I'd met him.

I'd walked away from my job search without a pause, thinking it would be so easy to make it work in music. And there I sat without a gig in sight.

I'd given up my apartment on the assumption I'd find another. And there I sat in my "struggling artist" brother's apartment with a handful of my belongings.

I'd moved away from my family and friends on the hope of what? Finding happiness on my own with a guitar?

Who had I become? A month ago, I would've begged Keith to let me keep my job. I would've been content playing music with Micah from time to time. I would've kept going out with Stacy and Kelly.

And, of course, I would've been miserable.

So there I sat, miserable without all of that.

And I blamed Adam.

As I walked to Micah's, imaginary e-mails wrote themselves in my brain until I was able to sit down on the sofa with my laptop to dump out the words, thinking I'd write it out but never send it.

Adam,

I'm sorry, but the truth is that if you weren't a highly sought after rock-star sex god, maybe I would have had more courage to tell you everything up front. I know it offends your need for authenticity, but as soon as I learned who you are, the power dynamic shifted in your favor. Of course I assumed you would break up with me as soon as you found the first flaw. You can have any girl you want. And of course I assumed you would blame me for tricking you into wanting to be with me. How else could a person like me end up with a person like you?

When you walked out on me, my own worst fears were confirmed. Did you ever stop to think that maybe I had my own demons?

I'm glad you've come to believe I was telling you the truth when I said I didn't have a clue who you were when we met. And honestly, after my brief brush with minor fame, I understand why you wouldn't trust people, but part of me just wants to say 'boo fucking hoo.' When I worried about getting negative press, you were quick to tell me it's no big deal, just a price to pay in your world. Well, so is the insecurity of wondering what people want from you. Before you preach trust, you could have started by trusting me. You have a tattoo to remind you to have faith in others. Have you already forgotten?

Eden

Writing the letter had made me angrier. I hit Send the second I'd finished it. Fuck him. He hadn't spoken to me for nearly two weeks even though he knew he was wrong.

Whatever. I had other things to worry about.

Still, before I went to bed, I checked my phone, hoping for a response from him. Nothing. Their show would've ended hours before. He had to have read my e-mail. I hoped he might at least text me, but so far, silence.

Since Tobin had ignored all my texts, I went to the club on Tuesday to ask him face-to-face whether he could get me a show. He put me off again. "Eden, I'll contact you when we have an opening, okay? If you want to open on Friday, I can hold the spot for you."

"Second opening act?"

He shook his head. "That's already booked." He took my hand. "It takes time, Eden. You can't rush it."

On Wednesday, the phone rang while I was in the shower, so I didn't hear it. I saw the notification light flashing as I toweled my hair dry. I swiped the screen to find a voice-mail message and missed-call icon. I touched the missed call.

Adam. My shoulders dropped. Damn.

I dialed into my voice mail. There was no message, just the sound of the call terminating. I could picture him listening to the outgoing message, waiting until the last second, trying to figure out what he wanted to say, and then finally deciding he couldn't say whatever it was to a machine.

Should I call him back? Where were they? Shouldn't he be getting offstage? I looked up his tour schedule to see. They'd played Rome the night before. They had a night off before playing Nice the next day. They were either traveling or recuperating in the south of France.

I started to weigh my options, but my fingers were hitting the Call button before I'd even formulated the available actions. It rang once, twice. I held the phone out, meaning to cancel the call, but the screen switched from dialing to connected, and I heard his voice. An ocean washed through me.

"Eden?"

"Adam?"

"Eden. I tried to call you."

"Yeah, I saw. I'm returning your call. Where are you?"

"Monaco."

"Oh, fancy night off, huh?"

"Yeah, I just lost money at the casino." He laughed. "I should never gamble."

"Is Micah with you?"

"Eden, I don't want to talk about Micah."

I fell on the sofa and put my feet up on the cardboard box that held my throw blankets. I asked quietly, "What do you want to talk about?"

"Are you alone? Do you have a minute?"

"Yes. You've got my full attention."

"Good. Listen. I keep going over everything that happened with us. I keep having to remind myself I didn't even know you until a few short weeks ago. How can we have gone through an entire relationship in a month? What the hell is wrong with us?"

I'd never considered that, and I had no answer. "That's . . . Wow. Yeah. And backward, too."

"It's sort of ridiculous. I've spent the past couple of years worried about meeting a girl and never knowing if she liked me or the image of me. And then I have this whole different problem."

"What problem?"

"Well, I know you never fell for the image of me. But since I discovered your company's shit, I've been trying to figure out if you even liked me at all." He laughed. "I never once expected to have this happen. Careful what you wish for, right?" His words sounded slurred, like he'd been drinking.

"You're not making any sense, Adam. Of course I did. Remember how I told you I'd never date a struggling musician? Or a guy named Adam?"

"Of course," he whispered. "And then I pushed myself on you, and you just rolled with it. You should've just broken it off if you weren't into it." I could barely hear him.

"Adam, you didn't push yourself on me." I gathered my thoughts, listening to him breathe. "I've always processed every single guy in the world through a filter of rejection. And they've always come up short. They have the wrong name. They have the wrong job. They read the wrong books. And then you came along. And you were perfect."

His breathing had become slow and rhythmic.

"Adam?" No answer. I waited another few minutes for him to answer, but he'd clearly fallen asleep. I hung up.

I didn't know how much he'd heard before he passed out. And that made me question whether he'd even remember calling me. For all I knew, he'd been drunk off his ass. That left me feeling kind of shitty, that he'd have to be wasted to call me. On the other hand, maybe it meant he was thinking about it all the rest of the time.

And then it hit me. He was insecure about *my* feelings for *him*? He had girls throwing themselves at him. He could have anyone anytime. But he chose not to. He said he had before, and I thought of Jacob's attention at the club. How easy it would've been to let him seduce me. It was flattering as hell. But Jacob didn't know me. He was attracted to me, but why? He'd obviously felt that way before he ever spoke to me. I could see how Adam could've been tempted early on in his career, but then how he might've grown skittish about women who followed Adam, the rock star, without knowing him at all.

When he met me, he found someone who saw him through all of that, and who was thrown off by the image more than attracted to it. Was that what attracted him to me? I'd never know that. I was going to have to learn to trust him.

But how was I going to get him to trust me?

The only thing I could think to do was get out of my comfort zone and do something I'd fought against since I found out who he was: chase him.

I opened my laptop and pulled up the tour schedule. The last night of the tour was in Barcelona, Friday night. I logged on to my travel account and priced tickets. All the flights were overnight, and the best I could put together was leaving the next night with a stop in Oslo. I'd be in Spain by Friday morning, though. I could be in Barcelona by noon. With the money I wasn't spending on rent this month, I could easily justify the expense. I'd have plenty of time to get to the ticket office before the show. Then I could text Micah and have him let me backstage.

I walked through my options.

Option one: I could stay here and wait for Adam to come

home. There was a chance he'd come home from his tour and look me up. He might take me out and try to patch things up. The fact that he'd called me this week gave me a sense that this was a remote possibility. It felt like the safe option, but it was in fact a risk. He'd clearly been trying to avoid talking to me for two weeks now. I worried that the only thing I'd hear from him when he came home was that we were broken up.

Option two: I could call Adam now and tell him everything. Apologize, confess, and talk it all out. That would be easy enough, but something told me I needed to make a more dramatic statement.

Option three: I could take the flight to Barcelona. I'd be putting everything on the line in one shot. Fear settled in as I pictured Adam closing the door on me permanently, with no recourse. I'd be flying home all alone with no hope of him reaching out to me once I got here. It scared the shit out of me. And that's why I knew it was the only choice.

With a dozen clicks, I'd purchased a one-way ticket and a hotel room.

Chapter 22

After several delays, mechanical difficulties, and reroutes, I arrived in the Barcelona airport at six p.m. And the concert started at eight.

I hoped to see Micah perform, but I couldn't very well take my luggage to a concert. There was no reason I needed to be at the arena right when the doors opened, so I grabbed a taxi to the hotel and spent roughly thirty minutes showering, shaving, primping, and dressing until I looked ready to rock.

At seven thirty, I was in a taxi on my way to the venue.

I made it to the ticket booth almost exactly on time, but when I asked for a single seat, the woman behind the glass waved up over her head at a sign that said AGOTADO in big red letters. She didn't even bother to glance up from her gossip magazine. I didn't know any Spanish, so I said a little louder, "I just need one ticket, *por favor.*"

"No ticket," she said. "*Agotado.*"

A man in a red and yellow soccer jersey approached me. "They're sold out. I can sell you one for three hundred euros."

I didn't have that kind of money on me. And besides, I didn't need the ticket. I fished out my phone and texted Micah, *I'm outside the stadium. Can you get me in?*

I hadn't come to see the show, anyway. I just needed to find Micah or someone who knew me enough to get me backstage.

A pair of giggling girls headed to the side of the building. I remembered the scene outside the bus at the other shows and followed them. Sure enough, there was a blocked-off area behind the stadium, where the buses waited. Security guards kept people back. The crowd near the steel barricade grew as the night wore on. It was complete insanity.

About an hour after I'd arrived, the back door opened, and Micah came out. He lit up a cigarette and walked toward the bus. I yelled out, "MICAH!" and he glanced over. The girls around me screeched, "MICAH!" He waved and kept walking until he disappeared onto the bus. I was going to have a talk with that boy about catering to his fans. But it hadn't slipped my notice that he looked exhausted. The constant touring and performing had to be wearing him down. And if they were partying on their nights off, he'd probably run himself into the dirt. But the tour was coming to an end, and they'd be going home.

I texted him again, hoping he'd emerge from the bus and find me. Maybe he'd gone straight to sleep. The bus doors stayed resolutely closed, and I waited.

Time wore on. Adam had taken the stage at some point, and the crowd inside could be heard through the concrete walls of the stadium. Every once in a while the decibels would literally go through the roof.

My feet hurt, and the cold night air bit into my skin. The excited girls around me chattered in Spanish. They clutched markers and T-shirts and CDs. I wondered how many had, like me, simply failed to get tickets and how many fans intentionally skipped the entire concert just to stalk the buses.

The jostling began about the same time people began to leave the stadium in small groups of twos and threes. As the doors opened, music poured out like liquid, in waves. The departing crowd thickened, and soon instead of sound, people flowed from the exits. More gathered into the increasingly tight stalking area, and I was pressed up against the barricade. The energy grew with the waiting. Girls who had just spent two or three hours in the cold, hoping for a chance to meet the members of a band they hadn't seen perform, were shoved aside by the new-comers, jockeying for better positions. An elbow dug into my side, and I found myself back a row, no longer against the barri-cade. The security patrol doubled. I searched for any familiar face, but I'd only met Paul once, and none of these men looked like Paul. Not that he'd been very helpful in the past.

Members of Adam's band came out, one at a time. Girls screamed for them, but not by name. I called out, "Hervé!" and "Charles!" hoping to catch them by surprise. But my voice was just one more layer in the insanity. Others picked up the chant as I yelled, "MARK!" My voice was going hoarse, but for naught. Each of the band members would smile and wave. They weren't the stars of the show, so they ducked their heads and climbed on their buses.

More time passed. Twenty minutes. Thirty minutes. Fans fell off and left. The number of girls had nearly diminished to the original group. I could no longer be sure who had been there from the beginning besides me.

At long last, the back door opened. Adam stepped out, fol-lowed by a tall, thin blonde in a too-tight sweater and stilettos.

My stomach dropped down to my shoes. What was he doing with her? I turned to ask someone next to me, but aside from the lack of linguistic compatibility, I doubted my companions would be any more versed in the motives of Adam Copeland than I apparently was. Besides, the girls around me were busy tearing their own faces off with hysteria and crying. I fit right in. Adam walked the groupie halfway across the parking lot. She touched his arm and asked him a question. He stopped and pointed her toward an awaiting bus. As soon as she climbed on, he headed in the direction of the waiting fans.

Finally.

And I wished I were anywhere else. Oslo. Madrid. Edison, New Jersey.

My mind shone a flashlight through the attic at all my worst fears. I had such a clear memory of him depositing me on his bus in the exact same way. After we'd made the fans wait. After we'd had frenzied sex on the floor of his dressing room.

I took a step back and hid behind the front line of fans, forcing oxygen into my lungs.

Quickly, ever so quickly, I weighed my options. *Think!*

Option one: I could catch a taxi to my hotel, fetch my things, and then be on the next plane back home. It might take me another fifteen hours to get there—fifteen hours of worrying about what the hell was happening back in Spain. My feet were already pointed that direction, but it was cowardly. I flashed back to my mom's party, when Adam had appeared and I'd planned to flee into the house that first—no, second—time I'd felt jealous of Adrianna.

My feet wouldn't move.

Option two: I could stand there and demand an explanation. He wanted me to talk out my anger? I could call him out right there in front of a group of fans, who would certainly take it to the Internet. It would take a few hours to make it across international borders, but by the following day, the gossip rags would have something to talk about. That might not be cowardly, but it would be unfair.

Fight or flight? Which would it be?

A small voice suggested a third alternative. I could finally overcome my fears, put myself on the line, and risk getting shot down right there after traveling so far. Making myself so vulnerable terrified me, like exposing a jugular vein to the executioner. But I'd already come so far to do just that.

He'd asked, "*How can I trust you if you don't trust me?*" Why had I flown all the way over to Spain if I hadn't wanted to show him I did? Whatever was going on with that groupie, I was sure there was an explanation. He'd always had a good one before.

If I was ever going to prove anything, I'd have to risk everything.

So I stayed. And I waited.

He was feet away, working his way down the line from the end, approaching.

And he was so beautiful. His skin glistened from the exertion of burning off thousands of calories rocking out. His hair flopped in mysterious ways no product would ever be able to tame. It was sex hair. His eyes crinkled sweetly as he listened to the exact same sentiment in different words from each of his fans. I doubted he spoke a word of Spanish, but he shook hands, took pictures, and smiled that exact same smile. All charm.

When the fan to my right shoved an iPhone into my hands and said, "*Tomad mi foto,*" I found myself separated from Adam by one smartphone. I said, "Smile," and snapped the picture just as recognition registered.

"I'm sorry. This picture didn't turn out very good," I said, holding it out for him to see the shock on his face. "Let's do that again."

He pulled the fan in tight, and this time, the smile on his face stretched from ear to ear. This fan was going to have something special to show her friends. She took her phone back, speaking rapidly as she immediately worked on uploading the picture.

Adam stepped in front of me and grabbed my hand. "We've got to stop meeting like this."

I dropped my eyes to my feet, suddenly shy. "You're a hard one to reach."

"You could've called."

"I texted Micah. He must not have seen it."

"Of course. Seriously, what are you doing here?"

My courage flagged, and I reached for a quip. "I was in the neighborhood."

His smile faltered, and I knew I was going to have to take the risk now or never.

"Adam. I flew here to confess something."

He took another step forward. His face was inches from mine. "Yeah?"

I closed the gap and rested my head against his. I brushed a dark lock off his forehead and gazed into his eyes, seeking permission or promise. Anything to give me the courage to bare my soul.

When he squeezed my hand, my anxiety broke, and my trust in him was total. "I love you."

The girl next to me shrieked. "I love you, Adam!" The chain reaction was instantaneous. "*Te amo*, Adam! Adam!!"

I doubled over and put my hands on my knees, trying to control my laughter. "You've turned me into a fan girl. How do you like that?"

He laid his hands on my shoulders, and I fought to gain control of my emotions. Hot tears streamed down my face even while I stifled my giggles.

Light-headed, I straightened back up and screwed my face up as serious as I could manage. "Say something, would you?"

He wiped a tear from my cheek and flashed his wicked smile. "So you're saying you want me?"

My breath hitched. "Oh, I want you."

"Good, because I'm crazy about you."

He jumped the barricade, and gasps sounded around us as the girls in the line lost their minds. He wrapped his arms around me and pressed his lips against mine. Time stood still as I lost myself in that kiss. Then the frantic screaming and jostling of the fans became too overwhelming to ignore.

Adam waved to the security guard and asked to have the barricade moved to let me through. He gave me a single order: "Don't go anywhere."

He stayed on the same side of the barricade as the fans, who were falling all over themselves to hug him and pose with him. The girls waiting to see him had forgotten me as they kept their laser eyes locked on him. The girls who had already had their Adam time all stared at me with their mouths open. This rumor would cross the ocean before we'd crossed the parking lot. I knew Adam had to know it was a possibility. And yet he'd kissed me in public before his most ardent fans.

My stomach flipped. I gawked at him, no better than one of

the fans. Hell, I'd been one of them for the past several hours. No better than a stalker.

At last, he was finished greeting fans, and he twined his fingers through mine and led me toward the buses. As we neared the one he'd pointed the groupie to, I naturally drifted in that direction out of muscle memory. His bus usually sat on one end. When I tugged slightly, he yanked me back. "My bus is over here."

He snaked his arm around my waist and squeezed me against him. "So how'd you wind up in Spain?"

I looped my finger into one of his belt loops. His body felt amazing. "I had an epiphany."

"Clue me in."

"I lost my job, gave away my apartment, and couldn't get another." Still giddy from before, I chuckled at how awful everything was. "Instead of looking for work, I took a risk and started pursuing the life I've always dreamed of—making a career out of music. I tried to play my own music, but I couldn't get a single decent gig. Needless to say, it hasn't panned out, yet."

He stopped outside the bus doors. "So I was your backup?"

"God, no." I leaned against the metal paneling. The vibrations from the motor purred through my shoulders. "I hated my job, and I no longer belonged in New Jersey. It turns out what I'd always thought would be this huge risk wasn't a risk at all. I'm not homeless or broke. I have Micah's apartment and savings in the bank. And the gigs will come. Thanks to you, I believe in myself enough to keep plugging at it. I'll start at the bottom and work my way up."

Adam lifted my hand and kissed the tips of my fingers. "I'd like to do that right now."

Chills shot up my arm, but I had more to say, the hardest thing yet. I sucked in my lower lip and worked up my courage. "I figured out that this drastic life change wasn't what scared me most." I swallowed. "Adam, ever since I found out about all this"—I rolled my hands to indicate the tour bus, the arena, the rock-star persona I'd gotten mixed up with—"I've been terrified of letting you see how much I wanted to be with you. I was afraid of scaring you."

"Scaring me?"

"Adam, you couldn't possibly need me as much as I need you. *Everyone* wants you."

"But they don't want *me*, Eden. That's what I've been trying to explain. I'd rather be alone than adored, or used, or even loved for anything other than who I am."

"And I've been worrying that you only liked me because of some cheap trick."

He grazed my lips with his. "I think our chemistry speaks for itself."

I closed my eyes, wanting to say it all before the moment passed. "The paranoia played into every fear I had about you, on tour, with Adrianna, even when you were with me."

"Adrianna?"

"Even Adrianna. Mostly Adrianna. I constantly feared I'd lose you when you figured out you'd been unwittingly seduced."

He put one hand above my shoulder, against the bus, and leaned in. "Eden, the minute I laid eyes on you, you knocked the wind out of me. Believe me when I tell you, I was quite wittingly seduced."

"After you called me from Monaco, it finally clicked. If I don't let go of myself, I'm going to lose you. And you're the one thing I want. And that's why I came to Spain—to put my trust in you."

He bent forward and kissed my forehead. "Eden, that's all I've ever wanted to hear you say. And I'm sorry, too. I know I should've trusted you, but I'm far from perfect."

"Do you forgive me?"

"I already did. Come on, it's freezing."

He climbed up two steps at a time and said, "Townsend, Mc-Cord, go ride the other bus."

Mark stuck his head out of the folding doors and stared at me. His shoulders slumped, and he exhaled. "Seriously, Adam? One second." He ducked in and returned with a duffel bag.

"Hi, Eden. What're you doing here?"

Charles followed, grumbling. "There's no room on the other bus."

Adam didn't take his eyes off me. "So go get a hotel. We're not going anywhere tonight."

"Why don't you two go get a hotel? I was almost asleep."

Adam ignored their griping and pressed his body hard against mine while Mark and Charles cleared out.

As we climbed aboard, I remembered. "My stuff's at the hotel."

"It's okay. Seamus can get it in the morning before we go to the airport."

The doors closed, and he put his arms around my waist and slowly walked me backward down the aisle. I took one step at a time, deliberate, not wanting to move so fast as to put any distance between our bodies. His lips brushed against the top of my head, and his hands slid down my sides. "I've fantasized about this every night since we've been on the road."

Although everything seemed the same as before, there were subtle differences. The fabric on the benches was the wrong color orange. The curtain between the front and back parted as my shoulders split the fabric and my legs hit the edge of the platform bed.

It was a different curtain.

Realization hit me hard. "This isn't the bus we were on before."

Adam lifted me up and then followed. He lay down, but I stayed upright, legs crisscrossed, facing him in the darkness. Through the window, I could see roadies dragging equipment to the gear bus. "Why are you on this bus, Adam?"

"Someone else got my bus." He reached over and laid his hand on my thigh.

Images of him and that blond groupie riding that bus together for however many days, fucking, always fucking, crossed my mind. "Shit. I'm an idiot."

He broke contact with me and rolled up onto his elbow. "What?"

"That girl I saw you with. God, I'm such a fool." My first in-clination was to bolt. I started to drag myself out of the alcove, but Adam put his hand on my forearm.

He sat up. "Eden, do you trust me?"

My eyes involuntarily returned to his face, and I focused on him. "I want to, Adam. But I don't understand. Why's she riding your bus?"

"Listen. I've never lied to you."

"Never lied. But you're the master of omission, Adam. What haven't you told me?" I scooted back against the wall, scared of hearing what I didn't want to know.

His eyes moved back and forth, gazing into mine. Finally, he took a deep breath and let it out through his lips. "Don't ever tell Micah I told you."

Oh, God. "What do you mean?" I caught my breath. "Micah's got a groupie?"

He burst out laughing. "Yeah. Micah's got a groupie. Her name's Anna. Nice girl. I've been riding this bus with Mark and Charles for a week now."

I sat for a minute, processing. "Why was she with you, then?"

"She wanted to use the showers."

"Oh." I believed him. The road was a dirty place to be. "I'm so sorry. I don't know why I get so jealous. I saw that girl walk-ing with you, and it reminded me of us in Paris. And I just thought . . . I assumed—"

"You never need to worry about the groupies. But before, when you said you were jealous of Adrianna . . . Is that true?"

The back of the bus was dark, quiet except for the purring of the motor, intimate. Adam's form was an outline, illuminated only by the industrial fluorescent lights of the parking lot. A perfect setting for baring one's soul.

"Adam, you can't deny there's something between you and Adrianna. She calls you to New York for some emergency, and you drop everything and go. Then she thumbs a ride with you to

Ireland and shows up in London." I twisted the fabric on the mattress. "It's hard not to feel a little jealous."

The shadows playing on his face reminded me of the first night we met. His hood had been pulled up, obscuring his features. For the first time, it became clear he'd been trying to hide his identity that night. But he hadn't hidden from me.

"Adrianna's a good friend, and she'll always be a part of my life, Eden. But you don't need to feel jealous of her."

"Why'd you both take so long to put an end to the rumor you were a couple, then?"

He put his hand over mine. "Actually, that day I met her in New York, I told her about you. I wanted to put an end to that stupid rumor, then. But she'd called me there, freaking out about another tabloid making accusations that she's transgendered."

I remembered thinking the same thing when I first saw her. "Is she?"

He narrowed his eyes, but didn't answer my question, exactly. "Eden. It's hard enough being a public figure without having your identity subverted as well. We thought a fictional relationship would give her a place to hide for a while."

"That kind of backfired for you though, didn't it?"

"Yeah. The media only became more interested in me. And I'd kind of hoped a fake engagement might discourage groupies, but the fan girls never stop pursuing me."

"Ouch." The ache of jealousy was becoming a familiar friend.

"Single, engaged, or married, I'm going to be turning down unwanted advances until I'm no longer selling records. Or dead." He stroked my thumb with his. "Comes with the territory, unfortunately. Trust is going to be critical, Eden. I can't promise you'll never have reason to doubt me. The gossip columns will make sure of that. I can promise I won't give you any reason to doubt me."

I wanted to trust him, but he'd sidestepped me again. "You've still avoided my first question, Adam. What stopped you from ending the rumors?"

"I'm getting there. When I told Adrianna I wanted to, she reminded me I was about to go on an extended tour in Europe. She pointed out that as soon as we made any kind of announcement, someone would get curious and sniff you out. And I didn't think you were ready to be shoved into the limelight yet. She suggested we keep up the pretense a little while longer to distract the media away from digging into *your* personal life until you and I had a chance to figure things out."

"But the tabloids did investigate me after you took me to dinner. Reporters came to my work place."

His teeth flashed white in the darkness. "And then they quit. Think of it like an inoculation. The reporters did a little digging, and when they found nothing, they left you alone. Or at least they would have if I hadn't let down my guard in Germany."

I drew up my knees and wrapped my arms around my legs. "I liked it when you let down your guard. It felt nice to be out in the open with you like that for a change."

"Yeah. I liked it, too. It made it that much harder after you left."

"You could've called me. I wanted you to call."

He shook his head. "When you got in that limo in Copenhagen, I thought that was it. I was going to have to become a celibate monk."

I laughed despite myself. "That would've been a tragedy."

He crawled across the mattress and propped himself next to me, his face inches from mine. "Speaking of tragic celibacy, can we talk about all this later?"

He brushed his lips against my neck, leaving a trail of goose bumps. I picked up the edge of his shirt and touched his side until I found his ribs. "Mmm. Adam's ribs."

Clothes fell to the wayside, and when I slid off his leather pants, he had nothing on underneath.

"Did they steal your underwear again?"

He didn't answer me. Instead, he pushed me onto my back and gazed into my eyes with dangerous intent.

"Adam," I ran my finger down his stomach. "Are there any condoms on this bus?"

"Oh, fuck!" He jumped up and threw on some boxers. "I'll be right back."

I lay in the dark, in his tour bus, listening to the double doors open and close, hearing the few remaining fans squealing at the sight of a half-naked Adam Copeland running from one bus to another across the parking lot. I hoped one of the other guys was better prepared than Adam.

Epilogue

Tobin stood onstage in front of the wall-to-wall crowd. I knew they were all there hoping to catch a glimpse of Adam, but I wouldn't regret an audience member, whatever reason had brought them out to see me perform. And for all they knew, he wasn't even there. I'd played my first set to a great reception. My new CD had just been released, and while I didn't get any spins on radio, yet, our agent, Jane, thought it was only a matter of time. With some touring at smaller clubs and radio stations across the country, I might be able to support it enough to push my single "Just Me" onto the charts.

For now, I was content to be sitting on a stool, strumming my guitar, singing almost every night. Tobin was happy to have me come back to headline the Friday night show. I hadn't played here in several months.

I pulled my stool up to the mic and scanned the expectant faces. This part never grew old. Whenever Adam had a night free and we were in the same town, he'd try to drop in on my shows. And I did the same for him. Not that people obsessed over my schedule to find out when I might show up in an arena the way they'd follow Adam's movements. They'd go out of their way for a chance to see him perform in a small club.

The second microphone sat beside me the entire show, like a promise. And when I started out, "Friends, it's with great pleasure"—the audience erupted with delight—"that I invite Adam Copeland to join me for the next set."

These were special nights because we were able to try out the songs we were writing for our collaboration CD. Adam bounded onto the stage, grabbed his guitar, and slid onto the stool next to me. "Thank you. It's always a privilege to perform with Eden."

He strummed, and I came in with my arpeggios. And we sang in harmony.

The song told the story of Tristan and Iseult on the surface, bonded together through the love potion they'd taken by mistake. We'd twisted it enough to tell of a magnetism that couldn't be broken, despite the physical distances brought on by touring, despite the misunderstandings the gossip columns tried to fan, and despite a history filled with doubts and mistrust in the powerful strength of that bond. His voice still gave me chills. And it turned me on like nothing else.

Tonight, we'd get to sleep in our own bed in our walk-up in Brooklyn. But when the set ended, and Adam walked offstage, I knew we'd never make it back to the apartment. The fans would have to wait in line until we came out to greet them. That nasty sofa was about to get a little nastier. I made a mental note to buy Tobin some new furniture.

But whenever Adam performed with me, the demand for an encore was overwhelming. Our shenanigans would have to wait another song. And since we knew they'd likely demand it, we always saved "Compulsion" for last. We'd released it as a single last December, a few weeks prior to Christmas, and it was a surprise holiday hit. The naughty but religious message dovetailed with other Christmas love songs, and we'd performed it live on a number of TV shows.

I left the stage and met Adam in the green room. He pushed me against the closed door and kissed me hard to the backdrop of fans stomping on the floor, yelling for us to come back out.

My hands dug into that mess of hair. "We could make them wait ten more minutes?"

He crushed against me. "Yeah? Don't you think they might

crash down the door if we don't get back out there? And besides, I'm not done singing with you tonight."

I let go of him, and he straightened up. I glanced in the mirror hanging on the green-room bathroom door. "Oh, God. I have lip hickeys."

Adam opened the green-room door, and I followed him out and up onstage to a loud cheer that broke as we grabbed our guitars. My hand caught on something along the neck, and I cast my gaze down, expecting to find a capo attached. This song didn't require one though, so I reached to unclip it. But instead, I found a small box tied by a ribbon. Perplexed, I looked up at Adam, who stood with his eyes wide.

I untied the ribbon and pulled the box off the guitar. He took it from my shaking hands and popped it open. And then he knelt. I nearly passed out, but the audience broke out in applause.

The microphone had been adjusted to his kneeling height, and as he spoke, his words carried through the entire room.

"Eden Sinclair. I met you here one year ago tonight. Somewhere between the merchandise and paradise." He chuckled at his own bad rhyme. "Somehow I knew from the moment I laid eyes on you that you were something different, something special, one in a million. And thankfully, you saw past all this"—he gestured to himself—"and fell for me, too. The loneliest I've ever been in my entire life was when I thought I might've lost you. I want you by my side. Always. Eden, will you marry me?"

With his last word, the room became eerily silent. Dozens of faces watched us, and the complete lack of noise freaked me out a little. I dropped down on my knees in front of Adam.

"You tricked me."

He smiled. "A little. I figured you couldn't say no in front of all these people."

I spoke into the microphone. "I'm taking requests up here. What do you all think I should do?"

The crowd burst out in cacophony, but I clearly got the message. "Say yes!"

My mom was going to be so happy. I smiled at Adam and said, "Yes. Yes, of course! I love you."

He placed the ring on my finger and kissed me to thunderous applause. Then he picked up the guitar, and right there on his knees, he played the song he'd written for me nearly a year before. And the crowd sang along.

But I only heard his voice.

Acknowledgments

This novel began like a song I couldn't get out of my head. I furiously scribbled down the words, like so many notes and lyrics, until I had something akin to a demo tape that eventually grew into a finished recording through much studio production. I could never have achieved this alone, and I have so many to thank for making the music come alive.

Kristin Wright, you've been my maestro, the conductor of change, both dramatic and subtle. With a wave of your stylus, you've helped orchestrate order from my chaos. Thank you for your always caring direction and helping me tune up my act.

Kelli Newby, you are the rhythm section, the heart of my band. Thank you for your steady backing and for letting me know when it's time to turn the beat around. Twue Wuv.

Laura Heffernan, Susan Bickford, and Rachel Reiss, you are fantastic critics. Thank you for providing wisdom and guidance through so many iterations of this book.

Shout-out to the CD, featuring Elly Blake, Kelly Calabrese, Kellye Garrett, Jennifer Hawkins, Margarita Montimore, Kelly Siskind, Summer Spence, and special guest Ron Walters. You are my biggest champeens. Thank you for constantly making me laugh long and hard.

Special thanks to Alex Trugman for allowing me to eavesdrop on your songwriting and for pushing me to take a leap. I wouldn't have had the chutzpah to set my first word down if you hadn't been so amazingly open and encouraging about the creative process.

Brenda Drake, I can never express my awe and gratitude for how hard you work to help make dreams come true for so many writers. It was through entering Pitch Wars in 2014 and later mentoring that I've met almost all of my writing friends. Thanks as well to the Pitch Wars ToT for your constant support. And to my Pitch Wars mentor Jaime Loren for everything.

I owe an enormous debt of gratitude to my agents, Rachel Stout and Jane Dystel, for seeing the potential in this story. And to my ever harmonious editor, Wendy McCurdy, for taking a chance on my debut novel, and for investing so much time and effort into transforming it into an honest-to-god novel. I'm so thankful to each of you for challenging me to level up.

Huge thanks to everyone at Kensington. I'm so happy with the beautiful cover (art, design, and copy) by Monika Roe, Kristine Mills, Lorraine Freeney, and Tracy Marx. And I'm in debt to the eagle-eyed Brittany Dowdle for editing expertise and to Paula Reedy for shaping this into a real live book.

Thanks especially to my husband and two daughters for putting up with my long bouts of immobility even when you weren't sure I was doing anything productive.

I'm a fan girl at heart, and I couldn't have conceived of this book without having followed musicians around until at least one was forced to ask, "Haven't you been to enough shows?" I appreciate every musician who has let me hang around and experience a small corner of that universe.

And to all the friends who've shared my love of musicians enough to chase after bands with me and to everyone who follows independent artists and live music like lunatics, thank you for your support. We are the music makers, for we are the funders of dreams.

SOME KIND OF MAGIC

Mary Ann Marlowe

About This Guide

The suggested questions are included
to enhance your group's reading of
Mary Ann Marlowe's *Some Kind of Magic*.

DISCUSSION QUESTIONS

1. If you could make anyone fall in love with you, who would it be?

2. If there were really such a thing as an irresistible pheromone perfume, would you want to wear it?

3. How would you feel if you discovered that your spouse/boyfriend/girlfriend were wearing such a perfume?

4. Do you think that Eden makes the right decision about telling/not telling Adam about the perfume?

5. What do you think of Eden's deal-breaker list?

6. Do you agree with her assessment of musicians, plumbers, proctologists, and salesmen?

7. Who would be on YOUR deal-breaker list, and why?

8. Given Eden's "rules" about who she is interested in dating, and the assumptions she makes about Adam, what is it about him that leads her to break her own rules?

9. Why do you think that Adam is attracted to Eden?

10. How do you think Adam's fame affected his previous relationships, and how is it different with Eden . . . or is it?

11. Have you ever had a crush on a rock star? How hard is it to imagine him or her as a regular person?

12. If you were famous, would that affect your trust in prospective romantic partners? Can you empathize with Adam's reactions?

13. How would you feel if you discovered that the person you have just started dating is a celebrity? Would you handle it exactly as Eden does? What things would you do differently, if any? Would it make a difference if you were already a huge fan of his or hers ahead of time?

14. If you had a famous boyfriend/girlfriend, would you be able to resist spying on his/her activities online? Do you think this would create any problems?

If you loved *Some Kind of Magic,* watch
for Micah's story in Mary Ann Marlowe's
next romantic novel

A CRAZY KIND OF LOVE

available from Kensington Books in fall 2017!

Read on for a preview. . . .

Stalker. When you put it that way, what I did for a living sounded despicable.

Paparazzi had a nicer ring to it. Slightly.

My editor, Andy, said I was too fresh to work the street. The way he told it, I still had the stink of human about me. *"Josephine, you have to figure out if you want to work in this profession or have a soul."*

That Andy was a joy to work with. But I'd seen him in action, walking backward down the sidewalk, shooting pictures and asking questions, right up in the faces of people who behaved as though he were completely invisible. He still hadn't let me live down the one time I apologized to a mark before taking her picture. In my defense, it was my first week on the job, and she'd just come out of the hospital with fresh bruises.

That was months ago, and I'd hardened up.

I'd been called "loser" and told to "get a real job." One time, an innocent bystander intentionally blocked my shot of an incognito Jeff Daniels slipping through the airport unnoticed. In addition to ruining my chance to call it a day, said good Samaritan accused me of being a vile parasite before sitting back down to ogle Jennifer Aniston in another entertainment magazine's photo spread.

Most people assumed it was an exciting line of work. But

while I clocked more celebrity sightings in a week than most people would their whole lives, most days, I simply leaned against a brick wall for hours, shoulder cramping, hoping the stars would align. Literally.

On other days, like today, a tweet would take me on a journey to Brooklyn, where I'd narrowly missed getting a shot of Emily Mortimer rehearsing her lines in Prospect Park. Cursing the waste of the morning, I had no choice but to head back to the subway with nothing to turn in to my editor. But as I rounded a corner, I spotted Maggie Gyllenhaal coming out of the Park Slope Food Coop with her two daughters. I raised my eyes to the heavens in gratitude and then steeled myself for the kill.

I wore two cameras strapped across my chest bandito-style. When Maggie stopped to adjust her bags, I grabbed my work camera off my right hip and caught her in my crosshairs. I disengaged my conscience and prepared to pester this person whose only crime was to have achieved a level of celebrity that made people willing to pay money to read about her and invade her privacy. It was my job to cater to that need.

Centering her in the frame, I got off one shot just as some oblivious jerk crossed right in front of me, completely obscuring my line of sight.

I threw my hand in the air. "Seriously?" Aggravated, I angled myself around the interloper for a better view of Maggie, but as I peered through the eyepiece, my viewfinder filled with a plasma-colored blob that auto-focus slowly resolved to reveal Mr. Oblivious now staring directly into my lens. I let my camera drop against my sternum with a growl of frustration, but my new friend didn't register my impatience.

Rather, he moved in closer with a disarmingly friendly smile. "Who are you shooting?"

"It's Maggie Gyllenhaal." Still irritated, I spoke too loud, and a nearby woman gasped and repeated the news. My heart sank as the whispers grew, and I watched my last chance at a celebrity sighting disappear into a vortex of autograph-seeking passersby. A long exhale left my body along with my hopes of returning with anything Andy might want.

I glared at my nemesis, but even as I formulated a murderous plot, I became aware of how deliciously pretty he was. With his blond hair, blue eyes, broad shoulders, and tanned skin, he should have been holding a surfboard on a poster for a California travel agency. He really was too perfect to be roaming the streets without a chaperone.

But none of that mattered. He'd thrown a wrench into my morning, and I arched my eyebrow a fraction higher in reproof.

And yet, he continued to stare at me with a look of curiosity, as if somehow *I* were more interesting than the famous person half a block away. A famous person I still couldn't see for the crowd surrounding her. He pointed at my camera. "Are you paparazzi?"

His fascination made sudden sense—he'd probably never seen the paparazzi up close and impersonal. I sucked on my teeth and considered the situation. "Look. I'm sure you don't care, but you've cost me a candid shot of that actress, and that's my bread and butter. The least you could do is give me a boost so I can maybe bring something back to my editor."

His eyes narrowed for a beat, and he glanced down the block, then back at me as he pieced together my dilemma. I wasn't short, but I'd need to stand on a bench to see over that crowd. A slight smile played on his lips. "You want to climb on my shoulders?" He waggled his eyebrows salaciously.

The idea seemed preposterous, but desperate times and all. I'd gone to greater lengths for less in the past. And somehow I felt like this guy might be a good sport. He'd maintained a devil-may-care grin throughout this entire exchange. And I really needed that shot. I closed my eyes and swallowed my pride. "Would you mind?"

He dropped to one knee with the speed of an eager suitor, and I winced as his bare knee hit the concrete. He merely bowed his head and said, "At your service."

I couldn't help but giggle at the absurdity. But then he lifted his eyes, and my laughter caught in my throat. Until that moment, he'd just been an annoying interference, but his smoldering gaze brought me thundering to reality. I took a half step away and drank in the beauty of my kneeling knight. Golden hair glinted in the late morning sun. Bright blue eyes shone with mirth and intelligence. Well-muscled biceps peeked out of a T-shirt that stretched across his broad chest. Thigh muscles flexed, and his smooth, taut skin cried out to be touched.

I swallowed.

He held a hand out toward me. "Come on, then. I don't bite. Well, not in full daylight."

I circled around him, hearing everything my mom would say in this situation. But this total stranger didn't appear to be suffering from typhoid, and I hadn't seen a gutted panel van in the vicinity, so I felt reasonably confident this wasn't the way I was going to die. I laid my hand on his left shoulder and immediately yanked it away from the shock of how toned and solid he felt.

He twisted back and looked up at me. "You don't need to be scared. I carry equipment all the time. I've only dropped a few." His lips, lips I noticed for the first time, grew into a full-fledged smile, white teeth flashing like an ad for Crest, and I wondered if I could muster the nerve to climb on this beautiful man.

One of Andy's many lectures came to mind: *Get the shot at any cost.* And just like that, fear of losing my job overcame my self-respect. Honestly, I'd been chipping away at that virtue ever since I traded art school for tabloid photography.

With a last farewell to my dignity, I swung my right leg over that mouthwatering shoulder. As soon as I felt his hand on my shin, I hopped up and sat square across the back of his neck. My human crane held my legs tight and stood.

And wobbled.

My free hand instinctively latched on to his hair, and he yelped. "Sorry," I hollered down. A hint of coconut wafted up, and I fought off an overpowering visceral reaction—the desire to touch him, smell him, even taste him. I wanted to lean forward and plant my face into the top of his head.

But I'd spent months focusing on preserving my job and wasn't about to crumble just because I straddled a Fifty-Most-Beautiful-

People level of beautiful person. With those sexy lips. And his hands on my legs.

Focus, Jo.

The crowd below had begun to thin, and I was tempted to abort plan A, but I couldn't take the chance that Maggie would walk away once she'd signed the last autograph.

I lifted my camera and zoomed in. There in the center stood my target. And she was facing the wrong way.

Crap.

I yelled down, "I can't even tell it's her from here. Do you mind walking closer?"

He began to move down the sidewalk, and my self-control faltered thanks to his neck now rubbing against my inner thighs—and more. His shoulders tensed and relaxed beneath my legs, heat intensifying in the most intimate way. My fingers gripped his neck, and goose bumps appeared. He lifted his arm and caught my hand in his. It was a miracle I didn't fall from a spontaneous swoon.

Despite our conspicuous approach, we'd nearly reached our destination, when Maggie turned her head up and locked eyes with me. I quickly lifted my camera, but the appearance of a desperate pap precariously perched on a lumbering accomplice must have spooked her, because in the time it took me to point and aim, she'd lifted her bags, grabbed her youngest daughter by the hand, and fled down the block in the opposite direction.

I palmed my forehead. Unless I'd inadvertently captured something during that mortifying display, I had nothing at all.

My accidental hero lowered me back to the street, and I found myself out of breath even though he'd been the one exerting himself. He ran a hand through his hair, and I followed it with greedy eyes, already regretting my descent to ordinary earth after my perch atop a golden god.

He eyed me with equal interest. "Perhaps we should be formally introduced? I'm Micah." He stretched out his hand. "And you are?"

"J-Jo." I took a deep breath and let it out.

"Jo Jo?" In ordinary circumstances, his constant teasing might have put me off, but Micah had an air of easygoing charm about him. And he had just agreed to be used as a parade float for no other reason than generosity.

"Jo," I repeated, a bit more confidently. "Josie."

"Well, Jo-Josie." His hand gripped mine, and his half smile hovered somewhere between charming and devilish. "Where are you from?"

I took a shuddering breath and tried to get my heart to stop galloping in my chest. I prayed my lack of composure had nothing to do with a sudden drop in my blood sugar, please, God, and rather everything to do with the proximity of the most attractive man I'd possibly ever laid eyes on. And I'd seen a lot of attractive people in my line of work. "Georgia," I said, then clarified, "Atlanta."

He gently pushed my shoulder. "Get back, Jo Jo."

I snickered at the dated song reference as though that joke hadn't fallen from the lips of every class clown I'd ever known. I put on my twangiest Southern. "You shooin' me on home?"

His blue eyes crinkled at the corner, and his playful smile stretched all the way to flirtatious scamp. Dimples emerged in his tanned, smooth cheeks, beneath a hint of blond stubble. His skin looked as soft as a baby's. "Absolutely not." He reached over and pulled one of my ash brown curls out straight, and I shivered. "It's just, you don't look . . ." He bit his lip and seemed to think twice about finishing that sentence. "You barely have an accent. I wouldn't have guessed you were Southern."

" 'Fraid so. DeKalb County, born and raised." I took a step closer. "And you?"

"Actually, you've wandered into my kingdom." He twirled his hands out as though to present his domain. "Might I ask, what is your quest here?"

I gave him points for nerd humor and chuckled. "I seek the holy grail. Have you seen it here about?"

"Alas, no." He winked. "I was just on my way to find it when I was accosted by a fair maiden in distress." His bratty-little-brother smirk felt like a challenge.

"Is that so?" I flashed him a smile. "And do you make it a habit of photo-bombing innocent maidens?"

He exhaled with surprised laughter. "You might say that."

I narrowed my eyes at him and, before he could react, lifted my camera, and clicked the shutter. "Aha! I've captured a consolation prize." I shook my camera at him, defiant. "Now we'll see what you go for on the open market."

He made a gesture as though to swipe my camera away, dramatically failing and clutching at his chest. "Touché. But I can tell you it's not much."

Thoughts of payment hit my stomach like a runaway freight train and sucked all the fun out of this enchanting encounter. The probability of running into yet another celebrity in this part of Brooklyn was slim. I needed to head back to the office immediately and do more research to scout my next lead. Maybe I could still bring something to Andy before the end of the day. I couldn't afford to let him down again. I knew he'd begun counting down the days until he could fire me—I could feel it. And I needed this job.

I frowned. "I have to be getting back."

Micah chewed on his pretty lower lip for a beat, then said, "Hey, you wouldn't happen to have a business card? You know, in case I'm ever in the market for my own personal paparazzi."

That made me laugh again, and my momentary gloom lifted. I reached into my camera bag and produced a plain white card with just my name and contact info. "And you?"

Micah patted his pocket and came up with a wallet. He slid a card out and held it toward me. I started to scan it when he laid a finger on my shoulder, and my eyes closed for a beat as I leaned my head against his hand. What had come over me?

"It was good to meet you, Jo-Josie from Georgia, Atlanta. I hope I see you again." He looked into my eyes once more, more serious than before. "And don't let this business change you."

He gave my arm a quick squeeze, then turned and headed away from me, and I stood planted in that spot enjoying the view as he walked away. I sighed, hoping maybe he'd asked for my card so he could call me. I dropped my eyes back to his and read, "*Micah Sinclair. Theater of the Absurd.*"

My jaw dropped.

I'd been talking to Micah Sinclair for a good thirty minutes. *Micah freaking Sinclair.* My head fell back, and I stared at the clouds passing. He'd been in my clutches, and I hadn't asked him a single hard-hitting question. And the picture I'd shot—I didn't want to think about it.

My boss would eat me alive. If I didn't kill myself first. I could have delivered a click-bait-worthy photo if I'd had the first clue I'd been hanging out with a sought-after commodity.

In my defense, I didn't have an encyclopedic mind like Andy's. And I didn't have the experience to recall every single minor celebrity who'd graced the tabloids. In fact, I had to wrack my brains to think of the last thing I'd even heard about Micah. Something about a girlfriend, I thought. It didn't matter. None of my excuses would hold water in the court of Andy.

I considered chasing after Micah. I could take a picture of his backside. It was a worthy subject, in my estimation. But I was already going to catch hell for the one crazy-ass shot I'd taken— especially without a printable quote. I could have deleted the picture and pretended this never happened. But Andy would make my life even more insufferable if I returned altogether empty-handed.

An ember of hope began to bloom as I remembered I had Micah's contact info. What if I called and sweet-talked him into a quote? I lifted his card again and read the words, "*Please contact my agent at—*" And all hope died.

Fixated on Micah's last statement, I trudged back toward the subway. "*Don't let this business change you.*" All along he'd known I was missing a golden opportunity, and he must have been laughing at me the whole time. I squared my shoulders and decided to chalk it up to a learning experience. Yet another one.

Ordinarily such a humiliation would have left me near tears. But as I walked, I began to laugh. At the very least, I'd have a hilarious adventure story to tell Zion. And in spite of everything, it had been the most fun I'd had since I couldn't remember when. Micah had turned out to be the bright spot in an otherwise cursed day.

As I neared the entrance to the subway, a young girl wearing face paint and holding a bright red balloon caught my eye. I reached left and switched to my personal camera, pressing the shutter to capture a burst of images. Bright sunlight created a halo in her wild curly locks. Her parents hunched over a map, blind to the masterpiece of their child. The girl glanced up and saw me. I knelt on the sidewalk and winked at her. She tilted her head and looked directly into the camera. A guileless smile broke out. She was missing her front tooth.

Click click click. Beautiful.